Thomas H Duncombe

The Life and Correspondence of Thomas Slingsby Duncombe, Late M.P. for Finsbury

Vol. 2

Thomas H Duncombe

The Life and Correspondence of Thomas Slingsby Duncombe, Late M.P. for Finsbury
Vol. 2

ISBN/EAN: 9783337094904

Printed in Europe, USA, Canada, Australia, Japan

Cover: Foto ©Andreas Hilbeck / pixelio.de

More available books at **www.hansebooks.com**

THE

LIFE AND CORRESPONDENCE

OF

THOMAS SLINGSBY DUNCOMBE,

LATE M.P. FOR FINSBURY.

EDITED BY HIS SON

THOMAS H. DUNCOMBE.

IN TWO VOLUMES.

VOL. II.

LONDON:

HURST AND BLACKETT, PUBLISHERS,

13, GREAT MARLBOROUGH STREET.

1868.

CONTENTS

OF

THE SECOND VOLUME.

CHAPTER I.

PRINCE LOUIS NAPOLEON.

CHAPTER II.

A FRIEND OF THE DRAMA.

CHAPTER III.

THE DUKE OF BRUNSWICK'S HEIR.

CHAPTER IV.

THE PRESIDENT AND HIS FRIEND.

CHAPTER V.

A TRIBUNE OF THE PEOPLE.

CHAPTER VI.

POLAND AND HUNGARY.

CHAPTER VII.

FRANCE AFTER THE COUP D'ETAT.

CHAPTER VIII.

LIBERAL LEGISLATION.

CHAPTER IX.

ITALY AND MAZZINI.

CHAPTER X.

SPECULATION.

CHAPTER XI.

MILITARY ABUSES.

CHAPTER XII.

THE EMPEROR AND THE DUKE.

CHAPTER XIII.

AUTHORSHIP.

CHAPTER XIV.

THE POPULAR MEMBER.

APPENDIX.

LIFE AND CORRESPONDENCE

OF

THOMAS SLINGSBY DUNCOMBE.

CHAPTER I.

PRINCE LOUIS NAPOLÉON.

Birth of the Prince—His education—Expelled from Rome—Joins in the Italian revolution of 1831—Escapes to France—Visits England—Retires to Switzerland—Writings and studies—Fails to raise an insurrection at Strasburg—Sent to America—Returns to England—Becomes intimate with Mr. Duncombe—Moves in the higher circles of English Society—Letters of Count Walewski and Count Morny—The Prince at Eglinton Castle and at Bulwer's Cottage, near Fulham—The Boulogne Expedition—The Prince imprisoned in the fortress of Ham—Literary pursuits—Extinction of pauperism—Mr. Duncombe opens a communication with the captive—Letter from him—A confidential agent sent to Ham—Conditions of mutual assistance between the Duke of B. and the Prince—The prisoner escapes from the fortress—Secresy—Louis Philippe and the Baroness Feuchères—Bonapartists in Paris—Wheels within wheels—Flight of the King—The Prince's visits to Paris—Elected a member of the National Assembly, and President of the French Republic.

Louis Bonaparte, King of Holland, brother of Napoleon I., had three sons by Queen Hortense, daughter of Josephine by her first marriage. One died in infancy in 1807 ; another survived till March,

B

1831; the third was born in the Tuileries on the
20th of April, 1808, and was christened Charles Louis
Napoleon.   After the restoration of the Bourbons
Hortense, bearing the travelling name of the Duchess
de St. Leu, with her son, retired in succession to
Bavaria, Switzerland, and Rome; and as though
to prepare the youth with republican pretensions,
Prince Louis was placed under the scholastic super-
intendence of M. Lebas, son of Robespierre's devoted
adherent, who shot himself rather than survive his
friend.

When Charles X. was expelled by the Parisians, the
expatriated family assembled at Rome, under the conviction that their turn was coming.   Prince Louis so
conspicuously prepared himself for eventualities, that
the authorities had him forcibly carried out of the
Papal dominions.   The Prince and his elder brother
then joined those Italians who were organizing a
general insurrection.   Farini does not allow the
Bonapartes any prominent share in the Italian revolution.   He states that they were volunteers without military rank.   He calls it a stage revolution,
and accuses the Provisional Government of endeavouring to propitiate the King of France by con-
fining the two Princes at Forli, where the elder
succumbed to an attack of measles, after a few
days' illness.   The Italian historian describes the
movement somewhat contemptuously, as neither
displaying energy nor gallantry, generalship nor
patriotism — in short, was so tame an affair that
it appeared a public merry-making rather than a
political revolution.   Nevertheless the new Pontiff,
Gregory XVI., was dethroned in Rome, and his

temporal dominion declared to be at an end for ever.*

With his mother Prince Louis contrived to reach the French capital; but Louis Philippe would not allow him to remain in France. They then proceeded to England, remaining only a few months.

Whether Mr. Duncombe made the acquaintance of the Prince at this first visit, as he was then well acquainted with Counts Mornay and Walewski, we are not certain; but as he was well known in the fashionable world, wherever the son of the Duchess de St. Leu presented himself, they were pretty sure to meet. In August, 1831, both mother and son proceeded to Arenenberg, in the canton of Thurgovia, where the Prince apparently devoted himself to military studies. In 1833, he wrote a book about artillery practice, and accepted a captaincy in a Bernese regiment. He had friends and correspondents in France—De Persigny, Lafayette, Carrell, Odillon Barrot, Vaudrez, and was eager to turn them to account. He made an attempt on the 28th of October, 1836, to create an insurrection at Strasburg. With only a couple of officers and a few privates he raised the cry of "Vive l'Empereur!" But the nation was not ready for such an appeal—assuredly the garrison were not—for he was taken prisoner, and after a brief detention shipped to America. There, however, he did not long remain.

The exile declined to remain on the other side of the Atlantic. The serious illness of the Duchess de St. Leu afforded him a good pretext for returning to Europe; and he once more sought the

* "The Roman State from 1815 to 1850." Translated from the Italian by the Right Hon. W. E. Gladstone, M.P. I. chap. iv.

convenient retirement of Switzerland. This he was presently forced to leave in consequence of the uneasiness of Louis Philippe, whose Government had already become unpopular.

He was again amongst his friends in London, sunning himself in the bright glances of the Countess of Blessington, or enjoying the pleasant fellowship of Mr. Duncombe. He was still of opinion that the French people were impatient for his advent; therefore, went to Switzerland that he might be near enough to the frontier to take immediate advantage of events. The remonstrance of the French Government had induced the cantons to require his withdrawal.

The Prince remained in England nearly two years. It is at this period that he is reported to have given himself up to dissipation. All that can be said with truth is that, like other young men of rank, he was curious to see the different phases of English fashionable life, and enjoyed the diversions of English gentlemen of good position. Mr. Duncombe met him at the race course, as well as in the club-room, but quite as frequently at the houses of his friends, Lady Blessington, Lady Holland, and others. The two ladies were rank Bonapartists, and were sure to encourage Napoleonic ideas.

It was the former Moore caught in a dreadful state of distress, with a handkerchief before her eyes; and when he inquired the cause of her grief she replied, " It is the anniversary of my poor Napoleon's death." Lady Holland did not regret the dead emperor quite so piteously; nevertheless, his nephew was sure of a cordial reception. Many similar establishments were open to the Prince ; and though he still studied hard he found plenty of amusement.

He was the guest of Lord Combermere,* of the Hon. Colonel Dawson Damer, and of Lord Alvanley. To them he was always social and communicative, smoking and conversing deep into the small hours. He made no secret then of his aspirations and intentions, but was regarded as a dreamer of dreams. He engaged in some secret conferences with one or two individuals whose appearance some of his English friends thought betrayed a strong intimacy with Leicester-square. Their names were obscure at this period, however famous they became a few years later. One or two were on confidential terms with Mr. Duncombe, to whom they had applied when they wanted any little social service rendered to any of their friends ; as in the following :—

Ce Mardi matin, Oct. 21, 1828.

Vous me pardonnerez, cher Monsieur Duncombe, si je prends la liberté de vous importuner, mais j'ose compter sur votre complaisance en le cas ci-dessous mentionné.

Lord Alvanley et plusieurs autres membres avaient promis *au Comte Lobolewski, premier secretaire de l'Ambassade de Russie à Londres,* un de mes amis intimes, de le faire recevoir membre honoraire du Club de St. James, à la première réunion. Il y a aujourd'hui un comité, et aucun de ces messieurs n'est en ville ; je prends donc la liberté de prier de vouloir bien vous charger de le faire admettre aujourd'hui. Vous voudrez bien me pardonnez cette démande, et agréez d'avance tous mes remerciments.

Tout à vous, LE CTE. A. WALEWSKI.

* See an interesting account of the Prince in Lady Combermere's "Memoirs" of her husband, vol. ii. p. 267.

Ce Mercredi, Août 24, 1830.

C'est aujourd'hui plus que jamais que je chérirais la liberté si elle pouvait m'être rendue, mon cher ami ; mais malheureusement je ne suis pas maître de moi pour Jeudi, et un engagement antérieur me prive d'aller figurer parmi ceux qui savent vous apprécier et qui vous rendent justice. Croyez donc à tous mes regrets et à mon bien sincère attachement.￼ MORNY.

He was invited to the grand fête at Eglinton Castle, intended to revive the institutions of chivalry. Everything was provided to insure the success of the experiment. There were valiant knights in full armour, riding magnificent steeds; and beautiful ladies in the brightest mediæval array, to do duty as the Queen of Beauty and her attendants; there was even a professional fool or jester, in a suit of motley; in short Lord Eglinton provided everything that money could procure—except fine weather; and the remorseless rain cooled the gallantry of the heroes, deluged the finery of their fair spectators, and extinguished the jests of the fool. In an interval of leisure from the programme, while under shelter, the Prince crossed swords with an English knight. It has been said that they amused themselves with such ardour that they were obliged to be separated.

One of the parties that Prince Louis Napoleon joined while in London assembled at a pretty villa on the Thames, near Fulham, then owned by Mr. Edward Lytton Bulwer, M.P. There were present the editors of the *Examiner* and the *Literary Gazette*, Count D'Orsay, Messrs. Disraeli, and George Bankes, M.P., with several ladies, literary and artistic. It was a *déjeûner*, and a very pleasant one, as have been all the reunions arranged by the same talented and amiable host. The

Prince was taciturn, as usual, and amused himself with a row on the river.

It has been stated that before he quitted London for the Boulogne expedition he contrived to have interviews with Lord Palmerston and Lord Melbourne. The Duke of Wellington, in relating this *on dit*, in his own honourable way adds—" If I can answer for anything where I can know nothing, I should say that those ministers had never heard of his intentions."* Of course they never had. Had either entertained any suspicion of the project he were sure not to have admitted him to an audience. It is most likely a Paris report, manufactured after the event. No member of the Government was likely to have been in the Prince's confidence. He professed republicanism; and if he had any Englishman of good position in his confidence, that person would inevitably have been selected from such politicians.

It was on the 6th of August, 1840, that Prince Louis, attended by between forty and fifty companions, landed from a steamer at Boulogne. They proceeded to the barracks, but the soldiers not responding to his appeal, and the National Guard having been called out, they presently retreated to their place of landing. A collision, however, took place before they could reach the steamer; they were fired at; some fell mortally wounded, and the rest were arrested.

Lenity was thought to be thrown away on so determined an offender; so the Prince was at once tried by his peers, found guilty of conspiracy, and sentenced to perpetual imprisonment. He was then consigned to the fortress of Ham, to the lodgings formerly

* " Correspondence of Mr. Raikes," 144.

occupied by Prince Polignac and his colleagues. Here he amused his leisure with literary pursuits. Among these employments was the drawing out an elaborate scheme for the extinction of pauperism, by cultivating the waste lands in France. The projector touched upon agriculture and industry, taxation, and the advance of the funds; and then went into figures to prove that a proper use of two-thirds of the nine millions and a hundred and ninety thousand acres of uncultivated lands in France might provide employment for twenty-five millions of French workmen in different agricultural colonies, each of whom should, at the end of twenty-three years, realize a profit of thirteen millions eight hundred and ninety-one thousand eight hundred francs.

The second prisoner of Ham, with whom Mr. Duncombe had held communication, was not less interesting to him than the former one; and he often compared notes respecting him with the Prince's cordial friends at Gore House. It was not easy to let the captive know that he had still warm hearts on which he could rely; but this was accomplished in time. A note was received in the prison, and thus answered :—

Ham, 14th August, 1841.

My life is passed here in a very monotonous manner, for the rigours of the authorities are unchanged; nevertheless I cannot say that I am dull, because I have created for myself occupations which interest me. For instance, I am writing 'Reflections upon the History of England;' and also I have planted a small garden in the corner of the yard in which I am located. But all this fills up the time without filling the heart, and sometimes we find it very void of sentiment.

I am very much pleased at what you tell me of the good opinion which I have left behind me in England ; but I do not share in your hope as to the possibility of soon being in that country again ; and indeed, notwithstanding all the pleasure I should have in again finding myself there, I do not complain in the least of the position to which I have brought myself, and to which I am completely resigned.

"LOUIS NAPOLEON BONAPARTE."*

Another letter from the illustrious prisoner had previously been addressed to Lady Blessington ; and notwithstanding that both betrayed an extremely philosophic spirit, his friends knew him well enough to be satisfied that if an escape were practicable, he would listen to it with eagerness. Written communications on such a subject could not be thought of ; but a safe medium must be devised before any steps for his liberation could be taken.

The first point to be gained was to get the French Government to relax the severity of the prisoner's confinement ; and with this object, the latter addressed to them a moving representation of the hardships he was made to suffer. He reminded them that the ministers of Charles X., when confined in the same dilapidated chambers, were not so rigorously dealt with, and that his claims by birth to consideration were higher than theirs had been. Though Louis Philippe bore him no affection, he responded to the appeal by removing some of the restrictions. The Prince's valet was permitted to leave the fortress for the neighbouring town. Confidential and secret communication with the prisoner was now deemed possi-

* "Portraits Politiques," par M. de Gueronnière.

ble, and the object was to seek out some person with whom the Prince might communicate through his own servant without having recourse to writing. Mr. Duncombe soon supplied and prepared a trustworthy agent.

He had too great a regard for him and the name he bore to remain indifferent to his fate. He had liberated one illustrious prisoner from those gloomy walls; but it required very different measures to succeed in the present instance. Louis Philippe knew the value of the proverb, "Safe bind, safe find," and possibly suspected that the House of Commons if appealed to on the subject would very likely return a coroner's-inquest verdict of "Served him right."

Mr. Duncombe set to work in another way. In the first place, he secured the co-operation of the wealthy Duke of B——, who wanted a Bonaparte to assist him to maintain important claims; and then having obtained the sanction of the prisoner to the conditions on which his freedom might be obtained, sent his own secretary to Ham, with instructions to negotiate the following treaty:—

à Ham, 1845.

Nous C. F. A. G., D. of Bk., nous Prince Napoléon Louis Bonaparte, convenons et arrêtons ce qui suit:

ART. I.—Nous promettons et jurons sur notre honneur et sur le St. Evangile de nous aider l'un et l'autre, nous *C. D. of Bk.* à rentrer en possession du Duché de Bk., et à faire s'il se peut de tout l'Allemagne une seule nation unie, et à lui donner une constitution adaptée à ses mœurs, à ses besoins, et au progrès de l'époque; et nous *P. N. L. Buonaparte* à faire rentrer la France dans le plein exercice de la souveraineté nationale dont elle a été approuvée en 1830, et à la mettre à même de se prononcer librement sur la forme de gouvernement que lui convient de se donner.

ART. II.—Celui d'entre nous qui le premier arriverait au pouvoir suprème, sous quelque titre que ce soit, s'engage à fournir à l'autre, en armes et en argent, les secours que lui sont nécessaires pour atteindre le but qu'il se propose ; et de plus, à autoriser et faciliter l'enrolement volontaire d'un nombre d'hommes suffisant pour l'exécution de ce projet.

ART. III.—Tant que durera l'exile qui pèse sur nous, nous engageons à nous aider réciproquement en toute occasion, à fin de rentrer en possession des droits politiques qui nous ont été ravis ; et en supposant que l'un de nous peut rentrer dans sa patrie, l'autre s'engage à soutenir la cause de son allié par tous les moyens possibles.

ART. IV.—Nous engageons en outre à ne jamais promettre, faire, et signer aucune rénonciation, abdication en detriment de nos droits politiques ou civiles; mais, au contraire, à nous consulter et à nous soutenir en frère dans toutes les circonstances de notre vie.

ART. V.—Si par la suite et lorsque jouissant de notre pleine liberté, nous jugerons convenable d'apporter au présent Traité des modifications, dictées soit par notre position respective, soit par l'intérêt commun, nous nous engageons à les faire d'un commun accord, et à reviser les dispositions de cette convention dans tout ce qu'elle contienne de defective par suite des circonstances sous lesquelles elle a été faite.　　Approuvé, &c. &c.,

In the presence of G. T. Smith,
and Count Orsi.

By this time, years of imprisonment had rolled silently on, and the Prince remained a captive. His dying father at Florence had implored permission to embrace his son, but was denied ; the philosopher of the dungeon would not give Louis Philippe the required guarantee, and he was kept in durance. It was then that Charles Thelin, the valet, and Dr. Conneau, the physician, were apprized of a plan for effecting the Prince's escape, while the Prince was made aware of what was in contemplation, and the conditions on which he might be a free man. The strictest confidence was insisted on : it is but justice to say, that so completely was this respected, that in the different narratives that were published, not a word was allowed to suggest that the captive had assistance of any kind outside his prison walls, or that any one, foreigner or native, had held any secret communication with him during his captivity.

The Prince made his way out of the fortress in the dress of a workman carrying a plank, while Dr. Conneau procured a figure to rest on the sofa in the position of an invalid.

So well were the governor and the jailors deceived, that the prisoner, provided with a Belgian passport, was in the railway, proceeding across the frontier from Valenciennes, before his escape was discovered ; and on May 29, 1846, was safe in London, writing a letter to Count St. Aulaire, the ambassador from Louis Philippe, giving him the first information of the adventure. He wrote also to Sir Robert Peel and Lord Aberdeen much to the same effect ; and then went into society to receive the congratulations of his friends, the warmest coming from him who is believed to have planned and carried out his rescue.

Mr. Duncombe was delighted with the success of the plot, and particularly with the concealment of his complicity in it. Up to the present time the name of none of the real parties to the escape has been suffered to transpire.

Louis Philippe has incurred no small amount of

odium from his acquisitiveness; to enrich himself and
his sons seemed the one object of his life. The
trickery displayed in the affair of the Spanish marriages lost him many friends in England; but the
most fatal blow to his reputation was his alleged intimacy with the Baroness Feuchères (*née* Shaw), an
Englishwoman, who was mistress of the Duke of
Bourbon when the latter was found hanging. A will
was produced that gave the bulk of the property of
the deceased to the Duc d'Aumale; and ugly rumours
were circulated as to the manner in which the old duke
met his death. The antecedents of the baroness were
. rather equivocal; and it was stated that she had been
induced to hasten the end of the testator when aware
that he intended altering his will. We are not satisfied with the assertions that have been put forward
as to the duke's inability to hang himself; nevertheless the case excited strong suspicions of foul play.

The Prince remained in England, enjoying the
English life he loved so well, under the auspices of his
zealous friend, yet far from being an unobservant
spectator of more interesting proceedings going on on
the other side of the Channel, of which he had constant information from his adherents. Louis Philippe
had imprisoned his physician and his valet : but there
was in Paris one whom he never thought of molesting,
because he was never suspected, who was a more busy
and a more secret conspirator, and had the means of
getting at state secrets by a key that could open the best-
secured bureau in the palace of the "citizen king."

There were other earnest adherents equally active
in preparing society for an adaptation of Napoleonic
ideas. Of these, the principal held a conspicuous

place in the gay world of Paris, was an adept on the turf, and seemed to think of nothing beyond the enjoyment of the present moment in his favourite pursuit. He was reputed to be a near connexion of the Prince; but M. de Morny was considered to be so absorbed in horse-flesh as to have less time than inclination for politics. The French Government does not appear to have suspected him.

In another circle there existed a Pole, who was quite as decided and quite as active a Bonapartist. M. Walewski also contrived to keep in the background, but added another wheel to the complicated machinery that was being secretly put together. In due time there were wheels within wheels acting in unsuspected localities: everywhere they were going on without noise, without display, in the faubourgs, in the garrisons, in the theatres, in the churches—always concealed from observation, always in concert.

All the while the King, on the brink of a precipice, seemed blinded by his own egotism and avarice. He would not believe that he was an object of general detestation and ridicule. Attempts at assassination followed each other in rapid succession, and caricatures were becoming more and more daring; yet in the face of these signs he had the supreme folly to cause the remains of the Emperor Napoleon to be brought from St. Helena to Paris, stirring up the Bonapartist feeling throughout the country, that common sense ought to have told him must be antagonistic to Bourbon rule.

In addition to this suicidal policy, he chose to display his intense greediness and craft at the expense of his only trustworthy ally, while permitting one of his sons to publish a braggadocio letter, suggestive of invasion and conquest. The indignation in England was only exceeded by the general disgust; and with the patriotic feeling thus excited, there was often a trace of Napoleonic ideas.

Mr. Duncombe's friendship for the Prince caused him to watch the course of public opinion in both countries with more than ordinary interest. That a crisis was impending he must have known. as he was in confidential communication with the Prince and with many of his most attached friends. He must have been aware also that the wheels within wheels, whirling on secretly in Paris, were accumulating a motive power that was ready to act with irresistible force on French society; and seems to have had some trouble in restraining the impatience of his friends to make the mechanism seen as well as felt. In the latter years of his diary the entry "*Burnt Letters,*" frequently repeated, accounts for the paucity of documentary evidence of his close intimacy with the Prince at this period; nevertheless some papers have been preserved that will be found sufficiently confirmatory of the fact.

The decisive *émeute* that put the Orleans family to flight, was regarded by Prince Louis Napoleon's anxious friends in England as a golden opportunity. He was ready to proceed to the scene of action and aid his active adherents by his presence. But Paris was at that time a whirlpool where straws were coming to the surface—only to be sucked down. A knot of revolutionists had made themselves masters of the situation, and caution was necessary in dealing with their imperial prejudices and an excited population that might be induced to repeat "the reign of terror." It was essential to his success—as a Republic had been proclaimed—that the Prince should lay aside his rank, disavow his motives, conceal his intentions, and assume the position of a patriotic citizen. He hastened to Paris, and was presently in the whirlpool, struggling manfully to make his way to the surface.

On the 24th of February, 1848, "the king of the barricades" was dethroned by the same power that had elevated him at the expense of his kinsman, and on the 28th M. Louis Bonaparte was merely "one Frenchman the more" in the capital, and at once recognised the Provisional Government—"*faisait acte de bon citoyen.*" Here, however, he shortly ascertained, through his agents, that his appearance was premature. The revolutionary fever was at its height, and there was danger in remaining in such an atmosphere. Having ascertained this, and communicated personally with the most influential of his secret agents,* the good citizen judiciously swam out of the whirlpool and left the floating straws to their fate.

He returned to his friends in London, receiving good counsel from one, if not more, enjoying himself at Gore House, at the clubs, everywhere. Society began to recognise him as a rising star, and to acknowledge in him the only dissolution of rapidly increasing European complications caused by the action of the Revolutionary Government in Paris. These imbeciles were evidently of the same opinion, for whilst permitting the banished Bonapartes to return to France, they excepted him by name. Of this blun-

* Tremblaire.

der he was not slow in taking advantage. As an unjustly persecuted man, he addressed the National Assembly in a letter dated 23rd May, 1848, complaining and disclaiming with equal effect. The document was of course published, and produced as much excitement among his enemies as among his friends. The latter now more boldly came forward to ridicule the democracy and suggest the revival of the empire. A proclamation extensively circulated in June, thus concluded:—

"Let us place at our head the only man who is worthy of us—let us place there LOUIS NAPOLEON. *Vive l'Empereur!*"

It was posted generally in the department of the Ardennes, no one knew by whom; other appeals were made equally conspicuous in other places; no one could trace their origin. The Republican Government could discover no trace of foreign interference and foreign inspiration, and the chief instruments in their overthrow were never suspected. Disturbances in the capital followed each other in rapid succession, and the name of the banished man became a rallying cry in every direction. The Prince, again impatient, was for heading a conflict, as a decree of the Executive Committee on the 12th of June declared that the law against him should be enforced. Prudent counsels again prevailed, and he retired once more, addressing the President of the Republic by letter, in which he intimated that if the people chose to impose duties on him, he intended to fulfil them. It was published, and the hint it contained at once acted upon: several departments simultaneously electing him to a seat in the National Assembly, notwithstanding the assurance expressed in the document that he would rather remain in exile than disturb the peace of France.

The opposition of the imbeciles became so intensified at this decisive proof of their decline, especially as Paris was one of the places for which the Prince had been returned, that again he listened to his trusty counsellors. It was obvious that the Republican Government were unintentionally playing into his hands; and the longer they continued to oppose his election, the more popular he was sure to become. The Prince wrote from London, June 15th, with much self-denial surrendering, for the tranquillity of France, the advantages he had acquired, and professing a desire to be permitted to return as the humblest of her citizens. This was answered by Corsica electing him almost unanimously. The game was seen to be his own if he would only wait; therefore there was no difficulty in persuading him to write to the President, again announcing his resignation, and again expressing sentiments of moderation. As the new elections were to take place on the 17th of September, it was evident that nothing would be lost, and much might be gained, by permitting the decline of Government influence for two or three months. On the eve of the election he made public his desire to take his seat among the representatives of the people. The result was that the Department of the Seine gave him 110,752 votes; and though four other departments returned him by large majorities, he preferred the first, as he should represent his native city.

The republicans in power were furious, but the

republic was already showing signs of collapse. On the 26th of the month, *le bon citoyen* was not only in Paris, but in the Chamber of the Assembly, where he read a speech from the tribune of so conciliatory a character, that, notwithstanding an effort made to prevent his aspiring to the Presidency, the opinion of the Chamber was evidently in his favour. A still more violent repressive attempt was made on the 25th of October, with a like result. It could scarcely be concealed from themselves that the Government were playing a losing game.

On the 24th of November, 1848, Prince Louis Napoleon issued an address from Paris to the people of France. There are certainly some points in it that challenge inquiry, particularly where he assures his compatriots that he is not an ambitious man, and that at the end of four years he would make it a point of honour to leave to his successor the consolidation of a republic with liberty untouched. But at this highly critical period there was a Bunkum in the old world as well as in the new—it might be said that there were a good many Bunkums—but the Bunkum Magnum was assuredly the good city of Paris. The language of virtuous profession had almost been exhausted since the expulsion of Charles X.; and the new candidate for the presidency was obliged to frame his sentiments to the popular form. Materials for the pavement of a certain place remarkable for the warmth of its temperature, were not more conspicuous in this declaration than in the oratorical extravagances of Lamartine, or the ruder appeals of Cavaignac.

The attractions of the new applicant for the suffrages of a great nation were put forward prominently;

his name was announced as a symbol of order and
security, as he stated in his opening sentence. A
slight reference to the growth of that name would
have shown that its development as a political power
was owing to the exercise of physical force, which
trampled out the republic, and on its ruins laid the
foundation of the empire. It is quite true that the
name Napoleon was a symbol of order and security,
but it was that order and that security which the
Emperor established—not the First Consul. If the
French people chose to accept the symbol, they were
bound to put up with the consequences.

On the 10th of December the Presidential election
was to take place, and the good citizen at once expressed his views and intentions, in the same conciliatory spirit that had been so prominent in his
preceding manifestoes.

More than five millions and a half of Frenchmen
voted in his favour. His competitors were completely
distanced in the race—Cavaignac coming in second
with little more than a quarter of that number of
votes. The others were comparatively nowhere—
Ledru Rollin obtaining only 371,431 votes, Raspail
looming in the distance with the insignificant number
of 36,964; while the late President, the most fortunate of French *littérateurs*, was just visible with
17,914 of his greatly diminished admirers. Finally,
the republican general, Changarnier, tailed off with a
poor 4687 votes.

The 20th of December, 1848, was a great day in
modern French history—a memorable day in the
annals of the National Assembly. M. Marrast, the
president, in the name of the French people pro-

claimed Citizen Charles Louis Napoleon Bonaparte, by an absolute majority of suffrages, President of the French Republic. The latter was then seated, dressed with a kind of compromise between democratic simplicity and imperial display. He wore a fashionable suit of black, a diamond star, and the grand cordon of the Legion of Honour. Like his friend in the House of Commons and on the hustings, his personal appearance left no doubt as to the value he set upon the social pretensions to which he was born. He then mounted the tribune, and M. Marrast read to him the oath to remain faithful to the democratic republic. "*Je le jure!*" he exclaimed, holding up his right hand; then made another conciliatory profession of faith, and retired amid unanimous cries of " *Vive la République!*"

In his next address, after taking the oath as President of the Republic, there were necessarily more professions. Between the citizen representative and their now acknowledged head there could not be any difference of opinion—he would strengthen democratic institutions. He paid a compliment to Cavaignaists, conciliated the Red republicans, and satisfied the ' moderates and the religious with his concluding sentence: " With the aid of God, we will at least do good, if we cannot achieve great things." Of course it was all Bunkum. Every Frenchman acquainted with the history of the century must have regarded such professions as symbolical.

In the account of an eye-witness* of the sanguinary struggle against the military force of the executive

* Captain Chamier: a " Review of the French Revolution of 1848." Two vols.

under Changarnier, nearly contemporary with the first appearance of Prince Louis Napoleon in this very sensational drama as a member of the National Assembly, justice is done to the moderation and good sense the Prince displayed in that crisis of terrible interest; but the writer considers that there was a mystery in the supply of money and munitions of war to the republicans. Could it be shown that the Prince furnished the funds, there would then be some difficulty in proving whence he got them. If it be suggested that another agreement like that entered into at Ham had been established for the purpose of placing the liberated prisoner in a position to assist his liberator, it must then be accepted that both, who equally detested democracy, encouraged the blouses only to insure their destruction. There is no evidence of such an agreement; and as the *ouvriers* had had a long time to prepare their movement, they could have collected the necessary supplies.

It is impossible to read a trustworthy report of that half-farce half-tragedy, the French revolution of 1848, without coming to the conclusion that the more sensible Parisians, as well as the more sensible Frenchmen, were getting tired of democracy, and eagerly seized on the name of Napoleon, as drowning men in a storm catch at the first solid support that floats in their way. The respectability of France had suffered enough at the hands of the incompetent adventurers who had assumed the government of the country since the expulsion of the "citizen king." Even supposing the Prince again had recourse to his wealthy friend, the subsequent prosperity of France must be placed among the profits of the investment.

The lower orders of the population of Paris had long been in a state of chronic revolution; and the narrowness of the thoroughfares, and the quickness with which a tolerably strong fortification could be improvised, combined with a knowledge of the success that had attended former insurrections, gave them confidence in their numbers and resources. But they now possessed as a ruler the nephew of that Bonaparte who had contrived to overthrow a revolution, and he soon proved that he could turn the lesson to profit. This was the special constable who had been sworn in to oppose the London chartists.

Mr. Duncombe was staying at Sidmouth for the benefit of his health during the year 1849. He made one journey to London, in June, to consult Dr. Latham, but returned in a few days.

When it became known that Louis Napoleon had been elected President of the Republic, he could no longer look on passively. A private communication apprized him of the position of the Duke of B—— during the excitement that prevailed in the French capital, and while despatching a confidential messenger to his assistance, he gave him instructions to communicate with the President. As the person so employed was the same who had effected his escape from the fortress, there could be no doubt of his reception. He bore the following letter :—

Sidmouth, December 21st, 1848.

My dear Prince,—I cannot allow my secretary and friend, Mr. Smith, to visit Paris for the purpose of having the honour of an interview with the President of the French nation, without availing myself of this opportunity of offering you my sincere congratulations upon your recent triumphant election, and of wishing you every success and happiness in the proud position you are called upon to occupy.

Be assured that at all times I shall as heretofore be most happy to forward the interests of one whom " a people delighteth to honour."

Believe me, my dear Prince, yours sincerely,

THOS. S. DUNCOMBE.

CHAPTER II.

MR. DUNCOMBE had long established a claim to be
considered a friend of the drama, and was eager to
join in any scheme for its advancement. The most
useful of these was under the direction of Mr. E. L.
Bulwer, M.P., and was before Parliament in the shape
of a committee, organized for the purpose of inquiring
into the laws affecting dramatic performances. Mr.
Bulwer was the chairman. The subject, too, had
attracted the attention of the highest person in the
realm, whose enjoyment in theatrical performances
had been unequivocal ; to him Lord Brougham wrote:

The Chancellor, with his humble duty to your Majesty,
begs permission to submit the result of the consideration

which he has been able to bestow upon the memorial of
Mr. Arnold, of the patent theatres, of the Haymarket, and
of Mr. Greville, which your Majesty was graciously pleased
to direct should be referred to him.

In order to arrive at a sound conclusion on the subject
matter of the memorials, and to give satisfaction to the
parties, as well as to the public, the Chancellor requested
the assistance of three learned Judges,—the Vice Chancellor, the Chief Justice of the Common Pleas, and
Mr. Justice James Parke. They were pleased to attend
the hearing, which took place at six several meetings in
his Honour's court at Lincoln's Inn, and after conferring
fully with these learned judges, the Chancellor has the
honour to lay before your Majesty the opinion which he
has formed, and in which they unanimously concur.

It was not denied at the hearing by any of the parties,
that a licence from the Crown is necessary in order to
authorize the opening of a theatre within the precincts in
question. Whatever doubts may have ever been entertained
upon this point, had it been urged, no question was made
of it by any one.

The question, how far the patents already granted preclude
any new grants, whether by way of patent or licence, was
argued; but the Chancellor has no doubt whatever on this
point, nor had any of the learned judges; and it may be
taken as quite clear, nor indeed in the end was it much
disputed on the part of the patent theatres, that your
Majesty has the entire power by law to make whatever
changes your Majesty may think fit in the rights already
granted to those theatres, or to revoke those grants altogether, or to grant to other parties rights inconsistent with
those granted to the patent theatres in former times.

After taking into full consideration the relative position
of the parties, *the claims of individuals connected with the
patent theatres,* the *sums of money* invested in the concerns
of *all the theatres,* and the *interests of the public,* the
Chancellor humbly submits to your Majesty, with the con-
currence of the learned judges, that it may be desirable to

grant Mr. Arnold an extension of his licence so as to include the whole of the months of May and October.

All which is humbly submitted to your Majesty for your royal consideration.

L. SHADWELL.　　　　BROUGHAM, C.

N. TINDAL.

JAMES PARKE.

In Liverpool there had long been two theatres, one having a patent, under the management of Mr. Hammond, and the other, with no patent, having as manager Mr. Desmond Raymond. The proprietor of each establishment felt aggrieved by his rival, and brought their complaints before their member, Mr. William Ewart. He here states that he laid them before the committee, and refers to the progress of the proceedings :—

London, June 13th, 1832.

SIR,—The committee on the laws which regulate the drama has met again to-day.

I have taken this opportunity of representing to Mr. Bulwer, the chairman, the case of Messrs. Hammond and Raymond, as more precisely stated in your last letter.

I have also mentioned the willingness of the parties to give evidence, their expenses being paid as usual; and I have delivered up your letter for the consideration of the committee.

Mr. Bulwer promises that every attention shall be paid to the statement it contains.

The committee has not yet arrived at that portion of their subject which includes the case of the provincial theatres.

I think it probable that the metropolitan theatres will occupy them some time longer.

I shall be glad to communicate anything further which is considered of importance to your clients, and remain, Sir,

Your faithful servant,　　WM. EWART.

London, May 28th, 1832.

Sir,—It will afford me great pleasure to present the petition of Messrs. Hammond and Raymond, and to support its prayer.

I entirely coincide in their views of the impolicy and injustice of the existing laws which regulate, or rather which obstruct, the drama.

They are doubly injurious: to the individuals who conduct our theatres, and to the public who frequent them.

The time at which petitions are presented is regulated by ballot; and therefore dependent upon chance.

You may rely, however, on every endeavour on my part to present the petition of Messrs. Hammond and Raymond before Mr. Bulwer's motion is introduced; and I will confer with Mr. Bulwer on the subject of it.

I feel much obliged by the kind expressions which you use towards me individually, and I remain, Sir,

Your faithful servant, WM. EWART.

Mr. Bulwer was influenced by many important considerations to make this praiseworthy attempt to reform the laws affecting the English drama. It was not merely that the best interests of the performer as well as of the performance were at stake, but the rights of the originator of both. As a dramatist he had no ordinary claims to take the lead in establishing the value of dramatic composition. *The Lady of Lyons* was, we think, not on the boards at this time; but the author may have waited for a state of things better adapted to secure its success when represented. There is no doubt, however, that the strong claims of the subject were fully recognised by him, and that his labours for the advancement both of the art and the artist were as zealous as they were disinterested. He is here his own witness :—

Matlock, Derbyshire, October 3rd, 1832.

My DEAR SIR,—I have been in France and at Lincoln—very busy in both—since the date of your letter, which must excuse a delay in replying to it. I write now in a great hurry, and having mislaid the letter you enclosed to me, I must trouble you at once to forward this in answer to it.

My own wish in any Bill on the dramatic question would be to render it obligatory on the magistrates in their jurisdiction, as it would be on the Chamberlain in his, to license *any* theatre for which the majority of resident householders in the town or parish should petition. This will suffice to emancipate the provinces as the metropolis, and mete out justice to both. But there will be great difficulty in this addition, from the opposing voices of many of the committee. What has already been won was no easy matter. If I can hope to carry all, I shall try all; if not, I should be unwilling to risk much for the chance of getting more.

I would advise the parties in question, Messrs. Raymond, &c., to petition Parliament at its opening; to get the petition strongly supported. They might also correspond with other country managers to the same effect. This will show the House that to emancipate London is not sufficient, and will give additional strength to my hands.

As yet the Bill is in abeyance. Not knowing whether I shall be in the next Parliament, I cannot presume to prepare for it. But if I should be in the next Parliament, and think it prudent for the general cause to introduce regulations for the country managers, I will correspond with Messrs. Raymond on the subject.

Yours in great haste and truth,   E. L. BULWER.

The exertions of Mr. Duncombe were not without results. In this instance they were really great and unremitting, as they were in every important case he took in hand. He made himself master of the entire history of the theatre in England, and particularly of

the origin and progress of the influence of the Lord
Chamberlain in restricting performances. Having accomplished this, he wrote to a member of the Government enclosing the opinion of one of the most eminent
counsel at the bar; but it does not appear that he
obtained much encouragement from him. Mr. Ewart's
note is added :—

The Albany Court-yard, March 11th, 1837.

MY DEAR SIR,—According to your request, I enclose you
Sir James Scarlett's opinion, given in 1833, with a copy of
the petition. The Killigrew patent, and the twenty-one years'
licence granted to Messrs. Whitbread and Company, in
1816, are to be found in the appendix to the Dramatic
Literature Committee's Report, made in 1832, pages 239
and 240. The only Act of Parliament that at all bears
upon the subject is the 10 George II. c. 28, whereby a copy
of every dramatic entertainment is required to be sent to
the Lord Chamberlain fourteen days prior to its representation, under a penalty of 50l., or a forfeiture of the licence
or patent; and there is no other Act whatever specifying
the days upon which performances are to take place. You
were quite right when you stated that it has been long the
custom for theatres to close on Wednesdays and Fridays
in Lent; but this custom has within the last few years
ceased to exist as regards the minor theatres within the
Lord Chamberlain's jurisdiction, and has only continued to
be observed by Drury-lane on account of its having heretofore suited the lessee's convenience to remain closed upon
those evenings. I believe I am only expressing the wish of
the gentlemen connected with the patent theatres, as well as
of the public at large, when I say that they do not desire
that theatres should be open on the following days, viz.,
Ash Wednesday, the whole of Passion-week, Christmas-
eve, and of course Christmas-day. But when we know
what is going on in every portion of this metropolis upon
the days now in dispute, all parties consider the restriction

attempted to be placed upon Drury-lane Theatre a gross
piece of humbug, and, as I contend, a stretch of power on
the part of the Lord Chamberlain's department unsanc-
tioned by law. Permit me also to observe that on last Ash
Wednesday, a day that I propose all theatres should be
closed, the Brighton theatre, which is licensed by and under
exactly the same jurisdiction—viz., the Lord Chamberlain—
as the theatres in the city of Westminster, and the Court
at the time residing at the Pavilion, played *Charles the
Twelfth, The Maid of Switzerland*, and *The Vampire*. If I
might therefore be allowed to suggest what I think would
be the best course at present to be pursued, looking at the
defective state of the law, and taking into consideration
what has already passed, it would be this, that in the event
of Drury-lane being opened on Friday next, which in all
probability it will be, that no one should give themselves
further concern about it, and the subject be allowed to
drop. I will not, therefore, trouble you further upon the
subject, unless Lord John Russell or yourself should wish
for further information; in which case, if either you or he
will communicate your wishes, they shall be immediately
attended to by   My dear sir, yours very faithfully,

THOS. S. DUNCOMBE.

[CASE.]

Temple, February 19th, 1833.

The patents to Killigrew and Davenant, granted in 1662,
were, about the year 1792, in the possession of the proprietors of Covent-garden, and Drury-lane was then performing
under a limited patent, granted for twenty-one years from
the year 1795, and which would therefore expire in 1816.
Under an arrangement made in 1792, regulating the Opera-
house and the two patent theatres, under the sanction of
King George III. and the late king, then Prince of
Wales, Killigrew's patent was purchased by Drury-lane
Company from the Covent-garden proprietary for 20,000*l.*
In consequence, however, of some circumstances, not here
necessary to be detailed, the Drury-lane Company did not

complete their title to Killigrew's patent till the year 1813.
See the accompanying Acts of Parliament affecting Drury-
lane Theatre—50th George III., cap. 214, 52nd George III.,
1st George IV.

In 1812, the limited patent for twenty-one years from
1816 (a copy of which also accompanies this case) was obtained by the Drury-lane Company.   This was done because
the patent granted 23rd George III. had then only a few
years to run ; and as litigation was then going on as to
Killigrew's patent, in consequence of which Drury-lane
Company could not complete their title to it, it was by the
company deemed necessary therefore to obtain this limited
patent in order to give confidence to and protect the public,
from whom they were obtaining subscriptions at this time
to enable them to rebuild the theatre.

Subsequently to their doing this, and about the year
1813, the company completed their title to Killigrew's
patent; and from that time, therefore, they have had the
double authority in their possession of Killigrew's patent
and the last granted limited patent.

A case formerly laid before counsel as to the powers of
the Lord Chamberlain is left herewith as a reference to the
different Acts of Parliament.

It has been the usage of the two patent theatres to restrict their performances on Wednesdays and Fridays in
Lent to the representation of oratorios, and to the same
representations on the anniversary of the martyrdom of
King Charles.

In consequence of a theatrical performance having been
advertised at Drury-lane for the evening of the anniversary
of King Charles's martyrdom, in the present year, the
Lord Chamberlain gave a notice prohibiting the performance.

In consequence of this circumstance, a Captain Polhill,
the lessee of Drury-lane, is desirous of being advised—
Whether the Lord Chamberlain has any power to interdict
dramatic performances on the nights of the days mentioned,
and what his powers are, having reference to both patents,

in case Captain Polhill should perform on any of the nights mentioned.

[OPINION.]

Temple, 19th Feb., 1833.

I find nothing in the patents to restrain the authority of the patentees upon the subject, nor am I aware of any Act of Parliament that relates to it. The usage has been very long, and it is possible that some general words may be found in some Act of Parliament for the observance of these days which may support the usage; but unless the statute is suggested to me, I have not time within the period when this case is required to look for it.   J. SCARLETT.

MY DEAR SIR,—I delivered your letter, together with the case and opinion enclosed, to Lord John Russell and to other members of the Government, and it was their opinion that if the parties interested in Drury-lane Theatre were to perform on Wednesday or Friday, they would expose themselves to all the penal consequences of persons playing *without licence.* How far this might affect them, or even the patent, I do not venture to inquire. I return the case and opinion.   Yours very truly, my dear sir,

T. S. Duncombe, Esq., M.P.   T. SPRING RICE.

Committee-room, House of Commons, June 12th, 1833.

DEAR SIR,—I am sorry to inform you that it will not, I fear, be possible to extend Mr. Bulwer's Dramatic Performances Bill beyond the limits which he has already prescribed for it. I have thought it my duty to move for a general extension of the bill to the provinces in the committee (on the bill) in which I am now writing. On a division, the general opinion of the members of the committee was against further extension without further inquiry. They considered that evidence, both on the part of the proprietors of patent theatres and of minor theatres in the provinces, should be heard, before the power suggested in your amendment is conferred on the chief magistrate of the provincial towns. Another objection was taken on the ground of the projected change in our existing corporations, and the projected establishment of new ones in towns where no corporation exists at present.

I am disposed to think (as it is clear that we cannot *now* carry our point) that a motion should be made for a select committee to inquire into the state of the provincial theatres. On this point I shall be happy to hear from you, and remain, dear sir, Your faithful servant,

WM. EWART.

At the commencement of the session of 1837, Mr. Duncombe brought forward his bill for the regulation of theatres. It was to amend an Act that explained and amended another Act for reducing the laws relating to rogues, vagabonds, sturdy beggars, and vagrants into one Act; and it provided that the Lord Chamberlain's preventive authority should be restricted to Sunday, Christmas-day, Good Friday, and Passion week. As it was not permitted to pass, it did not settle the vexed question.

The Lord Chamberlain on the 2nd of March prohibited the new play of *Fair Rosamond* in Lent. This produced the following intimation :—

The Albany Court-yard, Monday Morning,
March 6th, 1837.

MY DEAR CONYNGHAM,—The enclosed copy of the Drury Lane petition has only just reached me, or I would have sent it to you sooner, in order that yourself and your department might be put in possession of the grounds of the lessee's complaint, &c. Under these circumstances perhaps it would be more convenient to Lord C. Fitzroy if I postponed the presentation of it until Friday, within which time, perhaps, some arrangement may be made that will preclude the necessity of its being presented at all. Anything that I can do for peace I shall be most happy. And believe me

Yours most truly, THOMAS S. DUNCOMBE.

The Vice-Chamberlain now came forward. The manager of Drury Lane had announced the performances of Italian operas, and the Lord Chamberlain would not permit them. The following correspondence ensued :—

Lord Chamberlain's Office, May 13th, 1837.

The Vice-Chamberlain having been informed that, notwithstanding his letters of the 11th instant, Mr. Bunn perseveres in advertising the performance of Zingarelli's opera of *Romeo e Giulietta* for Wednesday, 17th instant, requests to know whether the continued advertisement of that performance at Drury Lane Theatre may not be a mistake.

T. R. D. L., May 13th, 1837.

MR. BUNN, in reply to the Vice-Chamberlain's letter of this day, begs to state that he has deemed it of sufficient importance, in so unprecedented a case as the suspension of the power of a Royal Patent, to memorialize his most gracious Majesty, and that the announcement of *Romeo e Giulietta* will be continued until his Majesty's final pleasure shall be known.

Lord Chamberlain's Office, May 14th, 1837.

SIR,—I have it in command, in answer to your memorial for permission to perform Italian operas at Drury Lane Theatre, to refer you to my letter of the 11th instant; and agreable to the directions contained in that letter you will be pleased to conform.

I have likewise to inform you that the Lord Chamberlain's Office is the proper channel of communication with his Majesty on the subject of theatrical representations.

I have the honour to be, sir, your obedient servant,

CHARLES FITZROY, Vice-Chamberlain.

A. Bunn, Esq.

Mr. Duncombe displayed the interest he felt in the drama by moving in the House of Commons on the

1st of March, 1839, the following resolution :—"That it is the opinion of this House that, during Lent, no greater restrictions should be placed upon theatrical entertainments within the city of Westminster than are placed upon the like amusements at the same period in every other part of the metropolis." It was put to the vote and carried by a majority of twenty. This was a great boon to members of the profession engaged at the principal theatres, who had annually been deprived of their salaries on Wednesdays and Fridays during the entire term. The spirited manner in which he had overthrown a long-lived prejudice gained him golden opinions from the Liberal press; and Lord John Russell, who had quoted episcopal authority for maintaining the custom for depriving actors of a third of their salaries, was sharply attacked.

The Lord Chamberlain was determined not to allow his authority to be set at rest; and again in 1839 a correspondence took place on the subject between the lessee and another of the Lord Chamberlain's officials. The latter asserted that "her Majesty's Ministers had decided that, until further instructions to the contrary are issued, no other than the usual performance of oratorios can be sanctioned in Lent." It was quite in vain for Mr. Bunn to state in his reply, that he could not without heavy loss comply with the pleasure of her Majesty's Ministers.

Another year promised another warfare between the contending powers; but in the first month the manager of the English Opera House thus addressed the member for Finsbury :—

31, Golden-square, 31st Jan., 1840.

Sir,—It is with extreme regret I am induced to intrude on your privacy at such a moment on a matter of business; but as the subject affects the interests of so many individuals, I trust I shall stand excused in so doing. On applying to the Lord Chamberlain's office, I have reason to believe it is the intention of Lord Uxbridge to prevent the promenade concerts at the English Opera House, as well as the performances at the other theatres under his jurisdiction, to take place during the Wednesday and Friday nights in Lent.

As such a prohibition appears to me totally opposed to the understanding which took place in the House last session upon the discussion introduced by you, I am led to hope it may not be too late to prevent it.   I therefore, as the period is drawing so near, with extreme reluctance trouble you on the subject, to know if it is probable that you will be enabled to bring the question again before the House with reference to the approaching Lent; and to request, should you be precluded from so doing, that you will kindly furnish me, if you can do so without inconvenience, with the day of the month on which you introduced the subject to the House.

Your most obedient servant,   A. S. Arnold.

On the 9th of April, 1840, Mr. Duncombe addressed the House on the presentation of a petition signed by 1400 gentlemen, who had been in the habit of taking their families to hear an astronomical lecture delivered at the Opera House during Lent, in Passion week, &c., which entertainment had been prohibited. He described the number of performances in the shape of oratorios, ventriloquism, Shakspeare readings, and orreries, that had been open to the public in Passion week; in the face of which, he said, to stop an illustration of the wisdom of the Creator, such as the lecture offered, was nonsensical. Mr. Fox Maule and Lord Robert Grosvenor opposed; nevertheless, in a division, Mr. Duncombe was again in a majority, for his motion for an address to Her Majesty, to oblige the Lord Chamberlain to withdraw his prohibition was supported by 73 members; there being but 49 against it. He now, determined to bring the matter to a satisfactory issue, addressed himself to another influential quarter, with what result will be seen in his reply :—

The Albany, Feb. 4th, 1840.

My Lord,—The numerous and respectable applications that have recently been made to me in consequence of the part I took in the House of Commons during the last session of Parliament upon the subject of theatrical performances in Lent, will, I hope, be a sufficient apology for my troubling your Lordship upon the present occasion.

It is stated to me, that although it was universally understood and agreed to last year, " *that no greater restrictions ought to be placed upon theatrical entertainments during Lent within the city of Westminster than are placed upon the like amusements at the same period in any other part of the metropolis,*" yet it is apprehended that no alteration will take place this year.

I have uniformly represented to parties expressing such fears to me that I felt confident their apprehensions were unfounded.

Your Lordship would, however, confer a great favour upon those who originally did me the honour to place their cause in my hands, if your Lordship would, at your earliest convenience, inform me if I am correct in the conclusion to which I have come, in order that all doubts and misunderstandings upon this subject may be immediately removed.

I have the honour to be,

Your Lordship's obedient humble servant,

THOS. S. DUNCOMBE.

The Earl of Uxbridge.

Windsor Castle, Feb. 13th, 1840.

DEAR DUNCOMBE,—I send you the formal reply which you are anxious to have, and hope it is what you want.

In haste.   Faithfully yours,   UXBRIDGE.

Windsor Castle, Feb. 13th, 1840.

SIR,—In answer to your letter which I had the honour of receiving last week, on the subject of the theatres being closed during Lent, I beg to inform you that I have sent letters to the managers, stating that it will only be necessary to close them during Passion week and on Ash Wednesday.

I have the honour to be,
Your obedient servant,   UXBRIDGE.

Mr. Duncombe took the chair at the Shaksperian Club Festival, held at Her Majesty's Theatre on the 23rd of March, 1841, when he was supported by many distinguished patrons of the drama. His successful efforts in behalf of the theatrical profession were gratefully acknowledged. They subscribed for a handsome piece of plate. On the 4th of March, 1841, a deputation, including Sheridan Knowles, Benjamin Webster, James Wallack, and Frederick Vining, members of the Haymarket company, waited upon Mr. Duncombe, and presented him with a silver cup, cover, and salver, beautifully chased, with his armorial bearings engraved on one side, and an appropriate inscription on the other. Sheridan Knowles made an eloquent speech on the occasion, and Mr. Duncombe an effective reply.

We complete the correspondence with a few notes from persons who were prominent in the proceedings that had taken place on behalf of the drama :—

Mulgrave Castle, 19th October, 1841.

SIR,—I have received your letter of the 16th instant, and regret to learn that there is any difficulty as to granting a patent for a second theatre in Liverpool—a measure which I had consented to recommend after considerable inquiry. It is, however, impossible for me to do anything in the matter; and I can only suggest that you should address Sir James Graham on the subject, representing the expense which you state you have incurred, under the impression that the patent was to be granted, and the loss you will sustain if it should be now determined to withhold it. I am, sir, your most obedient servant,

NORMANBY.

Grosvenor-place, December 13th, 1842.

LORD MAHON presents his compliments to Mr. Raymond, and begs to inform him that he has no intention at this time, or for the approaching session, to introduce a bill for the regulation of the drama. Nothing can be more defective than the present state of the law, but it involves so many and such complicated interests, that Lord Mahon has some doubts whether an effort for its reformation will be successfully made, except on the part of Her Majesty's Government.

Queen's Elm, February 22, 1843.

MY DEAR SIR,—Our petition is printed, and Lord Mahon presents it. A word from Mr. Duncombe to his lordship would effect your purpose.

The petition of the dramatic authors prays " The repeal of the Act of George the Second, and to place all the theatres on a fair and legitimate footing; to prohibit theatrical performances in the taverns ; and to place all theatres under a censorship, so increasing their respectability."

There is also a petition from another party, numerously signed, leading to the same object.

I am, dear sir, yours very truly,   R. B. PEAKE.*

* The well-known dramatist.

5, Bow Hill Terrace, North Brixton, Feb. 20th, 1843.

Sir,—Permit me to say that within the last few days the proprietors of the Theatre Royal, Liverpool, have issued a writ against Mrs. Honey for seven performances at the Liver Theatre, to the amount of 350*l.*, in addition to a former 50*l.* penalty, from which she has appealed. This has frightened her so much that her attorney has advised her to present a petition to the House from herself alone, in addition to the general one.   Mr. Watson (I think member for Kinsale) has kindly undertaken to present it. *I* am advised to get Mr. Ewart to present one from me individually ; Mr. Buckstone in the same way ; and we are further advised to have them all presented on the same evening, and together, if possibly convenient to the members who have kindly undertaken to assist us.   My legal adviser in Liverpool thinks it desirable to have the general petition sent up so as to lose no time, for the actions will be tried at the assizes in Liverpool next month. I will do myself the honour to wait upon you to-morrow, when perhaps it may be convenient to you to name an evening that may be most desirable for the presentation of the petition. I could then name it to the other honourable members.

I have the honour to be, your very obedient servant,

R. Malone Raymond.

T. S. Duncombe, Esq., M.P.

During this long period, Mr. Duncombe's experience of the drama as a looker-on had permitted him to see singular changes in some of the *dramatis personæ*. Blooming *figurantes* had become hobbling grandmothers, and flying fairies sedate matrons. The new dramatic generation had either less attraction than their predecessors, or he had become indifferent. He had long ceased to go behind the scenes; he seemed to have forgotten his way to the Green-room.

The English theatres found him becoming a rare visitant, and the Italian Opera no longer possessed the charm that had drawn him nightly to his box. In the season of 1846 a vacancy occurred in the omnibus-box, and, as will be seen from the accompanying note, a member of the royal family particularly partial to the lyrical drama and the ballet, sought admission into the select circle :—

Lowndes-street, Feb. 27th, 1846.

DEAR SIR,—I beg to acquaint you that his Royal Highness Prince George of Cambridge has expressed his desire to fill the vacancy in the box occasioned by the resignation of Lord Charleville, and that having consulted with Lord A. Fitzclarence, Col. Wildman, Hon. J. Macdonald, and G. Wombwell, Esq., &c., they consider it right that his Royal Highness should be at once admitted without being subject to a ballot.

I have the honour to remain yours,

DONEGAL.

At last, Mr. Duncombe's ill health necessitated a surrender of the most prized of his social gratifications. He gave up his nightly attendance at the theatre—a serious deprivation to him, in consequence of his deep interest in the drama, and the gratification he had for a long course of years been in the habit of enjoying in theatrical entertainments. It was also with sincere regret that he surrendered his seat in the opera-box, in which he had continued " the observed of all observers" for so many seasons. The regret of his friends at this proceeding was evidently as genuine as his own. The Marquis of Donegal again writes :—

Lowndes-street, Sunday.

MY DEAR DUNCOMBE,—I cannot tell you how truly and sincerely grieved I was to receive your note giving so unfavourable an account of your health, and expressing the determination it has imposed upon you of no longer belonging to our box. If it be a consolation to you, I am confident that I speak the sentiments of every member of it when I say that they one and all deeply lament the retirement of one with whom they have been so long associated, have passed so many happy and agreeable days, and whose loss they never can replace. For myself, my dear Tommy, I can only say that from my earliest intimacy with you, I have never had but the feeling of sincere friendship, and as far as in my power lay, I ever strived to prove it. If for a moment that feeling received a check, I regret it; I did all I could to repair it, and I hope and trust that it is long since forgotten. Sincerely do I hope that you may derive benefit from the mild air of Devonshire; and God grant that you may return to your duties in the spring as fresh and strong in health as I can wish you. I will with pleasure write to you all the news I can collect, and shall experience real and sincere gratification in so doing if I can for a moment contribute to your amusement.

Adieu, my dear Tommy, and believe me ever yours truly,
DONEGAL.

CHAPTER III.

THE DUKE OF BRUNSWICK'S HEIR.

Royal Families of Brunswick and England—Marriages—Arrival in England of Prince Charles—His English education—He is deprived of his tutor and recalled to Brunswick—The Prince Regent's animosity against his wife's relations—Appropriates the property of Prince Charles—He attains his majority—Revolution in Brunswick—Duke of Brunswick's flight and deposition—Fails in an attempt to re-enter his Duchy—In Paris—Failure of William IV. and the Duke of Cambridge in the French courts of law—The Duke in England—Consults Mr. Duncombe—Slanderous attacks—One of the Duke's calumniators sent to Newgate—The Duke's Bill of Complaint in the Court of Chancery—His appeal to the House of Lords—Mr. Duncombe's mission to the King of Hanover—Letters of Baron de Falcke and the Duke of Brunswick—His Petition to the House of Commons—Letter to Mr. Duncombe—The Duke's will—His valuables.

THE relations of the Royal Family at Brunswick with that of England were rendered closer by two matrimonial alliances—one, that of the Princess Augusta, the youngest daughter of Frederick Prince of Wales, father of George III., with Charles William Ferdinand, Duke of Brunswick,* whose second son (the

* On Princess Augusta, eldest sister of George III., being married to the Duke of Brunswick:—" Be it enacted, &c., by authority of same: That his said Highness, Charles William Ferdinand, Hereditary Prince of Brunswick and Luneburg, be to all intents and purposes whatsoever deemed, taken, and esteemed a natural-born subject within this realm, any law, statute, matter, or thing whatsoever to the contrary notwithstanding."—4 Geo. III. c. 5, 1764.

first had died without issue) was killed at Quatre
Bras; and that of his sister the Princess Caroline with
George Prince of Wales (George IV.) The heroic
Duke left two sons, Charles, born at Brunswick on
the 30th of October, 1804, and William, eighteen
months younger. (At the breaking out of the first
French Revolution the Duke of Brunswick had fled
to England with all the available property he could
carry with him, and invested the proceeds in the
English funds.)

Any one familiar with the court annals of this
duchy must be aware that some of the members of the
reigning family had peculiar characteristics, indulging
in extravagances of behaviour which our insular
notions condemned. As Prince Charles arrived in
England in the year 1809, he was too young to have
betrayed any of these failings offensively; he therefore was honoured with a state reception on his landing at Greenwich, and treated in every respect as a
member of the Royal Family.

His father desiring that he should receive an
English education, a talented clergyman of the
Church of England, the Rev. Mr. Prince, was appointed to be his tutor in 1812; and they not only
worked harmoniously together, but became attached to each other. Prince Charles appears to
have been brought prominently before the English
public in the year 1814, when he was selected to lay
the foundation stone of Vauxhall Bridge. As he
could only have been ten years old at this period,
such a performance is scarcely to be commended. In
the same year occurred the visit of the Allied
Sovereigns, his godfathers, their ministers and

generals, by whom the heir to the Brunswick duchy must have been regarded with considerable interest.

The Prince was getting on very well with his tutor; when, owing apparently to the reigning Duke of Brunswick taking offence at the behaviour of the English Royal Family to his sister the Princess of Wales, he was abruptly recalled to Brunswick. His separation from his tutor affected him profoundly; and a sense of wrong and injustice obtained possession of his boyish mind which gave a morbid irritation to all his after life.

The Rev. Dr. Prince seems to have been badly used in this transaction. Apparently under this impression, the Duke of Kent appointed him his chaplain, and took him to Brussels, where he remained for several years as English resident clergyman, taking pupils, and writing pamphlets detailing his grievances. He subsequently returned to London, and died at Old Brompton.

The Prince Regent extended his hatred of his wife to all her relations, and contracted a particular dislike to Prince Charles of Brunswick, because when he was sent for to Carlton House, and prohibited visiting his aunt, he dared to reply, that his father had directed him to pay his respects to her Royal Highness once a fortnight, and that he should continue to do so till commanded to do otherwise by the same authority. The Princess Charlotte appeared to entertain a regard for her cousin; and on his birthday, 1812, presented him with a " History of England" as a keepsake.

On his way to Brunswick Prince William learnt the death of his father; and by the arrangements previously settled by the Congress of Vienna, he succeeded to the duchy. Such a position on a young and ardent imagination, suffering from recent excitement, still further unsteadied his mind. It was the Duke's misfortune to have placed over him, in 1819, ostensibly in the post of tutors, a couple of intemperate pedants, who appear to have done their best, by their tyranny, to keep the temper of their pupil in a state of chronic irritability. The money in the English funds was seized, and the conduct of the King (George IV.) became so equivocal that the Congress of Verona required explanations. The young Duke complained loudly, and a war of abuse raged between the printing-presses of Hanover and Brunswick; till the Germanic Federation, in 1828, strove to put an end to the scandal by a decree against the younger, and less powerful offender.

When Duke Charles could escape from surveillance a reaction in his feelings led him occasionally to throw off all restraint. But that he could conduct himself as became his exalted rank was evident; when his Royal Highness attended at Hanover to witness the marriage of the Duke of Clarence with the Princess Adelaide of Saxe Meiningen, and subsequently entertained the royal couple for eight days at his castle in Brunswick.

It has been affirmed that a design was entertained by George IV. for causing Brunswick to become a portion of the kingdom of Hanover; and that his detestation of his brother-in-law not only made him readily approve of any scheme for the appropriation of its revenues, but caused him to spare neither trouble nor expense to place the youthful Prince in such a position as would render this appropriation easy and safe. It should, however, be borne in mind that these are part of the statements subsequently made by the Duke. The following memorandum also proceeded from him :—

The Duke never could [obtain] any money during the life of Geo. IV., and only obtained the same from Wm. IV. after the Revolution of 1830.

One most extraordinary fact is that the Duke Charles has never been able to see the testament of his father, and therefore does not to this day know the exact amount, although he has received contradictory extracts from the will. Wm. IV. admitted that he had only paid a portion of the money into the funds, and retained the rest for Prince William, who already had seized the Duke's fortune.*

Duke Charles complained that at the age of eighteen he was allowed only three francs a-week pocket money, and was kept as badly in diet; and that having been ordered to go to Lausanne, he was taken to all the lunatic establishments *en route.* It is to be inferred from these revelations that his violence had led to his being pronounced and treated as insane. It was also alleged that though, by the laws of Brunswick, he had then attained his majority, he was not permitted to assume his rights, that he might not offer an asylum to his aunt. On George IV.'s visit to Hanover, Prince William was sent to Göttingen, and Prince Charles to Carlsruhe. He subsequently went to Vienna, where he renewed his acquaintance with Prince Metternich, to whom he had been introduced in London in 1814, and made an arrangement to be guided by his advice for three years. He also had an

* MS. in the Duke's handwriting.

interview with the emperor, who was convinced that there existed no reason for considering him insane.

In October, 1823, he entered his capital amidst general rejoicings, and shared the private property of the family with his brother. He then visited Hanover and the Duke of Cambridge; subsequently Italy, France, and England. While here he received the freedom of the city of Edinburgh, and returned to Brunswick in March, 1826. He went again to the Austrian capital, and again had a conference with Prince Metternich; but in 1830 was in Paris when the revolution broke out which overthrew the elder line of the Bourbons. This movement spread to Belgium, and subsequently to Brunswick; where he returned only to be the victim of a conspiracy. He was obliged to fly to England; and at his departure his palace was burnt, his banishment and deposition decreed, and his brother elected to rule in his stead.

During this interval there appear to have been serious charges brought against him; but after making due allowance for revolutionary exaggeration, and for the animus of those who would profit by his overthrow, he seems to have conducted himself in a way anything but creditable. Still it is doubtful whether on such grounds he ought to have forfeited his civil rights. The case of the late Mr. Windham was characterized by much the same recklessness, but his relatives failed in their efforts to deprive him of the control of his property.

The duke received in England assurances of support from William IV. and the Duke of Cambridge; and the Duke of Wellington advised him to abdicate for a term of five years, retaining the title of sovereign and an income of a million francs; but two or three months later he resolved to return to his duchy, having first communicated with the Emperor of Russia and the King of Prussia. On his way he narrowly escaped drowning in the Channel, and assassination by the knife at Osterode, near Hanover. He reached Gotha, and offered attractive promises to his subjects, but without success. He then proceeded to Paris on the 12th of December, Prince Metternich having assured him that his private property would be respected. He claimed certain funds in the hands of bankers, but ascertained that the money had been stopped by William IV.

Duke Charles then returned to London, and subsequently started for Spain. After having been welcomed to Madrid by King Ferdinand, he wintered at Nice. He was now assailed by all sorts of accusations—among others, by a charge of recruiting soldiers for the Duchesse de Berri. The duke returned to Paris, whence he was directed to withdraw, on the accusation of aiding legitimacy; but remained in concealment until February, 1833, when he purchased a mansion, and gave 10,000 francs to the poor. He was favoured by Lafayette and Odillon Barrot. At this period it was that William IV. and the Duke of Cambridge endeavoured to move the law courts in France to sanction their guardianship of the property in the possession of the duke.

The Duke of Brunswick having taken a residence in Paris in January, 1835, he was cited to appear before the *Tribunal de Premier Instance*, to surrender all his property into the hands of the Duke of Cambridge, in accordance with an arrangement entered into between the reigning duke and William IV. The duke defended his own cause; and the tribunal decided that it had no jurisdiction. As the costs were necessarily paid by the unsuccessful party to the suit, the duke's satisfaction was intense.

He was in England in the summer of the following year, and consulted Mr. Duncombe. The duke placed great confidence in his judgment, and conferred with him as to the disposal of the property of which his relatives had tried to dispossess him. This, according to his own statement, was enormous.

"Throw dirt enough, and some of it must stick," seems to have suggested the slanderous attacks now made upon him. There is no doubt whatever that some of it did stick. It was also well known that the duke was rich, and might be induced to pay liberally to stop these slanders. The annoyance they caused could not but have been intolerable, for go where he would he was sure to be the object of as much curiosity as a state criminal. Notwithstanding all the merciless accusations brought against the duke while in England, the only one supported by a shadow of proof was—that he wore *a beard!* It is almost incredible the use made of this now familiar appendage for the purpose of exciting a prejudice against him. When certain Sunday newspapers failed to convince their readers that he was a murderer, they had only to refer to his hirsute chin to satisfy the Anglican mind of that time that he was an ape and a baboon.

At last the duke turned upon his enemies, and commenced a criminal prosecution against two of the most infamous, in December, 1842. True bills were duly found by the grand jury. It is impossible to imagine a more humiliating course than that taken by the offenders, alternately threatening and wheedling their prosecutor. His friends were overwhelmed with the most scurrilous abuse, and everybody known to have the slightest acquaintance with him assailed by name with the grossest insinuations. It came out that the animus of one of his assailants was derived from a supposition that the duke had caused him to be hissed off the stage, he having ventured to appear before the public as a candidate for theatrical honours.

Yet after all this vituperation, when the trial came on, he pleaded "guilty." The case was one of the most aggravated kind, and the libeller was sentenced to imprisonment in Newgate.

The libels were not stopped by this punishment: calumny had been too profitable to be easily surrendered. The editors of the more respectable newspapers began to appreciate the disgrace which these dealers in scandal were inflicting on the profession, and openly denounced the offenders. Then the most notorious of them thus assumed the office of censor:—
"The press of this country, and of the metropolis more especially, is influenced by the most despicable feelings of malignity: it is truly a house divided against itself, since its individual members, instead of elevating and extending its influence by the display of lofty and generous feelings, rarely omit an opportunity of wreaking the petty vengeance of personal hatred, no matter whether it be at the expense of truth, justice, and honour!"*

Thus wrote the convicted libeller, of those journals that had held him up to public scorn!

* *Satirist*, 7th January, 1844.

On the 1st of August, 1843, the duke filed a bill of complaint in the High Court of Chancery, Lord Lyndhurst being Lord Chancellor. It mentioned the revolutionary movement, and the decree of the Germanic Diet directing Duke William to assume the temporary government of the duchy; the compact between him and William IV. to take Duke Charles's private fortune out of his control, by placing it under the guardianship of the Duke of Cambridge, then viceroy of the adjoining State of Hanover. This agreement was not only signed by the king and duke William, but by the dukes of Cumberland, Sussex, and Cambridge. He complained that, by this illegal instrument, the viceroy had taken possession of the entire Brunswick estate, and bought and sold, and received large revenues, without rendering him any account, though there must be a balance in his favour to the amount of several hundred thousand pounds—refusing to give such account—appointing certain administrators to the property, and giving them instructions.

Further on the bill states that the defendants to the suit and their agents seized the following private property — " Cash at your orator's* bankers, at Brunswick, Messrs. Sussmann, Herniman, and Co., to the amount of 20,000*l.*, or thereabouts; Prussian Bonds, in the custody of your orator's said bankers, to the value of 20,000*l.*, or thereabouts; Bonds of the Cortes of Spain, in the custody of the said bankers, to the amount of 10,000*l.*, or thereabouts; Austrian Bonds, also in their custody, to the amount of 8000*l.*, or thereabouts; Brunswick State Bonds to the amount

* Quoted from the subsequent Appeal to the House of Lords.

of 100,000*l.*, or thereabouts; furniture, plate, jewels, private museums, horses, carriages, and divers other particulars, to the amount in value of 100,000*l.*, or thereabouts." Together with the rents and profits of the following real estates, also private property— "The palace of Richmond, with its park, near Brunswick aforesaid, of great annual value; several private houses, and other buildings in Brunswick, also of great annual value; and the park and other estates in Brunswick aforesaid, devised to your orator absolutely by the will of your orator's grandmother, Augusta, late Duchess of Brunswick, the sister of his late Majesty King George III., also of great annual value."

Then the bill relates the legal proceedings taken against Duke Charles in France, to secure property of his then in that country—their failure, and the payments in consequence the Duke of Cambridge was compelled to make; excepting a balance left unpaid, for which Duke Charles sued him in England in the Court of Common Pleas, and, after putting in several pleas, he submitted by paying 2000*l.* in September, 1848. All these sums, it was complained, were derived from the rents and profits of Duke Charles's private property at Brunswick.

The bill then describes his being mobbed and stabbed in the town of Osterode, in the kingdom of Hanover, while proceeding to visit his dominions, whence he was compelled to fly for his life into Prussia, leaving behind him at his hotel in the town "cash and notes to the amount of 34,000 crowns, or about 4500*l.* sterling—consisting of about 8500 crowns in Prussian paper, 2600*l.* in English bank-notes, and

4000 francs in notes of the Bank of France. These sums were delivered to the Viceroy and withheld from him, and only accounted to the Duke of Cumberland when the Duke of Cambridge gave up "the guardianship" to the former on his becoming King of Hanover. To be relieved from this control the bill prays for the interference of the Court, as well as for its assistance to recover all necessary documents.

The King of Hanover applied to be discharged from the process; this was refused by an order from the Court (12th of August, 1843). Then on the 31st of the same month he replied by a demurrer, which was argued before the Master of the Rolls in the following November; who gave judgment on the 13th of January, 1844, allowing the demurrer, with costs. As this defeated the suit on the plea that the Court had no jurisdiction, Duke Charles appealed from the judgment of the Master of the Rolls to the House of Lords, for the following reasons: because the respondent (King of Hanover) was a peer of the realm, and subject to the jurisdiction of the Court; because the appellant is a subject of the realm, domiciled in England, indisputably entitled to claim relief from an English court of justice; because his complaint is cognizable in an English court of justice, and because his bill makes out a case for equitable relief.

It was after a review of all these transactions in the duke's career, and with the fullest conviction that his royal highness had been grievously wronged, that Mr. Duncombe determined on becoming his advocate. Before bringing the case for discussion in the House of Commons, he advised that an attempt should be made to effect a private arrangement. It was impossible for him, after a careful scrutiny of the facts of the case, to doubt that the duke had been treated after a fashion that neither law nor equity could sanction. The award of the Cour Royale in France proved how an independent court of justice would deal with such arbitrary proceedings. The more recent defeat in the Rolls Court on technical grounds was equivalent, in his eyes, to a denial of justice. Still he desired to take up the subject in a courteous spirit; and sent his secretary on a private mission with the following letter to the King of Hanover:—

The Albany, December 1st, 1845.

SIR,—His Serene Highness the Duke of Brunswick having been advised to appeal to the British Parliament for redress of the various wrongs and illegal deprivation of private property which he has sustained, I have been requested to present, at the opening of Parliament, a petition to the House of Commons, embodying at considerable length, and in very elaborate detail, the grievances of which his Serene Highness has reason to complain.

But I feel that I should be wanting in courtesy and respect to your Majesty and the rest of the Royal family, were I to present this petition without first endeavouring to assure myself that his Serene Highness had exerted every means in his power, previous to an appeal to Parliament, to bring about an amicable adjustment of all matters in dispute.

With this view, and for this purpose, I have taken the liberty of despatching Mr. George Smith (my private secretary) to solicit the honour of an interview with your Majesty, trusting that your Majesty will receive this communication, as well as any that Mr. Smith may make to your Majesty, in the same spirit.

I have the honour to subscribe myself,

Your Majesty's very obedient humble servant,
THOS. S. DUNCOMBE.

The secretary started on his confidential mission. There was much tact demanded for the successful issue of the delicate negotiation entrusted to him. He could not be unaware of the impracticable character of the potentate to whom he was accredited, nor ignorant of his unpromising antecedents, but was entirely ignorant of the constitution of the Hanoverian court, and the small probability that existed of his mission being entertained by either king or ministers. The first, independently of all other considerations, had had more than enough of the House of Commons when Duke of Cumberland and the head of the Orange lodges; now he felt himself secure from such control, and was ready to treat the idea of parliamentary interference with him with becoming dignity. The secretary's report and the ensuing correspondence express the fate of the negotiation :—

British Hotel, Hanover, 14th December, 1845.

I am not getting on here as fast as I could wish, and very much doubt whether I shall see the king. I have had interviews with the Baron Malorty, and also with his Excellency the Baron Falcke, and I have received a letter, the copy of which is annexed; and on seeing the Baron Falcke this day, he has promised to speak to the king to-morrow morning, and to call upon me at one o'clock. Unfortunately the Duke William of Brunswick comes here to-morrow, to join the king in a wild boar hunt, to which I have been offered permission to go; they are going to kill 200 boars in the "Zoll Park." You would be astonished how well the Grahamising has made you known on the continent. In fact you are popular here.

Copgrove, Boro'bridge, December 20th, 1845.

MY DEAR DUKE OF BRUNSWICK,—I have just received the enclosed, which I take the liberty of forwarding, knowing

that your Serene Highness must be anxious to hear how my
ambassador at Hanover is getting on.   He appears to be
well received by the authorities, but to experience, as I
anticipated, much difficulty in obtaining the required audience.   However, I feel confident that he will do all that
can be done to carry out your wishes; and I think the
ministerial changes here will be favourable to them.

Has your Serene Highness heard a report of the probability of Prince Louis' speedy release?   If so, what will be
the effect of it on public opinion in France ?

I have the honour to be,

My dear Duke of Brunswick, yours very faithfully,

T. S. D.

The King of Hanover, as soon as he learnt the
business of the messenger from England, stood upon
his dignity :—

[ENCLOSURE.]

Hanover, the 13th day of December, 1845.

Major General Deering presents his compliments to Mr.
Smith, and begs to acquaint him that he has received his
Majesty's most gracious commands to say, that, as his
Majesty cannot communicate with any person, on the sub-
ject alluded to in Mr. Duncombe's letter, with whom he is
not personally acquainted, therefore requests that Mr. Smith
will address himself to Baron Falcke, his Majesty's Privy
Counsellor, who will naturally make his report to his
Majesty, and receive his commands.

Mr. Duncombe, on receiving these communications,
forwarded them to the duke.   Another arrived shortly
afterwards, and this settled the affair :—

Copgrove, Boro'bridge, December 21st, 1845.

MY DEAR DUKE OF BRUNSWICK,—Since I had the honour
of addressing you yesterday, I have received the enclosed
official communication from le Baron de Falcke, which has

been forwarded to me from the Albany, where it was left by a special messenger. Pray oblige me by reading it and returning it to me, and, at the same time, by informing me what you think of it, and what you wish me to do. My reply will of course be entirely guided by an anxious desire to promote your interests.

I hope they will not dispose of the Sr. Smith among the 200 boars which, in his letter of yesterday, he says he was invited to see shot.

Yours, &c. &c.,   T. S. D.

[ENCLOSURE.]
Hanovre, le 15 Dec., 1845.

MONSIEUR,—Relativement à la lettre par vous adressée en date du 1er du courant à sa Majesté le Roi de Hanovre, dans l'intérêt de son altesse sérénissimé monseigneur le Duc Charles de Brunswick, et dont le Sr. Smith, votre secretaire, a été porteur, le roi mon auguste souverain m'a ordonné de vous informer que, quoique loin de méconnaître ni l'attention que vous lui avez temoignée en cette circonstance, ni les bonnes intentions qui vous auront guidé, le roi s'est vu dans l'impossibilité d'admettre Mr. Smith en sa présence par rapport à une affaire qui n'est aucunement de nature à pouvoir de la part de sa majesté être traitée d'une manière particulière et clandestine.

Veuillez agréez, monsieur, l'assurance de mon considéra-tion très distinguée.   LE BARON DE FALCKE.

à Mr. T. Duncombe, M.P. Anglais, à Londres.

Brunswick House, this 23rd December, 1845.

MY DEAR MR. DUNCOMBE,—I return you with many thanks the enclosed letter from Hanover, which you where (*sic*) so kind to forward for my perusal. Receive, my dear Mr. Duncombe, the assurance of my distinguished consi-deration.   DUKE OF BRUNSWICK.

I this instant receive and likewise return the message

from Hanover under your address. I thought it would be so, and mentioned as much to the Sr. Smith, but he would not part with either my letter or my message but to the person's *own* hands. In every other respect you will deal with or answer Mr. Falcke at your pleasure.

It does not appear that Mr. Duncombe took any further trouble in the way of correspondence with the King of Hanover or his minister. The secretary came back safe; and after hearing his further report, all the documents were carefully read and arranged for ready reference. In these were included a draft of the appeal to the House of Lords, which, when printed, extended to twenty-two folio pages. Mr. Duncombe made abstracts from all, and took a great deal of trouble to be master of the case.

On his return to town for the session he conferred with the duke and his solicitors, and then drew up a petition to the House of Commons with the object of presenting it, and moving for a committee of inquiry.

In the session of 1846 he presented a petition from the duke to the House of Commons, complaining of the injuries he had suffered at the hands of his relatives, and including documents in support of his allegations.* He also complains of having fruitlessly had recourse to legal proceedings, as well as addressed unavailingly the German Confederation to insist on the carrying out of the sixty-third article of the treaty of Vienna, by which

---

* The one printed by order of the House of Commons for the use of members, 10th July, 1846, abounds with errors. We have one before us carefully corrected by the duke's hand.

his duchy was guaranteed to him; and now appeals, as a last resource, to the justice of a British House of Commons.

The petition is dated the 28th of May, 1846. Afterwards Mr. Duncombe moved, "That the petition of his sovereign highness the Duke of Brunswick, &c., be referred to a select committee, to report their opinion thereon, together with the evidence, to the House."

It may be advanced that the allegations put forth by the Duke are entirely *ex parte;* but it is long since they were made public, and no disproof of them has been attempted. The result of the trials in the French courts of justice sufficiently indicates the legal opinion of the case in one properly constituted tribunal, and the judgment in the analogous Windham case, in another. Whatever may be the amount of eccentricity or the degree of moral turpitude a man may exhibit, in no country does this constitute a right of interference in the disposal of his property by his relations, unless clear evidence can be established of his being mentally incapable of managing his own affairs. This was the view likely to be taken of the case by the readers of the duke's petition to the House of Commons. On the back of a printed copy we find in his handwriting the following memorandum :—

It may be remarked by Mr. Duncombe that as England deprived me of my duchy *and private fortune,* if it will not get the latter back for me, I should have as much right to a considerable pension from this country as the Indian princes whom England deprives of their country, and who enjoy considerable revenues for their loss, and a much greater right than those members of my royal family who, already enriched through my spoil, receive moreover large revenues from England in the shape of pensions, *vide*—

Cumberland and son, at *Hanover;* Cambridge, son, and daughter; while I actually spend what I have HERE.

The presentation of the Duke of Brunswick's petition did not produce the desired effect. Mr. Duncombe was unremitting in his exertions to serve him; but owing to his injudicious and eccentric spirit, success was difficult. His temper was uncertain, his judgment capricious, and his ideas were as frequently under the dominion of personal vanity as of personal prejudice. Mr. Duncombe was again induced to present a petition from the duke to the House of Commons in the following session. Again he laboured to induce Parliament to interpose in behalf of his client; but his client had contrived to create so general an impression of his being a *mauvais sujet* as well as a *mauvais souverain*, that little advantage was to be anticipated. The appeal to the House of Lords had been withdrawn till the effect of Mr. Duncombe's motion for inquiry had been ascertained.

Towards the termination of the session of 1847 the result of Mr. Duncombe's advocacy began to bear fruit. Negotiations were again opened under the happiest auspices. He was anxious to leave the important questions at issue to the settlement of Prince Metternich and Lord Palmerston, and the secretary's services were again in requisition. But the prince, it appears, did not approve of the terms submitted to him, and Lord Palmerston in consequence was likely to decline acting as referee, as proposed. In reply to a suggestive communication from the member for Finsbury, the duke wrote :—

Brunswick House, this 10th of August, 1847.

My DEAR MR. DUNCOMBE,—I hasten to acknowledge your letter of yesterday afternoon. Several conversations and some writings have taken place on the subject it discusses, between your secretary, Mr. Smith, and myself. He will have informed you of my views, and placed in your hands my writings. I will add a few new facts which have struck me. You say with great justice in your letter that an opportunity must not be given to Lord Palmerston to oppose my claims in Parliament on the ground that negotiations are going on elsewhere; but when do you think will he be better able so to do, now that Prince Metternich has refused those terms Mr. Smith was instructed to submit to him? and which you will have a right to say he refused, not because of any particular claim named, for Smith was only instructed to demand my fortune, and Lord Palmerston as an umpire, to decide in what that fortune consisted; so you clearly see that the pecuniary claims cannot be meant when Prince Metternich writes, " Proposals such as you make," or when such negotiations should actually have been set on foot and not brought to a close. That is all my enemies want, and nothing will be easier for them than to protract for 17 years longer a state of things that dates since 1830.

Receive, my dear Mr. Duncombe, the assurance of my distinguished consideration.

DUKE OF BRUNSWICK.

It is not easy to understand by what legal authority the duke was deprived of his private fortune at Brunswick; for even in the case of dispossessed continental princes such property has almost always been respected. The law of might, whether exercised by the Germanic Diet or the King of Hanover, can scarcely be considered sufficient authority in the nineteenth century, and according to the German legists consulted by the duke there was no other law to be referred to. It is a pity that the case was not submitted to independent arbitration, that the scandal of these criminations might have been avoided, for those by whom they have been read have been forced to come to the conclusion that royal families are not free from the unworthy feelings that create quarrels about money or money's worth among humbler folk.

The whole of the next paper is in the duke's handwriting :—

Legal Opinions of Sergeants-at-law, Lynkeer of Brunswick, and Nicol of Hanover, on the Non-competency of the Tribunals of those Countries to decide in the Robbery Question of Duke Charles's Private Fortune :—

In olden times, and before the dissolution of the Holy Roman Empire of Germany by Napoleon, the reigning princes of Germany could only be sued before the imperial high court of justice. Since then, they can only be sued before their own tribunals in questions of their private estates, or such cases into which they could likewise have been involved if they had been private individuals, but they cannot be sued for anything they have done in their capacity of sovereign, or for any goods they are only come possessed of in that quality. Well aware of these facts, both William IV. of England, as King of Hanover, and William the Usurper of Brunswick, issued their joint interdiction of Duke Charles, and the seizure of his highness's private fortune, in the shape of a treaty, and had this treaty inserted into the laws of Hanover and Brunswick—laws against which the tribunals of the countries are not only powerless, but which they are obliged by oath to enforce, good or bad. The question if a law or an order in council has been legally given or not, is beyond the competency of the tribunals, and ought to be answered by the German Diet. In our opinion, Duke Charles can only make good his claims at the German Diet, or otherwise politically. The King of Hanover and Prince William of Brunswick may pretend they only acted in pursuance of directions from the German Diet, although they certainly do *not* mention doing so in their treaty of the 6th and 14th of February 1833, and although the decree of the German Diet of 2nd December 1836 does *not* authorize them, for it only mentions the government of the duchy. There is no doubt that the right of high guardianship which used to be exercised by the Emperor of Germany, in the style it is in England by the Lord Chancellor, has become invested in the sovereign princes of Germany; but then again the legitimate sovereign of Brunswick *alone* could ordain a guardianship over a member of his family, and *no one* else. But here again the question would have to be decided, who is the sovereign of the duchy of Brunswick? This question is evidently *not* one for the competency of the Brunswick or Hanoverian tribunals. Prince William has usurped and exercises the sovereign power with the consent of the German Diet, and under the protection and acknowledgment of Hanover. The subservient tribunals of those countries cannot, and would not, interfere in favour of Duke Charles of Brunswick.

On the 7th September 1830 a revolution broke out against the sovereign Duke Charles of Brunswick, which had been long before prepared by a conspiracy, at the head of which was the Duke's only brother, the Prince William. This conspiracy was countenanced, ay, even wished for, by the Fourth William, then King of England, and his brothers, the Dukes of Cumberland, Sussex, and Cambridge, who thereby came one step nearer to the rich inheritance of a sovereign duchy and an enormous private fortune; for by the existing state and family treaties the surviving branch of the house of Brunswick is to enter into possession of the states of the other, and, by being the nearest relation, also in possession of all *private property, if not particularly* otherwise disposed of. It now so happens that there are only two remaining princes of the elder branch of the house of Brunswick, Duke Charles and Prince William. The first, put aside by force, the second alone remains, easy to remove by stratagem. But now, under what pretence could William IV., or his successor, the King of Hanover, put himself in possession of the private fortune of Duke Charles, who certainly, if left to himself, would *otherwise* dispose of it, even after having by force seized his duchy? For it has never been admitted that the right of making a revolution extends to robbing the Prince of all means of existence. So we see in France, Charles X. and his family remain in full possession of their private fortunes; yes, even Napoleon was left in the undisturbed possession of his fortune in France, after the loss of his crown. Not so with the Duke of Brunswick; against him the following plan was adopted to empty his, and fill the pockets of his royal relatives. The Prince William of Brunswick is a man of weak understanding, and was therefore, in so far, easily fooled by the King of England that the latter got all power over Duke Charles's private fortune to himself alone. It was given to understand by the King to Prince William, that he should make the Parliament of Brunswick seize upon his brother's private fortune in that country, under the pretence that this sovereign had sold estates, forests, palaces, and so forth, which he had no right to dispose of. This first step taken, the second, also by advice of the King, soon followed; this was, for the Prince William to declare to the Parliament that they should give up to him all goods, estates, palaces, and cash seized by them belonging to Duke Charles, for which Prince William would make himself answerable towards the Parliament. Now comes the thing most serious, and last step taken by Prince William and King William together in *public*, before *which* till then, as appears by this account, King William had not yet done anything till he thought his moment was arrived.

On the 6th and 18th of March 1833, both issued a deed or treaty under their respective seals and signatures, declaring that their much beloved brother and cousin, Charles Duke of Brunswick, was insane, and that they therefore had felt it their duty to take upon themselves the heavy burden of his private fortune, and appointed the Duke of Cambridge as the keeper as well of the *property* as his Highness's *person*. To this deed the Prince and the King had invited and obtained the consent and signature of their Highnesses the Dukes of Cumberland, Sussex, and Cambridge. The private fortune belonging to Duke Charles,* seized at Brunswick, and now under the control of the Duke of Cambridge, amounts to a large sum—to several millions of pounds sterling.

The Duke during the period he lived in London occupied Brunswick House, New-road, and enjoyed all the *agrémens* of town life. He mixed much in gay society, though permitting few intimacies, and was in his expenses a curious compound of extravagance and parsimony, of prodigality and avarice. While investing enormous sums in the purchase of precious stones and foreign stocks, he is said to have neglected paying accounts that had long been over due.

He executed a will in favour of Mr. Duncombe, to whom he professed a profound attachment. The member for Finsbury had often given him good advice, and quite as frequently had endeavoured to keep him out of scrapes ; but whatever was the extent of regard these services may have inspired, his Royal Highness's detestation of his nearest relations influenced him more than anything in such a disposition of his property. Mr. Duncombe by the provisions of this testament was left the whole of the Duke's personality, the value of which we will presently show. The will appears to have been made in good faith, and with the understanding that Mr. Duncombe was

* His Serene Highness Prince Charles Frederick Augustus William, Duke of Brunswick and Luneburg, and a General in the British service.

the heir, not only of what the testator possessed, but of all to which he had a claim—the securities, the precious stones, and the territory of his duchy.

We append the document:—

I, Charles Frederick Augustus William, Sovereign Duke of Brunswick and Luneburg, now residing at Brunswick House (late Harley House), Brunswick Place, New Road, Regent's Park, in the parish of Marylebone, in the county of Middlesex, being in sound mind and health of body, do declare this to be my last will and testament. I do hereby revoke all other wills and testamentary papers by me heretofore made. I desire, after my death, that my executors hereinafter named shall cause my body to be examined by three or more proper surgeons, or physicians, to ascertain that I have not been poisoned; and thereupon to report in writing the cause of my decease; then to be embalmed, and if found advisable for the conservation of my body, 1 wish to be petrified according to the printed paper enclosed with this my will. I further desire that my funeral shall be conducted with all the ceremony and splendour becoming my legitimate position of Sovereign Duke of Brunswick, as far as the same may be allowed or is permitted in England; and that I be deposited in a mausoleum to be erected of marble in Kensal Green Cemetery, and whereupon a statue and monument shall also be erected, according to the drawing to be hereafter annexed to or enclosed in this my said will; and that my executors shall cause the said statue and monument, or mausoleum, to be erected and made of the materials described in the document so annexed or enclosed, and that the work of art thus described shall be executed by some of the first artists in England. And I also direct, that all my just debts, funeral, and testamentary expenses, be paid and satisfied by my executors hereinafter mentioned *as soon* as conveniently may be after my decease, and subject to the condition that they shall enter into no compromise of any sort with my unnatural relatives (the usurper, William of Bruns-

wick, the King of Hanover, the Duke of Cambridge), or any
of my family, their servants, agents, or any one else; but,
on the contrary, I direct my said executors to use all
means, both legal and parliamentary, to possess and recover
my property in Brunswick and elsewhere after having seized
that in England; and subject to their respecting and carrying out any codicil or codicils I may further leave in favour
of those who may console my last moments. And whereas,
Thomas Slingsby Duncombe, Esq., M.P. for the borough of
Finsbury, and George Thomas Smith, Private Secretary to
the said Thomas Slingsby Duncombe, having severally
afforded me great assistance in prosecuting my case in the
House of Commons, for the purpose of vindicating my
character from the vile aspersions and slander which has
been so industriously promulgated by the members of my
family, and taking the above into my consideration, as well
as any further valuable trouble, and perhaps necessary outlay, in executing this my last will and testament, I do
hereby give and bequeath unto the said George Thomas
Smith the sum of thirty thousand pounds, sterling money,
from my general personal estate, to be paid to him the
said George Thomas Smith, free from legacy duty,
immediately after my decease, for his own absolute use and
benefit. And further, I do hereby give and devise unto
the said Thomas Slingsby Duncombe, *all* and every—the
castle, houses, messuages, lands, tenements, hereditaments,
whatsoever and wheresoever situate; my diamonds, jewels,
plate, pictures, horses, carriages, china, household furniture,
linen, wearing apparel, books, papers, correspondence; and
also all and every sum and sums of money which may be
in my house, or about my person, or which may be due to
me at the time of my decease; and also all other—my
monies invested in stocks, funds, and securities for money,
book debts, money on bonds, bills, notes, or other securities; and all the rest, residue, and remainder of my
estates and effects, whatsoever and wheresoever, both real
and personal, whether in possession, remainder, reversion,
or expectancy, particularly that important part of my for-

tunc retained by force in my hereditary Duchy of Brunswick, for his own absolute use and benefit. And I nominate, constitute, and appoint the said Thomas Slingsby Duncombe and George Thomas Smith to be the executors of this my last will and testament. And I do hereby further direct that my executors, immediately after my decease, shall enter into my present residence, or any other place of abode at which I may be residing at the time of my decease, and shall forthwith take into their custody and possession all my said estate.

And I declare this to be my last will and testament.

In witness, &c.

Dated this 18th day of December, 1846.

Witnessed by Mr. CHÁS. F. ARUNDELL, solicitor.

Mr. WALTER E. WM. GOATLEY, solicitor, and
Mr. JOHN MILES, clerk to Mr. Arundell,
3, Cork Street, Burlington Gardens.

The provision in this document for the preservation of the testator's body after death, is one of those eccentric fancies to which his mind was constantly submitting. The process of petrifaction is so well known, particularly to the visitors at Knaresborough, that it need not be described. We are not aware, however, of its ever having before been selected for the purpose to which the Duke of Brunswick seemed desirous of applying it. As regards the bequests, they will doubtless be considered equally extravagant. They are only to be understood with reference to his Royal Highness's intense desire to disappoint the expectations of his relatives, and as, in the testator's opinion, a proper way of showing his sense of the inestimable services that had been rendered him by the legatees.

The Duke of Brunswick, in his contest with his assailants, could not be satisfied with replying to the

libels complained of. He insisted on conducting his
own case, and when addressing the jury, chose to detail the whole of his history. He also printed his
speeches, and circulated them as widely as he could.
The effect was quite contrary to what he had desired.
The juries and the public became tired of such repeti-
tions, and considered that he was merely taking these
opportunities of coming before the public for thrusting
his quarrels with his family down their throats. A
prejudice against him was the consequence, under the
influence of which it became in vain for him to continue his prosecutions. In one instance a shilling
damages was the award he obtained. This did not
deter him from pursuing the same course in another
case. It was in vain the judge during the trial
warned him of the mischief he was doing himself.
Sir Frederick Thesiger, the opposing counsel, took
advantage of his imprudence, and the jury returned a
verdict "for the defendant."

Unfortunately for the duke, when he wrote about his
grievances, he could not resist the impulse to employ
language as offensive as it was intemperate. This
served to keep aloof from him persons whose influence
and talents might have been advantageously employed
in his behalf; it also caused others who entertained a
favourable opinion of his case to withdraw their support. While judicious friends were endeavouring to
bring the quarrel to an amicable settlement, he would
suddenly give fresh provocation. For instance, at the
very time when Mr. Duncombe was most desirous to
propitiate the House of Commons, the duke issued a
manifesto in English, and a longer one in German, in
a style that inevitably suggests to the indifferent and

calm-minded reader a certain melodramatic hero. We quote the English version:—

Duchy of Brunswick.—Proclamation.

We, Charles, by the grace of God Sovereign Duke of Brunswick and Luneburg, do hereby declare as follows:—

Whereas it has come to our knowledge that the present revolutionary Government, which succeeded in the year 1830 in establishing itself in Brunswick by an attempted assassination of our person, setting fire to our palace, and subsequently seizing all our estates and real property, under the pretext of a curatorship for our benefit, aided by those self-elected curators who render no account of their curatorship, purport defrauding not only ourselves, but also the citizens, peasants, and others of Brunswick, by attempting to parcel and sell in lots those our domains; as a caution to any person or persons who may so attempt to purchase, we hereby forewarn all such parties as may feel so disposed, that we shall not recognise such sales, but re-seize all such our lands and domains, in whatever hands we may find them, they being our rightful property inherited by us from our forefathers. We have never given up our domains to any one, and, therefore, all purchasers will be punished with the utmost severity of the law as aiders and abettors of the said revolutionary Government of Brunswick and those self-elected curators to whom the above refers.

In regard to those swindling traitors who wield the arbitrary power of robbers at Brunswick, they are fully aware that the scaffold and the headsman await their doomed heads, and that their estates, enriched through our spoil, will be confiscated to answer for their larcenies. We here again repeat, in virtue of those sovereign rights secured to us by the treaty of Vienna, and guaranteed by all the Powers of Europe, and which we never have and never will abdicate, our annual protest against that infamous usurpation and foul state of things in our legitimate Duchy of Brunswick. In proof of which we have hereunto set our hand and large state seal at London, this first day of the month of January, in the year of our Lord one thousand eight hundred and forty-seven, and of our reign the thirty-third. (L. S.) CHARLES D.

The duke had an irresistible passion for diamonds, and had already made a superb collection. His wealth in securities was also very large, and all had been secured in bags ready for removal. The following is a list that was given to Mr. Duncombe on the 11th of May, 1847:—

Schedule of the Duke of Brunswick's Valuables.

Mississippi and Maryland	£16,000
Massachusetts	50,000
Louisiana, A	20,000
„ B	10,000
„ C	10,000
„ D	10,000
„ Planters' Association. . .	14,000
Brazilian	15,000
Russian	50,000
Bullion	150,000
F. Rentes	40,000
Belgique	20,000
Ingots	20,000
Notes and bills	200,000
	£625,000

Jewellery and plate, &c.	£300,000

To Mr. Duncombe's secretary was confided every particular respecting the number, nature, and value of this property ; and he was to have charge of the whole in any emergency that should oblige its possessor to absent himself from its place of deposit, or require its removal. That emergency came in 1848, and the following narrative describes the feelings of its temporary custodian while taking possession :—

Monday Afternoon, March 13th, 1848.

On Saturday night I was occupied for five hours making a catalogue of the bonds, &c., now in my care. I have money to the amount of 200,000*l*., and gems, &c., to the amount of 90,000*l*.,* and all was safe at my house this morning when I left, and I hope will be there when I return. You will say, " Where is the rest ?" I will tell you as far as I know. First, the bankers have just purchased for him at a low figure, 40,000*l*. Russians ; therefore they have not yet been delivered. Then Andlau has the 90,000*l*. Three per Cents., French, which he is going to change in Paris for Five per Cents. Aridore, the Belgian agent, has 62,000 Belgians to change either for others or to be paid off; but where the 60,000 Louisiana are I know not—at least, I could not ask him too much, or he would have got frightened. I have only one saddle-bag, No. 4, and if your brother Henry will lend me his brougham to go in, *I will show him all.* Now, then, for your assistance. After he had decided what he would entrust me with, he started; in fact, he told me that before then his fear had been of my house being destroyed by fire, and the paper-money thereby lost. I, fearing to lose the opportunity, said I had got (which I have) an iron chest, but alas! mine is too small, and I am compelled to keep the saddle-bag in a cupboard—perfectly safe, except against fire. I want your permission to move your iron chest, till I deliver up the treasure again. My reason for making this curious request is this: he might perchance come to my house to look and see that it was all safely deposited in iron. I fear, on looking at your iron box, that I shall not be able to get the saddle-bag in, but I may the money, &c.

---

* Or thereabouts ; in fact, I believe I have *all* the diamonds and also all his other gems.

by packing close; and the most important part of the subject is this: the 50,000 Massachusetts coupons are due the 1st of April, and he said—"You can bring them to me and I will cut off the coupons." I said—"If your highness has no objection I will do so." He said—"Yes, that is capital; all those large bonds you might (if your box will hold them) take charge of, and cut off the coupons as they fall due and pay them to me." This opens the door to the following arrangement, viz.: he said—"You might manage all those matters for me should I go to Paris, and even if I remain here in London all the large loans might be so deposited; but," he added, "I will think about it." One thing is a fact; that I have in *genuine* good securities a tolerable good sum now in my house, and really if he would allow all the large loans (and which he does not for the present purpose think of changing) to be at my house it would be a grand thing for us at his death, and they would be just as safe as with him, for I would not touch one shilling until I felt I was entitled to it *by his death*. After all, he cannot be so suspicious as *we* fancy, else why should he trust ME with so large a sum? The only thing he seemed to fear was the possibility of incurring a debt to me for the trouble, and I assured him that it would be a pleasure to do so for him, which fact I think you can testify. He begged I would not bring them to 5A, for fear, he said, of Sloman & Co. I left his house at 1 o'clock after midnight, and was compelled to walk to Oxford Street before I could get a cab. When in the cab my fancy ran upon the excitement I should feel if the bags with the treasure had been with me in a cab under different circumstances, viz. the starting to join you. I cannot but think it a good omen that some of it should be with us, and it must, I am sure, please you to think that his confidence has not in the least diminished. Pray don't forget to say whether I may use the iron box *at my house;* there is nothing in it but THE WILL, and where so fit a place as that which contains the documentary powers of disposing of the money, for the money? You recollect, no doubt, some years ago a political work called " The Adventures of a Guinea," in which the guinea holds conversation with all the other pieces of coin he meets in the pockets of his different owners ; taking that view, I should like to hear the conversation between the will and No. 4 saddle-bag.   It would of course begin as to the right of precedence ; the will arguing that it ought to be kept at the top, and not run the risk of being crushed by base, sordid, filthy lucre—all those terms are applied to both good and bad bonds. However, to humour the will, I think it ought to be at the top.

P.S.—What a strange coincidence that I should be on the point of asking his permission to submit the gems to H. J. D. and that they should come into my possession without my having to make the request.   The Sunday post came all safe, on the DAY INTENDED.

CHAPTER IV.

THE PRESIDENT AND HIS FRIEND.

DURING the years 1848-9 Mr. Duncombe's continued ill-health prevented his taking any prominent part in politics. He rarely visited town, and remained only a day or two—staying in the country, and constantly having recourse to his physician. His secretary visited him repeatedly, and went to Boulogne and to Paris several times on private missions. It became necessary to forward as much as possible the carrying out the arrangement entered into between the high contracting parties to the treaty made at Ham. The negotiations were continued by the same agent. He was in Paris in November, 1849, whence he forwarded this despatch, taking with him a silver eagle as a present from the Duke to the President:—

6, Rue Duphot, St. Honoré, December 5th, 1849.

I have this instant left the President, and on my return here found your note, which delighted my heart, I assure you. I have settled the treaty matter—I have arranged for the letter of invite—I have got back the "national shares," and on which there is 200*l.* to receive on the 15th instant; and, in fact, I have done all but raise troops, which, being the point most wanted, will be the most difficult to satisfy HIM upon. However, L. N. has I say behaved very well. He has pointed out to me how little power he has while the present Chamber exists; for they are as *puissant* as him, and can make laws and issue ordonnances without him. Therefore, he says, until it is dissolved he can do nothing respecting the treaty.

Figurez-vous the state they have been in for ten months —all soldiering, and no manufacturing, but selling all in foreign markets, and then you will understand how little of the usual Parisian novelties are to be found !

I have quite done here, but must write to England to D. B.* for an authority *re* the national; and as soon as I get that, and settle the matter with L. N.'s foster-brother,† I shall start for Angleterre. I shall see the regt. first, as L. N. has arranged for the date of the letter of invite, and that must not be too old when delivered. I think L. N. is well settled, and that in twelve months he will be an emperor—*ça c'est entre nous !*

The negotiations continued, the President too much occupied with the affairs of a great nation passing through a terrible crisis to devote to it much attention, but expressing willingness to come to a satisfactory settlement as soon as he could be put in possession of the nature and extent of the claim against

---

* Duke of Brunswick.   † M. de Mornay.

him. Lord Palmerston, it seems, was to be drawn into the arrangement, as well as the Emperor of Russia. This, however, refers to the projected restoration of the duchy, in which neither was likely to interfere :—

Extract from Count Orsi's* Letter of the 22nd February, 1850.

I have had a very long conversation with the P—— respecting the affairs of the D——, and I think that everything will be settled to the mutual satisfaction of both parties. I must say that I found the P—— in excellent disposition to act with energy and activity in this matter; but you must back him in a more effectual way.

It is the intention of the P—— to open an active negotiation with Lord P.,† and to induce his lordship to act jointly with him in this affair. He will do the same with Russia; for it would appear by the despatches *recently* received that you are not in the right channel.

Now if you will do what I tell you to do, and this quickly, and in a statesman-like way, I can assure you that the wishes of the duke will be satisfied; but act quick, and lose no time. You must forward, as early as you possibly can, " a memorandum containing the claims of the duke, and drawn in such a way as to put things in a straight, clear, and business-like view." This memorandum should be backed by a copy of all such documents (if any) as will put Lord P. and the P—— in full possession and knowledge of all the facts connected with it.

In printed copies of the President's addresses Mr. Duncombe has underlined or struck out certain passages. For instance, in the one dated "Elysée National, Nov. 12, 1850," he has crossed out the last four paragraphs, and underlined the words " sur-

---

* One of the witnesses to the agreement executed at Ham.

† Lord Palmerston.

prise or violence," in the following sentence :—" But whatever may be the solution of the future, let us understand each other, in order that it may never be passion, *surprise, or violence* that shall decide the fate of this great nation." And the words " may be perpetuated" in the following—" The most noble and the most dignified object of an elevated mind is not to seek, when one is in possession of power, by what expedients it *may be perpetuated.*" As well as the subsequent assurance, " *I have honestly opened my heart to you.*" He must have known that these were Napoleonic ideas, and have made allowances.

Mr. Duncombe's secretary was again sent to Paris in October, 1850, but made only a short stay. He was, however, frequently coming and going, and the important interests at stake were often discussed between them. There seems to have been little else going on for which Mr. Duncombe cared. All his former pursuits, all his old amusements, all his customary gratifications were rapidly becoming " flat, stale, and unprofitable ;" a drive in a pony carriage varied the constant medical visits and ever-changing remedies. Politics had little attraction for him. When the Whig government again fell to pieces, he writes in his Diary, " Lord John Russell and Co. resigned ;" and when they return to power, " The Russell clique back in office."

The Duke of Brunswick had returned to London, and had taken up aeronautics as a hobby. On the 3rd of March, 1851, his Royal Highness ascended with Green in a balloon, and descended at Gravesend ; and on the 24th he went with Mr. Duncombe's secretary to Hastings. The latter thence went to

Paris in charge of the duke's heavy baggage. The duke found himself in legal difficulties, and an application was made in his behalf for the interference of the British Government.

It was the receipt of this communication that made the duke resolve on taking up his permanent residence in France, apparently to evade some proceedings commenced against him in one of the English courts of law. He put the design in execution in a novel but characteristic manner, crossing the Channel in a balloon.

The answer to his friend's note to the Minister was as follows :—

C. G., 20th November, 1851.

MY DEAR DUNCOMBE,—I am sorry to say we cannot assist the Duke of Brunswick in the matter mentioned in your note. Foreign princes are, like our own, liable to the laws of this country while they are in it, and the Government has no power to interfere in regard to legal proceedings in which a foreign prince is concerned, or to stay those proceedings on the ground of his royal birth and position. Neither has the Government any power to send a foreign prince out of the country. In fact, the legal position of a prince of a foreign royal family, while resident in this country, is exactly the same as the legal position of a British subject. Yours sincerely, PALMERSTON.

The secretary had returned to England, but crossed the Channel again on the 2nd of December, having received a summons by electric telegraph to come to the duke in Paris, where he was in a state of excessive alarm created by the *coup d'état*. His proceedings there are described in the following reports from La Maison d'Orée, the duke's house in the Rue Lafitte :

Thursday Morning.

I arrived here this morning at five o'clock, and to my surprise found that the duke left this two hours after sending me the despatch, without exactly knowing where he would go. He requested me through his servants to remain here till further orders. He has only taken one carriage, and I suppose *our* bags—I do not know.

Things are serious here. While I was at breakfast at Frascati's I saw an aide-de-camp, right under my eyes, pulled from his horse and killed. Up to that moment all was quiet. Now the troops are on the Boulevards, and the cannon firing towards, I should say by the sound, the Faubourg St. Antoine. I have within sight at least 10,000 men under arms; and they say in Paris there is at least 180,000. I will send you the news as I can, and when I can, for it is already no joke, and had I not been fortunate enough to get home, God knows where I should now be; for the troops, I fear, are a little *too* anxious—as I saw this aide-de-camp, after disarming one man, actually ride after a person who really appeared like a gentleman going home, and attack him in the *back*. *Pensez à moi.* This Thursday has been a dreadful day, and I have been in the thick of it. I really hope that to-morrow I shall have better news. No getting out, even to buy bread. The news here says the slaughter has been dreadful.

I can write no more; only wish I was safely at North Park, *ou chez moi.*

Friday.

Since the above was written, the house alongside this—" Tortoni's "—has been taken, and the bullets flew about here as thick as possible. Two lancers were wounded, from, they said, my window. The soldiers came and seized all the duke's arms.

Saturday, December 6th, 1851.

I send you a copy of a letter (the first) just received :—

" Dear Sir,—I am safe at Anvers with——. Please stop and superintend my house, servants, horses, and property, and let me know how things go on. There can be, I am afraid, no SAFETY till the end of the month. Receive, dear sir, the assurance of my consideration. "D. of B.

"P.S.—My address is, 'Hôtel du Parc.'"

You will see by the above the state of things *re* the duke, and I quite long for a letter from you, and hope it may be to call me home, and I will give up all dukes and be quiet; for I do not choose to run such risks. as I have this time done; and to prove it is not the "white feather" I show, M. Blot, the duke's lawyer, says he is astonished to find me alive after all the reports, and all that has happened, of which I do not think it prudent to write. By some strange coincidence, this part of Paris, which in other times was always tranquil, is the most disturbed; and when I tell you that they cannonaded with 18-pounders within seventy yards of this house, you may judge of the state we have been in, However, thank God, all is over—I hope for permanence, but cannot say.

Poor Paris, the cigarette man, is dead; received two bullets. They make it out not many have been killed, but the waggons of dead prove the contrary. The prince, at any rate, has been successful, but the danger is during this state of siege. Accident may throw you among royalists or others, and, without knowing it, you are compromised with them, and shot on the spot, if they think fit; and the Elysée is so beset, that there are no means of communicating with the prince. You will have all reports from the papers till I see you.

December 8th, 1851.

Nothing fresh has happened since I last wrote to you; neither have I heard from the duke again. His lawyer called yesterday, and told me he had received a letter from him, in which he regretted having left England. I, knowing thereby something of his sentiments, wrote to him regretting he had ever left England, and stated that you also regretted it, and that you had no doubt you could settle all his troubles in England. I also informed him that Brunswick House was vacant, and that he could instal himself in his old quarters without fear or danger in two days, as he was before, and very comfortable, if he chose directly. I asked if I should, to carry out views, if he acquiesced finish up all here, join him at Antwerp, come to Calais, and cross in a calm to Dover in one hour and three-quarters.

He of " Netherby"* is so busy that one does not like to say too much. I shall be glad to be back, and if I have no riches to guard, which I almost doubt, I do not feel flattered by being placed in the position of a " broker's man," or a " man in possession." I wrote to the duke to say that I hoped my charge was worthy of being guarded by me.

There has been a good deal of conversation between lawyer and me, concerning testaments, &c., and also about carrying my banking plan into operation—I beg pardon, I mean your plan—and lawyer says he quite agrees with my —*i.e.*, your view, and has written this day to D. of B., in reply to D. of B.'s request that he would advise him the best to do to say bags to England yourself where you like. I wish I was on " Jerry," instead of on the Boulevard des Italiens.

December 10th, 1851.

I have this instant received a letter from the duke in reply to mine, in which he tells me, " I have nothing at Maison d'Orée of inestimable value, but should not like to lose my papers." He requests my advice as to what he should do for the future, which I have given to this effect: Go to England, and if you decline that, let me take the money portion of your fortune there, and then, in the event of your having to fly, you will only have the diamonds, which are easily concealed about your person, and your life to look after. The lady's maid has written to one of the servants here, stating that she has received orders to hold herself in readiness to return to Paris, as the duke is not quite decided whether *he* will not go to England. I suppose, if the truth was known, he is communicating with his lawyer before deciding.

* Sir James Graham.

Thursday, December 11th, 1851.

I must tell you that I was much annoyed to find I was in charge of *rien*. So great was my disappointment that I almost quarrelled with myself for making so much haste, and attaching so much importance to what ended in nothing. I am, whatever you may say to the contrary, "in possession." Strange to say, that I proposed the visit, and received a letter this morning thanking me for the suggestion, and saying that for the moment I had better remain tranquil at Paris, and see how all goes on, and I shall then be the better able to visit D. B. and give him advice from the knowledge I possess of events; but that if I leave just now, I shall be as unacquainted as D. B. himself, and, therefore, be giving advice in "the dark."

With respect to *bags* I told you yesterday of Blot's view, and he wrote as well as myself, advising that if D. B. made up his mind to return, that he should not for the future put himself in so perilous a position as heretofore by running the risk of being robbed of every shilling, and from the peculiarity of D. B.'s fortune he (B.) has suggested that it should not be entrusted to any trader or banker, but to some friendly but honest *ami*, and for this reason, stock brokers, merchants, or bankers, although they would not venture to use the money, they might perhaps do so indirectly, *i.e.*, give it as security for the fulfilling engagements at stated periods, and so peril the bonds.

I saw Conneau* yesterday, and am to have an interview with the prince in a day or two. I saw and breakfasted with Edwardes on Tuesday, and I am very sorry he is going from Paris.

In the letter I received from D. B. this morning he tells me to get some police agents, two for this place and one for Beaujon, to be under my orders, so that, he says, " being exposed to a second invasion by soldiers, who may be less civil, I may show that, as far as I am concerned, I take no part in affairs and ought not to be molested." He

---

* The prince's physician at Ham.

then gives me some orders as to what horses and what
carriages I may use, tells me that Veyrac has orders to
give me any money I want, or he says, rather, Veyrac will
lend me, and then finishes by assurance, &c.   Then comes
the following in the countess's handwriting:—

"Monsieur Smith est bien bon de s'informer de ma
santé à cette occasion : je ne puis que lui réciproquer la
même demande, et le remercier de son aimable intention à
mon égard en lui souhaitant un heureux séjour à Paris, et
mes salutations empressés.   LA COMTESSE ——."

The duke then adds, in his handwriting, the following,—
"The countess got hold of this letter while I left the room
for a moment, and threw all this ink over it."

December 12th, 1851.

" I have seen Mocquart* and Conneau, and they say
that the prince will the first opportunity grant me an
audience; they are all delighted, and say that the prince is
now certain.   I have heard that Lord P. has written to
the correspondent of the *Post* to write up L. N. ; of this I
believe there is no doubt.

I met the Duc de Guiche, who is all for L. N. ; in fact,
he says that is the only chance for France.

Paris is just as gay as though nothing had happened,
and actually the scene of carnage, bloodshed, and much
more, is become quite the centre of a fête, for all classes are
out visiting the different places, and everybody seems to be
boasting of the risks they ran.   For my part I have only
to say I was at Maison d'Orée, and the reply is "diable."
I saw quite as much as I wish to see.   Nobody can tell how
many killed.   Johnson said this morning 7000; everybody
but Government says 3000; and Government says in all
about 800.

December 15th, 1851.

As you will no doubt see by the public journals, there is
really no news here, except that all is perfectly quiet, and I

* The President's private secretary.

think on the whole the people seem satisfied with the state of things as they suppose they will be after the elections, and as they are at present.

I am paying visits to the Ministre des Finances for the purpose of getting the permission required by our friend to enter France, so I hope he will soon come back here and let me return to England.

I have not yet seen the prince; I am invited to go to the reception this evening. The President will, I have no doubt, have a tremendous quantity of votes; some seem to think not less than 8,000,000, the whole of the persons entitled to vote being only 12,000,000.

December 16th.

The authority here will not grant D. B. the police, so that I presume D. B. intends to return here directly after the election, as my letter of yesterday would tell you that I had been to make preparations for his passing the frontier. With respect to the police doing all "but use his equipages," they, the police, might and may use them for me, for I will not; for he, the duke, says the horses he allotted to me wanted breaking, but he did not tell me that they were vicious, so much so that my stock has been drafted to the Barrière, and not even allowed to stand in his stable; and upon my speaking to the head coachman, he said we had better put them in a water cart for a week, for they both jib, kick, and bolt.

December 19th, 1851.

I wrote to the duke and had a letter to-day from him, in which he takes not the slightest notice of my Christmas request. I should much like to get home, for I like home better than all, but from a letter I saw just now at his banker's from D. B. himself, I think I shall get away from here a day or two after Christmas-day, as he says in his letter, "I must return to Paris sooner than I intended, as Mr. Smith wants to go home, which rather perplexes me, as I have such confidence in him, and he has the door open to him at all the places."

The duke informs me that he has sent for his lawyer, first to make arrangements to receive some money to be paid by Lord Eldon as executor to his father, who was executor to George IV.; and, secondly, to carry out, if possible, legally, my " Harmerian " view; and in a letter of the countess to her " cousine " she says, ' I am rather uneasy, for Mr. Smith, to whom the duke listens much, has just made some propositions to go to England, and whether we go there or not I cannot tell.'

With respect to the prince, I think you must admit that he has managed well, and, no matter how, the funds have risen, and the people are actually pocketing the money, and everybody predicts four years of greater prosperity than France ever enjoyed, and they say in four or five years the people will again become excited.   Everybody is astonished that I escaped being " run through " when the troops made their *perquisition de chez moi*, and I tell you, so satisfied am I of the truth of the danger I ran, that I should require a large bribe to risk the same again.

December 22nd, 1851.

I have just heard from the duke, in which he says, " I am now beginning to get ready to return, but wish you to send me word whether, during the Paris election, you saw anything which indicated it would be unsafe for me to do so ; if you advise it I shall return either on the 26th or 28th," and he further tells me that I may use the electric telegraph whenever I think it necessary.

I have no news to tell you, seeing that we have none here ; all is quiet, and the election passed off in Paris more quietly than a borough election in England.

I saw the prince yesterday for five minutes, but his time is really so taken up that it is impossible to get to him, and as to talk with him privately, he has not for the moment the time to spare.   He looks very well, and is in good spirits.   I hope soon to be *en route* for Angleterre ; I shall start as soon as I possibly can, and, if I can, with the bags, and if not, I shall feel I have lost a great deal of time and run great risks for nothing.

P.S.—I hear Lord Normanby and L. N. are not as intimate as heretofore. I have just seen some of the returns for the departments, and they are favourable to the prince.

December 23rd, 1851.

I have just heard from the duke, who requests me to use the electric telegraph should it be necessary to communicate anything to him, as he purports being in Paris either Thursday or Friday, and after that event 'I shall, you may rely upon it, get away from this as fast as possible. The stake is large, and therefore I suppose the risk and trouble must be corresponding.

December 27th, 1851.

In the middle of the night of the 24th D. B. arrived, and of course I had to change my room to make place for him.

With respect to bags, &c. the " Baring " view now predominates : whether that will be changed for some other I know not, and shall be unable to tell you till I arrive in England.

With respect to L. N. it is difficult to get to him in private as heretofore, as he really has so much to do, and I am now quite at a loss what to say or do since Lord Palmerston's retirement, and do not know what I can promise on your behalf with the new Secretary of Foreign Affairs. I shall send this off to-morrow, Sunday, so that you will get it on Tuesday, and if you can give me your views by Thursday here I will try to carry out your wishes. Of this I will write again to-morrow, when I shall, perhaps, have been able to settle with D. B. as to his plans.

I see by *La Patrie* that the President has given public notice that he can receive no one, " no matter whom," till after the first week in the new year; therefore I am the more decided upon quitting this quickly, and waiting for nothing. Lord Palmerston's retirement is much canvassed and regretted here, particularly by the Elysée people, who, it appears, were delighted with him. I hope it will not affect us, and I hope he will, ere long, be called upon to form a Ministry, of which there is some talk.

It will be seen from the preceding account that the mission to Paris was unproductive of results. The Prince was in a position which, sanguine as he was by nature, he could scarcely have contemplated at Ham when this memorable treaty was concluded; and there were many things that made the carrying out of its provisions impracticable. The duke appears to be still more regardless of his obligations, and the sole legatee might reasonably entertain doubts of getting any portion of his magnificent provision. The secretary was sent home; and the duke continued to live his customary life, buying more diamonds and more stock. The alarm had passed; and the millionaire seemed to think that his ally having succeeded in his dangerous experiment, he might now be able to secure his restoration to the duchy, or the return of his property; so he resolved to remain where he was.

The intelligent agent employed by Mr. Duncombe was disappointed by this result. It will presently be seen by the reader what were the duke's ideas respecting his belongings. He had no intention at present of parting with any portion of them, but was still willing to recognise Mr. Duncombe's reversion. A trait of character is displayed in the arrangement of the travelling account; but the interest of the communication will be found in its comprehensive glance into the state of our foreign relations, and its anticipation of the policy of the President of the

Republic. It was not written till after the writer's return to London:—

January 5th, 1852.

I will now acknowledge the receipt of a letter I received from you at d'Orée on Thursday evening last, just before I started for the rail, and therefore was enabled to read and show it to D. B.; he was much pleased that you knew Lord Granville, and to hear your opinion of him. We quite agreed that you were right as to the " nasty feeling" which was springing up in England, and unless great changes and great concessions on all sides, no doubt a European war will arise from the present events, and I fear England will, for the first time, find herself in difficulties, for although there will be a European war, it will be Europe against England, for all treaties are set aside, and it would be folly to ask the other Powers to fulfil the terms of treaties they have broken between themselves. See the Cracow affair, and the Russian entry into Hungary ; these two little acts unite Russia, Prussia, and Austria, and I have no doubt but that recent events will add France to the trio. These four great Powers can, and will if it suits, swallow up the smaller German kingdoms and states, while Italy will, I fear, yet have to obey the same rulers she now does for a long time, notwithstanding " her friends ;" and these four will, perhaps, each become emperors, *i.e.* the King of Prussia and the President will be added to the now existing two, and will in that case for a while govern what they call " parentally," but we, despotically.

L. N. has the power at this moment to decide the fate of Europe, and I must tell you that I think for himself he would like to be allied with England, and encourage libera-tion ; but on the other hand he is bound to run with those who have aided in placing him in his present position, viz. the great Northern Powers, and he undoubtedly, by a species of " holy alliance," would be maintained and sup-ported in his position by those friends. Another thing which will prevent him ever being able to shake off the yoke of despotism, is the unfortunate alliance he has formed

with the Jesuits; he may at the present time think he is
only using them, but no man once well entwined in their
deceptive meshes has ever moral courage or strength sufficient to extricate himself: and hence, I fear, will L. N.
fall, in my opinion, by the assassin's hand, for the Jesuits
part not so easy with their prey as may be imagined, and
they, hating England as they do, will no doubt urge him
on till he has gone so far that he cannot recede, and then
he is their tool; and the feeling entertained by the soldiery
as well as that of the priesthood, will no doubt develop
itself in an attack upon England. The Catholic priests
have already got a pretty good footing in England; the
Lutherans in Germany have become atheists, and therefore
Catholicism has only to battle against Protestantism in
England.

These views have partly decided the duke for the
moment to keep his fortune (the whole) in France, but
with a distinct understanding that I am to hold myself
always in readiness to run over and fetch it. At present
he says he has no confidence in the Government, and until
after the explanation of what he calls the shameful "dismissal" of Lord Palmerston, which strengthens despotism
tenfold by showing the tyrants that even in England, by a
well-directed and continued attack, you, or rather they, can
succeed in upsetting the most popular minister of the day,
his very popularity being his unpopularity, proved by the
manner in which he steered England through the shoals of
1848, and which caused him to be envied and hated by
those sage ministers of other states, who dreaded his firmness and his courage.

For these reasons D. B. thinks for the moment he has
quite enough money in England, that is, in the shape of
dividends becoming due, and in reply to your intimation
that war will be declared as suddenly as the late "coup,"
he desires me to inform you that he quite agrees with you,
only that he does not think there will be any declaration,
but an attack made, and therefore he should, if he found
France asking that which England would refuse, prepare

himself according to the circumstances of the case, and with respect to "everything being made previously comfortable," he desired me to tell you that he should keep that as an open suggestion, as he might want some day to avail himself of what he considered a wise and friendly proposition.

The notice in *La Patrie* applied to everybody, as the Prince really had no time to see anybody, and I think I can fully satisfy you that it would have been impossible to have seen him in less than a week, and having made my arrangements to get off on New Year's Day particularly, because you should not imagine that I stopped for " *les agrémens*," which really were commencing, to the detriment of your requirements, I started, and you will say I did right when I have told all the details.

On New Year's Eve we went to the opera together, and on our return we arranged that my travelling accounts should be paid, as I was to quit the next day. Accordingly I made out my account, he deducting the carriage to Godstone, which he said he did not ask me to take, and then settled to the sous. He then hum'd and hah'd a good deal, and at last counted out ten sovereigns, which he handed over to me, saying, this will pay for your white gloves; and he said, allow me to seize this opportunity of telling you that I have long since felt that I have very inadequately remunerated you for many things you have done for me. He then entered fully into the history of the visit to Ham; how many times he had seen you, &c.; what you had done for him, and finished by saying, as a collateral remuneration, I have made my will in your favour jointly with Mr. Duncombe, and should I have the strength to see you before I die I will, independent of that will, make you a present worthy of your acceptance.

Mr. Duncombe's secretary had not been unmindful of the interests of his employer in another and a higher quarter. The attack of the English press upon the *coup d'état* had been so violent that if the object of them designedly refrained from any personal communication with messengers from the other side of the Channel, it ought to have surprised no one. The reckless directors of those crushing onslaughts could not appreciate the proverb, that "desperate diseases require desperate remedies." Paris had for years been in a condition of chronic revolution—no good government was possible in so hopeless a state of things—industry, intelligence, and religion were equally depressed. The only alternative was the repetition of the wars of the Republic. Seeing the results of the *coup d'état* in the prosperity of the French nation, it is probable that the journalists who attacked the President might now be ready to defend the Emperor.

We now add the following from Count Orsi to Mr. Duncombe's secretary :—

Paris, 28th January, 1852.

MY DEAR SMITH,—I need not apologize for my delay in answering your letter, for it would be an equivalent to the acknowledgment of my being guilty of indifference towards you, and you know, my good friend, how anxious I am to keep pace, in that respect, with your kind feelings towards me.

The fault has not rested with me, but with the extraordinary circumstances of our situation, which has unabled me to comply sooner with your request.

It was only yesterday that I had an opportunity of talking the matter over with *our friend*, who gives you *carte blanche* for all you will have to say on his behalf.

It is impossible either for himself or myself to say which is the best course for you to pursue. In order to fulfil the task you offer to undertake you should take beforehand a right view of his personal position with regard, first, to the difficulty of establishing in France, without a dictatorial power, a regular government amidst the different parties which have brought the country to the deplorable state it is in ; second, to show by skilful hints that all this row of the English press is not a blind advocacy of liberal institutions, but a regularly bribed and systematic opposition, unjustifiable under all circumstances ; third, to prove by facts and by the text of pre-existing laws (regardless of political necessity) that the decrees about the property of the d'Orleans family ·have been an act, not of revenge or of spoliation, but an equitable one, such as was practised by every French king who ascended the throne ; and, fourth, to warn the English public that the game played just now by the English press is the same as that practised by England against France during the Revolution of 1789, which kindled a war between the two countries, for the only object of supporting the cause of the Bourbons of the elder branch, whilst it has now in view to set the two countries dagger-drawn against each other for the most unwarrantable object of supporting the ambitious and unpopular claims of the members of the Orleans family, for which the despicable *Times*,* soon after their flight from France, made use of the most abusive language that ever man could imagine.

Such are the main points upon which you will have to ground your defence. It rests with you to give them such a form as to make them applicable to the nature of the discussion which this affair will create in Parliament.

I need not say anything about the falsehoods of the English press in general, and of the *Times* in particular.

The acts of the French Government were necessary to put down that spirit of disorganization which threatened to pervade and ruin the whole country. As to the arbitrary power which the *Times* calls " unprecedented," I beg to refer him to the English Revolution of 1688, when William of Orange took upon himself to accomplish it on his own responsibility to save the country, and for the success of which he was driven to that much-to-be-regretted necessity of governing the country in such a harsh manner as to dishearten his fiercest enemies.

Yours truly,   Orsi.

* With its usual talent the leading journal took the popular view of the case, which was unmistakeably hostile to " our friend."

The *coup d'état* excited a tremendous sensation in England. Naturally, the Liberal party regarded it as an arbitrary extinction of democracy, and denounced it in the severest language. The Whig and Tory leaders generally approved of it, as necessary to the establishing of good government, and to put an end to the schemes of anarchists and other reckless political adventurers. Here and there one, stimulated by the violent denunciations of the press, expressed indignation at the shameless disregard of obligations it betrayed. Mr. Duncombe, in his judgment of the transaction, felt two opposing influences—the one was the necessity of supporting his constituents in their opinion of the President of *a Republic*—the other, the natural inclination to admire a bold measure successfully carried out.

One or two public writers in England have distinguished themselves by the bitterness of their hostility to the deviser of the *coup d'état*, appearing to judge all his subsequent actions in the same intensely prejudiced spirit. In the first place, the name Napoleon was the essence of the programme he offered his countrymen: it contained the military dispersion of the Council of Five Hundred, and every subsequent act to the establishment of the first empire; and as the endorsement of such promissory note was seven million responsible signatures, what right can a foreigner have to protest against it? Mr. Duncombe considered that France was of legal age and sound mind, therefore capable of transacting the business referred to. Close upon twenty years have elapsed since its date, and as both the parties to it are flourishing, no one can have any legitimate pretence for finding fault with the proceeding.

One extraordinary political event arose out of the *coup d'état* that gave it a much deeper interest to him —this was the dismissal, as was alleged, at the instigation of the prime minister, Lord John Russell, of Mr. Duncombe's friend, Lord Palmerston, then Secretary of State for Foreign Affairs. During the debate on the address a lengthened explanation of this stretch of authority was volunteered by the head of the Government, in which it appeared that Lord Normanby, our ambassador at Paris,—certainly not distinguished as a diplomatist,—had complained that the Foreign Secretary had given him instructions at variance with the language he had held to M. Walewski, the French ambassador in London. In addition, some complaints had come from a higher source, respecting supposed irregularities in the discharge of his official duties. Whereupon, without consulting his colleagues, Lord John had ventured to dismiss the ablest and most popular statesman of his age.

Lord Palmerston presently rose, and gave his version of the story with his customary spirit, in which he proved that if he had committed any fault in expressing, during a private conversation, an opinion respecting the conduct of the President, he must share the blame with the Premier and the rest of the cabinet, for all had privately expressed their approval to M. Walewski in similar terms. In every way it was a successful defence; and the House unequivocally expressed their sympathy. It leaked out in the course of the discussion which followed, that the real cause of his dismissal was his having displayed a certain amount of indifference to attempts at interference with his duties, made by a personage closely connected with his Sovereign. The affair was regarded as extremely impolitic and damaging to the Government, and one likely to impair the good understanding that had hitherto existed between this country and France. Eventually both Lord John and Lord Normanby found out that they had made a mistake.*

Negotiations were going on between the President of the French Republic, represented in London by M. Briffault, and Mr. Duncombe, represented in Paris by his secretary; who, though only returned from

---

* That Lord Melbourne was an accomplished courtier convincing evidence may be found in a work recently published, in which the Minister's efforts to gratify his youthful sovereign constantly appear. In the Queen's marriage, and in the settlement of a Parliamentary grant on the Prince, this was natural and proper; but when it was sought to confound the distinction between the Queen's husband and a reigning king, his efforts to please were open to question. It is just possible that Lord Melbourne may have derived advantage from the suggestions of a statesman who had scarcely attained his majority; but that men of the most comprehensive political knowledge, who sat at the Council, could have profited by them, is not so clear. Yet it appears as if Lord John Russell had been content with the same inspiration.

"I always commit my views to paper, and then communicate them to Lord Melbourne. He seldom answers me, but I have *often* had the satisfaction of seeing him act *entirely in accordance* with what I have said."—*The Prince to his Father:* "Early Days of Prince Albert," i. 321.

one of his missions on the 3rd of January, was in the French capital again on the 29th. Mr. Duncombe had interviews with M. Briffault on the 5th and 18th. His representative merely reported his arrival. The observations he hazards respecting the warlike disposition of the French people appear to have been the result of a very brief stay in the capital. He did not remain there many days.

Hotel Britannique, 22 Rue Duphot, Paris,
Thursday, January 29th, 1852.

I have not yet seen anybody, but I am going to try the imperial cover first, and afterwards the ducal. From the few hours I have been here, and the little one can judge in so short a time, I am strongly induced to believe that all our English views of the feelings of the people of this country towards their Government are very much exaggerated, and they quite ridicule the idea of war, or anything like it. All they ask for is that the non-intervention principle may be strictly carried out, and they will not interfere with us, and hope to be left alone. I will write to you more by-and-bye.

Mr. Duncombe's agent was temporarily promoted to the secretaryship of " the Regent." The latter had seen in a Paris paper, copied from a Cologne journal, a paragraph in which it was stated that the duke had renounced his sovereignty. As this might be prejudicial to his rights, and prevent the imperial interposition in his behalf he looked for daily, the duke called the secretary into council; and together they drew up the following state-paper, which was sent to and inserted in the *Journal des Débats*, addressed—

Paris, le 4 Septembre, 1852.

Monsieur,—J'ai soumis à S. A. le Duc Souverain de Brunswick le paragraphe daté de Vienne, le 27 Août, extrait de la *Gazette de Cologne*, et contenu dans votre journal du 2 de mois; et j'ai reçu l'ordre de le démentir au nom de S. A.

Monseigneur le Duc Souverain de Brunswick ne renoncera jamais à ses droits héréditaires.

J'ai l'honneur d'être, etc.   G. Smith.

CHAPTER V.

A TRIBUNE OF THE PEOPLE.

Mr. Duncombe's improved health—Proposed as the head of a popular party—Again returned for Finsbury—Lord John Russell's Government overthrown—Mr. Duncombe on bribery and controverted elections—The Carlton Club—Our policy in the East condemned—The Peace Conference—Mr. John Bright, the Quaker—Mr. Duncombe's interview with Lord Clarendon—The Russian war—Rents Chateau Beaugaillard, near Tours—Lord Palmerston's letter announcing a conditional pardon for the Newport convicts—Mr. Duncombe's correspondence with Lord Palmerston on behalf of the Preston cotton spinners—His correspondence with the Duke of Newcastle on the campaign in the Crimea—Lord Clarendon on the Passport system—Letter of Sir John Tyrrell, Bart., M.P., on the Peace Society—Meetings in Hyde Park—Friendly letter of Lord Palmerston, and Mr. Duncombe's judicious reply—" Honest Tom Duncombe"—The letter-carriers—Letter from Sir Rowland Hill—Deputations of working men.

In the year 1850, Mr. Duncombe made an effort to resume his parliamentary duties; and his political friends saw him once more attentive to debates and divisions; but he was quite incapable of exertion, and constantly under medical treatment. In June he introduced his secretary to Lord Palmerston, with the view of forwarding the duke's arrangements. He exhausted himself by the little he was able to do, and was constantly obliged to remain in the neighbourhood of Hastings, where he generally resided. He was

eager to try any remedy suggested to him, but could
only get temporary relief from the ablest physicians.
A book came under his observation, written against
the use of salt; and he called upon the author. The
result is entered in his diary: "Mad—never could
have written the book." The man committed suicide
a short time afterwards.

It should be borne in mind that there were two
Conservative Administrations in 1852. Lord Derby's,
organized in February; and Lord Aberdeen's, in
December. In one the Chancellor of the Exchequer
was Mr. Disraeli; in the other Mr. Gladstone, amal-
gamating Lord Parlmerston and Lord John Russell
as Home and Foreign Secretaries; while Sir William
Molesworth, First Commissioner of Public Works,
threw a *soupçon* of liberality into the mixture. Apparently it did not flavour it sufficiently—at any rate it
did not recommend it to the popular palate.

There was much discontent among the masses, and
strikes and combinations were never more prevalent.
Mr. Duncombe had allowed himself to be announced
as the president of the National Association of United
Trades. This post he resigned early in the year 1852;
but when it became known that an improvement had
taken place in his health, it was suggested to him that
he might place himself at the head of a popular party.
Mr. Duncombe expressed his willingness to do this,
provided a party could be brought together with a
thoroughly liberal action and policy; and published
an address in which he developed his views of both.

Other prospects opened to him about this time, but
the still delicate state of his health forbade great
exertion or continuous excitement; and he contented

himself with the performance of his political duties in the House and out of it, to the satisfaction of his constituents. There were questions of the deepest interest connected with the preservation of civil and religious liberty, which were rising to the surface, and would have to be made more prominent by his advocacy. The Dissenters were complaining of the inadequacy of the State arrangements for education ; and the Roman Catholics remonstrating against State interference with their faith.

He took his share of duty in the exciting struggle that marked the commencement of the session of 1852 ; and records in his diary the melancholy history of Lord John Russell's new Reform Bill. He interested himself for the letter-carriers, whose case he warmly supported ; advocated the Maynooth grant ; and attended several political meetings. Feargus O'Connor, his old colleague, was committed to custody on the 9th of May ; and Mr. Duncombe visited him on the 14th. Parliament was prorogued and dissolved on the 1st of June. Then came the customary worry of a contested election.

Mr. Wakley finding his duties as coroner for Middlesex as much as he could perform, gave up Finsbury ; and Mr. Alderman Challis and Mr. Wyld, the mapseller, of Charing-cross, contested the seat. Much money was expended by Mr. Duncombe's competitors, and the result was not entirely creditable to the constituency—Challis, 7504 ; Duncombe, 6678 ; Wyld, 2016.

During the autumnal sitting of the House Mr. Duncombe was in his place, presented petitions, and spoke on several subjects. He also gave notice of a motion for considering the state of the elective franchise.   On the 10th of December he moved that the Speaker do not leave the chair; in which he was seconded by Mr. Walter, and a long debate ensued. He subsequently attended several public meetings, convened to express opposition to the Budget.   This was the session of the new Reform Bill.   Ministers were in a minority on the Militia Bill Report.   Lord John Russell resigned on the 23rd of February; on which subject Mr. Duncombe addressed the House on the 12th of March.   He divided on Hume's motion for Reform, on Grote's ballot, and constantly against the Government, assisting in making the majority against the Budget on the 15th of December. He was almost every day at the Reform Club, and evidently intent on doing the best he could for his party.

In June, 1853, there was a discussion in the House on Sir J. Tyrrell's motion that a writ do issue for Harwich, in the room of Mr. Peacocke, whose election had been declared void; in the course of which the member for Finsbury made a most effective speech, detailing the enormities of this place in the way of corruption.   The extent to which bribery was carried on at every election in that notorious borough, betrayed the inefficiency of the Reform Bill ; yet it was not disfranchised—247 members voting for the motion, and 102 against it.   In the same session he called the attention of the House to the defective state of the law for the trial of controverted election petitions, and brought forward the case of Colonel Dickson and the Marquis of Douro, who were unsuccessful candidates for Norwich.   Their petition against the return of their opponents had been withdrawn by a parliamentary agent without their knowledge. Mr. Duncombe made some amusing references to the Carlton Club, whose solicitor was the agent complained of.

In the month of September, 1853, M. Kossuth published a letter condemning the foreign policy of England as being worse than that of Russia in the East, and anti-liberal. Popular attention was being directed to what was called the Eastern question by the English Liberals. Mr. Henry Drummond, M.P., having been invited to attend a Peace conference in Edinburgh, wrote a letter for the newspapers, freely giving his opinions not only respecting the occupation of Moldavia and Wallachia by the Russians, but denouncing the aggressive designs of the Emperor of France, and the despotism of the Emperors of Russia and Austria, the Pope and his priests, the King of Naples, and all the minor absolute German princes. It was, however, most remarkable for its attack upon the principles of the party who had proposed the Peace conference. In the following month John Bright, M.P., the Quaker, who was the representative of that party, wrote in condemnation of the popular desire to drive the English Government into a war against Russia in defence of Turkey. The public were daily getting more interested in the discussion; Mr. Duncombe, therefore, called a meeting of his constituents, and having been voted into the chair, addressed them at considerable length, ridiculing the pretensions of the Peace conference, but recommending a calculation of the cost of war before entering upon a conflict. He then condemned the system of

secret diplomacy, and the foreign policy of Ministers.
The proceedings were interrupted by the appearance
of an Irish agitator, Bronterre O'Brien. The majority
of the meeting did not want to hear him, but a large
party of his friends did, and the chairman had some
difficulty in restoring order. Resolutions were proposed and carried in condemnation of the designs of
Russia, and of the Government system of secret
diplomacy. Soon afterwards a deputation, headed by
the member for Finsbury, had an interview with the
Earl of Clarendon, and presented an address from that
constituency, expressing their opinions on these
subjects, signed by Mr. Duncombe as chairman of the
meeting. His lordship defended the policy of his
Government, regretted the necessity of secresy while
negotiations of importance were in progress, and expressed the intention of his colleagues to preserve the
integrity of the Ottoman empire, and the national
honour. Some discussion ensued, supported by Mr.
Duncombe and one or two members of the deputation,
on the conduct of preceding Governments in their
negotiations with foreign powers; but his lordship
contented himself with defending his own. Mr.
Harney wanted to exact a pledge from the Foreign
Secretary that the English fleet should not be
employed to coerce the Turkish people; but Lord
Clarendon declined discussing so improbable a con-
tingency, and the deputation retired.

Mr. Duncombe took a profound interest in this
question, preserving every printed paper that threw
any light upon it, and marking the illustrative passages : the able dispatch of Lord Clarendon to Sir
G. R. Seymour, our ambassador at St. Petersburg,

dated July 16th, 1853, condemning the Russian invasion of Wallachia and Moldavia, and expressing an
intention of defending the rights of the Porte;
also the manifestoes of the Sultan, the Czar, the
Emperor of France; as well as the communications of
Count Nesselrode, and Redschid Pacha; the instructions
of the four great European powers, England, France
Austria, and Prussia to their ambassadors; the reply
of the representatives of England and France to the
Turkish minister's application for the assistance of the
combined fleets; the note of the four ambassadors;
and the protocol of the members of the Vienna conference; in short, every paper of importance that
appeared in the public prints. The quarrel became
less and less pacific; and notwithstanding the declared
intention of the Governments of France and England
to unite their forces by sea and land for the preservation
of the territorial rights of Turkey, the Emperor of
Russia maintained his position and his hold of the
property of "the sick man."

The Parliamentary attendance of Mr. Duncombe
was unremitting in this session. From the previous
November he had been in forty-five divisions;
in addition, he had a great deal of duty to attend to
in the way of interviews with deputations, taking the
chair at public meetings, and meetings with aggrieved
individuals, who desired his advocacy or his subscription. His health had somewhat improved, particularly after a sojourn at Tunbridge Wells and
Brighton, but he still suffered severely from
bronchitis.

For a few months in this year the state of
Mr. Duncombe's health necessitating a change of

climate, he was induced by very attractive representations to rent during the recess a chateau and vineyard called Beaugaillard, near Tours. It was let to
him furnished, with the use of the domestic establishment, " as a great favour," for 750 francs a month.
He paid 30*l.* in advance on the 28th of May, but
afterwards being advised to give up the idea of going
abroad he did so, convinced that the place would not
suit him, and therefore never resided at the chateau.

Early in the session of 1854 Mr. Duncombe made
another appeal to the liberality of the English Government in favour of the political convicts Frost, Williams, and Jones. Lord Palmerston promptly responded, and announced to the House that her
Majesty's clemency would be extended to two of the
Irish offenders, Martin and Dogherty. Mr. Smith
O'Brien had already been pardoned. An influential
morning paper, in announcing this interesting fact,
adds—" A sentiment of gratitude is surely also due to
Mr. Thomas Duncombe, whose question elicited this
declaration from the Home Secretary, and whose
unbought exertions in favour of the political transports have, during the last fourteen years, been ever
ready when there seemed any chance of inducing such
a result as is now brought about."

The condemned Chartists, Frost, Williams, and
Jones, were pardoned ; but the Government appeared
to think that they had left their country for their
country's good, and were not inclined to sanction
their return. Independently of the sort of triumph it
might be represented as giving to the Chartist party,
it would, they thought, invest the returned convicts
with a degree of importance they might find it very

difficult to resist in case another movement of the kind should be attempted. Mr. Duncombe looked upon the case as a philanthropist, and desired that the men should be restored to their families. He believed that with the experience they had so dearly purchased they would appreciate home too highly to risk it for the Five Points, or for a hundred. He therefore addressed a communication on the subject, which was thus answered :—

C. G., 13th March, 1854.

My DEAR DUNCOMBE,—The pardon to be granted to Frost, Williams, and Jones is to be a conditional pardon, like that to be granted to Smith O'Brien, the condition being that the person to whom the pardon is granted shall not return to the Queen's dominions. They may go anywhere else.

Yours sincerely, PALMERSTON.

There was one part of his duties as a popular member that Mr. Duncombe filled with singular success—that of being a medium between the more excitable operatives and the Government, when the former seemed intent on illegal proceedings. · His interference in behalf of the convicted Chartists of Newport is one case ; but now the cotton-spinners of the manufacturing town of Preston demanded his intervention. He had an interview with Lord Palmerston ; and having learnt his lordship's views, wrote good counsel to the spinners, as may be gathered from the following letter and reply :—

1, Palace Chambers, St. James's-street, June 3rd, 1854.

DEAR LORD PALMERSTON,—After the interview that you were kind enough to give me last night I had just time to send an answer to the Spinners at Preston upon the subject of the withdrawal of the indictments ; and as my object was to transmit as correctly as I could your views, I think it

better to send you a copy of my note to them in order that
should I not have reported the result of our conversation as
you wished, I may in my next letter correct any error into
which I have unintentionally fallen.   You will perceive
that with regard to any opinion that I have expressed I
give it as my own, not as yours; although I cannot help
thinking that if you were in possession of all the facts of
the case as I am, you would not entertain quite so harsh an
opinion of the conduct of these poor fellows, considering the
severe trials to which they have been exposed, which I
much fear you have been induced to form from the over-
charged representations of interested parties.

I have the honour to remain, dear Lord Palmerston,
Yours very sincerely, T. S. D.

Broadlands, 5th June, 1854.

MY DEAR DUNCOMBE,—Thank you for the copy of your
letter to the Preston men; it was quite right.   I certainly
should have no wish to keep up the dispute if the parties
concerned could agree to put an end to it, and no doubt
it would be best that they should come to an understanding on the subject.   Yours sincerely,   PALMERSTON.

Mr. Duncombe's health fluctuated; he got better,
and he grew worse.   He tried physician after
physician, and remedy after remedy; but if with a
favourable result, this was only transitory.   Having
exhausted the skill of Dr. Williams and Dr. Moore,
he called in Halse and his galvanic apparatus: then
Dr. Cronin and his dry cupping; after these a female
mesmerist, Mademoiselle Julia de Bouroullec, who
promised a cure, and failed.   He tried vegetable diet,
bread and milk, decoction of walnut leaves, and pills,
potions, and plasters out of number: but he could not
expect much amelioration of his symptoms while he
over exerted his delicate lungs with public speaking,
and continued to bring on attacks of bronchitis by

exposure to wet and cold. Every session found him less equal to his parliamentary duties, yet he was present at all important divisions. In July, 1854, he joined in eighteen, and spoke on all necessary occasions.

The campaign in the Crimea created a great deal of dissatisfaction. The military arrangements were generally condemned, and the train of evils that arose out of want of system and ignorance of the requirements of a large body of men in the country they had invaded, were much and savagely commented on by the opponents of Government. There certainly was an unusual display of blunders, as well as an enormous sacrifice of life, and a prodigious waste of property. But the member for Finsbury, though he strongly opposed the measures of the administration, far from desiring to bear hard upon their mistakes, spontaneously offered his aid when he thought advice might be accepted. He wrote to the head of the War Department :—

Preston, near Brighton, December 26th, 1854.

MY DEAR DUKE,—As it occurs to me that, from the senseless outcry and prejudice that has been so industriously raised against the Foreign Enlistment Bill, the next great difficulty that you have to contend with will be to select any locality where the force during its stay in England can be maintained and drilled without causing in some instances considerable annoyance and alarm to the neighbourhood, and in others, perhaps, danger to the public peace, I have taken the liberty of sending you the description of a district which, from my own personal knowledge for some time both since and when in the Guards, appears to me to possess all that can be required to enable you to place with care and safety in temporary barracks at least five or six thousand, if not the whole, of the intended force. I refer to the small village of Bexhill in Sussex; it stands high and dry, near the sea, within six miles of Hastings to the east, twenty of Lewes to the west, and about six of Battle to the north; has its own railway station, and a large common admirably adapted to drilling, &c. purposes close to the ground where the barracks used to stand. This ground is at present let out chiefly for pasture, but remains Government property, and can be resumed by the Crown, I am informed, on notice being given that it is required again for the public service. A small burial-ground is also attached to it, and is still kept up, though I rather think it is only now used for the interment of paupers.

Had I been in town I should have done myself the honour of calling upon you, but as I shall not be there until Parliament reassembles, and as time presses, I have ventured to trouble you through the post. If my suggestion is of any service to you I shall be glad, or if I can give or obtain for you any further information, I shall be happy to do so; pray do not therefore scruple in communicating to me your wishes.

I have the honour to be, &c. my dear Duke,

Yours faithfully, T. S. D.

To His Grace the Duke of Newcastle, &c. &c.,
Whitehall.

War Department, 28th December, 1854.

My dear Mr. Duncombe,—I am greatly obliged by your suggestion of Bexhill as a good place for encamping our Foreign Legion.

A better position could not be selected, but I am afraid the land no longer belongs to the Crown, but has been sold some years ago. I have, however, written to the Ordnance to enquire.

I was truly glad to find by your letter that you do not participate in those objections to the Government measure which lately united so many of those with whom you usually act, with the factious Tories.

Believe me, yours very faithfully, NEWCASTLE.

The Russian war brought trouble upon many; but the official administrator of the War department had a particular hard time of it; probably want of experience was to blame rather than want of capacity. The Duke of Newcastle, though young in office, gave himself up earnestly to the daily increasing labour of his post; things, however, went wrong, and his grace got blamed. Mr. Duncombe appreciated his manly and honourable character, and believed that if he had had fair play he would have been able to overcome his difficulties.

The evils of the passport system were felt by every traveller, and in some instances were intolerable. Englishmen never could be made to appreciate the overhauling, and scrutinising, and worry, and expenses attendant upon it; to be stopped, and challenged, and searched at the boundaries of every petty state, and turned back if there was the slightest irregularity in their papers, formed a drawback upon the pleasures of travelling that deprived them of more than half their zest. The case was a thousand times worse with foreigners who were in the slightest degree obnoxious to the Governments of the countries they desired to traverse. Doubtless the member for Finsbury heard many pitiful complaints on this head from Hungarian, Polish, and Italian exiles, who flocked to him as a friend. He therefore applied to the fountain head of authority to ascertain if some improvement in the system could not be effected. After considerable delay an answer came :—

Grosvenor Crescent, November 25th, 1854.

MY DEAR DUNCOMBE,—I have many apologies to make, and I must beg you to excuse my unintentional neglect *in*

re passports.   The fact is, I could do nothing in the matter
without consulting Palmerston, which was impossible during
the last days of the session; then came poor Jocelyn's *
death, and I did not see him again till he came through
London on his way to Paris.   I then went over the whole
subject with him, and I have since endeavoured to meet
your wishes, as I will explain to you if you will have the
goodness to call here any afternoon except Wednesday.

Very truly yours,   CLARENDON.

The progress of the Russian war was viewed with
different feelings by different classes of politicians in
England, much as the Peninsular war was regarded by
the Tories and the Whigs.   But now it was only the
knot of deluded individuals who called themselves the
Peace party who croaked about the superiority of the
enemy and the certainty of disaster in the campaign
going on in the Crimea.   Notwithstanding important
advantages, there were still reports circulated from
Manchester discreditable to our allies the Turks, and
in the highest degree laudatory of the Russians.   So
prejudiced were they, that the heroism of the band of
nurses superintended by Florence Nightingale scarcely
obtained recognition.   The accompanying note gives
some account of the unfair spirit in which the war was
judged :—

Boreham House.

MY DEAR DUNCOMBE,—I am writing from a sick bed,
where I have been for a few days, in fact a week; but
yesterday a thing came to my knowledge which I have
determined to send you.

The *Times* and the Government have long acted, as was
suspected by you, upon the principle of suppression and
mutilation of any Turkish success.   This at last has been

---

* Lord Jocelyn died on the 12th of August.

complete: the Turks have taken a Russian man-of-war, and have obtained other naval advantages; but there is no account of them. This letter was dated from Constantinople, and also expressed the disgust of the Turks that our Government were permitting vessels of war at this moment to be built, and they are building, on the Thames by the [*illegible*] . . . . . builders. This I have also confirmed from . . . . , but he enjoined his name not to be mentioned.

These Russians pay very large wages to the men. What I should like would be that you should advise what course is to be pursued. It appears to me, when the facts are ascertained as to the present status of the [*illegible*] vessels. I believe they are at Northfleet.

I have no objection to write a letter in the paper and put my name to it, addressed to the Peace Society, or any parties you may please. The case seems to me to be so good a one, and measures ought to be taken without delay, that if you satisfy yourself of the truth of the facts, you had better fire away directly.

I am writing in bed, and with most unpleasant feelings. While I am writing I am assured the account of taking the Russian vessel is in some of the papers, but not in the *Times*. I think the people might be brought to bear to permit the Russians to launch their own vessels. The Russian fleet might be most effectually attacked by the people of England in their own River Thames, and I a little suspect at Portsmouth. In fact, Aberdeen and the *Times* do all they can for Russia.

In haste, my dear Duncombe,

Ever yours,   J. T. Tyrell.*

Increasing dissatisfaction met the efforts of the Aberdeen ministry, and soon after the commencement of the session of 1855 Mr. Roebuck brought forward a motion on the state of the army. The member for

---

* Member for North Essex.

Finsbury was in his place in the House, and spoke as usual the popular sentiments on the subject. The Government was in a minority, and resigned—the majority being more than two to one. A new cabinet, with Lord Palmerston at its head, gave the nation assurance of a vigorous administration.

Mr. Duncombe was constant in his attendance at the House, especially at divisions, and spoke on every important question. In April of this year the Emperor and Empress of France visited her Majesty at Windsor, and stayed a week. In this month the member for Finsbury was much occupied by attending to the affairs of Lord Dundonald and Sir Charles Napier : the first had war plans to submit for inspection, the other to explain his ill success.

In the summer of this session the metropolis was much excited by large assemblages of the working classes, including the usual average of "roughs." They wanted to make Hyde Park their place of rendezvous, and seemed to prefer Sunday as their day of meeting. The member for Finsbury was regarded by the masses as their champion, and as a natural result he was made responsible for their proceedings. Lord Palmerston was not the man to sanction what he believed to be wrong. Eminently popular as a minister, he would not tolerate what looked like a systematic defiance of authority, however agreeable this might be to those to whom it was permitted. Before, however, he had recourse to the means at his disposal for putting an end to these popular demonstrations, he wrote the following highly characteristic appeal to his friend :—

144, Piccadilly, 7th July, 1855.

My dear Duncombe,—I write to you as a friend and not as a minister. You have been, in the House of Commons, apparently the organ of those who directed and arranged the meetings in Hyde Park on the two last Sundays. Proceedings of a similar kind are expected to-morrow. It is needless to point out the various ways in which such proceedings might lead to consequences which I am sure you would be the first to deplore. May I not be allowed to suggest to you that it would do credit to those who may have influence with the directors of these proceedings if to-morrow were allowed to resume the accustomed character of a summer Sunday ?

Yours sincerely,   Palmerston.

Mr. Duncombe's reply proves how completely he disowned the policy of those mischievous demagogues who, as long as they can have an opportunity of gratifying their vanity by placing themselves in a conspicuous position, care not who may be the sufferers. It is impossible to prevent contrasting the conduct of the minister of that day and a real representative of the people, with that of the minister of a later day and a popular leader of less experience and moderation. Under Lord Palmerston the government of the country was not likely to be brought into contempt; and Mr. Duncombe had much too practical a mind to risk a collision with the civil and military power while insisting in the face of a proclamation that so many thousand industrious men should parade his leadership in the most fashionable part of the town.

St. James's-street, Monday Morning, July 9th, 1855.

My dear Lord Palmerston,—Many thanks to you for your kind note, which I have only just received; but you wrong me in saying that I have been the organ of those who directed and arranged the meetings in Hyde Park, for I know not who they were. I have certainly been the organ of many, and some of them your neighbours, who either suffered from or witnessed the disgraceful conduct of some of the police; and I can assure you that immediately after the discussion on Friday, I anticipated your wishes, and I did my best to allay the exasperation and vindictive feeling that then existed, by entreating all those who expressed their intention of revisiting the park yesterday to abstain from doing so, and to wait with patience the result of the promised inquiry, and I am informed that placards to that effect were circulated and posted up at the East end. If there is anything more I can do at any future time and with the same object, pray tell me, and it shall be done.

I wish on the two previous Sundays that the police had conducted themselves in the same conciliatory and judicious manner that I am informed they did yesterday. I hear that the *glaziers* were at work, and ought to be punished.

I have the honour to be, my dear Lord,
Yours faithfully,   T. S. D.

The member for Finsbury had been among the most urgent for inquiry into the mismanagement of our army, and in March he moved for the correspondence of the Commander-in-Chief (Lord Raglan) and the Minister for War. Lord Palmerston replied that as a committee of inquiry had been granted that had the power of calling for papers, such correspondence could not be necessary. The motion was ably supported by Mr. Milnes, but negatived without a division. Fortunately for the country the reign of jobbery and bungling was nearly over, as well as the necessity of taking care of O'Dowd. Sebastopol was taken by assault by the French and English armies. The Czar having found consolation in the capture of starved out Kars by General Mouravieff, condescended to listen to terms of peace, and the remnant of our magnificent army left their hard-won conquests and returned home.

Some metropolitan members turned their popularity to profitable account. They advocated the interests of the people and looked to their own. Government secured their support by advancing them to dignities or employments, or permitting them to exercise extensive patronage. Very edifying was the change of some of these fortunate individuals from the loudest democratic sentiments to a quiet adoption of those of the aristocracy—from the principles of extreme liberalism to those more in accordance with a position in the Government. These changes did not always occur without severe comment. In one case the transition was thus noticed:—

> " We dreamt that to nobles he ne'er would bow,
>   Nor the people's cause disgrace,
> Till he crouched for a coronet rather low,
>   And wriggled at last to a place;
> And then when we fancied fight he must
>   'Gainst the taxes he used to blame,
> We found to our most extreme disgust
>   That his views were not the same!"

Mr. Duncombe might, when personal friends were at the head of Government or held influential positions in the cabinet, have made equally advantageous terms for himself; but as a tribune of the people he had accepted a trust, and remained faithful to it to the last. Let it also be remembered that his health had been totally destroyed by his devotion to his duties, and it was only by having constant recourse to medical aid that he could maintain his arduous Parliamentary duties. "Honest Tom Duncombe!" was the familiar appellation of the Liberal press, and he did his best throughout his public career to prove that he deserved it.

His zeal was untiring in his exposure of corruption, and he never omitted an opportunity of denouncing its evil effects in influencing the election of members of Parliament. · In the address to the Queen's speech, January 31st, 1854, the announcement that measures were in preparation for amending the laws relating to the representation was adverted to for the purpose of pressing the necessity of putting an end to corrupt practices. In the month of June he put on the notice-paper an amendment, in case a new writ was moved for the notorious boroughs Canterbury, Cambridge, Hull, Maldon, or Barnstaple, in which he referred to the proved allegations against them, and stated that nothing had been done in the way of correction. He then proposed as a remedy that for five years the voting in such boroughs should be taken by ballot. The reports of the several committees had hitherto remained a dead letter. Mr. Duncombe strove to spur the Government on to attempt something remedial.

The grievances of the postmen were brought under the notice of the House of Commons in February, 1855, by the member for Finsbury presenting 253 petitions from them and giving notice of a motion on the subject. The attention of the authorities was roused, and a little later the head of the department addressed Mr. Duncombe in answer to a note from him :—

G.P.O., 14th March, 1855.

My DEAR SIR,—I called at the Treasury this morning to enquire again about the Act, and was about to write to you when I received your note.

I should be happy to frame your question if I could recollect the object of your inquiry, but, if you named it, the matter must have escaped my memory.

The circulars informing the letter-carriers and others of their positions under the new arrangement will be in the hands of many of the men to-morrow, and in the hands of all by the end of the week.

I made inquiries about your "sick friend," and find that nothing can be done. He comes on duty at five, not, as you understood him, at three in the morning.

Faithfully yours,   ROWLAND HILL.

Thomas Duncombe, Esq., M.P., &c. &c.

In the month of February, this year, the cause of Reform lost an able and conscientious advocate in Joseph Hume; and a few months later, in poor Feargus O'Connor, many years editor of the *Northern Star*, and in 1847 member for Nottingham. In 1853 he was declared of unsound mind by a *Commissio de Lunatico Inquirendo;* and about a week before his death had been removed by his sister from Dr. Tuke's establishment, Chiswick. He was buried at Kensal Green, nearly 20,000 persons being present at his funeral. The loss of these earnest friends and fellow-labourers seriously affected Mr. Duncombe, and he became more excitable. He was much troubled with deputations of all possible kinds; and when he suspected that they were trying to dictate to him, or instruct him in his duties, his patience would occasionally give way. We will give a description of two, that the reader may be able to appreciate the

trials to which a popular member of Parliament is
subjected.

When Sir Benjamin Hall's Bill was before Parliament, it became necessary for a certain commissioner
of paving to have an interview with the members for
Finsbury. He wrote a report of this for a Sheffield
paper, from which our quotations are derived. He
was evidently a person of influence in the borough, and
thoroughly acquainted with the kind of life led by
his representatives. In his introductory observations
he asks—" To what can I liken the experience of a
member for a metropolitan borough ? There is no
torture to be compared to it . . . . The metropolitan
member may enjoy fame (if fame it be), but his fame
is the curse of Kehama—that is, accumulated torture,
and no death." He presently adds, " You must ordi-
narily spend 1000*l.* at least in legal expenses at each
election. You must lend money to all the slip-shod
orators in the borough, or you must be surety for
them ; or if you have patronage, you must get them
situations, or these men will review their own political
opinions ; those opinions without *solid argument* may
quickly change."

This intelligent commissioner sought and found the
members for Finsbury in a sort of cupboard, without
seats, near the lobby of the House of Commons. The
" interview" of the deputation shall be described in
his own words :—

" They shook us heartily by the hand, and expressed
their regret that it was so long since they had seen
most of us. Personally I believe they were happy
to see us ; but it is evident that such deputations
were a nuisance. Every attitude, look, word, inti-

mated that we must be brief. Our clerk, in his manly way, began his speech.

"'Could you not,' said Mr. Duncombe, 'embody it all in a petition?'

"Mr. Talbot said, 'We only wish to draw your attention to one or two points.'

"'Put on your hats,' said Mr. Duncombe.

"Another member named extra-parochial plans.

"'I should be happy,' interrupted Mr. Duncombe, 'to see you on the subject at Spring-gardens. Come and see me.'

"Several details of Sir Benjamin Hall's Bill were rapidly and confusedly referred to by all the members of the deputation *at once.*

"'I'll tell you what to do,' said Alderman Challis. 'Elect two from each parish; agree on your views; and we shall be happy to appoint a meeting; shall we not, Mr. Duncombe?'

"'We shall,' replied Mr. Duncombe.

"I drew Alderman Challis's attention to the clause which disqualifies commissioners if they should be bankrupts, insolvents, or if they should compound with their creditors; and I suggested that the clause should also comprehend collectors of rates.

"The alderman took a note and said, "You will be one of the two delegates.'

"All the deputation were now *speaking at once*—all were hurrying to make their suggestions—the members were distracted, not knowing who to listen to. At this moment the alderman luckily looked out at the door. 'Oh!' exclaimed he, 'here is the other deputation!' And in rushed a string of respectable looking gentlemen; and out went all of us in a crowd

without salutation, bowing to, or shaking by the hand
our excellent members.

"At a guess," adds the frank and good-humoured
reporter of the meeting, "we had speeches bottled up
that would have engaged our members an hour and a
half; as it was, our rush meeting was over in less
than ten minutes. I have no fault to find with our
representatives. What are men to do with fourteen
or fifteen thousand constituents, all like locusts round
them, on the spot? There is not in the House one
man—I say, not *one man*—so truly independent in
spirit as Mr. Duncombe."

The greatest trial to his patience were deputations
of working-men. These persons also came with
"bottled-up speeches," and insisted on wasting his
time by delivering their crude notions—also "all at
once." They were paid for their services, and their
"little brief authority" was pretty sure to invest
them with airs of importance. If they were not permitted to inflict their orations upon, or annoy with
their impertinence, their unfortunate representative,
appalling was their sense of injury, and dreadful their
complaints. We append an exaggerated report by a
member of one of these deputations :—

"On presenting our card to Mr. Duncombe in the
lobby he exclaimed, 'I am busy now,' and entered
the House. Five minutes after he came out, and
called upon us to follow him into the vote-room. We
commenced by stating that 'the question we have to
call your attention to——'

"Mr. Duncombe interrupted and said—'Well, but
stop! Where do you come from?—who sends you?'

"We answered, that we were sent by committees

established in various towns, whose objects *are strictly the investigation of home and foreign affairs !*'

" Mr. Johnson, of Stafford—' I act for a committee of working men in Stafford.'

" Mr. Duncombe—' Do you mean to tell me that the working men pay you for coming here? I say they are great fools if they do.'

" Mr. Duncombe abruptly broke off here, and left us, and then returned in company with, we are informed, his secretary. He began not where he left off on leaving us, but by saying, ' I will say nothing but what I say before another person.' He then said that ' the working men had better keep their money.'

" Mr. Johnson, of Newcastle, *interrupted*, and attempted to open the case.

" Mr. Duncombe, vehemently — ' Will you hold your tongue? I am not going to enter into the case with you. You came here to instruct me on Maritime Law !'

" We said that we did not come to instruct him or any other gentleman, but to appeal to him as an Englishman, having some interest in common with ourselves.

" He again interrupted,* exclaiming with great vehemence, ' Will you hold your tongue? *You* instruct *me!* I am the independent representative of an independent constituency. I know far more about it than you can tell me. You will have my opinion when the subject comes before Parliament.' He here suddenly relaxed (?) into his former *menacing* and

---

* A few lines back we are told that it was Mr. Johnson who interrupted.

insulting tone of speech, saying, " In fact, I will not hear you.'

" On our asking if he did not represent England, he said ' No, I don't. I represent a constituency.'

" We answered, ' Then that is not part of England ?*

" We were about to continue, but he stopped us, repeating his former words—' Will you hold your tongue ? I will not hear you. I tell you that you are imposing on the working men.' And then asked ' if we were not the followers of Mr. Urquhart ?'

" On our answering in the affirmative he said, ' Then I tell you at once, that I have no confidence in his principles, and still less in his foreign policy ;' and then entered into *a rambling statement* about it being presumption on our part [which it certainly was] to be calling on members of Parliament assuming to instruct them.

" We said that we did not wish to instruct, we desired them to assist in protecting the crown and the people, who are alike attacked by this innovation.

" Mr. Duncombe—' To set aside Lord Campbell and Lord Clarendon !'

" One of the members of the deputation said, ' We have nothing to do with Lord Campbell; we have to (*striking the declaration*) do with this. Here is a question that affects the crown of England, *as it does us*—and we come to you.'

" Mr. Duncombe again interrupted, declaring *passionately* that he would not hear us ; that we were imposing on the working men; and saying, ' I will

---

* These poor fellows had not learnt the familiar axiom, that a part is not equal to the whole.

tell them wherever I go. You may take down my words if you choose.'

" He then quitted the room abruptly without allowing the deputation to reply."*

Probably this is a bad sample of these intruders upon his time. They were not his constituents—the member for Finsbury had no sort of connexion with them—nevertheless, having imbibed certain peculiar notions on foreign policy from the pamphlets of a political lecturer, they had considered themselves justified in taking an experienced member of Parliament away from his public duties to listen to their " declaration" about a question which, as they represented, equally affected the interests of the crown of England and the Johnsons of Salford and Newcastle!

* *Sheffield Free Press*, June 21st, 1855.

CHAPTER VI.

POLAND AND HUNGARY.

It had now become well known all over the civilised
world that the member for Finsbury was the friend
of oppressed nationalities. It therefore occurred to
the exiled Poles to endeavour to enlist his sympathy
in their behalf. There had for some time existed in
this country a society expressly established to take
cognizance of their distress and afford them relief.
As is very often the case, the managers of this association, with the best intentions in the world, were
not popular with the body of unfortunates who had
to apply to them for assistance. A former chancellor

of the exchequer had brought a charge against the society of want of discrimination in affording relief to the Poles; but in August, 1840, having occasion to address the House of Commons respecting them, Mr. Duncombe referred to what appeared to him to be instances of partiality in the distribution of the funds. This elicited several long letters from Lord Dudley Stuart, the President of the "Literary Association of the Friends of Poland," in which he defended its administration. Mr. Duncombe wrote a reply, which was published in the newspapers.

There was another society organized for the regeneration of Poland, of which Mr. Ernest Jones was president, and Mr. George Julian Harney secretary. Mr. Duncombe also belonged to this society, and assisted them with all his influence. He presented a petition from them demanding the intervention of the British Government for the restoration of the nationality of Poland, on the 11th of March, 1846, and another the following year. The democratic committee issued a publication for general circulation at the price of a penny each number; but only two numbers were published. They then arranged that missionaries in pairs—the one an Englishman, the other a Pole—should be sent to all parts of the country to stir up the population with the wrongs of Poland. Messrs. Jones and Harney indulged in a good deal of "tall talk" on these occasions, but nothing came of it; they scolded the House of Commons, but nothing came of that; and they abused every one who did not adopt their views— with the same negative result.

There cannot be a question that Poland has been

badly used; but poems—though written by a Campbell—occasional balls, and societies like those we have
mentioned, can afford no real benefit. If "Freedom
shrieked when Kosciusko fell," she must have
swooned when the duchy of Warsaw was seized upon
and declared a Russian province : since when it looks
as if Poland had really become "a geographical expression;" but Europe cannot help her, any more
than it could help the gallant race of Circassians
when they were denationalized after the same fashion.
No amount of Lord Dudley Coutts Stuarts could have
stopped the giant state from absorbing its weak
neighbours.   Mr. Duncombe spoke for the Polish
exiles whenever his advocacy was likely to be felt;
but all statesmen of sound judgment knew that England could not interfere in their behalf to any profit.
He helped them also with liberal subscriptions.

The Magyars in Hungary, after the insurrection at
Vienna, when Georgey led them to revolt and the
down-trodden Poles hastened to their assistance on
the Danube, might have established their nationality
on the ruins of the Austrian empire, had not the
politic autocrat of the neighbouring empire inter-
posed, and with the assistance of the able Windisch-
gratz rescued the House of Hapsburg from destruction.   So enormous was the Russian force sent to the
assistance of Francis Joseph, that the Hungarians
were everywhere overpowered.   The fighting men of
the revolution retreated fighting till they were pushed
over the frontier into the country of the Turk, in
whose service they were glad to offer their well-
stained swords; the talking men of the revolution
fled talking into lands that enjoyed the blessings of

constitutional liberty, in whose service they superfluously offered their well-used tongues.

Lord Dudley Coutts Stuart took the fugitives under his protection, notwithstanding the trouble given him by the Poles. He appealed on their behalf to Mr. Duncombe, with what result he shall himself relate :—

34, St. James's-place, Tuesday,
August 7th, 1849.

MY DEAR MR. DUNCOMBE,—A gentleman has just called on me and brought me your note of the 6th instant, with 5*l.* from yourself for the Hungarians, and an order for 2*l.* from the liberal inhabitants of Keighley for the same purpose.

These subscriptions, for which I beg to offer my personal thanks, I will take care and have publicly acknowledged. I was delighted to see and to hear you in the House of Commons so much better than I expected, and trust this fine weather will promote the speedy restoration of your health.

Believe me, yours sincerely,
DUDLEY COUTTS STUART.

M. Kossuth arrived in this country, and shortly took upon himself the duties of a political Peter the Hermit, making tremendous appeals on behalf of Hungary. There was great enthusiasm excited for him at first, and it was thought that a new crusade was about to commence. They were certainly wonderful orations, those of M. Kossuth, and were extremely patriotic. The newspapers were full of them, and nothing was talked of but enslaved Magyars and Austrian tyranny. In course of time, however, this marvellous oratory ceased to be effective, and the speaker sought fresh audiences across the Atlantic.

In America his success was equally great, and his oratorical powers equally appreciated; but in time here too he exhausted the admiration of his enthusiastic friends, and returned to England.

He had not long reappeared before rumours were circulated that he was meditating a warlike demonstration against the Emperor of Austria, and it began to be whispered that munitions of war were preparing that were intended to do incalculable mischief to his imperial majesty. England was at peace with Austria, and her Government could not permit preparations for a destructive war against that power to be carried on in this country. Armed with a secretary of state's warrant, the police made a seizure of a large store of combustibles evidently collected for a destructive purpose. The newspapers in recording the facts stated also that the magazine was the property of M. Kossuth.

Mr. Duncombe was an earnest admirer of the Hungarian patriot, and it having been reported to him that the account printed in the journals was an exaggeration, and that an injustice had been done, on 15th of May, 1853, he addressed the House of Commons on the subject,* and endeavoured to prove that a Mr. Hall, who was an inventor of rockets, had been prosecuted for having a larger quantity of gunpowder in his possession than was permitted by law, and that not content with condemning him to penalties for his alleged transgression, they had accused him of being in league with M. Kossuth for establishing an arsenal to be employed against a sovereign with whom

---

* Diary—" Spoke on the Rotherhithe and Kossuth mare's-nest."

England was at peace, when in reality he was merely employed in completing a large order for *fireworks*.

The humour of this defence was extremely relished by the House; nor were they insensible to the reply of Lord Palmerston, given in the same spirit. The *Times*, in a leading article upon the subject the next morning, acknowledged the ingenuity of Mr. Duncombe's speech, but sanctioned the seizure of the fifteen hundred rockets and missiles known to have been manufactured by M. Kossuth's Hungarian friends. Mr. Hall presently acknowledged his culpability, and the Government not only let him off the penalty, but presented him with 870*l.* as compensation.

The Hungarian patriot, like Othello, found his occupation gone. The Emperor of France evidently considered one emperor at a time a sufficient opponent; indeed there seemed reason to believe that, provided he could bring the war with him to a successful issue by the capture of the great Russian stronghold in the Black Sea, he would be well content to come to an accommodation. The Emperor of Austria, doubtless with many congratulations that he was permitted to preserve his large military force for the maintenance of his hereditary dominions, was well content that his two imperial rivals should waste their strength against each other. The Emperor of Russia having contrived to make ridiculous an English admiral who had led a magnificent fleet through the Baltic, with the avowed intention of capturing St. Petersburg, and in the result had slightly varied the famous report of Cæsar—"He came, saw, and"—sailed away,—was preparing a demonstration in another direction, intended to terminate in a manner still more to the

honour of "holy Russia," and was in a mood to conciliate the most formidable of his allies, that he might
recover his *prestige* in Europe, while the potentates
not engaged in the struggle reserved their strength to
put down democracy in their own dominions. There
was therefore no encouragement for the eloquent
leader of an Hungarian revolt, so he employed himself
as an itinerant lecturer, while he scrutinized the progress of events from his own point of view. He was
solicitous to inspect treaties and blue-books, and
applied to the member for Finsbury to procure them
for him :—

8, South Bank, Regent's-park,
February 19th, 1856.

DEAR SIR,—Your obliging affability encourages me to a
request.

Has the treaty of alliance between Great Britain and
France (referring to this war), and the other treaty with
Turkey on the same subject, ever been communicated to
Parliament ?

If it has been you would very much oblige me by
lending it to me for perusal, as I never have seen these
fundamental documents. Upon your kind permission I
would send my *aide-de-camp* to fetch them, and return them
with thanks immediately after perusal.

If they were never brought under the notice of Parliament, then I really don't know what to say ; the fact is so
curious. How can an opinion be formed on the issue when
the basis of the whole transaction, and the engagements
England has entered [into], are unknown ?

With high esteem and particular consideration,

Yours most obsequiously,   · KOSSUTH.

That lookers-on see most of the game, is as applicable to the great game of war as to humbler and
more innocent pastimes ; and when such a spectator

as the ex-governor of republican Hungary takes a
deliberate survey of what is going on in that way, a
comprehensive knowledge of its past, present, and
future may be looked for as a matter of course.   M.
Kossuth disliked the war in the Crimea—it was not
undertaken for any purpose in which he could feel
interest; he therefore looked with disfavour on the
belligerents, and was ready to scrutinise the arrangements that led to it, in a hostile spirit.   Making
allowances for this, his criticism is not without a
certain illustrative value :—

Wednesday, February 20th, 1856.

My dear Sir,—I beg to return my sincere thanks for
the documents, and the obliging manner in so promptly
and so perfectly complying with my humble request.   The
documents are exactly those I desired to see.

The passage about the Sea of Azoff is to be found in the
despatch of the Earl of Clarendon to Lord John Russell,
dated April 3, 1855; it is the No. 2 of the additional
Vienna Papers presented to Parliament in July 1855, and
published in the *Times* of July 14th.

Perhaps you will allow me to invite your attention likewise to the following facts :—

1. Lord John Russell, in the debates of June 5, 1855
(previous to his compulsory resignation), made the following
statement; " The proposition suggested by the French
Government, though not regularly put in the form of a
proposition in the protocol, but more than once stated with
great eloquence and ability by the French minister,
M. Drouyn de Lhuys, was this, that there should be what
he called a neutralization of the Black Sea, that it should
be a neutral sea for the purposes of commerce, and, being
so, that arsenals and fortifications for the purpose of war
should be destroyed."

At present the word " fortifications " has been omitted
from the text of the third point.

2. In the original proposition of the four points (Eastern Papers, part xiii. 1855, Vienna Protocols, No. 1 and 2) the third point explicitly contained a double object, " to connect the existence of the Ottoman empire more completely with the European equilibrium," and to put an end to the preponderance of Russia in the Black Sea.

With respect to the first object, an Article has been agreed to " engaging to respect the independence and integrity of Turkey, and guaranteeing the observance of this engagement " (Annex A to Vienna Protocol, No. 11).

At present no reference is made in the preliminaries of peace to this first object of the third point, the connecting Turkey with the European system; the guarantee of his independence and integrity, is entirely dropped.

3. You of course are aware of the fact that the present fifth point is absolutely no new addition to the olden four points; only last year at Vienna it stood in the prologue, now it stands in the epilogue; but in connexion with the fact No. 2, alluded to above, there is again a curious modification in the text.

Now the fifth point is: The belligerent powers reserve to themselves the right of producing, in a European interest, special conditions over and above the four guarantees.

At Vienna last year the reservation stood thus (Vienna Papers, No. 1, Memorandum) ; " Austria, France, and Great Britain reserving to themselves the power to put forward such special conditions as may appear to them required beyond the four guarantees by the general interest of Europe to prevent the recurrence of the late complications."

You see the difference, " the prevention of the recurrence of the late complications " here, and " the connecting of Turkey with the European system " there, are omitted (diplomatists never change an expression accepted by common agreement without some design), while the right of producing new conditions, formerly reserved to the allies, now appears reserved for the belligerent powers, consequently for Russia likewise. Of course it was due to the dignity of Russia that should England dare to speak " Bomarsund,"

Russia should be in order when speaking, for instance, " Heligoland."

This forcibly recalls to my memory that despatch of Lord Clarendon to Lord John Russell (additional Vienna Papers, No. 1), wherein he speaks of Russia lulling her antagonists into security, and says that " while the navy of England were upon a peace establishment a Russian fleet of twenty-seven or thirty sail of the line might suddenly issue from the Baltic and sweep the British seas."

Oh, how the " big brother " (as Mr. Roebuck calls him) would chuckle should he succeed in making Clarendon a prophet, besides having gained his point now, which undoubtedly was never anything but " the legitimisation of his dynasty," not only not yet recognised until now, but rather outlawed by the 1815 treaties. Lord Clarendon had some presentiment of this issue when he wrote his despatch of March 23, 1853, to Sir G. H. Seymour (Secret Correspondence, page 19), but of course " drifted " is the word.

Still, since Lord Clarendon (House of Lords, May 25, 1855) acknowledged that " the four points would certainly have offered no security to Turkey," and since the conditions actually agreed to are nothing but those same four points, only milder in favour of Russia, it will be pleasant to hear how the Government will convince Parliament that the peace is " safe and satisfactory, and that it secures the future independence and tranquillity of Europe."

The Roman augurs laughed when they met each other. I wonder what those at Paris will do.

Excuse my chattering, and believe me to be, with distinguished consideration,

Your most obsequious servant, KOSSUTH.

By this time intelligence reached England of another failure in the allied operations against Russia; it was one, however, in which English interests were most concerned. The only general officer in our army who had conspicuously displayed generalship had been placed in command of an important post, with an inadequate Turkish garrison, and with the assistance of only one or two English officers, was left unsupported to abide the attack of an overwhelming Russian army, in the most perfect state of efficiency, and conducted by the ablest general in the Russian service. The heroic defence of Kars by General Sir Fenwick Williams, was, as every one knows, the most glorious event in that grand chapter of accidents, the Crimean war. How it was caused the Hungarian looker-on shall relate :—

8, South Bank, April 27th, 1856.

My dear Sir,—I leave to-morrow for Edinburgh, and hence on a three weeks' lecturing tour. I thought to get ready yesterday with my arrangements, but so many unexpected matters came between that I have absolutely not a minute to my disposition. It is, therefore, with very sincere regrets that I feel obliged to apologise for my being prevented to wait upon you.

As to Kars, as far as I can remember the Kars papers contain numerous indications that Kars has been designedly sacrificed. I have no time now to refer to them. I, however, am one of those who are wont to form their opinion rather on the logic of a given situation than on petty details. These are but symptomatic, great events walk on a broad track.

Now, thus much is incontrovertibly established: that the allies had 200,000 men in the Crimea absolutely idle, while Kars lingered in protracted agony (those 200,000 men were already consigned to winter quarters at that time, consequently idle), and the allies had immense means of sea transport. To relieve Kars they had not to go to Kars: no land transport was needed; they had only to land at Batoum. Please look to the map and you shall feel convinced that the mere landing of 30,000 men at Batoum

would have instantly forced Mouravieff to leave Kars in all
haste, and to retreat in forced marches towards his basis,
Tiflis, at least as far as Achalosik, or else he would have
been cut off, and caught like Mack at Ulm, with his whole
army.

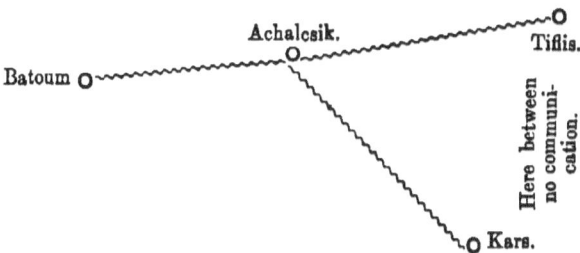

Well, the allies had men to spare, had countless idle
ships for transport, and had Batoum within easy distance
(50-60 hours), still they did not move.

Why? because the Czar wanted a victory to restore a
prestige to his arms, or else he would not have consented,
could not have consented, to negotiate.

But Bonaparte wanted him to make peace, for making
the new dynasty acknowledged, and for arriving at that
alliance with Russia, which was the only aim of war with
him.

Bonaparte was the leader in the war; his marshal commanded in the Crimea: England was but an auxiliary.

So he voluntarily sacrificed Kars to induce the Czar to
negotiations.

Please read the Russian proclamations, whereupon do
they turn? " I could make peace with honour, because I
was victorious in Asia; " thus says the Czar.

To this conspiracy fell Kars a victim.

This is the leading feature in my opinion.

And how came it to pass that Turkey was not able to
save it? please to read in one of the enclosed slips what I
marked " Kars," written in December. There is my explanation.

I have, besides, the honour to enclose another slip to
which I referred at our late interview. Its value is only

that it might facilitate the "*recherche*" amongst the ocean of rubbish "blue books."

I would request you to have these two slips returned, as I have no other copy, and like to file for my children my writings.

Many thanks for the Eastern papers.

I have the honour to remain, with very grateful feelings for your last benevolent allusions in Parliament to the cause of the nationalities (a ray of consolation while the horizon is all dark), and with very distinguished regards,

Your most obedient servant, KOSSUTH.
Th. Duncombe, Esq., M.P.

Walter Savage Landor, an author of some celebrity, who had occasionally come forward to give expression to liberal ideas, not unfrequently extravagant and exaggerated, in the month of March, 1856, published a letter addressed to the editor of the *Times*, in which he proposed the raising of a public subscription for Kossuth, who, he alleged, was in straitened circumstances. The communication was written in his customary style. The person for whom he required pecuniary assistance was thus described:—"The jewels of the Hungarian crown lay at his feet; he spurned them, as he spurned the usurper and perjurer who had worn them. * * * The representative of Mahomet saved the follower of Christ from the vengeance of the Apostolic : the caliph cast his mantle over the wounded, and defied the uplifted sword."

As if such inflated language was not sufficiently unpalatable to English common-sense, he went on to degrade and vilify one of the most honoured names in English history among liberal politicians.

"Mr. Fox had squandered a large fortune in the most pernicious of vices, gambling. * * * Mr.

Fox committed an act of treason, or very similar, in sending an agent to the Empress Catherine assuring her that she might safely take possession of Nootka Sound against the just claims of England. The speeches of Mr. Fox never elevated the soul, never enlarged the intellect, never touched the heart. He upheld the cause of France against England throughout the war, even while her best citizens were bleeding on the scaffold. Kossuth upheld the cause of Hungary, &c."

Such a comparison challenged a reply; and the editor of the *Times*, in a leading article of the same date, gave it in a way that made the idea of a public subscription for Mr. Kossuth totally out of the question, and damaged that "Daniel O'Connell of Hungary," as he is styled by the writer, irretrievably. It came under his notice, and he possessed penetration enough to see the mischief it was calculated to do both to his cause and himself. The same day he wrote to Mr. Duncombe, enclosing both the letter and the commentary cut from the newspaper, with this sentence referring to the former.

"I just see, with indescribable astonishment and grief, from the *Times*, that the sacred domains of my private life have been profaned by a public appeal—well intentioned, but sorely afflicting my feelings, and grievously inconsiderate. I beg from you to believe that not only have I had no knowledge of it, but that I would gladly sacrifice a goodly portion of the little life I may yet have in store could I make it undone."

He wrote a communication to the same effect for publication, but was never able to remove the injurious effect which his friend's mischievous comparison with one of the first and noblest of English reformers, had created.

Among the Hungarian patriots who were compelled to fly their country was Colonel Türr. On the breaking out of the Russian war, this gentleman obtained a commission in the English service, and was sent to Bucharest to purchase horses for the English Government. Here he was recognised and carried away a prisoner by the Austrians. On February 1st, 1856, Mr. Duncombe addressed a question to the Government respecting this gross violation of international law. Lord Palmerston replied that the Austrian Government, in deference to her Majesty's Government, having first tried Colonel Türr as a deserter, and found him guilty, had ordered him to be released. The colonel was permitted to return to his duty, and Mr. Duncombe had almost forgotten the individual for whom he had interested himself, when the latter called upon him towards the close of August of the same year, bearing a letter of introduction from his countryman, Louis Kossuth.

Colonel Türr's troubles recommenced, when he had reasonable hope for believing that they were at an end, and a prospect opening to him for a useful, if not a brilliant career, in the East. He had expressed his intentions to Mr. Duncombe, during several visits paid to him in the autumn of 1856, and the latter had engaged to forward his wishes as much as lay in his power. With that object he at once addressed his friend the Premier.

57, Cambridge-terrace, October 10th, 1856.

MY DEAR LORD PALMERSTON,—Colonel Türr, in respect of whose illegal arrest by Austria, while in the service of

Great Britain and on a neutral territory, you may possibly recollect I asked a question during the last Session, has called upon me and is very anxious that I should bring him to you to enable him to thank you personally for your intercession upon that occasion in his behalf, which I would willingly do did I not feel convinced that your time must be much better occupied at present than by receiving our visits; but as he is desirous of returning to Turkey in a few days, and wishes to obtain employment, civil or military, either under the Sultan or the British Government, perhaps you would have no objection to kindly furnish him with a recommendation for that purpose to Lord S. de Redcliffe.

If you can consistently do so, I am confident that you will not only be doing a kindness but an act of justice to a most ill-used and honourable man.

The director-general (Colonel McMurdo) appears to think most highly of him, has passed all his accounts, and very properly, in my opinion, recommended the secretary for war to authorise the liquidation of his arrears of pay during the period of his Austrian persecution and imprisonment.

I may add that Colonel Türr has recently become a naturalized British subject.

I have the honour to be,

My dear Lord Palmerston,

Very faithfully yours,

THOS. S. DUNCOMBE.

In due course a reply reached him :—

Broadlands, October 16th, 1856.

MY DEAR DUNCOMBE,—If I had been in town I would have seen Colonel Türr, though I could not have been of any use to him.

It would of course have been impossible to give him employment in the British service, and I fear there is little chance of his obtaining service in the Turkish army, as we have not succeeded in regard to Polish officers who have stronger claims upon us than Colonel Türr. The Colonel

was very ill used, but he was indiscreet in placing himself
in a situation which rendered him liable to ill-usage.

Yours sincerely, PALMERSTON.

Mr. Duncombe experienced a very severe attack of
illness in the autumn of 1856 that confined him to
his room for thirteen weeks. Among the few persons who had access to him was Colonel Türr, who
came several times previous to his return to the East.
That he felt a profound interest in the colonel was
evident, for as soon as he was permitted to leave the
house he called at the Foreign-office and had an interview with Lord Palmerston and Lord Clarendon on
his account. Questions of inconvenience or even of risk
were never permitted to interfere with the performance of friendly or public services. Indeed, there
cannot be a doubt that this unselfishness of spirit
often aggravated his disorder; but it had never taken
so serious a turn as in the last attack. It had become
essential to his safety that he should seek a warmer
climate, but he could not be induced to listen to such
suggestions.

There remained now nothing for the colonel to do
but to get his passports and proceed to Constantinople.
But here, as in many other sublunary matters, the
first step was the greatest difficulty. He was hardly.
then aware of the troubles that beset an alien on quitting its shores. Although he was a naturalized subject, the Foreign-office could only regard him as a
foreigner, and looked jealously to his antecedents
before they would in the smallest way become responsible for his future. The following announcement, and the communication that follows, apprized
his friends that the authority essential for his depar-

ture from England had been withheld. The clerks in the Foreign-office had detected some passages in a book published by Colonel Türr that did not accord with his application for a passport. Lord Clarendon therefore demurred.

16, Leicester-place, Leicester-square,
Octobre 26, 1856.

MONSIEUR,—Je reçu à la fin un lettre de Foreigne Offize, dans lequel on me dit de venir Mercredi le 29 Octobre, pour mon passport : je tâcherais partir ce même jour. Si vous verais un fois le Lord Palmerston, je vous en prie de lui presente ma malheureuse situation, et de l'engagée de fair quelque chose pour moi. Un photografist a voulu fair mon portrait, et il m'envoye aussi deux copies : veuillez accepté un, en signe de profound respecte ?

Agréez, cher monsieur, les homages de
Votre sincèrement dévoué, E. TÜRR.*

16, Leicester-place, London,
Octobre 29, 1856.

MONSIEUR,—Je suis alléz chez Mr. Lenex Conynham dans le Foreigne Offize, qui pour me donner un passport, ma fait savoir que Lord Clarendon me refuse le passport, pour le raison suivant.

1. Que je suis devenu sujet Anglais par le temoignage que j'abite l'Angelter depuis 5 anne ; qui n'est pas exact.

2. Que je suis allez l'anné passé en Valachie, ou j'etais arrêté pour le delit militair par les autorité d'Autriche, qui à causéz beaucoup d'enbarass au Governement, et amené d'aigrement entre le Gouvernement d'Autrich et le Gouvernement Britanique ; après quand j'etais mis en liberté je suis partis de Constantinopel tout suit dans le voisinages du quartier-general Autrichien, que a causé de nouvel protestation.

3. Que je declaré d'avoir l'intention de reste en Angelter, qui est en contradiction avec le demand d'un passport pour Constantinopel. Pour finir, le Lord Claren-

* We print the colonel's letters as they are written.

don dit pour n'avoir pas de nouvelles question avec
l'Autrich le Gouvernement me refuse de donné un passport.

Je repondé aujourd'hui au Lord Clarendon, et je lui fait
voir qu'il a tort, et que le raison qu'il me donne sont pas
exact. C'est conu que j'abite l'Angelter depuis 1850; ce vrais
que j'allée suivant resté plusieurs mois a Turin, Suisse, ou
en France. Le 2—3 imputation vous mieux aprecié que
person. Je suis faché que un minister Anglais me dit que
j'etais arrete pour delit militair, et que le Gouvernement a
ou d'enbaras;—et moi? j'avais un sort inviable en prison
pendent 4 mois. Je part demain, Jeudi.

Agréez, Monsieur, le gratitud eternel

De votre tout devouc,   - E. TURR.

Lord Clarendon's reason for refusing Colonel Türr
the opportunity for obtaining that of which he was
in search, employment in Turkey, seems to have been
based on an apprehension that he was going elsewhere.
His lordship no doubt was well aware of his intimacy
with Kossuth, and evidently suspected that he was proceeding on a mission that might involve the English
Government in unpleasant complications. The colonel
had already established a character for imprudence,
and might again place himself in Austrian hands.
The Foreign Secretary thought that gentleman would
be out of harm's way at home, and considered that a
naturalised subject should be naturalised only to settle
in it, in accordance with the Act "To amend the
laws relating to aliens," section vi. We give Lord
Clarendon's declaration on the subject:—

Foreign Office, November 3rd, 1856.

SIR,—I am directed by the Earl of Clarendon to acknowledge the receipt of your letter of the 29th ultimo, and to
inform you that it does not explain the inconsistencies
which appear to exist in your case, nor is there any

attempt in it to account for the discrepancies between your printed accounts of yourself and the statements as to residence in your own letter. You state in your letter that in 1850, 1851, 1852, 1853 you resided chiefly in London, though part of that time your affairs obliged you to visit Turin, Switzerland, and France; on the other hand you state in your pamphlet, page 10, that between September, 1849, and October, 1850, "you resided partly in Switzerland and partly in Piedmont" until October, 1850, subsequently to which date you conducted, "on foot to Havre," a party of Hungarians. You then state that "you remained in Europe, residing alternately in Piedmont, Switzerland, and now and then in Paris and London, until the month of February, 1853, when you went into Italy." The revolution in Milano having failed, you state that you were arrested and kept in prison forty days; that you were afterwards sent to Tunis, whence you had an opportunity of reaching England. You further state that when the war broke out between Russia and the Western Powers in March, 1854, you went to Turkey, and you make no allusion to any subsequent residence in England till August, 1856.

There is nothing in these statements with respect to the past which bears out the allegation that you resided five years in England; and, with respect to the future, you have informed Lord Clarendon of your intention of seeking employment in the East, in a manner which is wholly incompatible with the supposition of a residence in this country.

His lordship does not feel it necessary to enter into any argument as to whether or not your conduct, after you had been provided by the British Government with employment, was or was not judicious, or likely to lead to the difficulties which were subsequently created by the course you pursued; but there was certainly nothing in your case to justify Lord Clarendon in departing from the course he would pursue in any similar case, namely, of refusing to grant a British passport to a naturalized subject in virtue of a certificate of naturalization obtained upon statements which appear to be incorrect.

It was open to you when you were informed that your statement of residence was incorrect, as it is open to you now, to offer any explanation of the conflicting statements you appear to have made.

You were not informed at this office, as you seem to imply, that your becoming a British subject " debarred you from ever leaving British soil ;" but I am directed to inform you that until you can satisfy Lord Clarendon on the points to which I have alluded, he cannot feel himself justified in granting you a passport.

I am, Sir, your most obedient humble servant,

SHELBURNE.

$\frac{911}{880}$. War Department, November 8th, 1856.

SIR,—In reply to your letter of the 21st October I am directed by Lord Panmure to acquaint you that the payments to Colonel Türr cannot be exempted from the charge for Income duty.

I am, Sir, your obedient servant,

(Signed)   JOHN CROOMES.

Colonel M'Murdo.

Je vous transmets cette copie en vous disant que person des employées etranger du Land Transport Corps n'a pas payée l'income taxe. Par exception particulière je n'étais pas conté parmi les heureux, et je du la payer.

The next communication the unfortunate Hungarian received from the English Government was to announce to him the surprising fact that, although he had become nationalised in England, he had not been de-nationalised in Austria ; therefore he was still an Austrian subject.

Lord Clarendon finding that Colonel Türr could not give a satisfactory explanation of his errand to Turkey, was obliged to come to the conclusion that this was only an assumed destination. The colonel again applied to the member for Finsbury, and Mr. Duncombe again had an interview with Lord Palmerston. Whether the Foreign Secretary became satisfied that the Hungarian had a legitimate object in travelling at this particular period, cannot be stated on sufficient authority; all that we are aware of is, that he did obtain a passport, and that a short time afterwards, first as chief of the aides-de-camp, and sub-sequently with the rank of general, was serving gallantly with Garibaldi in the French and Sardinian war with Austria in Italy.*

General Türr gained great credit for a brilliant achievement in that glorious campaign, in which he was wounded. At this period Mr. Duncombe, at the request of Mr. Edwin James, the eminent barrister, wrote a letter of introduction to the general, and another to Baron Poerio, Mr. James having decided on going to the seat of war. These were not the only services of the kind he rendered military amateurs. Mr. Francis George Hare, formerly of the 2nd Life Guards, received such a recommendation as procured him employment immediately. He was present at the battle of Volturno, for his gallant conduct got promoted to the Staff, and was made a captain.

The general had the command of one of the divisions of the army of Sicily, and Mr. Duncombe's legal friend met him at Naples, in the full enjoyment of his well-deserved success, but suffering much from indisposition.

---

* General Türr's other letters to Mr. Duncombe will be found in the Appendix.

Naples, Sunday, September 9th, 1860.

MY DEAR DUNCOMBE,—This evening I gave your letter to Colonel Türr. What a scene we have had here ! no pen can describe it. I entered Naples with Garibaldi, and came by special train with him from Salerno. The popular enthusiasm knows no bounds.

I have been with him three times, and like him much. Türr seems very ill; he desired his kindest remembrances to you.

Garibaldi will pass on to Rome at once.

I shall remain here about ten days. I want to see Garibaldi give the Bavarian troops a good licking.

           Ever sincerely,   EDWIN JAMES.

I have been very well, but the heat is fearful.

Garibaldi was not permitted to continue the campaign to its crowning triumph. Italy was won; but Rome, as usual in its extremity, protected by the chapter of accidents, had a reprieve in the eleventh hour.

The war was over, and the heroes retired on their laurels till they should again be wanted. In the following year one of them published the following announcement amongst his friends :—

Turin, Septembre le 11°, 1861.

Le General Etienne Türr a l'honneur de vous faire part de son mariage avec Mademoiselle Adeline Bonaparte Wyse.*

The public interest in Kossuth waned in England from the time that more impartial accounts of his antecedents and of the civil war in Hungary began to circulate. They varied materially from the narrative

* Daughter of Madame Lætitia Wyse, who wrote the letter to Mr. Duncombe to be found in a preceding chapter.

of himself and his partizans. Perhaps the one most
damaging to him was the Baron Prochazka's " Revelations of Hungary," published in this country in
1851. A memoir of Kossuth was added, that represented him as anything but a hero, and his proceedings as anything rather than beneficial to Hungary.
No doubt there was a strong bias in its tone ; but the
facts related were indisputable, and these getting
diffused through the newspapers aided materially in
divesting his name of that romantic interest with
which it was clothed on his arrival in England after
the termination of the revolt he had assisted in creating and helped to maintain.

Hungary became less and less attractive in England. Kossuth persuaded "The Friends of Italy" to
combine the Hungarian with the Italian cause. This
idea in November, 1851, was brought before the
members of the society. On the 12th of that month
Mr. Duncombe wrote a letter to the secretary, Mr.
Daniel Masson, stating that he would approve of the
change provided it had the sanction of Mazzini as
well as of Kossuth. The desired sanction was ob·
tained; moreover, a joint appeal was made for a
shilling subscription on behalf of Hungary and Italy,
to be handed over to the two patriots; but as events
made their projects more and more hopeless, more and
more lukewarm became their admirers.

Kossuth, though he had no pretensions to patrician descent, in all his communications signed with
his surname only, as though the representative
of a noble or princely house. His name was Lajos
Kossuth, the Hungarian christian name agreeing with
" Louis," and complaints were made of his haughti-

ness during his short-lived power. The murder of Count Lamberg threw as much odium on the cause of the Hungarian revolutionists as that of Count Rossi did on the Italian.

Early in the year 1861 public attention was again directed to Kossuth by his being a defendant in the Court of Chancery, the plaintiff being Francis Joseph Emperor of Austria and King of Hungary and Bohemia. It was caused by the manufacture in this country of paper money for circulation in the kingdom of Hungary, signed "Louis Kossuth," in the Hungarian language, and bearing the royal arms. On the affidavit of Count Apponyi, the Austrian ambassador, that the amount of such paper money attempted to be thrown into circulation in the emperor's dominions would exceed a hundred millions of florins, for revolutionary purposes, an injunction was prayed for and granted by Lord Campbell. The result was that Messrs. Day and Son, who had been made defendants in the suit with Kossuth, had to surrender the whole of the notes they had manufactured, and to pay the costs of the injunction.

Kossuth was as much discomfited by the treaty of Villafranca as by the injunction in the English Court of Chancery. According to a statement in a communication addressed by him to a friend in Glasgow, published in the newspapers, he had been organizing a revolution in Hungary which, just when success was certain, was extinguished by the unwelcome compact between the imperial belligerents; and we learn under his own hand that he never obtained one of the notes printed by Messrs. Day. Mr. Duncombe was not disposed to give the Government so easy a victory, and followed the same course with the Kossuth notes he had taken with the Kossuth rockets. His proceeding elicited the following comprehensive reply :—

7, Bedford-place, Russell-square,
March 18th, 1861.

MY DEAR SIR,—I beg to express my most sincere thanks for your so ably and so warmly protecting my good cause.

I am going instantly to take steps that I hope will give me authority to put into your hands conclusive evidences to substantiate the facts to which you have been pleased to refer in the House of Commons on Friday last, and I shall not rest till I get the authority required for the production of said evidence.

I think Lord John's explanation about " the interests England has in the Adriatic " was very illogical and very weak. What possible connexion there can be between England being in possession of the Ionian Islands and Lord John using the authority of England for deterring Count Cavour from liberating Venice from Austrian thraldom, no man in his senses will ever understand, nor will Lord John ever be able to explain. " *Baculus in angulo ergo pluit,*" says the culinary Latin proverb.

The " I do not remember " of Lord John, about his ordering Sir James Hudson " to keep an eye on my doings at Turin," is not dignified. It puts one in mind of the notorious " *non mi ricordo.*" He had notice of the question, he has had time to refresh his memory by referring to his papers ; he must therefore say yes or no, and can't be allowed to evade the question with a " *non mi ricordo.*" Perhaps he is playing on the word " despatch ; " the order in question may go by some other denomination in the diplomatic phraseology : they may call it not despatch but " note," or " inquiry," or " communication," or " letter," &c. Be its name what it may, he *did* write to Sir James to the effect.

His answer with regard to the " *mesquine* " interference

with the railroad business misrepresents the facts.   It was never proposed or intended (therefore it is not true that the project, it having never existed, could have been afterwards abandoned) to concede the railroad in question to anybody upon the condition that a large sum should be paid to me. Quite the contrary ; I made inquiries whether that railroad was yet open to concession, and to competition for a concession, and I was answered in the affirmative.   I was told that any man or company may apply for it, but upon the express understanding that the affair can only be treated exclusively on its own ground, and any application for said concession will only be decided on its own merits, and not on any political considerations.   Upon this I got up amongst my city friends a company which offered to construct the railroad on certain terms.   I myself was not a director of the railroad, I only had brought the matter under the consideration of some English capitalists, and they remained connected with them, when Lord John remonstrated against the concession being granted to a company with whom I was connected.

So my lord did not threaten that he will not allow any expedition from Italy into the Adriatic ?   Well, I shall use every possible exertion to procure you the proof.   In the meanwhile I may say that the very despatch of August 31 bears out the fact, because there he speaks of England having gone already too far in blinking at armed expeditions, declares that in future they would be considered as organised with the consent of the Government, and winds up with referring to the interests of England in the Adriatic.

Now either Lord John must say that he wrote words without any meaning at all, or else the only possible meaning of his words is,—that in the past England allowed armed expeditions (for Sicily), but her indulgence will go no farther, and for the future she will not allow any such expeditions to start from Italy, especially for the Adriatic, because there England has interests (the safety of Austria) to guard.

This is the only reasonable construction that can be put on those words, especially as they were shortly followed by a concentration of a powerful fleet (800 guns) before Corfu, that concentration implying a " *de facto* " preparation, to give effect to the menace implied in the despatch of August 31.

I can positively assert that this is the sense in which the said despatch and the said concentration was understood, not only at Turin and Paris, but also at Vienna.

Lord John should be pressed to produce the instructions issued to the admiral on his being ordered to concentrate so large a force before Corfu. I am perfectly confident that we should see contained in them the order to stop or not to let pass any armed expedition from Italy for the coast of Dalmatia, and the order closely to watch for this purpose the " Levante " coast of Italy.

I instructed Messrs. Day to send you a copy of his affidavit. The statement of Sir Cornewall Lewis about his having had no translation of the body of the note is not correct; Sir Richard Mayne positively told Day on their first interview that he, Sir Richard, had a translation made of the note; therefore Government knew that the notes are neither forgery nor imitation of any note in existence before the police had been ordered to interfere with the work.

I have the honour to remain, with very high regard and esteem,

In great haste, yours ever truly and gratefully,

KOSSUTH.

It is very evident that the proceedings of Kossuth were closely watched by the English Government; and the police having secured evidence of his culpability, by means generally considered unjustifiable, another prosecution against him was commenced. A note was said to have been purloined, and the case was made to assume such an aspect that several of his English friends formed themselves into a committee for undertaking his defence. This Mr. Duncombe joined; he moreover from his seat in Parliament did his best to excite public indignation against a prosecution so conducted.

The writer of the accompanying notes was a barrister of Liberal principles, who seems to have been extremely zealous in the cause :—

Highgate, March 26th, 1861.

MY DEAR SIR,—How thoroughly I enter into the course you have taken you will best see by the copy note which I now enclose, and also by another of mine which ought to appear in *Star* of to-day. The fact is, we must " bother " them in every way we can, and, luckily, we have got the whip-hand of them both on the facts and the merits.

We must not let Mr. Ashurst consider whether to prosecute; we must insist on the prosecution. Between ourselves I have had to take this course throughout, or the game would have been entirely spoiled. I had myself to prepare Kossuth's affidavits, or they would have been a disgrace to us all, and the only trouble I now have comes of one affidavit which I let Ashurst prepare, thinking he could not blunder, but he has made a dreadful mess of it.

I am disgusted with Bright (I have often been so before). I happen to know that he was specially communicated with. He had in his possession facts by which he could have shown up Lord J. Russell's lying about the *Banshee*.

I cannot express warmly enough my thanks to you, as an Englishman, a lover of liberty, a hater of espionage and conspiracy, for what you have done, and for your promises of continued help. I am spending the Easter " holiday " [!] in working the matter. We will be too much for the rascals yet.

Believe me, my dear Sir, very faithfully yours,
TOULMIN SMITH.

T. S. Duncombe, Esq., M.P.

Highgate, March 25th, 1861.

Sir,—It having been stated officially that the stolen Kossuth note was brought to you by a policeman, and as this policeman must have either stolen the note himself, or received it knowing it to have been stolen, I beg to ask whether steps have already been taken by you to prosecute this policeman, as the law requires, or, if not, when those steps are about to be taken. I will not allow myself to suppose that you will allow so base and flagrant a crime, committed immediately under your eye and within your special jurisdiction, to pass without prosecution and punishment. I have, &c. TOULMIN SMITH.

Sir R. Mayne.

The affair did not turn out so damaging to the Government or to the police as the indignant writer of the foregoing had anticipated; but this result was in no way owing to the want of spirit of Kossuth's friends. They did their utmost in behalf of their client: unfortunately for him his popularity had vanished, and public opinion—except a small but active band of reformers—was averse to his projects. In truth, there was a powerful party strongly sympathizing with Austria in her reverses, who regarded the Hungarian patriot as a firebrand, and this opinion was shared by several members of the Government, who were determined to extinguish him rather than permit a conflagration.

The mystery about Kossuth's note admitted of easy explanation: but it was one no member of the Government would have given or sanctioned. They had secured evidence of a spurious issue of paper money, produced at the instigation of the Hungarian patriot. Mr. Duncombe was indignant at their

finesse; other friends of Hungary were equally so.
We quote a communication from one to show in what
light they regarded the general support afforded to
the executive in this transaction.   The correspondence between the member for Finsbury and the
Secretary of State for the Home Department shows
the spirit that existed in that quarter:—

Highgate, March 24th, 1861.

My DEAR SIR,—I entirely agree with you that there
never was such a lick-spittle House of Commons.   Every
day serves only more and more to show this.   Why you
were not backed up is inexplicable ; Collier wrote to White
and Layard, and I sent them copies of the petition.
Bright was both seen and written urgently to.   It is
thoroughly disgraceful that men who pretend to be liberals
and lovers of freedom put little personal jealousies before
public duty.   One man did go down on purpose to support
you, and that was Mr. Horsman.   He had been out of
town ; he found my note on his return on Friday, late in
the afternoon, and instantly went down to the House, but,
owing to other men having broken faith, the thing was over,
and it was too late.

But an invaluable result was got.   It is now admitted
(1) that they dare not let the public know how they got
the note ; (2) that they alone supplied the evidence to the
Austrian Embassy, and so are entirely responsible for the
proceedings.   To have got this out is of the highest
importance.   I have handled Sir G. L.'s flimsy pretences
in " Remembrancer."

Very faithfully yours,   TOULMIN SMITH.

March 25th, 1861.

SIR,—To save time and further trouble on the reassem-
bling of Parliament I shall feel much obliged to you to
give me the name, number, and letter of the policeman
from whom Sir R. M. received " the K. note ; " also to

inform me whether the aforesaid policeman is still on the strength of the Metropolitan Force, if not, when he left it.

Your obedient humble servant,   T. S. DUNCOMBE.

Home Office, March 30th, 1861.

MY DEAR SIR,—In answer to your letter of the 25th instant I beg leave to say that I do not feel justified in complying with your request, and in furnishing you with the information which you desire.

I remain, my dear Sir,

Yours very truly,   G. C. LEWIS.

T. S. Duncombe, Esq., M.P.

The member for Finsbury, so far from being deterred by the hostility of the Government to the Hungarian patriot from aiding in his defence, now proceeded to make powerful appeals in the House of Commons in favour of the Hungarians. Though they produced no decided effect in England, as they were translated and reproduced in the continental papers, they were very favourably received in Hungary. In the course of the next three or four months Mr. Duncombe received about a dozen addresses from patriotic assemblies in that country acknowledging the value of his advocacy, and expressing a grateful sense of obligation.

The provincial assemblies in Hungary that evinced so lively an appreciation of the advocacy of the member for Finsbury conferred on him the distinction of being an honorary member of the General Committee, a distinction occasionally conferred on distinguished foreigners, of whom one was the late Prince Consort. It is curious that among extreme reformers in the House of Commons there should be two retained in antagonistic services. One by repute at least filled the office of counsel for Austria, the other thus publicly became the leader on the opposite side. Mr. Duncombe was now an Hungarian by a higher authority than that which made Lord John Russell a freeman of the city of London, and the honour was well merited, and could be worn without reproach. There was no assumption of republican sentiment in those who thus chose to regard their English advocate as one of themselves. They desired only in a constitutional way to preserve the institutions many generations of Hungarians had been permitted to enjoy.

The proceedings of the Foreign Office were watched with great jealousy by the refugees in England, and if any transaction occurred that they disapproved of, through every accessible channel complaints were sure to be made that the Government was acting in opposition to the true interests of the country. Kossuth kept quite as keen a glance upon their doings as they maintained upon his, and having a popular representative in the British House of Commons to whom to state his impressions, he was not without hope that he should be able to check any manifestation of Austrian policy that came under his observation. Lord John Russell was in his eyes the *bête noir* of the Government, and he lost no opportunity of expressing his opinion of the darkness of his doings.

2, Cromwell-terrace, Harrow-road, W.,
April 7th, 1861.

MY DEAR SIR,—I think Government should be asked to lay before Parliament all the diplomatic correspondence referring to the subject of certain arms carried under Sardinian flag from Genoa to the East, and of Her

Majesty's ship *Banshee*, ordered to bring some of those arms back to Genoa from Galatz, where they had been seized by the Moldo-Valachian Government.

This is a very, very important affair. Either Lord John will place the papers complete before Parliament, and then they will afford the best possible opportunity for reviewing the philo-Austrian policy of the Foreign Office, or else Lord John will resort to the usual trick of garbled extracts, and in that case I shall not rest till I put you in possession of the whole, though I may have to send to Constantinople for the papers.

You very likely have heard from Mr. Ashurst of what has come to pass with regard to the notes. I have not heard of Mr. Ashurst for two days, and am therefore not quite *au fait*. It requires to be considered how far the new disclosures may or may not interfere with further steps to be taken with regard to the policeman over whom Sir G. Lewis is so deliberately throwing his protecting shield.

Most faithfully yours,   KOSSUTH.

T. S. Duncombe, Esq., M.P.

In his own country Kossuth's name and cause were equally neglected, and in England his few supporters were rapidly diminishing. The surrender of the Austrian rule in Italy appears to have strengthened the emperor's hold over Hungary, and the reverses subsequently met with at the hands of the King of Prussia have so intensely excited Hungarian chivalry, that the recent magnificent coronation of the emperor as their king has been cordially accepted by the entire nation. Francis Joseph has since published a political amnesty.

CHAPTER VII.

FRANCE AFTER THE COUP D'ETAT.

A slice off the magnificent reversion—Another secret mission—
The Duke attacked with apoplexy foudroyant—The President
and the new treaty of commerce—The will—The Duke and
the retrospective clause—Horse exercise—Fould and Persigny
—The President signs a Decree in favour of the Secretary's
scheme — Preparations for the Crimean War — The Duke's
health—The camp at Helfaut—Iron barracks—Mr. Duncombe's
secretary in great request—Ideas on climate—Letter of the
Duke—Marshal Vaillant—Disaster at the Camp—Probable
destination of the Camp du Nord—Conduct of the Emperor and
the Prince Consort—An impromptu engineer—The Poles considered under a new aspect—Reinforcements for the French
army in the Crimea—The greatest men in Europe—What is
Mr. Duncombe's secretary to become?—Charges against the
Emperor.

Two objects of special interest to Mr. Duncombe still
remained in Paris, and his secretary was still in requisition as a medium of communication with both. The
magnificent reversion, however, began to be enveloped
in an atmosphere of doubt. Nothing seemed more
probable than that, with a disposition so uncertain,
the Duke should entertain other views; and as if to
prepare him for such a change in his prospects, the following announcement was sent him to authenticate :—

The Sovereign Duke of Brunswick has this day informed
us that he has left in the hands of the Baron Andlau the
following bonds and securities, viz. :—

50 Bonds Russian English Loan 5 per Cent. of £1036 each.
5 Bonds „   „   „   4½ pr.   „ £1000 each.
45 Bonds Danish Loan, 1849, 5 per Cent. „ £1000 each.
15 Bonds „   „   1850, 5 per Cent. „ £1000 each.
2,000,000 francs 5 per Cent. French Rentes; as also a scaled portfolio.   And his Sovereign Highness has been pleased to command that in the event of his death the Baron Andlau shall take therefrom the sum of twenty thousand pounds sterling money as a legacy; and which donation we promise to respect as his Highness' testamentary executors.

London, this 15th day of March, 1851.

Signed,   T. S. D.
G. T. S.

The Sovereign Duke of Brunswick has this day informed us that he has left in the hands of Mademoiselle Lucie Victorine Bordier six bank notes of £100 each as a legacy in case of his death, which donation we promise to respect as his Highness' testamentary executors.

London, this 15th day of March, 1851.

Signed,   T. S. D.
G. T. S.

The indefatigable secretary was again in Paris towards the end of July, and returned on the 2nd of August, and was off for the same destination on the 20th.   The narrative of his proceedings, which we will now place before the reader, requires very little commentary.   He will see, however, that besides the objects he had previously in view in these visits, there was now an addition in the shape of another mercantile speculation quite different to the last.   The idea apparently was to introduce the system of bonding and warehousing employed by English merchants; and it was sought to establish a company under the auspices of the Government, to put this into a practical shape in Paris.   How he fared in bringing his scheme before the President and his principal ministers he fully describes:—

Hotel Britannique, Rue Duphot (St. Honoré),
Saturday Morning, Augt. 28th, 1852.

I have delayed writing to you, having nothing good to say, but that we had arrived safe ; for unfortunately, the ministre d'état with whom I have had to do has gone to the Pyrenees, and I can do nothing during his absence.   He waited for me, it appears, as long as he could ; consequently, I suppose my affair will go on well, as far as the President and Ministers are concerned.   I have, however, had great difficulties to encounter, for I found out that my position in the affair was not quite as it ought to be; and I have, therefore, been compelled to employ a lawyer, and have been very busy with him all the week endeavouring to place myself in the proper position, in which I had understood myself to be already.   However this morning, at seven o'clock (strange hour !) we all met, accompanied by our professional men, and made a notarial act in my favour, deposited in the hands of a third party, defining the sum I am to receive, and my position in the affair.   I am indebted to you for the discovery, for it was in pressing and persisting in my right to name a friend as administrator with myself, to form two of the English board, that I found out I was dependent upon others, owing to my not having been present when the first notarial act was made.   However, all is now, I think, well settled, and Blot has got my act deposited with him.

I have sent off yesterday, or rather ordered to be sent off, twelve bottles of wine to Mr. Durham, six bottles of St. Emelion, a perfectly pure wine, and said to be the best wine for invalids of any ; and I have great hopes it will be found for you highly beneficial, as it is invigorating without being stimulating, and as it possesses nothing in the shape of spirit but that of its own formation.   I have not seen Ricord, but in talking with a chemist he says the reason why Spanish wines—or in fact any wines—prepared for the English taste and market, are bad for invalids, is the amount of alcohol they contain; and therefore, instead of generously nourishing the blood they inflame it, besides destroying altogether the digestive powers; and a pure wine, notwithstanding it may taste a little acid, aids the digestive powers, and, strange to say, the vegetable acid of the wine destroys, or rather counteracts the animal acidity of the stomach, and so produces healthy action. I hope St. Emilion may do so for you; it is only 2s. 1d. the bottle.

Hotel Britannique, Rue Duphot,
September 2nd, 1852.

You say I do not mention D. B.; it was an omission on my part, for I am always out with him at night; and his servant has just called to tell me (by the duke's command) that the duke has been " iceing" his head all night, and is lying in bed. Strange to say, he (D. B.) has those fits much oftener than heretofore, although he has less constipation. As soon as I have written this I shall go to him.

My affair has not yet commenced, in consequence of the ministre d'état; but he returns to Paris to-morrow or Saturday, and then I must work it quick, so as to get it done before the 15th instant, as the President leaves for the south on that day. In fact, if the decree of the concession is not signed before the 15th the thing will fall for the winter. I wrote the prince so the other day, by the desire of the chef du cabinet, of Fould.

Orsi has just got a concession of a railway and coal-mine, with a contract to supply the French navy with French coals, from a mine lately discovered, and said to be the best coals on the Continent, and nearly equal in quality to the English coals. He has found English capitalists to come forward and pay the caution money; and in a few days will pocket 16,000l., with a good annual income besides. I understand the prince is very desirous of doing my matter, and Fould is quite willing, so that I have great hopes. But after the trick I have been served, I do not like some of the people who are concerned in the matter with me, although I cannot expel them.

I think it a great pity that the *Times* should continue those unjustifiable attacks against the prince, and they become the more unjust because, to a great extent, they are untrue. I wish you would write a letter containing your views of the Claremont clique, so that I could show the prince, as it might happen that some day he might be useful to you.

To show you the highly civilized state of society, in passing "la Morgue" yesterday I went in, and saw three bodies lying there; two had been assassinated, bearing all the marks of the knife. The lookers-on were coolly remarking, that they "had got something for themselves." Surely such a people want governing, and are unfit to govern themselves. And hence the popularity of the President; they fear him, and consequently they love him; and he is certainly doing all he can to give the people employment, and thereby hoping to get them quietly settled down into a sober thinking and commercial people. Could he once manage that, he would make France the dread and envy of the world.

Everybody seems to be here: among the persons I have seen and met are Lord Granville, one or two Cavendishes, Sir R. Peel, Sir R. Inglis—I should say his first visit, because he had a guide with him—Mr. Blunt, Mrs. Maberly, Mr. Wilkinson, Lawyer, Dr. Lewis, Mr. Fortnum, and Marshal Haynau, besides a host of others.

Hotel Britannique, Rue Duphot,
September 3rd, 1842, 4 o'clock afternoon.

I write just two lines to say that the duke is very ill with an attack of "blood to the head." After I left him late last night I thought he would have had a better night, but this morning I was called up at four o'clock to put twenty leeches on his head. I have only just returned home; I am going again by-and-bye to put on twenty more leeches on the other side of his head, as I could only put them on one side, he being too unwell to sit up; therefore I put the twenty on the upper side. Strange to say, he will not have a doctor, but trusts to me—a very unpleasant responsibility. He is much frightened, as several persons have died lately of *apoplexie foudroyant*. I will report to you again when I can. It is most unfortunate, as I hope to-morrow to begin my work. The President goes to-morrow to Saumur; there has been a row there between the cavalry and the citizens. He will not return till Tuesday.

The duke made me tell him the news last night; and upon my telling him that the Secretary for the Interieure here is in London to negotiate the Act of Extradition, it affected him greatly. He counts much upon your aid in the House of Commons; and desires me to write to you, and so state. Report says that France offers to England a favourable "treaty of commerce," in lieu of her passing through the Parliament the Bill of Extradition as first proposed.

I saw last evening some of the Elysée people, who assure me that the treaty between the northern powers *re* Imperialism exists only in the imagination of the *Chronicle*.

With respect to Hopwood,* I told young Hopwood I was going to France, and requested he would do nothing till I returned, as he thought a deputation from the Alderman's committee† ought to wait upon your committee on the subject of the dinner. He thought he should like me first to sound them—*i.e.*, your committee—as to their views, so as to prevent the application on their part if there was any chance of refusal.

The duke's illness was not of that dangerous nature the doctors consulted represented it to be; but it appears to have been sufficiently serious to have frightened him into a reference to his testamentary arrangements. His royal highness did not give any indication of having changed his mind. As regards the other illustrious personage, equally the object of

---

* Under Sheriff.

† Committee of Alderman Challis, Member for Finsbury.

the secretary's hopes and anxieties, he gives some curious notices of his principal ministers. It will be seen that he had a difficult part to play; the duke wanting an amount of English parliamentary influence for his own purposes, it was more easy to promise, than safe to employ. The Convention Treaty to which he referred with such anxiety, was for the mutual surrender of criminals fled from justice; and the new clause introduced was to the following effect:—

Copy of the change, in English, proposed to the 14th paragraph of the Convention between England and France.

The stipulations of the present Convention shall in nowise be applicable to crimes or misdemeanours committed previously to the date of the present Convention, except for the crimes already named in the Convention of the 13th February, 1843, for which crimes this Convention will remain in force retrospectively till the 13th February, 1843.

The following is in the handwriting of Mr. Duncombe's secretary:—

Memo*.—The duke gave me this, written by Monsieur le Duc de Feumacon, and he desires me to inform you that this was the proposition of some noble lord, he does not know who. I again repeat 'tis most important you write to me on this subject directly.

We now give a series of his reports as forwarded to Mr. Duncombe:—

Hotel Britannique, September 7th, 1852.

With respect to D. B., he has now been in bed for the last six days, and yesterday he sent for a doctor, an homœopathist, who gave him some globules. This same man attended D'Orsay* in conjunction with Ricord; they dis-

* The fate of the Count is well known.

agreed, and you know the rest. However, I have taken an opinion with regard to D. B., and it is thought to be a breaking up of the constitution; they say, at his age, he runs great risk of a severe attack.

Last night the conversation between H.R.H. and self was the subject of the will; and he said to me, "If anything happens to me during this illness, over and above what you have by the will, I give you 50,000 Sardinians as a gift; and as there are 156,000 in the packet, it would be well to send Mr. D.* over the same amount, and place the remaining 50,000 in some secure place, to pay your joint law expenses which you would incur in insisting upon the whole of my Brunswick property being placed at your disposal." I then said (having a good opportunity), "Are you quite sure that the will is in perfect order to satisfy the French law?" He said, "I have always understood so; but you may ask Blot;" which I shall do as soon as he returns to town.

With respect to my own affair, it hangs fire most terribly. Fould has been absent all the time I have been here; in fact, it would appear as I entered Paris he quitted it. He came to town on Sunday, and started to see the Prince at St. Cloud, and has stopped shooting, but returns to-night; and the Prince says it is no good seeing me till I have settled with Fould, so I begin to think that it is absolutely necessary to kill partridges in September to prevent their assuming other forms in January; for all over Europe, whether constitutional or despotic, the government, the minister, and diplomatist quit their bureau to kill their partridges, leaving all business to take care of itself; and so, owing to the fine weather in the south, and the shooting here, I have been compelled to wait patiently with my important affair.

I send you the debates; you will see he† is corresponding with the press here as elsewhere. Strange to say, there is now always something in the *Augsburg Gazette* as well as the *Cologne Gazette* about D.B.

* Mr. Duncombe.   † Duke of Brunswick.

I now beg to call your serious attention to the following, which really may prove too much for us unless you can in any way nip it in the bud. The duke desires me to say to you that he is not at all easy about the treaty the French Government are seeking for with England; and he particularly desires me to call your attention to the fact that he shall not consider himself safe here, and consequently will not stop, if the English Parliament pass that Act ratifying the treaty with the retrospective clause cut out. But he thinks, considering the original proposition was for the retrospective clause, that there ought to be in the new treaty a positive clause stating that on no account shall the treaty be considered retrospective; for he says after that it has been proposed to be retroactive, and then, that clause merely omitted, would not be sufficient to decide whether it was intended to be retroactive or not.

I must beg of you to write me on this subject directly; for he says as soon as the bill has passed the Lords in anything like a doubtful form he will quit Paris, and will not stop for the passing of the Commons. So pray write me a letter for him on the subject, assuring him or me (as the case may be) that the English Parliament will not pass such a law, and promising him all he desires with respect to the retrospective clause, for in that and on that depends his danger. And if you can send him a copy of the clause you would propose, to mark it as not being intended in any way retroactive, it would do great good; and, *entre nous*, I think you might get some peer to move for the insertion of the clause in your words, and that would be of immense importance to us.

Hotel Britannique, Rue Duphot (St. Honoré),
September 8th, 1852.

Yesterday, the 7th, I called upon him, *par ordre superieure*, to read to him and to open his letters, and to reply thereto if any required a reply; and while there, his new medical man, the homœopathist, arrived, and we were both ushered to the royal bed together; and after the M.D. had prescribed for him, and given him orders positive that he must quit his bed, or that he would he so weaken himself that it would be a long time before he would recover his strength, the duke called me to his bedside, and requested me to ask the M.D. in the next room as he was going out, the name of his disease, which I did, and which the M.D. pronounced to be "cephalite." The M.D. cut me very short, merely giving me the name of the disease, and pronouncing that it was *très dangereux*.

Neither the duke or myself was to be done by the term "cephalite," which neither of us understood; but on referring to the dictionary we found it thus described:— "Cephalite—*inflammation de cerveaux*." The duke persists that I must have made a mistake; but I am quite sure of my correctness. You are as good a judge as I am of the nature of the disease, and therefore it would be presumption in me to attempt to describe it.

When the duke's M.D. was pointing out to him the necessity of his getting out as soon as possible in order to avail himself of the "tonicity" of the morning air, all of which D.B. pronounced "d—d nonsense," I made a few inquiries as to the most healthy and fitting time to take exercise, and the nature thereof; and the reply I got was, that morning exercise on horseback at this time of the year— in fact, at all times—had a doubly good effect, viz., to bring into action the lazy, torpid functions of the human frame (this applies to an invalid), and at the same time the "tonicity" of the air creates appetite, while the digestive powers are in action to digest it. All this is caused by the exercise on horseback.

With respect to my affair, I have an appointment with the Ministre d'Etat to-morrow; but in consequence of my detecting the fraud intended to be practised on me, one of the poorest but yet the most active of the parties concerned has taken umbrage, and we are divided; consequently great difficultes are thrown in the way. But I prefer spoiling the thing altogether rather than allow them to benefit themselves at my expense; for they (that is, one of them), was working hard to obtain the concession, and to deprive me of

the promised benefits; in fact, it was nothing less than a
fraud. I therefore have not quite made up my mind whether
I shall not explain all to the Minister to-morrow, and leave
him to decide upon the merits. The real difficulty is this,
that the party of whom I complain has so tightly got hold
of all the other parties concerned, that they dare not act as
I believe they would. Orsi is going with me to-morrow;
and he proposes that I should take the concession, and look
for other capitalists.

Hotel Britannique, Rue Duphot,
Saturday Morning, 11 o'clock.

I have this morning been to pay the other Dr. Cabanas, and I asked him the name of the duke's disease,
and he replied—"Cephalit," and the consequence, sooner
or later, "apoplexy *foudroyant.*" I said, then there is
great danger? He said—"Yes; great danger." And the
duke's life is not worth one moment's purchase, for when
he appears the best in health, then he is the worst. He
ought not to be left; but if he thought so, the nature of the
disease invariably makes them, *i.e.* the sufferers, suspicious.

My affair stands thus: admitted by all to be first-rate.
Fould made the report to the prince, and fixed last Thursday to settle the matter, so that the prince might sign the
decree before he leaves, which he does on Monday or Tuesday next; but when we met he admitted the reality of the
proposition, but regretted it was not belonging to his
ministry, and so threw us over. We are now handed over
to Persigny, who treated me very kindly, went to St. Cloud
to the prince, and is willing, if possible, to do it; but he
says, and truly, that he cannot draw a decree without
knowing something of the matter, and he feared we shall
have to consult the " Chamber of Commerce," the " Ville
de Paris," and the " Conseil d'Utilité Publique." He says—
" I am willing to shut my eyes as much as possible, but I
must know something of the affair." Fould has got all the
papers, and we have to make a formal demand to get them.

I have the prince's order for him to hand them to Persigny; but he can if he chooses take a day or two before so

doing, and then I am done. Fould is a banker, and doubt-less would like the thing indirectly himself. The prince is all for it, and I fear Fould—desirous, either under pretence of being a cautious minister, or wishing to have it himself—against us, and so has delayed the affair till the last moment in order that the thing may die a natural death by lapse of time, as all the contracts for the purchase of exist-ing monopolies will fall in in November, of which Fould is aware. I am going to-day to Persigny, who has promised, if he gets the papers, to study them to-day.

The duke is better, much better; but imprudently—in-stead of taking a drive, as ordered, in the open air—nothing would suit but he must drive to the theatre. He was so weak as scarcely to be able to walk, and when I left him last night complained of the pain returning again to his head. I shall see by and bye how he is; he has never before been so shaken.

Ricord has quitted Paris, I think to visit his friend in "New Orleans." Some say he retired with a large fortune. However, he is not here at present, and they say will not be here for some months.

I shall not stop here longer than this day week, for when the prince has gone I may go; however, of that I will let you know. Alderman Humphreys, late for Southwark, is here. He is a great "warehouser" in London, and I believe will be a director. I have not yet seen him.

Blot is gone to Spain, or the borders thereof, shooting. With respect to the document: if anything happened while I am here I should telegraph to you, and I fear your pre-sence would be also necessary, as I could not act for you, having no power beyond your letter, and being myself an executor. I shall learn this from a counsellor, as it is most important to know.

I was on the point of coming to England the other day for a few hours for D. B., when I should so have done, but his illness put it and the cause aside. Strange, the night he was taken he had been with me to the theatre, and after-wards we supped together at *Café Anglais*, and he appeared better than usual, full of fun and mirth, and you would have said had you seen him he never had been better; but the attack came on in the night—not, the doctor assures me this morning, the effects of the supper, but from natural causes, *i.e.* that the blood in his case has a natural tendency to flow to the brain, and will some day congest the same and produce apoplexy.   Nothing can save him but great exercise; and the duke says he is a d—d fool for his advice, for he will for no one get up at eight o'clock in the morning and not know what to do all day.

Thursday, September 16th, 1852.

With respect to my own affair, that has assumed a favourable position, and I think I shall get the decree signed in a day or two.   I was with Persigny yesterday, and he planned the form of the decree, and the prince desires to sign it at Lyons.   Whether I shall have to go there I know not; but I hope in a few days to settle all. The decree will be in the names of Messrs. Cusin, Legendre, and Du Chene de Vere.   I have not insisted on being therein, for reasons which I will explain when I see you.

Hotel Britannique, September 26th.

I send you by this post the *Moniteur* of this morning, and you will see the affair has been signed at Roanne.

I have taken counsel's opinion on D. B.'s matter, and I am sure you will be delighted at the information I have obtained as to our plan of action in the event of our being called upon to act.   I shall not be able to get away before Thursday next, as there is yet a great deal to do to carry out the decree.

On Sunday I go to Fontainbleau, and shall then see a celebrated trapper of *cailles de chasselas*, and will bespeak some for you.   They are in high perfection just now, and much sought after *par les vrais gourmets*.

Au Nom du Peuple Français.

Louis-Napoleon,

President de la République Française,

Sur le rapport du Ministre de l'Intérieur, de l'Agriculture et du Commerce;

Vu le décret du 21 Mars, 1848, concernant les magasins généraux pour depôt de marchandises;

Considérant que le commerce doit retirer une très-grande utilité de l'établissement de docks ou magasins destinés à recevoir en dépôt les marchandises dont on veut mobiliser la valeur au moyen de *warrants*, récépissés négociables par voie de simple endossement, et qui, sans cette faculté, restent souvent stériles dans les mains du producteur;

Considérant que ces docks et magasins profiteront non-seulement au commerce mais encore à l'ouvrier travaillant à son compte, ou, en cas de mévente, pourra déposer là ses produits et continuer son travail au moyen des fonds qu'il se procurera sur le récépisse délivré par la compagnie;

Considérant que l'expérience qui se fera à Paris d'un établissement analogue à ceux qui fonctionnent si utilement en Angleterre et en Hollande, est de nature à encourager la création de semblables établissements dans nos grands centres commerciaux,

Décrète :

"Art. 1er. MM. Cusin, Legendre et Duchesne de Vère sont autorisés à établir, à Paris, sur les terrains qui leur appartiennent près la place de l'Europe, des magasins dans lesquels les négociants et industriels pourront, conformément au décret du 21 Mars, 1848, déposer les matières premières, les marchandises et objets fabriqués dont ils sont propriétaires.

"Art. 2. Les marchandises déposées dans les dits magasins seront considérés comme appartenant à des sujets neutres, quelle qu'en soit la provenance et quelles que soient les éventualités qui pourraient survenir.

"Art. 3. Un règlement d'administration publique déter-

minera les obligations de la compagnie en ce qui concerne
la surveillance de ses magasins par l'Etat, les garanties
qu'elle devra offrir au commerce, et le mode de délivrance
des récépissés transmissibles par voie d'endossement.

"Art. 4. Le Ministre de l'Intérieur, de l'Agriculture et
du Commerce et le Ministre des Finances sont chargés,
chacun · en ce qui le concerne, de l'exécution du présent
décret.

LOUIS-NAPOLEON.

Fait à Roanne, le 17 Septembre, 1852.

Par le Prince Président :

Le Ministre de l'Intérieur,
de l'Agriculture et du Commerce,   F. DE PERSIGNY.

The secretary visited Paris twice in 1853, but
stayed only a few days. He again went, on 14th
April, with Baron Andlau, and returned on the 24th,
and repeated his visit on the 6th, returning on the
10th; left on the 4th of September, and did not return
till the 5th of October. He was off again on the 21st.
The only communications that have been preserved
commence before his last departure; and it will be
seen that he was now on a totally different mission.
The emperor desired his services to assist his military
arrangements for the Russian war. He gives the
following account of them, and of the duke. The
manner in which he procured the habitations required,
and set up the barracks, gained him great favour.

Chez-moi, October 9th, 1854.

You say I did not tell you anything about the duke; all
I can say is, that he was, if possible, kinder than ever, and
made me promise to spend a fortnight with him soon;
though how that is to be managed I know not, as I must
finish at the Camps, which will take twenty days, all of

which when I see you. But to refer again to the duke. We, although you have been absent, stand better than ever; I, on account of being so much taken up by the emperor while at Boulogne, which pleases his highness much; and he said, on parting, that he should be angry if I did not come and spend a fortnight at least with him. On my arrival at Beaujon he saw me directly. I then went out till he got up, rode out on horseback, and then went out alone* and dined with duke ———. He said, while I was sitting in his drawing-room, "I thought, about three weeks ago, you would have to be telegraphed for on account of my health;" and he then informed me that he had had a slight attack of apoplexy. It appears he was in better health than usual, dressing to go out; felt the room go round with him backwards, and fell out of his chair on the ground; and that is all he knows, but referred me to his valet for the rest. The valet said he was just passing his highness's cravat round his neck when his highness fell, and the force of the fall was saved by his being suspended in his cravat. He (the valet) eased him to the ground, sent off directly for medical aid, during which time the duke turned all manner of colours, and his tongue hung out of his mouth, and he was as cold as marble. The M.D. pronounced it as a bad omen, and said it was a slight fit of apoplexy; and although this one has done no harm, he is never certain when he might be again so attacked, as he will always have a tendency to such attacks, more now than ever.

The Prince of Armenia is at Mazas, and all the world— i. e., those who know us—say that I have done it. Be it how it may, he is secure for the present, and therefore the duke wants some one. How I regret your not being well enough to enjoy Paris life.

One good thing the duke said directly he recovered, which was at night :—" If I say Smith during my illness, that means send for him—he is now at Folkestone, Hotel Boulogne—and by telegraph."

---

* I mean without the countess.

Friday Afternoon, October 13th, 1854.

With respect to my matters at Boulogne, the tale would occupy many sheets of paper to inform you of its nature, and then the details would be uninteresting to you. In a few words, the camps from Equichen to Helfaut will exist all the winter; and the Emperor, being desirous that the troops should suffer as little as possible, is always ready to adopt any plan which he thinks will add to their comfort. During the sojourn of Prince Albert, he happened to mention that the Queen, being desirous of giving balls at Balmoral, had had a ball-room constructed of iron in ten days.

The Emperor, whom I had just pleased by my happy selection of some presents from him to the Duchess d'Alba and the Countess Montijo, in which I was lucky enough to give great satisfaction to him and the Empress, sent for me to England, thinking I had gone home. The letter was forwarded to me in due course, and I presented myself. The Emperor explained his wants, and sent me off to the north of England to purchase one of these buildings. I did not find one ready made, but by dint of pressure got a contract signed under demurrage to have one erected in six days. I returned to Boulogne without stopping in London, and in six days had the honour to receive their majesties and the generals of division in the completed house.

I was then sent three other times to England (once I crossed in a storm) but never slept, and entered into contracts, which will be completed and landed on the 21st, by the boat leaving Saturday morning, the 20th, and consequently I must be there to superintend the landing and erection at each of the camps, as all is under my charge; and on Tuesday next I must send an account to each camp of the number of men, horses, and *prolonge d'artillerie* I shall want, so as not to interfere with the organized service of the waggon train. You will see, therefore, that I am compelled to go on Sunday, the 21st, or I shall again throw away opportunities which may eventually prove of material benefit to me, and which might never occur again.

Hotel de Folkestone, Boulogne-sur-Mer,
October 29th, 1854.

When I wrote to you on Tuesday I could say nothing of my barracks, as they had been detained, and did not arrive till Wednesday night, in consequence of the dreadful storms in the Channel. I am now happy to say that they are progressing, but not so fast as I could wish.

I have not heard direct from the duke, but it appears that the Minister of War (Marshal Vaillant) wanted to communicate with me, and applied to the duke for my address in Boulogne, which the duke gave, and the minister sent his aide-de-camp from Paris to me, by command of the emperor, to consult about making permanent barracks at Marseilles. We sat up all night calculating, and the aide-de-camp has returned to Paris.

With respect to myself, I have been suffering from having got wet through two days in succession, being obliged to take long rides in the wet.

I write to-day to the duke to thank him. I have no doubt he will not fix a time till he knows I am free from the emperor.

P.S.—The Hon. H. Fitzroy is here, and has been for some time.

Hotel de Folkestone, Boulogne-sur-Mer,
November 3rd, 1854.

My business goes on slowly, from a variety of causes; but I hope the middle of next week to get to Helfaut, the camp near St. Omer, and after that I shall be guided in my movements entirely by what I hear from you. I wrote to the duke to know when he wished me to visit him, and to say that perhaps as the baron intended visiting Paris at Christmas, that his highness would prefer my availing myself of that moment; and further, that as I should have many visitors that perhaps that might be disagreeable to him. I enclose you a copy of his reply to me *verbatim et literatim.*

I have had a long chat with the medical inspector of the camps, with whom I happened to be the other day—a very sensible man, and of high standing in his profession. The subject turned upon the effect of climate upon certain diseases, and the susceptibility of some diseases, and how they are influenced by climate. A gentleman said to him— "What do you think of the climate of Montpellier? Are the hotels good?" &c. His reply, which first excited my attention, was—"Montpellier is a most delicious climate for persons in *good* health ; but you will find there nothing but *malades et des gens poitrinaires, envoyés là par les médecins Anglais pour mourir.*" I then began, and said—" Do you mean to say that the whole of the climate *du midi* is the same?" He replied—"Yes ; it is quite a mistaken notion to suppose that that beautiful climate is without its evils, and in the case of diseases of the chest very dangerous." He then as a reason gave the following—" You must know," he said, " that when the chest is affected the most delicate membrane of the whole frame is attacked ; and how can you suppose the fine climate of the *midi* can be beneficial to such, when I tell you that it does not rain sometimes for three months ? The earth becomes pulverized, and imperceptible but dangerous grit is floating in the air. This dust or grit exists to an extent fabulous to the healthy, but deleterious and deadly to the diseased chest, producing irritation to an extent, in the very weak, too much for them to bear, and consequently producing death. In the summer months the heat is too great for invalids or anybody else to go out in the midday, and the delicious evening cannot be enjoyed by the weak chest without producing certain death. The winter is beautifully temperate on the whole, but subject to sudden and violent changes : as, for instance, in one hour the mistrale wind will convert the most beautiful imaginable day in winter, when all appeared genial, to knives and daggers to the weak chest, and the thermometer will fall many degrees in that same hour, while the air is again charged with dust. This applies more or less to the whole length of the Mediterranean coast. Perhaps any other disease but that of the chest might be benefited by such a climate, in fact would be."

We then spoke of other places, and he said—" The

strange thing is that you have in England one or two places almost all that could be desired, viz., the Isle of Wight, Devonshire, and Cornwall in certain months, the shores of the Channel—perhaps the French side during a couple of months, about Dieppe the best." As a proof of this the Russian imperial family preferred 'those places to Italy. The things most to be avoided : unnatural air, dust, and smoke—the greatest irritants; and as a preventative to some extent of catching cold, avoid a thing which people, he says, have not the common sense to do, that is going out of broad sunshine into shade, or, to use his own words, " Jumping from Italy to Iceland, and back again, and then asking yourself why you caught cold"; and it mostly happens that when shade is the most agreeable that it is most dangerous; the sun itself rather good to bask in, when not overpowering, so as to produce a sunstroke, and never of any harm if the head is well protected; never ride in open carriages with the head up, as the head draws in the air; and above all adapt yourself as well as you can to things, and things to you—this last remark applies to physic and diet; move about, or rather remain no longer in any place than you feel comfortable—that means with respect to your health. Egypt a beautiful climate, but all the good things of the world not to be had there if wanted, and man cannot live on climate alone; many places in the centre of France, as also Italy, equally good." And upon my thoroughly describing your complaint, he said that you must seek for yourself; but that he had known many instances of persons being reduced to almost death, and after years of suffering, and by some sudden and unaccountable effort of nature, recover and live for years.

Copy of Duke of Brunswick's Letter.

Rue de Beaujon, November 1st, 1854.

MY DEAR SIR,—I thank you for your good wishes to my birthday ; but I have been unwell and unable to leave my bed since Thursday last with what Dr. Cabanas calls neuralgia. I prefer your coming this time, but that is no reason why you should not come when the baron comes. I have no objection to your receiving the emperor's and minister's people or messengers. I close this letter, as I am still unable to sit up long in bed. Receive, dear sir, the assurance of my consideration,   D. B.

(P.S. *to mine.*—Woodcocks are very plentiful at eight francs per brace. Quails all gone; I have seen none since I have been here this time. Would you like any woodcocks?)

Hotel de Folkestone, Boulogne-sur-Mer,
November 7th, 1854.

It is a great piece of humbug on the part of the Government. They have collected a double income tax for the war, and now lend themselves to supply their own deficiency and want of foresight in preparing proper means for every event by an appeal to the private charity of the nation, and her Majesty and Co. lending themselves to it, cause all persons in public positions to become marked if they do not contribute.

With respect to myself: I think as soon as I have finished my camps (and I hope to begin Helfaut early next week) I shall go while on this side to see D. B. He evidently wishes me to be there alone, and 'tis not often you catch him writing such a letter as that to me! so I shall write him to that effect. I am in direct communication with L. N., and have an *aide de camp de service* mostly with me. I have just declined the Marseilles and Algerian trip—not but what I should like it. Marshal Vaillant, le Ministre de la Guerre, has just informed me by telegraph that aide-de-camp Colonel Dutrelaine will be with me at six o'clock this evening from Paris. I have an orderly at my disposal, and am doing things quite *à la militaire.*

Hotel de Folkestone,
Wednesday, November 15th, 1854.

The weather being so bad retards very much my camp operations, and I had hoped by this time to be at Helfaut;

but from calculations made last night, I fear I shall not get there till next Wednesday.

After the receipt of your last I wrote to the duke to say that as soon as I had done I would join him in Paris, and received a reply written by the countess to say I was to give them notice of my arrival, in order that my room might be got ready; but not a word about the duke's health. I suppose he was still unwell, or he would have written himself. This is all I have heard since I last wrote to you. You may rely upon my keeping you *au courant* of all news in that quarter. All my other news would not interest you, or I have plenty of camp news.

My opinion as to the reason of the duke wishing to see me alone is this : no doubt the Camp du Nord, to which I am attached for the moment, will at early spring march into Prussia, and the duke may hope to be able to join them in some way when they go to Germany, and punish his brother, who is a general in the Prussian service. I think that something of this sort may be passing in his head, and that he will confide to me his bags while he goes there. What do you think of this view?

Sunday Afternoon, November 19th, 1854.

All was just upon the point of completion at the camps near this, and I had planned to start for Helfaut on Tuesday, when a courier arrives to inform me that the general who commands the Equihen division wanted to see me without a moment's delay. I mount on horseback and ride there, and find the camps all razed to the ground. Upon inquiry I find that the officers of engineers, to carry on some work, have so relieved the buildings of their supports that the wind has carried them away. What damage and what delay, cannot yet be told ; but we are all thrown on our beam-ends. The emperor every alternate day writes to urge us on, and now all is down, and when it will be again up, God knows ; for the frost and hurricanes have commenced, and it will be with great difficulty we shall get them up again. I had at first intended to write to the emperor and marshal minister; but they persuaded me not, and so I have not done so, and therefore they may get done quicker, to oblige me, as I have served them. It is the expense of thousands, and all the responsibility rests on my shoulders, although I cannot govern the elements or make fools wise men.

P.S.—I have written to the duke also to inform him of my accident as a reason why I cannot fix a time to join him. I know he is anxious to see me, as a person called *en route* for England—left no name, but I know it was Tibbey—to say my presence would not be disagreeable in Paris. I was at the camp when he called.

Tuesday, November 21st, 1854.

I am, with you, curious to be at Beaujon, and I might almost say anxious. I have a good deal of exciting news to tell him, as I really think—in fact know—that Prussia will be the destination of the Camp du Nord, unless the winter brings an arrangement, which I doubt. The prevailing opinion of the higher military men here is, that Menchikoff, by his lies and the despatches which were published, was only to throw us (the allies) off our guard, in order to deceive us as to the necessity of having a large army there during the whole time he was getting his reinforcements up, while we were only crying up that the Russian empire was made of carton. His *ruse de guerre* succeeded, and we have our work to do now, with a small, decimated army, and the winter at hand. I hope your nephew has escaped, although one can hardly hope that many of them will return.

I see by the papers, which sometimes fall in my hands, that Lord Paulet, whose chambers I went after in the Albany, has been scalped. I recollect when the Coldstreams marched, you, with something like regret, said—" If I had remained in the regiment I should now have commanded them instead of (I think) Bentinck." Permit me to congratulate you upon being even as you are, and a civilian, rather than in the Crimea.

The emperor has sent me word that I am to make a daily report of my progress, as he thinks of coming down. He has not been at Compiègne, nor has he had a dinner party since the commencement of the siege; and many people here say that 'tis bad taste of Prince Albert hunting and amusing himself as though nothing was occurring, while the nation is spending its best blood for the support of the honour of England and the power of the crown. Admiral Dundas is often called " Madame Dundas," while they say of Admiral Lyons—" He is *un vrai* lion." If this dreadful hurricane which is now blowing does me no harm I shall soon get from this.

P.S.—The waiter on bringing up your letter to me said— " Here are five letters for you, sir : one from the ministre Anglaise d'Orée." Your crest and envelope quite astonished him.

Thursday Night.

P.S. 2.—I send this by the boat. I have just returned from holding an inquest on two barracks blown down last night. When the blowing down will finish, I know not ; and it is my almost fixed intention, if an aide-de-camp does not come to me from l'empereur, to go up to Paris and explain all about it, for I am truly tired of it all.

Hotel de Folkestone, Boulogne-sur-Mer,
Tuesday, November 28th 1854.

You say, and apparently to you, with some truth, that you are at a loss to conceive in what my knowledge of erection can consist. I confess to you I am astonished at the same myself; but by dint of perseverance I have arrived at such a knowledge, and in a short space of time, that I attend the council of engineers, *i.e.* the military council, every Saturday, and I submit my plans, give rough sketches on the spot, and have them adopted ; and so pleased are all the commanding officers to whom I am accredited, that they three weeks ago reported to the Minister of War, and the said minister, by command of the emperor, sent his aide-de-camp to me here to make some proposals highly advantageous, which I declined for reasons that few would believe. But I again repeat to you I am myself astonished at what I have been doing, and where I learned it I know not, and in making any proposals I always give them the liberty to laugh at them if they appear foolish, as I remind them I am not an engineer, either military or civil.

What I am doing here for the moment is superintending and giving orders direct from the emperor and for the emperor, who has given me a *carte blanche* credit to a certain limited amount *outre de cela*. I have been offered (a continuation of the emperor's wishes to serve me) a very excellent appointment, which I have accepted, under terms of limitation and reduction, to enable me to fulfil my duties *chez vous*. In other words, I have proposed to reserve to myself the right of living in England for a period of say five years on half pay, and thereby to be able to act as heretofore for you, as after the finish of this affair at Boulogne an occasional run to France is all that will be required.

I shall not get from here to Helfaut before next week, and shall certainly be a fortnight there, and then to please D. B., to whom I have this day written to tell him I am still here, and promised to join him before I return to England.

With respect to the Poles, I should have nothing to do with them, for if the kingdom of Poland was again re-established as of old, it would be as great a blot upon civilization as a Russian empire, and the Poles are only fit for demonstrations out of which good subscriptions arise. Where are the Poles in the Russian service?—what move have they made? If they would only make a diversion, it would be something; but no, they are as passive as the purest Russian serf. And again, supposing they wanted to be certain that their brethren in England (a most disorganized family, by-the-bye) were up, what possible means of letting them know? Nicholas is too wide-awake to let the news in. If they (the Poles) are willing to do anything, let them organize themselves into regiments and then apply to the allied governments for means of transport and other requisite aid: although I should be sorry to see even that take place, for my opinion of them is, that they would take Russian gold to betray us, or anybody else. I never had any opinion of these gentry.

If Austria still plays false, then, if L. N. wills it, Mazzini would be powerful, and do the business; and humbug as Kossuth is, he might, as a rallying name for the Hungarians, be of some use. But the Poles have lost their nationality, and are become hired assassins all over the world: there are a few good men among their generals, and that's all. When Poland did exist it was quite as bad a despotism as Russia—serfs and nobles were the population, and the nobles actually wiped their feet upon the serfs to prove their humbleness, *i.e.* degraded position. It was a good stalking-horse for poor Lord Dudley.* Once you take them up, and the bank of England would not supply the demands upon your purse, and when you ceased to give, they would begin to denounce their patriotism, and their view of patriots is money.

Tuesday Night (after the Post).

You say why does not L. N. send troops directly to the Crimea; he is doing so, but we cannot expect him to send a sufficient force to gain the day without some arrangement with England, which doubtless is the object of Lord Palmerston's mission. We must incur some risk, either a money risk or men risk, and the question is asked here, suppose England pays for keeping of the men, their transport and accoutrements (the latter when injured), how is the man himself to be paid for? Suppose, as in many cases in the French army, he is the only son of hard-working parents, and he falls as a hired man, what compensation do you make for the man? or, as they say, and very truly, is the man counted as nothing? the value being only what he consumes while living, either in food or material? There must be some contingent for the surviving family, or there will be difficulty in managing the matter.

* Lord Dudley Coutts Stuart.

When I see you I will tell you a conversation I had with the Hon. H. Fitzroy; he did not think I knew him, and if the sentiments he expressed to me are really the sentiments of the English Ministers I really think they differ strongly with those of the English people.

I could, I have no doubt, get L. N.'s views as well as anybody, but I know there exists a feeling that you desire knowledge merely for your own personal pleasure, having never said anything for him when he wanted friends, although he gave you ample opportunities; now he has ministries and governments ready to aid him: therefore I will not attempt to do anything there in that shape.

I have been on horseback to Ambleteuse, and have been strongly pressed to go there next Sunday to assist at the ceremony of opening the first barrack; the generals all invite me, and I should stop at one of their houses all night. I have refused, to get back to London as soon as I can, and, notwithstanding my letter of to-day, if it is possible to get home sooner than I named I will, but I cannot then visit D. B.

General Rolin has sent me word to-day since I wrote that the emperor is quite satisfied, in fact, very much pleased with my efforts, and he finishes by saying, as soon as your work is over, and you present yourself at Paris, " *vous serez très-bien reçu.*"

I could, if I deserted my post, never expect to get received again by L. N., who is certainly the greatest man in Europe, in my opinion.

Wednesday Morning.

I have written to General Dubreton at Helfaut, informing him that I hope to be with him on the 5th and not later than the 6th proximo, and I propose stopping with him one week, in which time I shall set all in train for completion; this will bring it to the 12th or 13th. I then propose to go to D. B. and stop a week, which will bring it to the 20th, and then try to return home on that day, or to present myself the day after. Now, what I want in this arrangement is this, and the part I most particularly want you to answer is, whether I shall go to D. B. or return home. I think, under any circumstances, I must go to St. Cloud, and I only propose the returning home subject to your taking the responsibility of D. B. being offended, or not.

The reason of the delay has been the blowing down before completion, caused by the large surface presented to the wind, and the power the wind had on what presented a breach, it being impossible to do as much in a day or days as would prevent the wind getting in. The ground plan will give you some idea of the surface presented to the winds, and with an elevation of twelve feet it caused a great deal of difficulty. If, please God, the wind that is blowing now does no harm I shall be quite able to carry out the plan I propose.

21, Rue Beaujon, Champs Elysées, Paris,
December 29th, 1854.

I arrived here last night and was most kindly received by the duke and countess. Ure has been stopping in Paris and had taken his leave before I arrived, with the promise that if he remained over the night in Paris he would come to the duke's box " *aux Italiens*," but as he did not come I conclude he left for England, and so I did not see him. Strange to say, I had not been here half an hour before the duke said, " As you are here, and the baron is coming, we will dine at home sometimes, and you can write to England for some pheasants." I then said that his wish had been anticipated by you, and that some would be here.

I have, therefore, by this same post sent to Fisher for some in your name. I was very nearly starting for England this evening for the emperor, but I have telegraphed instead.

The weather is fine, but Paris itself dull. The duke seems in tolerable good health, but certainly I think from what he says is brewing something, as he feels an inclination to lie in bed for days at a time.

The reader by this time must have come to a con-

clusion that the writer of these reports had changed his
vocation. His secretariat must have become a sinecure,
whilst between two illustrious potentates he oscil-
lated like an uneasy pendulum, or a waiter upon
Providence, unable to make up his mind as to the
superior attractions of a millionaire royal duke or an
all-powerful imperial majesty. Whether he is to become
a military Paxton or a commercial Walewski, is still
in the womb of time; whether as the presiding genius
of the Camp du Nord he is to cross the Rhine, and
become the Bismark of a "young Brunswick," is
behind the curtain of coming eventualities; all that
the reader can be informed is, that while the clever
employé was making himself master of the situation at
Beaujon, at the Elysée, at the camp, everywhere, a
process of ratiocination was passing through the mind
of his invalid employer, which resulted in the question
—"If no man can serve two masters, how is it possible
to serve three?" This led to the suggestion, that there
might be a fourth, nearer and dearer to his agent,
who would inevitably secure the first consideration.
How the result affected Mr. Duncombe's interests will
presently be shown; we can now only state that
during the Crimean war the *entente cordiale* was preserved in France; and notwithstanding the charges
brought forward by a certain historian, we believe
that the conflict was maintained by our illustrious
ally in a spirit of perfect good faith and loyalty.

CHAPTER VIII..

LIBERAL LEGISLATION.

The Albert Park—Letter of Lord Robert Grosvenor—Mr. Duncombe and Mr. Roebuck—Correspondence of Lord Brougham
and Mr. Duncombe—Unconditional pardon of Frost, Williams,
and Jones—Contested Election for Finsbury—Mr. Duncombe
at the head of the poll—Cost of a seat in Parliament—Education—Untaught talent—Thorogood imprisoned for non-payment
of Church-Rates — Mr. Duncombe effects his liberation —
Catholics and Dissenters—Letters of Mr. Chisholm Anstey—
Cardinal Wiseman and the establishment in England of a papal
hierarchy—Mr. Duncombe's moderation—His advocacy of the
Jews—The Jews' Bill—Report of a Select Committee of the
House of Commons—Another triumphant return—Reform—
Sunday trading—Letters of Lord Chelmsford.

THE member for Finsbury did not restrict himself to
the performance of his political duties ; out of Parliament he was as active in advancing the public welfare as in it. Any scheme of real utility was sure of
his support ; but in no instance did he afford it so
heartily as he did to the plan for creating a public
park at Islington for the benefit of the northern portion of the metropolis. A communication from one
of its most active supporters describes it in detail:—

Moor Park, December 26th, 1853.

My DEAR DUNCOMBE,—As chairman of the public meetings held at Sadler's Wells theatre for the purpose of
promoting the formation of a park in the northern portion

of the metropolis, and having been since the organ of communication between the committee appointed at those meetings to carry out the resolutions then passed and the Government, I take the liberty of requesting your opinion on the following subject :—

The Government have sanctioned the introduction of a Bill into Parliament, and for the above purpose to propose an advance out of the public revenue, provided the larger portion of the expenses be borne by a rate. I may mention that to make a park worthy of the name, in the locality described, will require a series of advances altogether not exceeding 300,000*l.*, of which the half will be recovered in the course of a few years, so that the absolute cost may be estimated at 150,000*l.*

The inquiries going on at the present moment into the affairs and actions of the Corporation of the City of London will probably lead to a consideration of the subject of municipal government for the whole of the metropolis, including the method whereby future improvements in the capital of the empire shall be carried on ; and were it not for the peculiar position of the question relative to Albert Park, it would obviously be better to postpone the consideration of it until the general question shall be settled. But as every day's delay is most injurious, on account of the rapid absorption of every green spot for building purposes, so that for nearly four miles in a direct line north of the River Thames the whole is one dense mass of crowded tenements, and as great injury is accruing to a portion of the property proposed to be taken, from having been in schedule for two years, I shall feel obliged to you if you will say whether you think that the rate ought to be levied only upon the district likely to derive immediate benefit from the park, or upon the whole of the metropolis?

My opinion is that it will be most unfair, after all the other quarters of London have been improved and beautified with parks and commodious streets at the public expense, to suddenly limit the area of taxation to the immediate vicinity of any proposed improvement.

It would, moreover, be an entirely novel method of treating urban and suburban improvements of this nature, and my belief is that the inhabitants of London will consider that though their city must always be a matter of imperial concern, still that the cost of metropolitan improvements ought to be defrayed by metropolitan funds, raised not by parish rates but by a rate levied over the entire area of the capital. As this question is still unsettled, and as, for the preparation of the Bill required in the case of Albert Park, it should be arranged at as early a period as possible, may I request you will send me a reply at your earliest convenience, addressed to the Committee Room, Canonbury Tavern, Islington.

I remain, yours very faithfully,   R. GROSVENOR.

The member for Finsbury had a happy way of exposing jobbery that invariably carried the House with him. In July, 1856, during a debate on going into committee on the General Board of Health Bill, he made an amusing allusion to the comprehensive experiments at reform of Mr. Roebuck. He said— "He is going to set us all to rights, not only in Leadenhall-street, but in New Palace-yard, at Somerset House, at the Admiralty, at the Horse Guards, and at Downing-street. But if the honourable and learned gentleman would come to this neighbourhood he would find in a corner of a street a little hole, called the Board of Health (laughter), and where he would find comfortably ensconced a near relation of the Prime Minister, and the relative of another Cabinet Minister—all very snug berths for ministerial patronage to bestow." (Hear, hear.)

Mr. Duncombe then referred to the cost of the Board, and with such effect, that the Bill was lost on going to a division. That Bill had caused another deputation, of which Mr. Duncombe formed one. This consisted of all the metropolitan members except four, who waited on the Chief Commissioner of Public Works, at his office in Whitehall, on the 21st of April, 1856, to confer with him on the provisions of the Act. A long and animated discussion ensued respecting the proposed alterations affecting church-wardens and overseers, in which the member for Finsbury played a prominent part.

In the following month he took advantage of the return of peace to move again for a free pardon for political offenders. The Government had anticipated his appeal, and Lord Palmerston announced that pardon would be extended to all except those who had broken their parole, and fled to a foreign country. By an entry in the Diary, 13th July, 1856, we learn—"Frost called with Moore, having returned last night from transportation, to thank me."

In the course of Mr. Duncombe's speech suggesting an amnesty for political offenders, he had indulged in an eloquent reference to the philanthropic labours in the same direction of an old and distinguished political friend. He described the urgent interposition of Lord Brougham to induce Lord Melbourne to com-mute the punishment of death for that of banishment in the case of the Newport Reformers—"To no act of his life," he said, "whether as a vindication of the laws, or as an effort of humanity, would that dis-tinguished man look back with more cordial satis-faction."

This speech was read the next morning by the veteran statesman, and elicited a warm acknowledg-ment. We insert both the letter and reply:—

4, Grafton-street, 10th May, 1856.

DEAR T. D.—I am much obliged to you for making me remember (and for the kind way in which you did it) a good work, or part of a good work, which I had entirely forgotten. I now recollect all about it, and that it was merely taking my share in an act of strict justice. It was in like manner only as an act of justice that I once was of some help to you, of which you never could have the least notion, and which also I had entirely forgotten till this morning.

It is the chance of now and then having such opportunities of doing some little good that makes the burthen of long life less hard to bear.

Yours sincerely,   BROUGHAM.

57, Cambridge-terrace, May 13th, 1856.

MY DEAR LORD BROUGHAM,—Your letter having been directed to St. James's Street has only just reached me, which I hope will account for my apparent neglect in not thanking you sooner for so kindly noticing my feeble attempt in the House of Commons to do you that justice to which your noble and generous conduct in saving the lives of those misguided men in 1840 so pre-eminently entitled you. It grieves me, however, to hear you talking of the hardship of bearing the burthen of a long life, distinguished, as all must admit yours to have been, by so many acts of true philanthropy; but I trust that there are yet many more years of health and enjoyment in reserve for you before the country will have to lament your loss.

Permit me to remain, with best wishes,

Yours very faithfully,   T. S. D.

Mr. Duncombe took great interest in the proposed formation of Finsbury Park, and was assiduous in his attention to divisions, presenting petitions, asking questions. Government were beaten on Cobden's resolution censuring their proceedings in China, on the 3rd of

March ; and on the 5th the member for Finsbury spoke strongly in favour of Lord Palmerston. While attending a public meeting after the dissolution of Parliament, his watch was stolen. This loss was soon repaired. He had now to prepare for one of those scenes of excitement which seemed to become more frequent as he became less able to bear them. He could only take part in a contested election to a limited extent, and it seemed necessary that he should exert himself more than ever, party spirit running very high in reference to the defeat of Lord Palmerston by the Manchester section of the reformers, in conjunction with the Tories, against whom there daily manifested itself a strong feeling of indignation.

The Government having been defeated, an appeal to the country was as usual resorted to. In the general election that occurred in the spring of 1857, Finsbury was distinguished for the severity of the contest. Alderman Challis retired, in his parting address to the electors paying a cordial tribute of commendation to Mr. Duncombe. He wrote :—

"I take this opportunity of tendering my thanks to my honourable colleague for the kind assistance and co-operation I have at all times received from him ; and, were not his services and abilities so well known in this borough, I would venture to add my humble testimony to the energy, ability, and honour with which he discharges his duties. Ever fearless in the support of his honest opinions, thoroughly qualified by long experience, he well sustains in the Legislature the office of your representative in support of the principles of political freedom, and the practice of political honesty."

On this occasion there were four candidates in the field. There was a Major Reid, Mr. Serjeant Parry, and a Mr. Cox, a solicitor and common councilman. The latter had been canvassing nine months with an enormous staff and an unlimited expenditure. Mr. Duncombe had little more to rely upon than the services of his secretary, and a messenger employed a few days before the polling commenced, with his personal attendance at three public meetings. Nevertheless, he was placed at the head of the poll, and returned by an overwhelming majority, the numbers being :— Duncombe, 6922; Cox, 4110; Parry, 3954; Reid, 2378. The three last had professed similar opinions, and in their addresses had rivalled each other in the liberality of their promises; but it soon became manifest that their long-tried representative possessed the confidence of the constituency. Cox was accused of wholesale bribery, and the learned serjeant's cause damaged with some of the electors by a charge of having signed a petition to open the Crystal Palace and British Museum on Sundays, which he denied.

Lord Palmerston had issued an address to the electors of Tiverton, defending the policy in China that had produced the hostile vote in the House of Commons; and at a banquet given at the Mansion House he went more at length into his defence, sharply attacked the Opposition, and proclaimed the advantages the Government had gained by the result of the general election. All the leaders were then suitors for public confidence, abusing their opponents and lauding themselves. In one instance—Lord Malmesbury—a spirited defence was published in the newspapers; in that of Mr. Serjeant Parry, a political dinner was given by his friends, when he improved the occasion to the same effect. Mr. Bright was rejected from Manchester; and Cobden, Gibson, Fox, and Miall had also been unsuccessful in securing their return. The Finsbury election was a signal triumph to Mr. Duncombe; he had not been at the head of the poll since 1835.

The election cost him 412*l.*; Cox, 2308*l.*; and Parry, 790*l.* Major Reid's accounts were not published. The metropolitan constituencies were expensive luxuries, though much improved from former times, when Westminster has been known to cost 20,000*l.* A candidate may now hope to get returned for any sum between 2000*l.* and 8000*l.* Lord Dudley Stuart paid 7000*l.* for Marylebone in 1847; Lord Ebrington, his successor, 5000*l.*, and Mr. Bell, 3000*l.* Southwark election cost Locke 3880*l.*; Napier, 1219*l.*; and Pellatt, 684*l.* Lambeth cost Roupell 5339*l.*; Williams, 1706*l.*; and Wilkinson, 2688*l.* The Tower Hamlets: Ayrton, 1337*l.*; Butler, 1133*l.*; and Clay, 806*l.* While the City of London cost Lord John Russell 3222*l.*; Baron Rothschild, 1313*l.*; Duke, 1608*l.*; and Crawford, 999*l.* Added to this expenditure must be subscriptions to local charities, &c., which, in Middlesex, cost Mr. Byng 2000*l.* a year. In the boroughs the outlay varies from 300*l.* to 1000*l.*

For the diffusion of education there was no more earnest advocate than the member for Finsbury, but no one was better acquainted than himself with the evils of imperfect teaching on the working man, or had a more decided opinion of the injudicious and indiscriminate cramming of the poorer classes of children.

He had constantly before him fussy knots of ill-informed operatives, who had been rendered dissatisfied with their own social position, and were unfit for any other. His own constituency afforded abundant examples of the evil arising from the cobbler not sticking to his last. Such men would insist on being political censors, and were constantly calling him to account. He was quite as frequently obliged to administer a snubbing to them; and it was not his fault if it failed in producing a wholesome effect. He preferred education for the masses such as should render the boys good workmen, and, in time, equally good masters. There are some men belonging to the humbler classes who appear to have done much better without education than those who have been most carefully crammed with knowledge useless in their social position. Here is a portrait of one of them from a trustworthy source :—

" 'My guide, philosopher, and friend' was Abraham Plastow, the gamekeeper, a man for whom I have ever felt, and still feel, very great affection. He was a singular character. In the first place, this tutor of mine *could neither read nor write*, but his memory was stored with various rustic knowledge. He had more of natural good sense and what is called mother-wit than almost any person I have met with since; a knack which he had of putting everything into new and singular lights made him, and still makes him, a most entertaining and even *intellectual* companion. He was the most undaunted of men. I remember my powerful admiration of his exploits on horseback. For a time he hunted my uncle's hounds, and his fearlessness was proverbial. But what made him particularly valuable were his *principles of integrity and honour.*"*

Here are the elements of a hero and a Christian, here the model of a good citizen and a good man. If there is any system of government education that can produce better results, it ought to be made public, and the same plan adopted all over the world. Mr. Duncombe was always ready to extend educational advantages of the first class to all likely to profit by them; but his long experience assured him that a very small per-centage of those born to labour for their bread had either opportunity, talent, or inclination to secure them. The Abraham Plastows, on the contrary, are by no means so very rare.

He had endeavoured to obtain the liberation of a Nonconformist, who had been imprisoned in Chelmsford gaol for not paying his church-rates. There was a public meeting in Edinburgh, and the chairman forwarded the thanks of that assembly to him for having brought the poor man's case before the attention of the House of Commons. He was not the man to let such a case be cushioned, and took it up with such vigour that the Government caused the prisoner to be liberated without enforcing the obnoxious rate.

As early in his career as March, 1829, Mr. Duncombe, as an advocate for religious freedom, presented a petition to the House of Commons, signed by 32,000 inhabitants of Sheffield and the neighbourhood, in support of Catholic Emancipation. In this measure he took the deepest interest, speaking on various occasions with remarkable force, and by his disinter-

* " Memoirs of Sir Thomas Fowell Buxton, Bart.," p. 5.

ested labours doing more real service in the way of preparing the public mind for the removal of religious disabilities than any of the Irish members effected by their most imposing displays of oratory. He does not appear to have had any connexion with the Catholics; yet he continued their advocate as long as there was any question before the House that in the slightest degree affected their interests.

Though Mr. Duncombe was the son of a bishop's daughter, and had several of his nearest relations clergymen, he did not allow this connexion with the Church of England to influence his views of toleration and religious liberty. Of this he gave a striking proof during the session of 1840, by bringing forward in the House of Commons a motion for relieving Dissenters from their liabilities to the payment of church-rates. This was a grievance of which all persons of that communion complained. Jews, Catholics, Methodists, Quakers, and other sectarians could not reconcile themselves to being taxed for maintaining an establishment they never used, and did not want. In Finsbury the religious opinions of the electors varied much; but there was a large portion who did not belong to the Church of England, and were disposed to save the money they were obliged to contribute to its perpetuation. There was pressure from this quarter on the popular member; and finding himself supported by Dr. Lushington and Mr. Hawes, two of the most influential of the metropolitan members, from his place in the House he moved for leave to bring in a Bill to relieve from the payment of church-rates that portion of her Majesty's subjects who conscientiously dissent from the rites or doctrines of the Church of England. Leave, however, was refused, on a division there being only 63 for the motion, and 117 against it. The majority made up of Whigs and Tories.

This defeat did not do him any harm. The supporters of the church treated the attack indulgently, proving that they were not in the slightest degree alarmed by it; while the friends of religious freedom were delighted at its boldness, and enthusiastically applauded the daring reformer by whom it had been made.

As a friend to freedom of thought the member for Finsbury was regarded by the English Catholics as an excellent medium for bringing before the legislature what they considered to be their grievances. They were willing to admit the benefits they had derived from the great emancipation measure, but chose to regard it only as an instalment of their rights. They still laboured under some disabilities; and notwithstanding that, in this respect, they were infinitely better off than were Protestants in Catholic countries, and enjoyed indulgences they had never conceded to Protestants when the Catholic religion was in the ascendancy in this country, they were determined to agitate for equal privileges. The Roman Catholics of the metropolis, therefore, drew up a petition for the repeal of the Penal Code, and it must be acknowledged that they took very high ground, for they commenced with the extraordinary statement, that "the religion of your petitioners was until *a very modern period*, the religion of the whole of this realm." Three centuries had elapsed since the establishment of the Reformation; and many years previously thousands of earnest Christians had renounced the Church of Rome, through the arguments of Wicklyffe and his followers. The document equally ignores the existence of the Jews, whose religion in its claims to antiquity really made the Roman in its turn a very modern institution.

When the petitioners began to mention their grievances it appeared that these were in the shape of certain oaths, which were required from them as safeguards, as they professed allegiance to the Pope in the first place. Under the statute of Præmunire they were still liable to penalties for assisting in the introduction or circulation of papal documents. This law they forgot to state was passed by a Roman Catholic sovereign and a Roman Catholic senate, as a security against intolerable exactions and oppressions of the court of Rome. Then there was a grievance in reference to restraints upon religious orders, which they regarded as cruel to the Jesuits, Benedictines, Dominicans, and Franciscans, and "a foul stigma and reproach to their religion." There was also a complaint of interference in Roman Catholic marriages.

It will be seen from the accompanying note what Mr. Duncombe was expected to do :—

1, Plowden-buildings, Temple,
June 29th, 1842.

Mr. Anstey presents his respects to Mr. Duncombe, M.P., and begs to know whether that gentleman has any objection to undertake to present and support in the House of Commons a petition signed by 138 Catholics of the metropolis, praying for the total repeal of the remaining penal laws. Mr. Anstey encloses a copy of the petition as printed in the *True Tablet* of the 11th instant. It is desired that the member presenting the petition should manage to elicit a debate upon the points there set forth; a motion of some kind will therefore be necessary. The low estimation in which the English Catholic members are held in their own body prevents Mr. Anstey, who is entrusted with the conduct of the matter, from troubling either of them with it. Not being personally known to Mr. Duncombe (although as a committee-member of the Catholic Registration Society he assisted in canvassing Catholic votes for him last year), he begs to inform Mr. D. that he is a friend of the Reverend Mr. Macartney of Manchester,* whose case was so admirably managed lately by Mr. Duncombe in the House.

The petition was presented, and Mr. Duncombe's services thus acknowledged :—

> Erectheum Club, Wednesday Morning.
>
> Sir,—On the part of those whose petition you presented last night I beg to offer you my most sincere thanks. I have just read the reports of the presentation in the various newspapers; the *Morning Herald* is the only one that has reported it correctly. Will you have the kindness to give notice to-night (if you have not already done so), and ask Sir James Graham to-morrow whether it is his intention to act upon the report of the Criminal Law Commissioners, or to repeal the remaining disabilities of Catholics? It is of some importance that this should be done by to-morrow at the latest, in order that the *True Tablet* may make its comments upon Sir James's reply upon Saturday morning.
>
> I have the honour to be, Sir, your obedient servant,
> T. CHISHOLM ANSTEY.

In the year 1851 the entire Protestantism of the British empire exhibited the most frantic excitement in consequence of the Pope of Rome having published a letter apostolical, announcing in language of absolute

* A convert to Popery who complained of his wife having been immured in a convent.

authority the creation of a Catholic hierarchy in England, entirely ignoring the Established Church and its prelates. Since the Reformation the operation of the Papacy in this country had been generally (especially during the last century) quiet and unobtrusive. The community here in connexion with it had been governed in the most unassuming manner by vicars apostolic; but partly through the influence of distinguished English converts from the Church of England, and partly in consequence of representations of one or two of the dignitaries of the Roman Church officiating in England, the supreme Pontiff caused an entirely new and comprehensive arrangement to be carried out, in which the kingdom was divided into dioceses, each governed by a bishop, assuming a title from the episcopate, and all were to be governed by an archbishop.

This announcement took the Protestant community by surprise; although the important change had been contemplated by the court of Rome two or three years before, and they were not reconciled to it by the contemporary publication of a document quite as startling to Protestant readers, in still more extravagant phraseology, declaring the establishment of a Roman Catholic hierarchy under the direction of the writer, who signed himself "Archbishop of Westminster, Cardinal Priest of St. Pudentia, and Administrator Apostolic of the Diocese of Southwark."

It is impossible to exaggerate the impression created throughout the length and breadth of the land, not only by the purpose, but by the tone of these documents; and Lord John Russell increased the excitement tenfold by publishing an indignation letter to the Bishop of Durham, denouncing the innovation in the strongest terms, and threatening parliamentary interference. The press generally echoed his sentiments; and the two branches of the Legislature were called upon to save the country from popery.

Catholics explained that the papal documents were intended only for themselves; that the supreme Pontiff's intentions were purely spiritual; and protested against any tampering with the provisions of the Catholic Emancipation Act. There were zealots on both sides, who did their best to inflame the public excitement; there were also moderate men, who strove earnestly to lessen the wide-spread irritation.

Among the latter conspicuously stood the member for Finsbury. He had been instrumental in carrying the long disputed measure for relief, and was averse to any legislation in a contrary spirit. In the face of the popular agitation against the alleged encroachments of popery he raised his voice for toleration. During the debates in the House of Commons he spoke forcibly in deprecation of the spirit of reprisal that was then influencing a large body of his countrymen. In so doing, however, he laid himself open to the animadversions of the ultra-Protestant portion of the press, who could not appreciate what they considered to be a Protestant champion of popery. He was obliged to declare publicly his opposition to the spirit of the Papacy, and avow that, as a consistent advocate of religious liberty, he was bound to raise his voice against an arbitrary control of the privileges enjoyed by any portion of her Majesty's subjects. The moderation and good sense that influenced his interposition in favour of the Catholics may be gathered from the following motion, which we print from the original draft :—

Mr. T. Duncombe.—On motion for Mr. Speaker leaving the Chair to go into Committee on the Ecclesiastical Titles Bill,

To move,—" That whilst this House regrets that in the documents relating to the recent appointment of a Roman Catholic hierarchy in this country greater consideration was not shown towards the Protestant feelings of the people, yet this House, relying upon the solemn assurances that have been given, that neither slight nor insult was thereby intended to the sovereign or to the nation, will abstain from further legislative proceedings, unless it shall hereafter be found that those appointments are exercised in a manner inconsistent with the civil rights or the religious freedom of any portion of her Majesty's subjects."

The action of many of the Dissenters in this agitation was equally in opposition to the Church of England; and sectarian animosity declared itself by a cordial support of the papal and cardinalian manifestoes, mingled with virulent abuse of the State establishment. Among the Finsbury constituency there was a large element of dissent, and these electors got up public meetings, in which the conduct of their member was warmly commended by resolutions published in the newspapers. The chairman having communicated the result to Mr. Duncombe, the latter, in a letter dated 6th June, 1851, replied:—

I rejoice to learn that my opposition to the Ecclesiastical Titles Bill meets with such general approbation, for although Popery possesses no charms in my eyes, yet I consider that I should have been a traitor to those sacred principles of civil and religious freedom that I have ever advocated, as well as unworthy of the enlightened constituency I have the honour to represent, had I, by any vote of mine, basely succumbed to that bigot cry so industriously raised last winter throughout the land, and thereby deprived my Roman Catholic fellow-subjects, whether in England or in Ireland, of any portion of those religious rights and privileges conferred upon them by the Emancipation Act of 1829.

That these were Mr. Duncombe's real sentiments is evident from the fact that among his voluminous papers there is not a single communication from a Catholic priest or layman in favour of the manifestation of the Pope's authority in England which caused the Parliamentary measure he mentions. Had he permitted any consideration to interfere with his sense of duty, he would have taken the side of the Church of England, of which, as we have just stated, some of his nearest relatives were ministers.

He strove hard to allay the alarm that had been excited among the members of that establishment, and recommended their waiting and seeing if any mischief arose from the proceeding complained of, before they demanded a remedy. As every one knows, his anticipations were realized: the new Catholic bishops in no way interfered with the old Protestant bishops, and the greater novelty, the cardinal archbishop, found " ample room and verge enough" for the display of his dignity without incommoding either of the respective primates of the Established Church—while the much-abused Pio Nono, instead of upsetting both Church and State " in that famous realm of England" referred to in his bull, met with considerable difficulty in maintaining his own position in Rome.

The only person who really suffered during the controversy was Henry VIII., whom Dissenters and Catholics unanimously voted "a ruffian"; but as Mr. Froude has so thoroughly defended that zealous defender of the Roman Catholic faith, and still more zealous supporter of the Reformation, this practical application of the pleader's advice—"Abuse the plaintiff's solicitor!" cannot be said to have done the Protestant cause any harm.

As for Cardinal Wiseman—whose red hat at one time was regarded as not less revolutionary than the *bonnet rouge*—he turned out to be as harmless a personage as ever lectured at a mechanics' institute or presided at a teetotallers' demonstration: in truth, the obnoxious "prince of the church" lived to become the most be-photographed celebrity of the nineteenth century, and died absolutely more regretted by the antagonistic church than by his own.

Soon after Mr. Duncombe's return for Finsbury, he wrote, April 12th, 1835, to a gentleman of great influence (Baron de Goldsmid) offering to bring again under the consideration of Parliament the abrogation of Jewish disabilities. The Baron, then Mr. Isaac L. Goldsmid, replied that Dr. Lushington having offered his advocacy if they would place Sir Robert R. Grant's bill on the subject in his hands, his coreligionists had acceded to the proposal. The project slept in his mind for more than a quarter of a century, during which time he saw bigotry and intolerance triumph over every effort to obtain for the Jews the rights enjoyed by their Christian fellow subjects. There was no systematized agitation in their favour like that which rendered triumphant the claims of the Roman

Catholics and the Anti-Corn-Law League. They had to rely on their own fitness for the boon they asked for, and the strong sense of justice among the people of England. They did not rely in vain.

The proceedings of Lord John Russell since he had been returned for the City of London, with respect to the question of admitting Jews into Parliament, had excited a good deal of remark. There had been much said by him, it was alleged, and nothing done. Mr. Duncombe determined that the reproach should not fall upon other friends of religious liberty in the House, and put the affair in a right train for decisive action. He was probably stimulated by a leader in the *Times* of March 18th, 1858, from which we quote the following sentences :—

Mr. Duncombe may be rather too pressing and too ready for an appeal to the *ultima ratio* of a Representative House, but still it may come to that. Lord John Russell is losing ground and incurring a certain degree of ridicule by always appearing as the friend of the Jews, without being able to do anything for them. Thus he is always holding the wisp of hay before the poor jaded beast without ever giving it a mouthful. Is he in earnest? There are those who doubt it. There are certain costs and other disagreeables a man will submit to for the sake of being in Parliament, and Lord John Russell may carry a perpetual brief for Baron Rothschild as the price of his seat. The arrangement has gone on a long time, and the worthy Baron has already lost a good many years of his promised Parliamentary career. He may come to his estate at last, but meanwhile he has been deprived of the enjoyment of it for a most unreasonable period, and a short future does not always make up for a long past. So Lord John Russell is bound to do something effectual. He has only to put into exercise all the power he has in the matter, and all the influence he possesses with the Liberal party, and he can hardly fail of success. We hope to see the time when nothing but the natural preference of Christians for Christians will stand in the way of a Jew M.P. or a Jew Peer.

The member for Finsbury had been the earnest advocate of the Dissenters as well as of the Roman Catholics; now to show how perfect was his toleration, he took up the subject of the "disabilities of the Jews." Having acquired the necessary information, and communicated with the leading professors of that faith in England, in the sessions of 1857 and 1858 a bill for the removal of oaths was found necessary by the election of Baron Rothschild for the City of London. On its going to the Lords certain amendments were proposed to which the Commons would not agree, and the latter appointed a committee (Lord John Russell as chairman), which included Baron Rothschild, to draw out their reasons for disagreeing. Mr. Duncombe proposed this, as the penalties for disqualified persons voting in the House could not apply to their voting on committees. His motion was carried by 251 to 196. The bill, after much debate, was passed by both Houses. On the 26th Baron Rothschild was sworn upon the Old Testament, and took his seat. On the 3rd of March, 1859, he attempted to bring in a bill to amend the Act entitled— "An Act to provide for the relief of her Majesty's subjects professing the Jewish religion." An amendment was afterwards proposed that—"A select committee be appointed to consider and report to the House on the best mode of carrying into effect the provisions of the Act 21 and 22 Victoria, to provide for the relief of her Majesty's subjects professing the

Jewish religion." The select committee was granted,
Mr. Duncombe being the first on the list. It in-
cluded Lords John Russell, John Manners, and
Hotham; Sirs Richard Bethell, George Grey, James
Graham; Colonel Wilson Patten, the Solicitor-
General, and Messrs. Walpole, Byng, Henley, New-
degate, Dillwyn, and Adams. They had power to
send for persons, papers, and records.

The committee continued to sit from March 15th,
1859, to April 1st, when a draft report was prepared
by the chairman, the Right Hon. S. H. Walpole.
The only evidence taken was that of Mr. Erskine,
then clerk-assistant of the House, Mr. Duncombe
being present at each of his two examinations and
assisting in eliciting evidence.

A report from the select committee on the Jews'
Bill was printed on the 11th of April. In it is
stated that Baron Lionel Nathan de Rothschild presented himself at the table of the House at the previous session, the oath was tendered to him in the
usual manner, but declining to take it on conscientious scruples, he was ordered to withdraw, when a
resolution was passed, that as a person of the Jewish
religion entertaining conscientious objections to the
declaration on "the true faith of a Christian," such
words should be omitted, and he be permitted to take
his seat. He took the oath in that form, and subsequently sat and voted as a member of the House. A
day or two afterwards Baron Meyer Amschel de
Rothschild and Alderman David Salomons took such
oath and their seats.

The popular member for Finsbury was now more
than ever called upon to take the chair at public din-

ners and meetings, and to originate or support measures of public utility; among others, he moved
that the National Gallery should be thrown open on
Saturday for the convenience of those who enjoy a
half-holiday on that day, and succeeded.

His colleague, Mr. Cox, was neither popular in nor
out of the House, and therefore retained his senatorial
honours only a very short time. In the general election
this year, he was at the bottom of the poll, Mr. Duncombe beating him by a majority of nearly two
to one, having polled the extraordinary number of
8538 votes; Sir S. M. Peto, 8174.

Mr. Duncombe's ardour for reform was not confined
to voting when measures of the kind were brought
forward. He had no confidence in promises, and had
grown tired of professions, by which the country was
put off session after session. He never consented to
the cry of the Whigs, by which they sought to make
theirs a final measure—" the Bill, the whole Bill,
and—*nothing but the Bill.*" He was aware that a good
deal more was required to satisfy the requirements of
the occasion, but consented to take the full amount
by instalments, of which the Bill of 1832 was considered the first. "Finality John" laboured in vain
to persuade him that the Reform Bill was the universal panacea for electioneering ills, "the great last
cause, best understood" of legislative perfection; nor
would he accept as sufficient the attempts in the same
direction of either Whig or Tory ministers.

A Parliamentary Reform Committee was established
in London, consisting of Messrs. Clay, Fox, Miall,
Roebuck, Pease, Major-General Thompson, William
Williams, and other zealous reformers, with Mr. Morley

as treasurer. Mr. Duncombe was invited to join them in an attempt to ascertain the feeling of the country on the subject, or to state his opinions. A circular, bearing the signature of Mr. Roebuck, was issued by them in June, 1857, but the member for Finsbury did not seem desirous of co-operating with them. Indeed in December he wrote declining to sign their address, being of opinion that "any step of that description is premature at the present moment." In the course of a few months he had so far modified his first impressions as to address the honorary secretary in the following terms :—

March 10th, 1858.

Sir,—I have the honour to acknowledge the receipt of your letter of the 8th instant, and in reply beg to observe that since my last communication it must be obvious, I think, to every reformer, that an unfavourable change has taken place in the country's prospects of Parliamentary reform.

When I last wrote to you I considered we were on the eve of the Government redeeming its pledge to lay before Parliament a plan for the amendment of our representative system, and that to condemn or distrust its provisions before the country could judge of them was unfair, and calculated to discourage and to hamper any administration who had pledged itself to so difficult a task. I therefore declined appending my signature to the address, not from any dissent to the principles as far as they went, but solely on the ground that, in my opinion, the step was premature. A new Government has suddenly been called into power, composed of men who give no pledge upon the subject of reform, beyond, to quote the prime minister's own words, " That he should feel it his duty, in conjunction with his colleagues, to look into this important question, but he would not pledge himself or them to introduce either now or at any future time a Bill upon the subject." Now this declaration following upon the words that, " as far as he was concerned, he was content with things as they were, as, in his opinion, the present representative system had resulted in a House of Commons fairly and fully represent- ing the feelings of numbers as well as of the property and intelligence of the country," I consider, since the days of the celebrated speech of the Duke of Wellington against all reform, anything less cheering to ardent reformers has never appeared ; and if nothing should eventually be proposed by the Government, reformers ought not and cannot blame Lord Derby or his colleagues.

If I might, therefore, take the liberty of suggesting any- thing, it would be that the reform committee should issue a fresh address, based on the same principles as their last, but adapted to altered circumstances. I presume those who signed the former would not object to their signatures being transferred to the new, while a vast increase of fresh names would proclaim the people's disappointment and the nation's wants. And if I might be permitted at the same time to propose an amendment to the original address, it would be to add to its requirements a quarterly, or, at the farthest, a half-yearly revision of the electoral lists, founded upon a less vexatious and less expensive plan than the present.

Should my humble suggestions meet with the approba- tion of the committee, I hope that I need not add that I shall be proud and esteem it an honour to co-operate with those gentlemen who have so ably paved the way to secure the ultimate success of real Parliamentary reform.

I have the honour to be, Sir,

Your obedient servant, T. S. DUNCOMBE.

Of all forms of legislation, the most difficult to deal with was that which involved changes of custom and modifications of popular prejudices. The indignation created amongst Protestants by the papal division of England into Roman Catholic dioceses was not greater than the same feelings excited among the poorer

classes of both religions by the attempt to do away
with privileges they had been in the habit of enjoying
from time immemorial. Presbyterians and other rigid
nonconformists looked with horror on what they considered the desecration of the Sabbath by trading in
various London districts; and societies were formed, in
which a large proportion of the members were influential clergymen and prelates of the Church of
England, to put down the custom, while efforts were
made in both Houses of Parliament to render it
illegal. The Liberals were averse to any interference
with the privileges of the people; and if they found
it convenient to buy and sell on the Sunday, considered that no more harm would come of it than resulted in Catholic countries to the people by the same
practice. "The Sabbatarians" desired that the London
parishes should assume the aspect of a Scotch village
on "the Lord's day," and seemed determined to put
down not only trading but travelling. In their idea,
nothing was to be permitted but going to church or
chapel. The old Puritanic tyranny was to be enforced with extreme penalties; railroads were to be
stopped, omnibuses to cease to run; no dinners were
to be baked, no beards to be shaved; no houses
of refreshment to be open; the costermonger's barrow
and the itinerant basket were to be prohibited; and
another abortive effort made to force the lower classes
to become religious by Act of Parliament.

We append the views of the framer of one of these
attempts at moral reform :—

Eaton-square, May 7th, 1860.

My dear Duncombe,—Many thanks for your letter and
for the return, which you were quite right in supposing I

had never heard of. I agree with you that the Act of Charles II. has a most unequal operation in London and in country towns. I have been solicited by others to extend my Bill beyond the bounds of the Metropolitan Police District, but I am already upon a hornet's nest, and I do not know what would be the consequence of stepping out of the limits within which I propose at present to confine myself. If I make the law general, the statute of Charles ought to be repealed, and entirely new provisions substituted. This would be a large question, and one beset with difficulties, and I must be content at present to endeavour to apply a remedy to the place where the evil is most felt.

Yours very sincerely,   CHELMSFORD.

Eaton-square, June 13th, 1860.

MY DEAR DUNCOMBE,—Any one who undertakes a Bill relating to Sunday trading and expects to conciliate all parties, must be a very sanguine or a very silly man. The Scylla and Charybdis of such a measure are on the one hand the religious world, who object to the smallest relaxation of the law for observance of the Lord's day, and, on the other, those who are interested in Sunday traffic, and who consider any interference with their dealings an infringement of their liberties. Between these two extremes I have endeavoured to steer my course, but if I turned my head even a little to one side or to the other, I was sure to run upon a rock.

I have always been careful to guard against the notion that my Bill was intended either to enforce a more strict regard to the Lord's day, or that in any sense it was to be treated as a religious movement. What I kept steadily in view and always insisted upon was, that there were thousands and thousands of tradesmen in the metropolis who were anxious to have their day of rest, and that they were utterly deprived of the opportunity by a minority of their neighbours keeping open their shops, which compelled them in self-defence to do the same; and this, of course, entailed the same privation upon their servants and apprentices, who were not free agents. But when I proposed to close the shops entirely on Sundays I was met by the case of the poor man who, from the unfortunate practice which prevails (though gradually changing) of paying wages late on Saturday night, had no opportunity of making his little purchases for the Sunday before that day.

With respect to the sale of oranges, fruit, ginger beer, &c. before ten and after one, I cannot think that there ought to be any objection. To prohibit this would be to put a very invidious distinction between the poor and the rich man, and in that respect would be most objectionable. The same remark applies to pastrycooks. Eating-houses and cooks' shops are within the exemption in the 29 Car. II. As to periodicals, they have been my main difficulty; here the struggle has been between the bishops and the press. At first my Bill permitted the sale before ten o'clock only, and in this form it was approved by the Sunday Rest Association, of which the Bishops of London and Winchester are the presidents; the addition of " after one " was then made, and upon that clause, and that alone, the Right Reverend Bench rose in opposition. I do not care about keeping it, but it may be observed that it is the most harmless form of Sunday trading, so far as interfering with the day of rest is concerned, as a single person in the shop is all that is requisite to carry it on. I quite agree with you that it would have been better if I could have extended the Bill beyond the metropolitan district, but this would have entailed the necessity of repealing the statute of Charles II., which would have occasioned me many more difficulties than I can describe. I have applied my remedy where it was most wanted, and there are plenty of precedents for legislating only for this district. Of course there are objections to the Bill, as what measure was ever proposed without being exposed to formidable and even unanswerable ones? The question always is, whether the objections to the present state of things are not still greater. We must never lose the good by refusing everything which is not the best.

I am afraid I cannot look with favour upon your Jew Bill, nor excuse it according to the old story, because it is only a little one. Our arrangement was that each House should deal for itself with this matter, and I think it is a departure from the terms of our compromise to ask us to assist you with a Bill to regulate it for all time to come.

Ever yours sincerely, CHELMSFORD.

CHAPTER IX.

ITALY AND MAZZINI.

The Italian Liberals—Mazzini and "*La Giovine Italia*"—The
Sanfedists and the Roman Government—Revolutionary move-
ment—Mazzini and the Republic of Rome—Mazzini in London
—His letters to Mr. Duncombe—The Member for Finsbury a
Member of the Society of the "Friends of Italy"—Atrocities
committed by the Roman and Neapolitan Governments—
Petition to the House of Commons—Communications from
Mazzini—Kossuth on Cavour—Letters from Sir John Romilly
and Baron Poerio—Kossuth in Italy—Treaty of Villafranca—
Notes by Kossuth—Garibaldi's Conquest of Naples—Mr. Edwin
James at the Seat of War—Absence of Mazzini—Evacuation of
Venice by the Austrians—Republication by Mazzini of his
Writings—Italian unity yet imperfect.

MOORE, in his "Diary," gives a description of the
Italian liberals as they were in 1819, that is more
strongly characteristic of them many years later.
They were opposed to the English Government granting Catholic emancipation, because it would increase
the power of the Pope. They hated the papacy as
the worst possible form of absolutism; moreover,
they hated the Austrians — perhaps because the
despotism of one came more home to them than
that of the other. What religion they professed
was far from orthodox in character; it bore a strong
resemblance to Canova's ideal representation in St.
Peter's. "Religion with the spikes out of her head,"
writes a Catholic, "is a disagreeable personage."*

* "Diary and Letters," edited by Lord John Russell, iii. 48.

The first Napoleon is reported to have told Canova that he would make Rome the capital of all Italy. The idea has not yet been realized by Napoleon III. or by the Italian liberals under the inspiration of their celebrated chiefs.

Giuseppe Mazzini was one of the most active and enterprising of the Italian revolutionists of 1831. He was a native of Genoa, the son of a surgeon, and played so prominent a part in the movement that his countrymen readily adopted him as its director. He originated the idea of Young Italy, and in a periodical, in an association, and as a political cry, made such profitable use of it, that *La Giovine Italia* began to stir the pulses of the entire nation. He published a volume dedicated to Carlo Alberto, king of Piedmont, urging him to place himself at the head of a united effort of the Italians to drive the Austrians back to Germany, and made the most energetic appeals to his countrymen at home and abroad to induce them to combine in the same patriotic cause. He was an indefatigable conspirator, and caused his influence to be felt in every direction. The Governments at Rome, at Milan, at Florence, at Naples—indeed, everywhere in Italy—were kept in a constant state of alarm by a knowledge of his intrigues. The King of France, too, was as hostile as the Emperor of Austria. In short, he was regarded as a dangerous character.

The complaints of the inhabitants of the Pontifical States of the tyranny and bad faith of their ruler were recognised not only by the English Government, but by France and Prussia, even Austria uniting in a joint recommendation of reform to Pope Gregory XVI. Nothing, however, seemed more foreign to the nature of the Pope and his ministers than any concession. Instead of this they organized a band of miscreants, called Sanfedists, as pontifical volunteers, who were permitted to rob and murder the population of the Legations with perfect impunity. The historian Farini* denounces the infamous proceedings of the Roman court and its supporters. There cannot be a shadow of a doubt that the atrocities they committed justified the continued action of Mazzini, and the constant remonstrances of Mr. Duncombe.

Mazzini repeated his attempts to make old nations young, but with less and less success. " La Giovine Italia" did well as a suggestive title to a publication; "Young France" did less as a suggestion; "Young Switzerland" produced little effect; and "Young England" none at all. The propagandism was active enough in the mind of this republican—so active, that in every place in which he received shelter the first use he seems to have made of his security was to organize a plot for upsetting its political institutions; but it appears that wherever he went a counteracting influence rendered his labours nugatory. People began to suspect that the old lamp might be more trustworthy than a new one; and the cry of national renovation lost its charm. It was acknowledged that fine things could be said about republicanism, but that the working result might be drawn from the condition of the states of South America.

In 1848, the Prefect of the French police sent a communication to the Minister of the Interior announcing the arrival of Mazzini in Paris, and giving an account of his plans. Soon afterwards the movement recommenced in Rome; where Padre Gavazzi,

---

* Admirably translated by Mr. Gladstone, 3 vols. 1851.

then a Barnabite friar, gave as a sermon one of those stirring discourses that have since rendered him famous as an orator. The Jesuits were denounced, and changes in favour of laymen in the Roman cabinet conceded. At this crisis the expulsion of Louis Philippe in Paris brought a fresh access of agitation into Italy; and Pio Nono, Francis Joseph, Ferdinand, as well as the other established governments in Italy, were made to feel its effects. It caused Carlo Alberto to come forward as the leader of an Italian army; it also caused Mazzini, who was in France, to stimulate his friends, particularly in Rome, to activity in another direction.*

The revolutionary earthquake that shook French society to its foundation in the spring of 1848 was almost as severely felt in the neighbouring kingdoms and states. In Italy it caused the Austrian army to retire behind the Mincio. After the foreigners had been expelled from Milan, Venice proclaimed herself free, and Rome independent. Naples was not yet so fortunate, the Swiss mercenaries having made a good defence of the Bourbons for a time; and the patriots from the Abruzzi to the Alps began to talk of an united Italy as a grand republic, with its metropolis at Rome, and Pope, Kaiser, and Bourbon, utterly extinguished, annihilated, and forgotten.

Mr. Duncombe was not so sanguine as his friends of

---

* Farini's opinion of this reformer is not a very exalted one:— " Giuseppe Mazzini is a man of no common talent, remarkable for perseverance in his plans, for resolution under suffering, and for private virtues; but in these last crises of the Italian nation, he has confounded patriotism with self-love, or rather with selfish pride, and has chosen to risk seeing the temple of Italy burned down, because she would not dedicate to him its high altar."— Mr. Gladstone's translation, ii. 207.

the sweet South; and the triumphant return of Radetski, of the fugitive Pontiff, as well as the increased despotism of the King of Naples, confirmed his opinion that the hour of Italian freedom had not yet arrived.

Mazzini hastened to Rome after the flight of the Pope and the establishment of a republic. He was elected a member of the Constituent Assembly, which he addressed in a stirring speech on the 6th of March. He was received with acclamation, and his ascendancy became patent. His great idea was at once adopted, that Italy must be a single democratic state, having Rome for her capital. Unfortunately, as quickly as it was accepted as quickly was it laid aside. When Mr. Duncombe heard of his friend's pre-eminence in Rome, he heard of the practical extinction of Italian unity (for that time), caused by the battle of Novara, the abdication of the King of Piedmont, and the dispatch from republican France of an army under General Oudinot, to assist the Pope in returning to Rome.

The days of the Roman republic were then numbered, and Mazzini had once more to leave Italy, and recommence weaving his political meshes from a safe distance. After many vicissitudes as Carbonaro and revolutionary propagandist, in the spring of 1851 Mazzini was living at Brompton, but not inactively. His *Giovine Italia* had not been so successful as he had anticipated, and he had begun to entertain misgivings as to the possibility of establishing a democratic Italy. Still the idea was not to be abandoned. He now appealed to the good offices of his English friend to give the people of England a knowledge of recent events in Italy, and disabuse the public mind of unfavourable impressions created by adverse reports.

2, Sidney-place, Brompton, April 4th.

DEAR SIR,—The papers which ought to be published are the "Correspondence on the Affairs of Rome," from the month of November, 1848, to the July, 1849, when Rome fell under French invasion. The November ought to be chosen as the month in which the murder of Count Rossi took place, and things began to look gloomy. I feel sure— and that ought to be the ground for some remarks of yours —that all the accusations spread by Cochrane, the *Quarterly*, the *Times*, and all the reactionary men or papers here, concerning our "Reign of Terror," &c., would fall to the deep from which they sprung, through the reports of British agents.

I am sure that you have kept, for possible future occasion, the few notes I sent. But one designed thing was forgotten by me, concerning the Central Committee of European Democracy, about which there has been such a series of exaggerations. The acts of the committee have been *all* published in our organ; by other papers they have been quoted or translated, but always re-edited: the official appearance is in that French weekly paper. Now the paper is not published in London, but in France. The first number was seized on account of an article signed Ledru Rollin. The number was not containing a single act of the committee. The other numbers have, to the present moment, appeared in France; all our acts, proclamations, addresses being there—*not one has been seized*.

Should you wish for a number of our paper, I shall send it. You may have received before this a note from James Stansfeld.

With many thanks, I am, dear sir, now and ever yours,

Jos. MAZZINI.*

1. Mistaken point of view on the main question. There are no special duties for political exiles in England; no

* M. Mazzini's Letters are printed as they were written.

special concession to them from the Government; no special benefit imparted to them; in fact, no category of exiles—no exiles for England.   It is her beautiful privilege that her land is opened to every person chosing to come in; that no passport is asked, no declaration of quality called for, no special system established for anybody.   Foreigners are equalized to Englishmen ; they must abide by the laws, and benefit by them—nothing more, nothing less.   To talk about hospitality, and then to impose restraint on the utterance of opinions, and deny to foreigners rights of free-dom belonging to all men living in England, is equal to abolish the beautiful privilege which we are alluding to. The only exception could be when a Government grant, a special boon, is granted to exiles.   Even in that way it would be bad and un-English to be hospitable to the body and curtail the freedom of the soul.

2. We have committees—Central, Democratic, and Na-tional Italian Committees; but they have always been in existence, in France, in Switzerland—everywhere.   Polish committees have been existing, organizing, addressing, in Paris, at Poictiers and Versailles, during the whole reign of Louis Philippe, the central committee of the Democratic Polish Society, avowedly directing the national movement; the last Cracow insurrection, and the Posen movement, in which Nicolawski, a member of the society, was the re-cognised leader, has been during that time and after, until last year, residing in France; Nicolawski is still there. Has England applied to France on the subject?   The com-mittee are working publicly, printing and signing.   Do they violate English law ?—let them be tried.   More than that you cannot do.

3. There is now visibly a reactionary crusade against exiles and national causes going on on the continent. Exiles are persecuted, driven away from France, Switzer-land, &c., with a view to force them to America.   Is Eng-land to enlist in the absolutist crusade?   Exiles are at work for the national independence of Italy, Hungary, Ger-many: let them be blessed for that.   Do we not most cor-

dially sympathize with the efforts of those countries? And
it is not whilst French bayonets are keeping up the phantom,
whilst Austria possesses not only Lombardy but Tuscany,
the Duchies· of Parma and Modena, and the two-thirds
of the Roman Estates, whilst Austrian troops are overthrowing the Schleswig-Holstein movement, and garrisoning
Hamburg, where Austrian troops have not been seen since
the Thirty Years' War; whilst Russia has been trampling
on Hungary; whilst all powers are threatening, annoying
Switzerland and Piedmont, that we, who ought rather to protest
against such an infamous conduct, will stoop to foreign embassies, and persecute exiles for justice and truth. The
honour and European influence of England are much more
affected by brutal force overthrowing Italian and Hungarian
liberty, than by a few exiles testing the feelings of their
countrymen by raising a loan.

4. Klapka's proclamation was a mere, and not signed,
utterance of sympathy between Hungarians and Italians.

5. The National Italian Loan is raised not for the purpose of fitting up expeditions and initiating from without
the Italian movement, but for the purpose of supporting
and strengthening the national movement as soon as it
shall take place in Italy.

6. All the nonsense about a second Norman conquest
from the exiles, is worth the first of April.

7. I think you ought to avoid anything about the
dangers of discontenting foreigners coming for the Exhibition; it would be misconstructed into a threatening suggested by the exiles themselves.

For five or six days after the fall of Rome, everybody
knows that, to give the lie to all falsehoods about Republican reign of terror, &c., and against the entreaties of all
my friends, I walked alone day and night the streets of
Rome. I never did set my foot in Mr. Freeborne's house.

It is impossible to exaggerate the atrocities committed by Ferdinand and his ministers. A most intelligent eye-witness, Mr. Gladstone, in writing to

Lord Aberdeen in the year 1851, characterises them as transactions " more fit for hell than earth;" and in reference to the treatment of one victim, the Baron Poerio, stigmatizes it as emanating from " a system of government which is an outrage upon religion, upon civilization, upon humanity, and upon decency."

In his place in the House of Commons Mr. Hume, on the 11th of June, 1849, and the 9th of May, 1851, had brought the condition of Italy, particularly of the Roman States, before the Government; but beyond an expression of sympathy from some of the Liberal members for the wrongs the country was enduring, nothing was attempted. Mr. Duncombe also did his best to rouse the Foreign Secretary to active interposition; but no promise of interference was elicited. The vindictive Government of the Pope went on from bad to worse, committing the greatest atrocities. Some idea of the nature and extent of the misgovernment complained of, may be gathered from the following list of Romish eventualities compiled from the morning papers :—

ROMAN STATES.—1850.

New taxes on industry and commerce, November 7th.
Agreement of the Pope to the Treaty of 1849, respecting the free navigation of the river Po, November 11th.
Papal allocution against Sardinia, November 13th.

1851.

Alarm at Rome on hearing of the change of ministry in France, January 27th.
Note from the Papal See to the Austrian Minister of Affairs, demanding a supply of Austrian troops to defend Rome in case of another French Revolution, May 17th.

Increasing ill feeling between the French and Papal governments, June 23rd.

Return of the Pope to Rome from Castel Gandolfo, July 28th.

Concordat concluded between Rome and Tuscany, doing away with many of the restrictions on Church authority imposed in the last century by the Grand Duke Leopold, July 14th.

Extra taxes imposed by the Papal government, August 2nd.

" The invisible government in Italy," August 4th.

Trial of persons accused of being implicated in the burning of the Cardinals' carriages in 1849, September 3rd.

Attempted assassination of the Count Dandini—the trials respecting the Cardinals' carriages—insolence of the Papal police, September 11th.

Condemnation to the galleys for 20 years of Colonel Calandrelli, Minister of War under the Republic, accused of having stolen books from the Ecclesiastical Academy, September 22nd.

Condemnation to death of Signor Salvatori, in retaliation for the death of a Sanfedist brought to trial through his instrumentality, September 22nd.

Allocution of Pope Pius IX., held in the short consistory of September 5th, October 7th.

Fears at Rome in consequence of the Ministerial crisis in Paris, and efforts to subsidize the peasantry by reviving the system of centurioni, November 3rd.

Pardon and liberation of Diamelli (plunderer of medals in the Vatican); his services as a spy in prison, November 3rd.

Result of the labours of the Commissioners appointed to revise the claims on the treasury, November 18th.

Difficulties of recruiting for the Papal army, November 24th.

Instances of the corrupt state of the system of criminal justice, December 12th.

Effect of the news from France on the ecclesiastical authorities, December 17th.

Anxiety felt by the ecclesiastical authorities as to the ulterior development of Louis Napoleon's schemes, December 29th.

Flattering letter from Louis Napoleon to the Pope; his reply, December 29th.

1852.

More searches and arrests by the " sbirri ;" women searched in hopes of finding Mazzinian circulars upòn them, January 7th.

New organization of government spies, through tradesmen and family servants, January 28th.

Clandestine printing press seized; Ganarelli (editor of the *Saggiatore* in the time of Mazzini) expelled, January 29th.

Commission appointed by the Pope to inquire into the financial state of the country, January 31st.

Secret celebration of the anniversary of the establishment of the Republic three years ago, February 18th.

Additional particulars of the celebration of the anniversary, February 25th.

Arrest of individuals charged with attempting to throw grenades, &c., amongst the people during the Carnival; alleged discovery of a conspiracy connected with this attempt, March 5th.

Arrival of Prince Canino at Civita Vecchia—alarm of the ecclesiastical authorities, April 2nd.

Edward Murray sentenced to death, May 12th.

Petition to the Pope in favour of Edward Murray, May 13th.

Article from the *Giornale di Roma* defending the conduct of the Papal government towards E. Murray, June 12th.

Letter from Murray to the English people, written from the prison at Ancona, July 15th.

Rumours of the intended withdrawal of French and Austrian troops towards the end of the year, July 22nd.

Rumoured discovery of a long list of conspirators paid by the Revolutionary Committee in London, August 9th.

Interview between Sir H. Bulwer and the Cardinal Secretary of State—refusal of the latter to give up the documents relating to E. Murray's case, September 24th.

Reported object of Sir H. Bulwer's visit to Rome, viz., to obtain from the Pope a formal discouragement of the proceedings of the Irish clergy in political matters, October 22nd.

Execution of nine prisoners at Ancona, November 6th.

Commutation of the sentence on Edward Murray—further particulars of the executions at Ancona, November 8th.

Escape of Signor Corrado Politi from Ancona, November 16th.

First meeting of the Financial Council—some signs of an independent spirit, December 6th.

Proclamation of Napoleon III. at Rome—effect produced in the Papal Court, December 15th.

Further particulars of the proclamation of the French Empire at Rome—evident alarm in the ecclesiastical party, December 16th.

Numerous arrests of innocent persons under pretence of their having had some share in Politi's escape, December 16th.

Hungarian soldiers (serving in the Austrian ranks) shot for desertion, December 16th.

Aggressive spirit in the division of the French army quartered in Rome—against England, December 24th.

1853.

Military occupation of Rimini—fine of 2000 scudi on the inhabitants and banishment of several individuals, to avenge the insult offered to the Austrian vice-consul, February 19th.

Increased vigilance of the police in consequence of the recent events in Milan, February 28th.

Protest addressed to the Pope from the superior Council of the Order of Jesuits, against the expulsion of Jesuits in South America, March 3rd.

Questions asked by the Papal government of Nardoni (chief of the sbirri) as to the number of Republicans in Rome, March 11th.

Orders received by the French sentries to allow no one to approach them by night, and to make use of their arms in case of disobedience, March 15th.

Mr. Duncombe continued to display a warm interest in the affairs of Italy. The evils caused by the subjugation of its provinces by Austria were well known to him; equally familiar was the despotism of the Papal government. There was a society established in London with the title of the " Friends of Italy," of which he became a member of the council, at the solicitation of Mazzini, in 1851. It maintained communications with the Italian patriots in Rome and elsewhere, and held public meetings and published pamphlets describing the wrongs of Italy. The society caused a petition to the House of Commons to be drawn up, November 10th, 1852, giving a *resumé* of recent events in Rome and the Pontifical States, and praying for assistance to drive the French and Austrian forces that had lately marched into Rome, out of Italy. The petitioners denounced the conduct of a declared friend of Italian independence, who had joined with the worst enemies of Italy in bringing her again under an intolerable subjection, and prayed for interposition, that an end might be put to the unjustifiable occupation of Rome by France and Austria.

Mr. Duncombe supported the prayer of the petition. He was by this time well known to the leading patriots, and in frequent communication with the ablest of them.

November 24th, 1850.

Dear Sir,—I have been deprived of the pleasure of seeing you whilst I was in England. I do not think I shall be long before revisiting it, and you will then be one of the first persons I will endeavour to see; meanwhile, will you allow me to introduce to you one of my best friends, and of the most enlightened patriots I know, Mr. James Stansfeld, and ask your earnest attention about the subject of his conversation with you. This subject is my permanent thought—my own country. That, after what our people did in 1848 and '49, we are firmly bent on a renewal of our national struggle, you cannot have any doubt. What sort of help, what sympathies, we shall try to enlist in our cause before initiating this struggle, is left partly to the decision and to the activity of our friends in England. Mr. Stansfeld will communicate to you our present organization, and some of the acts of our national committee. Is there any means of establishing a public agitation whatever in favour of our national cause? could not a rather important public meeting be organized in London either concerning the general national question or the condition of things in Rome? Could anything be done to transform the actual useless, senseless, sectarian anti-Popish agitation into a political, logical one? Could we not avail ourselves of the opportunity offered to teach again the English public that all Italian questions are questions of independence? and to remind them that the Pope would not enthrone a Romish hierarchy in England from Gaeta or from any other place of refuge? Could we not elicit from such a demonstration a series of others both in London and provinces, and, from those, some support to our national loan? Upon these enquiries I call now your attention, so that my English friends can listen to what you suggest, and act accordingly. Whatever thing you advise or do for our cause will establish a new claim to our gratefulness and to my friendly esteem.

We are about issuing an address to England, signed by our national committee. Some of the members are residing permanently in London.

Believe me, dear Sir, with deep esteem and grateful friendship, yours ever truly, JOSEPH MAZZINI.

Mr. Mazzini wrote the following notes for Mr. Duncombe's guidance :—

I. That the Roman Republic, tried according to whatever principle, possessed all those claims which ought to accredit one Government in the eyes of others, and to secure for it respect and guaranteed existence.

(1.) In virtue of its constitutional origin, and credentials from the Roman people, municipalities, &c.

Tract on Terrorism in Rome, p. 5.

Printed Petition, p. 1.

Printed Collections of the adhesions sent in to the Roman Republican Government, after its establishment, by the Town Councils of the Roman States. (Large book in Stansfeld's possession.)

(2.) In virtue of its actual conduct when in power, conduct impressing all disinterested witnesses, and even English diplomatists, with the conviction of its moderation, fitness, and conscientiousness.

Tract on Terrorism throughout, where a sketch of the Republic is given, with references to its proclamations and legislative measures.

Mazzini's letter to MM. de Tocqueville and Falloux.

Passages in "Correspondence" from English agent, chiefly quoted in Tract on Terrorism.

N.B.—Under this head, while answering the common calumnies of "terrorism," "foreign demagogues," &c., reference might be made to the destruction of the Inquisition.

II. That, notwithstanding these perfect claims of the Roman Government on the recognition and support of all States, the Government of Republican France sent troops, which put down this Republic by force and restored priestly government, and that the then Government of England was directly an accomplice of the French Government in this iniquitous act.

(1.) The history of the French intervention.

Tract on Terrorism in Rome.

Mazzini's letter to De Tocqueville, &c.

Correspondence (quoted generally in Tract).

Note F, Appendix to Tract No. 4; i.e. Mazzini's Lecture to Society. (This note brings out the principle on which the French justified their intervention; i.e.

that the Papacy is an institution, the common property of all Catholic powers, and that the Roman territory as the seat of this institution could not be allowed to be invested with the usual right of nationality. Farther elucidation of this point in some speeches of O. Barrot, &c. &c. in French Chambers.)

(2.) Complicity of the British Government. Article in *British Quarterly Review* on " British Statesmanship " with regard to Italy, pp. 488-497. (Here a discrepancy is brought out between the views of Palmerston as minister and Lord Normanby as ambassador.)

Society's First Annual Report, pp. 10, 11.

N.B.—The British Government in this complicity could not plead the logical excuse of the French, being a Protestant power, and therefore bound to be delighted with the conversion of Central Italy into a nationality.

III. That, even allowing the actual suppression of the Roman Republic by France and Austria, with British complicity, to pass, yet that suppression was affirmed at the time to be purely conditional; all the three Governments coming under documentary promises that a good and free and acceptable Government would be established in Rome, and that the occupation of Rome by the French and Austrians was to be but a " temporary arrangement " till this should be accomplished.

Article in *British Quarterly Review*, pp. 494, 495.

Correspondence as quoted in printed Petition, pp. 2, 3, 4.

A speech of Lord Palmerston in May, 1851 (to be looked out).

IV. That these promises have not been fulfilled, and that the obligation of the British and other Governments to redeem their word remains.

(1.) Present horrors of Papal and Austrian rule; to be illustrated by abundance of facts and instances.

The cabinet in England did not patronize revolutionists of any country. The seizure of Hale's rockets had put an end to the belligerent aspirations of Kossuth; the French occupation of Rome was almost an extinguisher to Mazzini—nevertheless, he desired to make his English friend believe that Italy was again on the eve of revolt.

15, Radnor-street, King's-road, Chelsea,
April 7th, 1854.

MY DEAR MR. DUNCOMBE,—Events are fast approaching in Italy; these events will of course, if with a leadership, have nothing that can trouble your alliance with France. Our aim is now anti-Austrian, and certainly, with an armed neutrality which hangs, like the sword of Damocles, over both friends and foes, you cannot lament that we should summon Austria's activity somewhere else than on the Turkish frontiers.

I do not ask you to do anything for us now; you have done already most likely what you could in 1853, but Mr. Collett, a friend and colleague of yours, having told me some time ago that when the crisis approaches he would be ready to do anything that he could in accordance with your own feelings, I have applied to him; and I should ask you, if you continue to look upon our cause as upon a good and sacred one, to encourage him, in case he asks you, to do what he can for us.

Ever faithfully yours,   JOSEPH MAZZINI.

As there seemed little prospect of a revolutionary movement in Hungary, Kossuth turned his attention to Italy, as affording a better chance of stirring up opposition to the Austrian power. The Italians of Lombardy and Venice were waiting for an opportunity of throwing off the hated yoke; the people of Rome were quite as eager to get rid of the Pope; but Austrian and French bayonets kept down the spirit of patriotism. There was certainly a sovereign in Italy who entertained a dream of driving the Austrian from the Italian soil, and there existed statesmen who entertained the idea of a free and united Italy; but Victor Emmanuel could have scarcely felt, even after the seasoning his troops had had in the Crimea, that he could have overpowered the veteran Radetski, and his able minister, Count Cavour, was well aware of the difficulties in the way of the independence and union of his country. The assertion in the following letter respecting that minister was incorrect:—

> Montpelier House, Ventnor, Isle of Wight,
> August 28th, 1856.

My DEAR SIR,—You were so kind as to allow me to address myself to you in case I should want to consult the Parliamentary papers.

Just now I would very much want the Blue Books of 1848 and '49 respecting the affairs of Italy. Were it too much to ask the favour to have them lent for a couple of weeks, if it can be done without trouble and inconvenience to yourself? If delivered at my house in South Bank (No. 8), to Captain Frater there, he would forward to me hither the parcel in safety.

It may interest you to hear that Cavour is conspiring with Murat. I have it from a very good source.

The national Italian party at Genoa has opened in *L'Italia e Popolo* a subscription for 10,000 muskets, as a counter-demonstration to the subscription for the 100 defensive cannons of Alessandria. The argument is just: it is not by a defensive policy that the cause of Italian independence can be forwarded. The national party hopes, or rather would fain hope, that a demonstration of English popular sympathy will come to them in the shape of some shillings and sixpences for their muskets, while pounds are going towards the defensive cannons. Mistake! not one penny will they get. There is the most unconquerable darkness prevailing in public opinion here about the character and intentions of the Cabinet of Turin, though

Lord Palmerston told the world (thank him for nothing for so much) that it is only "by holding out a bright example of liberal institutions the Government of Turin would be allowed to work for the deliverance of Italy." I would like to know by what possible process can that "bright example" induce Austria to recross the Alps or the Pope to abdicate his temporal sovereignty, "the worst of human inventions;" and yet these two points constitute the Italian question.

However, curious matters are in process of brewing there in the Peninsula, not the least curious of which is, that "the champion of Italy at the Paris Congress, Cavour, is conspiring with Murat." Will the Cabinet of St. James's allow itself to be duped, or will it still continue to dance at the tune of Bonaparte? I fear they will. No first-rate Power can with impunity descend to a secondary position. It is Milton's bridge, leading "smooth, easy, inoffensive, down to ——."

Those who consented to abdicate an independent policy will of course glide whither they are pushed; counter-influence is impossible, but it would be good to know, at least, what they are about. I cannot so much as guess. May be, neither they themselves; very likely not.

Apropos of Colonel Türr; the Government has not paid him for the five months he was imprisoned in Austria. Is that generous or even just? Have they withheld the pay of General Williams while he was a prisoner in Russia? I don't think they did, though Williams surrendered and Türr was kidnapped in violation of international law. But, of course, he is but Türr the exile, and not Williams of Kars. Kmety may, by-and-bye, have a word to say about this.

Excuse my chattering, and believe me to be, with high regard and consideration,

Your most obedient servant,   Kossuth.

The anti-Austrian movement in Italy was now supported by the military power of France. The Emperor

ANTI-AUSTRIAN MOVEMENT. 239

Napoleon led an army in person with the avowed object of driving the Austrians out of Lombardy. England wisely determined on neutrality, though two opposing influences were strongly directed to engage her as an ally. Kossuth seems to have been apprehensive that the Government would be obliged to support Austria, and allowed himself to be announced as intending to address a public meeting to be held at the London Tavern on the 20th of May, the lord mayor in the chair, to which Mr. Duncombe was thus invited :—

10, Bedford-square, May 18th, 1859.

My DEAR SIR,—I am very anxious to secure your attendance and assistance at the meeting announced on the next page, and for which I enclose a platform ticket.

I have been with Kossuth this evening, and he joins his request to mine that you will be present and support a resolution in favour of our neutrality in this European war. He fears and I fear lest even before the meeting of Parliament the German sympathies in high quarters will have involved us in the strife, or induced us to enter into entangling treaties which may so involve us. Pray come.

Yours truly, C. GILPIN.

In July Mr. Duncombe in the House of Commons moved for the correspondence respecting the British officers sent to the head-quarters of the Austrian, French, and Sardinian armies, and by the return printed it became known that Mr. Mildmay, formerly in the Austrian military service, was to attend the Austrian army in Italy, while Colonel Claremont accompanied the head-quarters of the French army, and the Hon. Colonel Cadogan those of the Sardinian.

The decisive battles of Magenta and Solferino caused the Austrian army to evacuate Lombardy. Every one knows that the two emperors then came to an understanding, and that the French army marched home instead of following up its successes.

The rule of the Bourbons in Naples was more intolerable than that of Austria in Lombardy and Venice, and the revelations that appeared in the English press of the atrocities committed by the king created the strongest feelings of indignation in this country.* Mr. Duncombe entertained the greatest sympathy for the victims of oppression. Every exile had a sacred claim upon his attention, which he liberally acknowledged, and it afforded him the sincerest pleasure to be of service to them. It may therefore be imagined with what gratification he complied with the request of the Master of the Rolls in

* *Mr. Petre to the Earl of Clarendon.—(Received November 1).*

Naples, October 27, 1856.

MY LORD,—I regret unfeignedly in this, one of my last despatches to your lordship, to have to record the physical sufferings of Carlo Poerio [and first six years no pen, ink, or paper allowed, or relative seen].

For some time past he had been suffering from a tumour on the spine, arising in great measure, I believe, from long confinement and low unhealthy diet, and aggravated by the friction of his chain. An operation was performed very recently upon him, and he is now, I am told, in a more satisfactory state of health. But, if my information is correct, and I have no reason to doubt it, however revolting to humanity the fact, neither before, nor during, nor after the operation was Poerio's chain removed.

I have, &c.,   (Signed)   G. G. PETRE.

—(*From Correspondence Relative to Affairs in Naples, printed in 1857.*)

behalf of the distinguished Neapolitan thus recommended to his good offices :—

6, Hyde Park-terrace, April 25th, 1859.

MY DEAR SIR,—I venture on the slight acquaintance I
had with you in the House of Commons to make a request
in favour of Baron Poerio, one of the Neapolitan exiles, with
whom you are probably acquainted. He is very desirous to
see the proceedings of a contested election in England, and I
promised him that I would endeavour to obtain for him a
ticket of introduction to the hustings at Finsbury on your
nomination. If you can do this, and will send me a ticket
for him, I shall be much obliged to you both on his and on
my own account, from the great esteem and sympathy I
entertain for him and for his cause, and for that of Italy.

Wishing you every success, which I do not for a
moment doubt,

I am, yours very sincerely, JOHN ROMILLY.

Thomas S. Duncombe, Esq., &c.

15, Arlington-street, Piccadilly,
Londres, Avril 25, 1859.

MONSIEUR—Sir John Romilly a bien voulu m'honorer
d'une visite pour me faire connaitre les effets de votre bonté.
J'accepte avec la plus profonde reconnaissance l'offre si bienveillante et si aimable que vous avez bien voulu me faire
d'avoir l'honneur de vous accompagner à l'élection qui aura
lieu Vendredi prochain ; et je me rejoui d'avance du plaisir
que j'éprouverai en faisant la connaissance d'un personnage
politique si hautement placé dans l'opinion publique, et dont
la voix éloquente deployée en faveur de ma patrie rétentit
encore dans mon cœur. Mais je ne permettrai jamais,
Monsieur, que vous vous dérangiez pour moi venant me prendre
chez moi. Demain matin, Mardi, je me ferai un devoir de
venir vous presenter mes respects et mes plus vifs remercie-
ments, et me mettre tout-à-fait à votre disposition. Dans
le cas où vous fussiez dejà sorti à cette heure, c'est-à-dire
entre midi et une heure, j'oserais vous prier de vouloir bien
me laisser un petit mot, avec l'indication de l'heure et du

lieu où je dois me trouver Vendredi prochain pour avoir
l'honneur de profiter de votre aimable permission de vous
accompagner sur le lieu des élections.

Veuillez bien, Monsieur, agréer les sentiments de ma plus
vive reconnaissance, et l'assurance de ma considération la
plus distinguée et de mon plus profond respect.

Votre devoué,   CHARLES POERIO.

Count Arrivabene* mentions having met Kossuth
towards the close of June, 1859, at Brescia, when he
acknowledged that he was on his way to meet the
emperor. He was then travelling in company with
the Prefect of Police, Pietri—a curious conjunction;
but later events suggest that it was not an undesigned
one. The Hungarian patriot was evidently under the
impression that he was about to have the direction
of a formidable diversion against Austria on the
Danube. He had been sent for by Napoleon, and
nothing seemed more probable than that the latter
should take measures for making the most of his success at Solferino. About a week later it became an
established fact that a suspension of arms, followed
by a treaty of alliance, had been agreed to by the
Emperors of France and Austria. It can easily be
imagined with what feelings Kossuth retraced his
steps. He might have said, as well as Baron
Ricasoli — "After Villafranca I spat upon my
life!"

It is also stated by the same authority—"That
during the French-Sardinian war against the Austrians in Italy, the Emperor Napoleon sent a secret
messenger to Garibaldi with offers of assistance, that

---

* "Italy under Victor Emmanuel." By Count Charles Arrivabene, i., 104; 258.

were coldly declined : the republican general naturally distrusted the professions of the hero of the *coup d'état*. After the arrangement at Villafranca the distrust increased to detestation, which increased when he found his favourite enterprise, the capture of Rome, thwarted by the emperor's interference. The policy of Louis Napoleon was always imperial, however completely he might disguise it for a purpose. He invited Kossuth into Italy on pretence of arranging an Hungarian insurrection; but his anti-republicanism was shown as completely by throwing him over for the Austrian alliance, as by putting an end to the triumph of democracy in Rome and restoring the Pope."

The Hungarian patriot subsequently took a journey to Italy, ostensibly to obtain a concession for a railway in which he had a considerable interest. In this he was not likely to meet with success ; for however much the country may have wanted railway communication, its statesmen would not hear of them if supported by republican propagandists. The governments who fancied that they had as much to fear from Kossuth as a railway king as a Hungarian president, made anxious inquiries through their ministers, and the scheme was not favoured. The following, endorsed " Extracts of conversations and visits to Sir James Hudson," are in the handwriting of Kossuth :—

Turin, October 9th, 1860.—I called to-day on Sir James Hudson. He told me that the application for a railroad concession by an English Company, with whom M. Kossuth appears to be connected, had caused great alarm, both at St. Petersburgh and at Berlin ; since these two Governments were informed from London that it was intended here (Turin) to give, by means of this concession, money to

M. Kossuth for carrying out his political purposes. Sir
James wondered how any such rumours could have got
credit at the Foreign Office in London, since it was evident
that the Cabinet of Turin could never have thought to
resort to such "a clumsy way."   "Why!" said Sir James,
"if they want Kossuth they will most assuredly give him
the required money without looking out for any such
pretext."

Turin, December 29th, 1860.—I had a long conversation
with Sir James Hudson; he entered freely on discussing
the situation, and especially the affairs of Hungary.   He
declared that, as a servant of the Queen and an English
citizen, he certainly felt bound to support with all his
strength the maintenance of Austria; but that the European
Governments—England included—appeared to labour under
such delusions as were truly ridiculous.   They maintain
that the Sardinian Government and Prince Couza are allied
for preparing the Hungarian revolution in the Principalities
—the stipulated price being the future reannexation of
Bukovina to Moldavia.   Nay, Sir Henry Bulwer went so
far as to maintain that it was the Sardinian Government
which sent the (afterwards confiscated) arms to the Danube,
whereas it can be proved to satisfaction, and in fact he (Sir
James) had proved it, by referring to the dates, that it was Türr
who sent them, and the Sardinian Government could absolutely have had nothing to do with the matter.   But it was extremely difficult to impart conviction to the English Government—they actually keep an eye on Garibaldi at Caprera,
lest he might go to Turkey.   Yet it is evident that there
will be no war next spring : France does not will it, England
cannot allow it, Italy is not prepared for it, and as to
Garibaldi he could only commence the war on the shores of
the Adriatic, and there the English fleet is keeping a close
watch, and will not allow another such violation of international law as that in Sicily.   No, England will not shut
her eyes a second time so.

We now come upon the grand expedition of Garibaldi, whose fame as a republican leader attracted to

his banner Poles, Hungarians, and English in considerable numbers. The Italians flocked to him as to a liberator capable of finishing the great work the treaty of Villafranca had stopped; and the King of Sardinia readily consented to a nearer approach, with the popular general's assistance, to the sovereignty of a united Italy to which he had aspired. How the Neapolitan territory was invaded and the Bourbon despot forced to fly for his life, while his kingdom passed from his dynasty for ever, is well known. It will be found admirably described by an eye-witness, who though a non-combatant shared in the dangers of the Garibaldians, and for a time became a prisoner in the hands of their enemies.*

The result of Mr. Edwin James's mission to the seat of war, is amusingly told by Count Arrivabene. It appears that the learned counsel, not content with the credentials he had obtained from Mr. Duncombe, when he arrived at the head-quarters of Garibaldi gave out that he had been entrusted with a mission from Lord Palmerston. This secured him a most favourable reception from the Garibaldian officers, and access to every person or place of importance he desired to see. Lord Llanover, his predecessor as member for Marylebone, and the Hon. Evelyn Ashley, and several other Englishmen then at Naples, laughed at these pretensions; and having run some risks by getting too near the enemy, and inspected the Neapolitan prisons, the self-constituted ambassador took his departure from Italy.

In this achievement Mazzini took no part. Though

---

* "Italy under Victor Emmanuel." By Count Charles Arrivabene, 2 vols.

it was largely indebted to Young Italy for success, the great republican was forced to keep aloof from it. His disciples were foremost in the conflict, but the master nowhere. The fact is, the Government of the *Rè Galantuomo* could not risk the presence of the apostle of democracy under circumstances so exciting, among such materials as composed the army of invasion. However liberal may have been the general's sentiments, he was known to be loyal, and confidence was reposed in him; but the republicanism of the ex-triumvir of Rome was unmanageable, and there were ugly rumours afloat as to his system of propagandism that left Ricasoli and his colleagues no alternative but rigid banishment.

The condemnation of Mazzini is thus expressed by his countryman :—" The impracticable character of his political ideas, the virulence of his opposition to Cavour and to Piedmont generally, the recklessness of the various insurrections he has organized, and the violence of some of his followers, have naturally associated with his name an amount of unpopularity which the services of his earlier life are not sufficient to counteract."*

He had got a bad name—for worse actions than ideas—for which the talent he possessed, or the virtue he had displayed, could not compensate in the opinion of soberer-minded men. He was doomed to remain in exile, and note from a distance how barren of results the conquest of Naples was made in consequence of Garibaldi being prevented from marching upon Rome.

* " Italy under Victor Emmanuel." By Count Charles Arrivabene, ii. 211.

Mr. Duncombe read and preserved every particle of intelligence respecting Italy that appeared in the public journals, and was kept well informed from private sources. He was therefore able, when he addressed the House of Commons on the subject, which he did frequently, to surprise the members of the Government with the extent of his knowledge.

Both Mazzini and Kossuth were averse to any action on the part of England; in the former this desire for neutrality, however, evidently arose from opposition to the monarchical form which the movement for a united Italy had assumed.

The account given by Mazzini of his connexion with Gallenga, the intended assassin of Carlo Alberto, will be accepted by very few English readers as a satisfactory defence of the accusation brought against him—that he suggested the king's murder. By this explanation it is quite clear that he was not only cognizant of the contemplated deed, but gave a weapon with which it might be accomplished.* The indisputable fact, too, that Orsini was his colleague, joined to his notorious detestation of Napoleon, has left him open to the suspicion of having also been privy to the murderous attempt against the emperor. Lastly, the knowledge that for several years he was an active emissary of the Carbonari, with whom assassination is well known to have been an ordinary resource, caused him at last to be generally distrusted.

The spirit aroused among the Italians was not to be thus satisfied. The demand for Italian unity caused the entire nation to resort to arms, and Victor Emmanuel

---

* "Life and Writings of Joseph Mazzini," i. 348.

and Garibaldi led a well-appointed army against the
famous bulwark of Austrian domination in Italy—
the Quadrilateral. The surrender of Venice without a
siege completed the evacuation of Italy. Victor
Emmanuel was now king of all Italy except Rome,
the natural capital of that kingdom. There, in opposition to the Romans and to Mazzini, in opposition
to Victor Emmanuel and to Garibaldi, Pius IX.
ruled as sovereign and pope, supported by a French
army.

Mazzini had the support of men of high intellectual
attainments, many with names of European fame.
Sismondi afforded him cordial encouragement; Azeglio
assisted in endeavouring to work out his plans;
Alexander Dumas was eager to become a fellow-
labourer in the same vineyard. Thomas Carlyle gave
him the benefit of his recommendation; and Thomas
Slingsby Duncombe was his faithful and eloquent
advocate. Yet circumstances rendered nugatòry these
powerful aids. A momentary success, when one of
the triumvirate of republican Rome, was succeeded by
a complete overthrow. What was effected in the way
of Italian unity was done without his assistance.
His opinions became repudiated, his schemes were pronounced chimerical, and he found himself condemned
to the life of an exile, under surveillance as a dangerous character, making frequent appeals to his admirers with a decreasing effect.

Mazzini has since this further development of his
great idea lived to see the evacuation of Rome by the
French army; but it could have afforded him no
solace, for the metropolis of his nationality still remained the head-quarters of priestly misrule. The

pope maintained his temporal throne, somewhat dissatisfied certainly, but to all outward appearance as absolute, as intolerant, as illiberal as ever; more disheartening still, "La Giovine Italia" looked on and made no sign. Nothing therefore remained for him to do but to leave this imperfect Italian unity to its fate, while he occupied his time in collecting his various publications, and giving them again to the world, with an autobiography which is intended to be a defence as well as a life."*

He made one more effort to rouse his English admirers to afford him material aid by issuing a manifesto to raise the sum of 3000*l.*; but like the shilling-subscription plan in behalf of himself and Kossuth, the result was unsatisfactory.

Mazzini has ventured to state his disbelief "that the salvation of Italy can ever be accomplished by monarchy."† The present Italy he considers incomplete, the Papacy preventing the union of the provinces under one ruler, and the cession of Nice and Savoy to a foreign sovereign having severed a portion from the map. He might have added that the present Italy is dissatisfied, impoverished, and apparently decaying. That Naples begins to doubt the blessings of being a portion of united Italy, and Venetia is not certain that she has gained commercially by the withdrawal of the Austrian rule; that Lombardy misses the German markets for the produce of her rich fields; and Tuscany and Parma mourn the loss of their petty courts; while the rest of the pro-

---

* "Life and Writings of Joseph Mazzini." Vol. i., published in 1864.

† "Life and Writings," i. 53.

vinces of the peninsula, from the Alps to the sea, are looking in vain for the advantages they ought to have acquired by union.

Nevertheless, although the Italian unity is not a perfect success, it must be conceded that, from the Italian point of view at least, it may be regarded as an improvement upon the former state of things. The foreign domination is at an end; there are neither Austrians in Milan, Swiss at Naples, nor French at Rome; Italy can no longer be stigmatized as merely "a geographical idea." The country possesses claims to a nationality; and although Victor Emmanuel has met with difficulties in realizing his programme, and finds his resources insufficient for his requirements, he is well aware that great changes like the one he has directed cannot be brought about without considerable derangement in the economy of a nation circumstanced as it was a few years back. "Rome was not built in a day;" the Roman empire had a long and fierce struggle for its development. The Italian empire is but yet in its cradle.

CHAPTER X.

SPECULATION.

Spirit of enterprise very general in England — Influences Mr.
Duncombe—Secret information from Portugal—Joint-Stock
Wine Company in Paris—Railway from Madrid to Lisbon—
Letter to General Bacon—Letters of Count D'Orsay, and from
Messrs. Da Costa and Madden on the scheme—General Bacon's
report—Iron roads in England—The Railway King—Suit
commenced against him—Condemned to refund—Charge by
him brought against Members of Parliament of having accepted
bribes—Mr. Duncombe's speech—Railway for Ceylon—Letters
from Sir William Molesworth and the Right Honourable H.
Labouchere—A rival speculation—The scheme abandoned.

THE spirit of speculation had seized all who had anything to speculate with, as well as some who were
totally without resources. Among the first were the
Marquis of Hertford and the Rev. Sydney Smith,
both of whom made considerable investments in
America—the peer to the reputed amount of 300,000*l.*;
the wit had risked a much smaller sum.

There appears to have been a large element of enterprise in the composition of Mr. Duncombe; and
when all classes in England were under the same influence, there can be nothing surprising in his par-
ticipating in it. There is reason to believe that he
was associated in his ventures by a distinguished
personage, who bought largely in foreign shares. At
any rate it is certain that he had trustworthy infor-

mation from our embassies abroad respecting political changes or arrangements that might affect the funds. Lord Cochrane's escapade on the Stock Exchange must be familiar to the reader; but the member for Finsbury was not likely to engage in such proceedings. Don Pedro's design against Don Miguel created a large amount of speculation in the Government funds of Portugal. A friend afforded him the following notices of the progress of events:—

Wednesday, September 24th, 1834.

DEAR D—, —I should think there would be a rise in Port. Bonds. The accounts up to the 13th are very favourable. Palmella, Villa Real, and all that party have agreed to join Freire's ministry; Pedro is better, but in the event of his death there is to be a regency, of which Palmella will be the head; the Cortes have given Pedro unlimited power to conclude a marriage for his daughter, and a messenger has been sent from Lisbon to the Duke of Leuchtenberg to announce that the Duke is the chosen husband. What think you of this?

DEAR DUNCOMBE,—Torreno's plan, *en gros*, is to acknowledge and to create one fund of the whole foreign debt of Spain, a portion of it (two-fifths he thinks, though that must to a certain degree depend upon the Cortes) is to be what is called active debt, *i.e.*, bearing interest and in process of redemption; as soon as that is accomplished, another portion of the passive debt (which bears no interest) is to be made active, and so on till the whole is paid off. The particular stock which is to be made " active " is to be decided by lot, and the proportions in future to be made active will be greater as the resources of the country increase.

Saturday, September 27th, 1834.

DEAR D—,—Pedro is dying, and was at his last gasp on the 21st. Donna Maria had ordered Palmella to form a ministry with Freire, who had not quite determined upon joining Palmella. The Cortes had declared Donna Maria of age. I hope this will reach you before you go. Send it with all speed to our friend.

Sunday, September 28th, 1834.

DEAR DUNCOMBE,—I told you yesterday of Pedro's approaching death, of the fact that Donna Maria had been declared of age by the Cortes, and of her having sent for Palmella to form a ministry. When she sent for Palmella (on the 19th) she named Terceira, Freire, and Carvalho to form part of his government. After some discussion Palmella went to Queluz, on the evening of the 21st, to name to the Queen a ministry, consisting of himself as president of the council; Villa Real, foreign affairs; Terceira, Freire, Carvalho, finance; and Saldanha, commander-in-chief at Pedro's death. There is little doubt that Donna Maria will agree to this, and nothing can be better or more likely to satisfy every one. Donna Maria has shown great decision and firmness, has declared she will be married, and has already signed full powers to proceed with the marriage negotiations with the Duke of Leuchtenberg begun by her father. France may raise some objections to this match, but will offer no real opposition, and England is delighted with it. By-the-bye, Donna Maria was proclaimed of age in consequence of Pedro's resignation of the regency, owing to his ill health. I send this under cover to E. The Spanish Government is particularly well disposed towards the Cortes' bondholders, and has promised that their claims shall be considered first, and with the utmost liberality.

One of the most promising of Mr. Duncombe's commercial ventures took the shape of a Joint-Stock Wine Company, in Paris under the direction of Messrs. Stork, in London under that of Mr. Charles Conyngham. It appears to have been carried on with considerable success for many years; but in 1839, Mr. Duncombe wishing to withdraw from it, received

2000*l.* for his share. The company were liberally supported by noblemen and gentlemen in England, for among the customers are the names of Lords Alvanley, Belfast, Donegal, Bathurst, Adolphus Fitzclarence, Chandos, Hastings, &c. They also had consignments to New York, Jamaica, Limerick, Bristol, Liverpool, Quebec, Glasgow, Belfast, Dublin, Rome, and London.

The reign of the railway king had commenced, and the marvellous rapidity with which a small tradesman in York had contrived to be the reputed possessor of millions, and the arbiter of the fortunes, if not of the destinies of much of the rank, fashion, and wealth of the kingdom, suggested to other speculators the advantage of seeking a similar road to unlimited wealth. As this must be in a country where iron roads did not exist, and where a commercial spirit in the middle and upper classes might be relied on to support their development, the Peninsula was selected. A grand scheme was drawn up for uniting the capitals of Spain and Portugal, and abundant patronage secured, a well-selected and influential board of directors published, and the speculation launched.

A railway to connect the two kingdoms having been determined on, it became necessary to secure the services of some person of superior talent and social influence to visit the Peninsula, for the purpose of reporting on the best line, and of collecting such information respecting the probable traffic as might be of advantage to the shareholders, as well as useful to the managers of the company. Among those distinguished persons who were applied to to give the enterprise the advantage of their patronage, was the

Duc d'Ossuna, whom Mr. Duncombe had met in the gay circle that so long flourished in the smiles of the beautiful Countess of Blessington.*

General Bacon had greatly interested himself in the undertaking, and there were special reasons for selecting him as the intelligent agent the directors required. The letter now printed is a testimonial that carried great weight :—

London, May 15th, 1845.

My dear Bacon,—I spoke to Dietz, and I had no doubt of the King writing to his cousin. He expressed himself kindly respecting you.

The movement for the railway project is most favourable; there is the greatest disposition to give impulse to works in this country to be undertaken by companies. But in dealing with these people it is right to consider what is likely to influence them, so as to be prepared at once by anticipation to overcome certain obstacles. If you should come out, I recommend that the project be as matured and complete as practicable at present to make, particularly as to terms; but there is one suggestion which I would make to you who understand these people, which is to give them as direct an immediate interest in the undertaking as possible. The way to do this would be either to purchase the privilege by a sum or by shares in the Company gratis; or to allow the government a per-centage on the profits—say 10 per cent.; or to allow them to share the profits equally, after indemnifying the shareholders for the outlay—say at 6 per cent.— that is, when the profits may be 12 per cent. 6 would go to the shareholders, interest on capital, and the other 6 divided.

The Government should be offered a share, say one-tenth, not as a gift, unless this should be the bonus proposed instead of a per-centage, and there should be a portion left open for Portuguese capitalists ,say for three or six months; this with a view to overcome the feeling which will be

* For his reply, see Appendix.

attempted to be excited by the Obras Publicas Company against foreigners: when the offer is made, the greater the publicity given to it the better.

There are two ways of dealing with the Obras Publicas Company—one to make them friends at once, or if intractable to declare war against them, and to decide to expose the bubble character of their projects and the onerous terms they impose upon the country.

There are already parties here about a railroad, Messrs. Clegg and Lowe; but for the moment nothing will be decided, to afford time to receive other proposals.

Yours sincerely,   H.

This is all quite private, as from me, though the substance is for your guidance and consideration in treating the matter with others.

There were many wealthy men who countenanced the scheme, and there were men whose names were not held in anything like the same respect on the Stock Exchange; nevertheless the projectors of important speculations were sure to have recourse to them if they possessed much social influence. It was in the power of these favourites of society to advance such objects materially. They generally had friends or relations whose support would be of the first advantage as a recommendation. In this respect no one was better qualified than the writer of the four following letters. He was known to every one who figured prominently in society, almost all of whom at his solicitation would readily lend their patronage to any project of utility in which he professed an interest:—

Friday Night.

My dear Tommy,—Bulwer came again to-night; he will go to see you, and you will ascertain by yourself that he is very anxious to assist us. He lives at 36, Hertford-street,

May-fair; go to see him if you have a moment, as I am afraid that he may call on you when you are out. He will tell you that Colonel Stopford spoke to him about a railroad from Spain to Portugal, and he advised him to see our company. I know Colonel Stopford very well. You may be sure that Bulwer will do all he can for us, and that he is anxious to see you.

Yours faithfully,   D'ORSAY.

Gore House, June 13th, 1845.

MY DEAR TOMMY,—Will you have the kindness to indict Keily for forgery, and to tell him that he is an infernal liar (although a good Catholic), as the Duke d'Ossuna writes to me that he is excessively obliged for my contradicting that he ever put his name to any papers concerning railroads; if he had, it would have been for ours. He will exert himself and do all he can to serve us; we have only to point out what he is to do. Make a point to see at once Norman and Co.   Yours faithfully,   D'ORSAY.

P.S.—Try to get me some good news about railroads.

Gore House, July 5th, 1845.

MY DEAR TOMMY,—An intimate friend of Lady B. and me asked me to ask you not to impede this Bill; he knows that on Wednesday you will be the great opponent. Can you find some reason to abandon that question, which, after all, is not of great consequence to Old England? You will oblige us. Say that Baughan and C$^{\text{ie.}}$ required your attendance.

Have you seen Bulwer, and what are you going to do? Shall we be satisfied with our Portugal grant, without caring for Spain? or will it be necessary to send my nephew to Madrid? Will you come and dine with us on Friday? I will ask Bulwer. My brother-in-law, the Duke of Grammont, dines here; he will be glad to see you.

Yours affectionately,   D'ORSAY.

My dear Tommy,—I hear that you are quite discouraged
with the prospect of the Portugal business.   I cannot conceive why, precisely at the only moment when it has a good
appearance.   I could easily understand your disgust at the
beginning, when all the predictions of Frankell failed; but
now we have a chance.   Bacon has succeeded so far as to
obtain the names of the king and queen as patrons, which
is an ample compensation for d'Ossuna.   He has also the
first names of Portugal; and if we find difficulties as to
procure the capitalist, we have a chance of joining with other
companies.   Bulwer told me again yesterday that he was
anxious to make me meet Colonel Stopford, who has a great
deal to do with a railroad in that direction, and who would,
I think, join us.   We have gained another great point,
which is to have nothing to do with Spain, which is so dis-
credited in England.   Courage, mon ami! run well and
straight in distress, otherwise you would not be the real
good, straightforward Tommy.

Yours affectionately,   D'Orsay.

P.S.—I have heard from Bacon; he will be here directly.
Therefore we will judge soon of our position, present and
future.

It may be gathered from the last of these characteristic notes of Beau D'Orsay in the novel character
of a man of business, that Mr. Duncombe began to
appreciate the difficulties of the gigantic enterprise.
Spain had a bad name in the share market, and a railroad was likely to be looked upon as coldly as her
stocks.   Nor did Portugal at this time afford much
promise of success for an undertaking that demanded
a large capital and an enormous amount of labour.
It is amusing to find the Count, who had nothing to
lose by failure, encouraging his friend.

. The scheme attracted general attention in Spain

and Portugal as well as in England; but there were persons who knew the governments of the peninsula well and could not help entertaining misgivings respecting their cordial support. A project set on foot by foreign adventurers would naturally be regarded with suspicion by the ruling powers in both countries, unless these were quite satisfied that they might calculate on deriving from it some extraordinary advantage. It was therefore imperative to secure their co-operation, however extravagantly the company might be obliged to pay for it.

We append communications from an eminent Portuguese merchant, and a well-known English traveller and *littérateur*, who, though they regarded the scheme from different points of view, evidently viewed it in the same light of practical common sense.

Lisbon, July 19th, 1845.

SIR,—Having for many years given my attention and my capital to roads in this country, and having seen your name announced as one of the directors on a railway proposed to be constructed from Lisbon to Oporto, I take the liberty of addressing myself to you that you should have the goodness to give me any information that you may think meet thereon, for me to form my judgment of the enterprise, and co-operate in it if I find that it can be accomplished.

I presume that no one has the data that I may furnish on the general statistics of Portugal, having pursued the subject for many years, and could carry out your views with more efficiency, if they are earnest, and if it is not your condescension alone that has engaged you to allow you to have your name placed on the list of directors.

I speak with so much frankness, because I know from authority that Government will not lend its countenance to any scheme that may not rest on the most solid basis. The other gentlemen who came here and have gone away, are aware of this. Of one of them, with whom I had the pleasure to hold one or two conferences, I can assert it as a fact. Great care must be taken also with politics, and on which side you start, for if you join any body adverse to the party in power you will be only for your pains for the whole of your trouble.

I am, sir, your most obedient humble servant,
CLAUDIO ADRIANO DA COSTA.

6, Salisbury-street, Strand, Friday.

MY DEAR COUNT D'ORSAY,—I read the letter, and return it. My opinions may be erroneous, but they remain unchanged. If the concessions be obtained, they must be got by money from a venal Government. The Obras Publicas obtained their privileges by very large *empentros*, bribes, and theirs were nominally exclusive privileges.

They must be outbid and bought to get the Government to throw them over. All this is a hateful kind of language to me, but there is no other in which the real state of the case can be told. The whole question is—with the Portuguese Government—what party can be turned to most account.

As to the injury done to the project represented by Gen. B—— by Col. Fitch, the statement of the foreman is quite correct, and I have little doubt so are his statements of the heavy expenditure in Lisbon. As to his exertions to effect the objects of the Company, they have been unremitting ; and if any similar exertions could have been successful, backed as they are by the favour of the Court and the patronage of Terceira, his ought to have been so. But the kingly power, the governmental power, are in the hands of the Cabrals, and all that power is exercised for one end—to make a purse.

If I can be of any use to you in Lisbon, command me at all times. In more than the ordinary sense of the words I would be most happy to be made useful to you.

Yours ever, my dear Count, most faithfully,
R. R. MADDEN.

General Bacon having received his instructions proceeded to Lisbon, where he immediately placed himself in communication with the Government. A narrative of the progress of his mission will put the
reader in possession of the history of the affair up to
its date.

Memorandum of the proceedings of General Bacon's mission
to Lisbon, in June last, on the part of the Great Madrid
and Lisbon Railway Company.

Rusham House, Aug. 7th, 1845.

I arrived in Lisbon on the 18th of June, and returned
on Monday last, the 4th inst.

On the day of my arrival I waited upon the President of
the Council to inform his Excellency of the purport of my
visit, and was received in the most flattering manner.

On the following day I proceeded to Cintra to see Lord
Howard de Walden, who had already exerted his influence
in our favour, and with his lordship settled the terms of our
proposals.

On the 16th of the same month I attended a Council of
Ministers, to deliver my proposals and credentials, and to
explain the views of the Company.

The proposals were most favourably received, and on the
following day I attended their majesties' levee, and handed
to the king a copy of the proposals. His majesty was
pleased to give his sanction to the Company to use the
royal patronage so soon as the necessary arrangements
should be completed with the Government, and also to
signify his intention of becoming a shareholder.

In consequence of the Company's engineer not having
arrived from Madrid, I was unable to define the proposed
line, but on the 23rd the arrival of Mr. Emelie, after having
completed his survey much to my satisfaction, enabled me
first to examine the outlet from Lisbon and fix the terminus,
and next to forward the engineer's report,* together with my

* The report was forwarded to London.

distinct offer upon the part of the Company to construct the line by the valley of the Tagus. This was done on the 25th.

I was now opposed by the Obras Publicas Company; but I had established such a sound footing that I had not much to fear, as the sequel will prove. To bring together the Government and Opposition party was the great desideratum; and this difficulty, after much discussion, I at last succeeded in overcoming.

The Obras Publicas Company neither has, nor ever had, any intention of constructing the railroad themselves; their obligations are so extensive, that their whole nominal capital is insufficient to complete the works already undertaken; their sole desire is to sell their pretended privilege.*

Prior to the general election, they put forth a claim in virtue of their contract to make all public works, whether specified or not in their contract. This was, at once overthrown in one of the many interviews I had with the directors of that body, and they admitted that they only claimed a priority in the construction of the railway to the Spanish frontier—a loose wording; and in consequence of the many proposals made to the Government for railways, the Obras Publicas Company was called upon to define their line. They asked time for their decision, and the Government has confined them to the left bank of the Tagus, thus leaving open the whole country between the Tagus and the Douro; or, in a few words, confined them to their original proposal to construct a railway from Aldea Galleja to Badajoz. This is their undisputed right, provided the Government approves their estimates; and I have no doubt that some arrangement is contemplated between them and the Central of Spain Company, for I know they have been in constant communication with one another, of which my letter would have apprised the directors. An understanding between the Central and our own company would have greatly facilitated my operations in Lisbon.

I considered it right to send to Madrid to ascertain

* *Vide* article in the *Correio* of the 26th July.

whether the Spanish Government would entertain our proposals as regarded the project of constructing the whole line by the valley of the Tagus to Madrid; but my overtures, although not refused, were received doubtfully; in short, they depend upon the ability of the Central Company to perform their contract. It is thus clear that our proposal to make the railroad from Madrid to Lisbon is at present undecided.

It is difficult to explain to persons unacquainted with the country the position of the Government of Portugal with regard to the various public companies, which, although having different objects in view, are all linked together for the purpose of getting the Government as much as possible in their power by means of loans of money. The formation of some of these companies has been illegal, and the Government is desirous of shaking off its trammels; but it has been so bound up with them, that previous to the general election no decided measures could be adopted. These being over, the Government is free to act. In compliance with the laws of the country, all public works must be subject to public competition; and the Government has decided to put forth the conditions upon which they are ready to receive tenders for the construction of railroads. These conditions were handed to me at a Council of Ministers, which I attended on the 13th ult.; and after discussing some points, I received the positive assurance from all the Ministers that my proposals, as well as those of Mr. Clegg, would be accepted, so soon as the necessary forms were complied with; but that at the same time I must bind myself to construct the railroad to Oporto, to which I readily assented.

A meeting of the directors in Lisbon was called, and the noblemen and gentlemen whose names are in the footnote* having signed a paper accepting office, decided that Mr.

---

* Duke of Terceira, Marquis of Loulé, Viscount de Sá da Bandeira, Baron de Barcolinhos, Don Miguel Ximenes, Sr. Fereira Pinto Bastos, Sr. Castro de Guimaraes, Sr. Costa Souza, Sr. Duarte Cordoyo de Sá.

Duarte Cordoyo de Sá should hold my powers of attorney, as my further presence in Lisbon for the moment was unnecessary, every point having been settled with the Government satisfactorily. The last five named are among the richest capitalists of Portugal ; and I am fully authorized to state that a very considerable portion of the capital will be subscribed in Portugal.

I was led to believe by the projectors of our railway company that an agent was established in Madrid, and that a Sen. Carvalho Silva, of Abrantes, was applying for concessions from the Portuguese Government. In the former capital no such agent ever appeared ; and in the latter no such person as M. Silva has ever made any offers whatever to the Government, for I have seen all the proposals.

It would appear advisable to make some announcement to the shareholders ; but as my communications have been in some measure confidential, care must be taken not to compromise the Government or my friends in Lisbon.

The line given to me from Lisbon to Oporto is to be carried by Thomar ; and a clause is inserted giving to the company the option of constructing all branches and extensions. We have thus two-thirds of our originally proposed line to the Spanish frontier by the valley of the Tagus ; and my firm impression is that we shall have the concession for the line to the Spanish frontier, whether by the valley of the Tagus, or by crossing the river at Santarem to Badajoz.

The title of our company must be changed, but cannot be decided until the extent of our lines is made known.

ANTHONY BACON.

General Bacon returned to England, but it does not appear that the enterprise turned out profitable to him. It is evident, however, that he had not exhausted his inclination for speculation, and was still sanguine.

Hermitage, November 10th, 1849.

MY DEAR DUNCOMBE,—I have only now got your note of the 6th. The Lisbon water affair is going on with ;

most of the arrangements are concluded with the Portuguese Government, the capital required is subscribed, and I hope to get such remuneration for all the anxiety and trouble the whole concern has caused as will repay a portion at least of the sums advanced by N. and yourself. You say I have paid nothing; true, I have only taken 25*l*. of shares, but I borrowed 500*l*. when I last went to Lisbon, and a further sum of 200*l*., all of which was spent in furtherance of the objects, and both of which sums I must repay. It is an unlucky thing that the Portuguese Government did not conclude this arrangement when it was first offered; I should then have had 20,000*l*. to divide amongst us, Crawshay's own agreement with me; the times are now altered.

As soon as we are in a position to call for the money I will see you or let you know, and no time shall be lost in settling with Mapleson, Draper, &c.

Believe me, sincerely yours, ANTHONY BACON.

I have also another resource, from which I hope to be able to get money very shortly.

Of all the forms of speculation that of iron railroads proved the most attractive: mines had lost their metallic interest, pearl fisheries had ceased to interest even the jewellers, canals seemed to be thought of by no one but as a convenient means of thinning the feline race, bridges were apparently produced exclusively for an anti-tollpaying population, banks appeared to be established only to break, cemeteries were opened as sepulchres for the broken-hearted directors—in short, every kind of investment had become hopeless to the brokers on the Stock Exchange, when travelling by steam on an iron road at tremendous velocity and risk renewed the gambling mania that had in a preceding age produced the "South Sea bubble."

Many of our readers must remember the magnificent mansion by the handsomest entrance to Hyde

Park, to which the *beau monde* were invited; and the equipages of those who responded to the appeal choked Knightsbridge almost to Piccadilly. The possessor of that edifice had become a member of the Imperial Parliament for an important constituency, and was said to hold in his hands the fortunes of half the English aristocracy. Never was there such an illustration of Mammon-worship since the invention of money. Almost every one who had available funds placed them at the disposal of the successful speculator, and seemed ready to worship him to propitiate his assistance for securing a tenfold return.

When the folly had become in the highest degree frantic, a reaction commenced. The favourite investments fell in the market, and the investors began to get ruined. The amount and extent of the losses in a short time attracted a large share of public attention. Inquiries were instituted and a suit commenced against the railway potentate—"The York and North-Midland Company v. Hudson"—when his accounts were scrutinized. Among other items disallowed was the sum of 6300*l.* "in respect of shares stated by Mr. Hudson in his answer to have been distributed by him to certain persons of influence connected with the landed interest and Parliament for the purpose of securing their good offices in connexion with the operations of the railway company." Judgment was given against him, and the sum he was condemned to refund was 54,590*l.* !

The charge which Mr. Hudson thought proper to bring against members of the House of Commons was an apparent repetition on a smaller scale of the bribery practised by the promoters of the South Sea scheme;

but though the sum alleged to have been expended was considerably smaller, the excitement the accusation produced was infinitely greater. Every member repudiated any knowledge of the transaction, and the storm of indignation the accuser created became so violent after the delivery of Mr. Duncombe's remarks, that Hudson was obliged to attempt something in the way of explanation—a defence it could not be called. He had the effrontery to say that he had made no charge against any member of the House, and invited the most searching criticism from his cradle, to detect a discreditable action in the course of his career.

No one had experienced the desire that very few had been able to resist, to a greater extent than the member for Finsbury; but from different causes he had kept as much as possible out of the vortex into which his friends had been rushing. He was himself a Yorkshireman, and was therefore not likely to be indifferent to whatever offered such a cornucopia of advantages to his native county as the iron roads that were to traverse the length and breadth of the shire; but his own venture in them was small. Some of his friends had invested largely, and their losses probably induced him to look sharply after their seducer. The opportunity occurred that he had been waiting for, and he availed himself of it with his customary fearlessness. In his place in the House of Commons he entered upon a thorough exposure.

Mr. Duncombe's speech was circulated throughout the kingdom; and among other comments, public and private, produced the following :—

Honoured Sir,—You have my and, I may say generally, the public thanks for bringing the conduct of that notorious

man, George Hudson, before the House of Commons.
Hudson, as no doubt you are aware, was a linendraper in
York; the firm was Hudson & Nicholson, or N. & H.
When in this trade there was an old man of property, of
the name I think of Botterill, who lived out by Monk Bar,
not far from Hudson's shop, who had an only sister living
between Burlington and Driffield upon a farm belonging to
the ancient family of St. Quintin; she had a pretty large
family. This sister was, I believe, about if not the only
relation the old man had. The old man had a house-
keeper, to whom, I have heard say, Hudson was in the
habit of presenting from time to time a gown-piece, and
that through this woman, Hudson wormed himself into
favour with the old man, who by his will left Hudson all
or the bulk of what he had. Among other things a valuable farm of some hundreds a year at Hutton Cranswick,
near to the market town of Driffield in Yorkshire: this
farm Hudson sold to my Lord Londesborough. The old
man left his relations nothing, or next to it, if anything,
who were naturally disappointed. Hudson was in no way
related to the old man.

Hudson to talk about an investigation from his cradle to
the present time, is an unblushing bounce.

If you want to know anything further about Hudson
you will, I believe, get every information from the editor of
the *Yorkshireman* paper published in York.

If you want anything further from me, for the present
address A. Z., through the London *Times*.

May success attend you honourable endeavours.

Memorandum in Mr. Duncombe's handwriting :—

Posted at Leeds February 10th, 1854, and received Feb.
11th.—T. S. D.

Mr. Duncombe's enterprising spirit was manifested
in the share he took in the year 1855 in organizing a
railway for Ceylon. Having arranged a company
with Mr. W. P. Andrews, chairman of the Scinde

railway, and Mr. J. A. Yarrow as engineer, he addressed his friend, Sir William Molesworth, then at the head of the Colonial Office; from whom the next day he received a reply as under:—

Colonial Office, August 16th, 1855.

My DEAR DUNCOMBE,—I am inclined to look very favourably upon the establishment of railways in Ceylon, and will give the subject an early and careful consideration.

Believe me, very truly yours,   W. MOLESWORTH.

T. Duncombe, Esq.

The Colonial Secretary was at the time in bad health, suffering apparently from overwork. He went into the country to recruit, and died soon after his arrival. Mr. Duncombe then applied to his successor, from whom he received the following communications:—

Colonial Office, November 29th, 1855.

My DEAR MR. DUNCOMBE,—I have delayed answering your note about the Ceylon Railway of the 24th instant until I could find a little time to look into the question. It is obviously of the utmost consequence to the prosperity of that island to give it the benefit of this means of transporting its produce with as little delay as possible. I find that negotiations with another railway company have already made some progress; still I shall be quite ready to listen to any observations or proposals which the gentlemen connected with the Scinde Railway Company may desire to make to me. If they will communicate with my private secretary I will appoint an early day for seeing them.

Believe me always, very sincerely yours,

H. LABOUCHERE.

Stoke Park, Slough.

My DEAR DUNCOMBE,—I assure you that I have not forgotten your friends, but it is impossible to conduct railway matters (especially when you are acting for a distant colony) at a railway pace.

What has occurred is this : I find that negotiations were going on with the Ceylon Railway Company when I came to the Colonial Office. I have desired certain questions to be put to them in order that I may learn what their prospects really are, and at the same time I have told them that I hold myself quite free to go to any other company if I think I shall do better for Ceylon in so doing, or make the railway in any other mode on behalf of the Colonial Government; in short, that I shall do the best I can for the colony. I have received a memorial signed by most of the merchants and planters in this country interested in Ceylon, urging me to make use of no railway company at all.

In short, though I am most anxious not to delay this business more than I am obliged, it is one which obviously requires great care.

Until I have received the answer of the Ceylon Company I see no use seeing your friends, but I will take care that they shall be informed whenever the business is in a state which will enable me to ask them to come to me.

Ever yours sincerely,   H. LABOUCHERE.

The rival speculation, " The Ceylon Railway Company," issued a prospectus, with the names of directors and engineers, and mentioned their communication with the Government with so much confidence that the projectors of the new company thought it most prudent to abandon their undertaking. Nothing could have been more unfortunate for the enterprise than the death of Sir William Molesworth; much more reliance being placed on his shrewd, straightforward intelligence, than could be bestowed upon the dilatory habits and crotchety ideas of his successor.

Mr. Duncombe now seems to have had enough of such enterprises ; he ceased to interest himself about them.

271

CHAPTER XI.

Case of Lieut.-Col. Bradley—Mr. Brougham's account of it in a
letter to Mr. Duncombe—Place the tailor—Want of interest at
the Horse Guards—Career of another soldier of fortune—
Lieut.-Col. Lothian Dickson—Commissioner at the Cape of
Good Hope—Harsh Treatment by Lord Grey—Deprived of his
appointment—Appointed Lieut.-Colonel of the Tower Hamlets
Militia—Dismissed at the complaint of Lord Wilton—He
appeals to Mr. Duncombe—Court of Enquiry—Case of Dickson
v. Wilton—Letters of Right Honourable S. H. Walpole and
T. S. Duncombe—Verdict and damages—Correspondence
between the Earl of Derby and Mr. Duncombe—Lord Combermere—Mr. Duncombe presents a petition to the House of Commons—Court of Enquiry on Lord Wilton—Lieut.-Col. Dickson
withdraws his charges—Terms of settlement—Mr. Duncombe
declines further interference—Lieut.-Col. Dickson publishes his
charges against Lord Wilton—H.R.H. the Duke of Cambridge.

THOUGH a civilian, Mr. Duncombe felt so deep an
interest in the service to which he had belonged, that
he was peculiarly sensitive to any wrong done a
brother officer. This made him ready to accept the
advocacy of any one who considered himself wronged;
and a zealous and powerful advocate he was sure to
become. The first case he took up was that of Lieut.-
Colonel Bradley, who had had a misunderstanding
with a senior officer in the service, while under
the impression that the latter had been reduced to
half-pay; and had been placed under arrest. He peti-

tioned the House of Commons, and made out a strong case; but the most acceptable account of it we now lay before the reader from a most trustworthy source.

Berkeley-square, July 28th, 1855.

My DEAR DUNCOMBE,—Lieut.-Colonel Bradley has put into my hands a report of a debate in which it is represented, I suppose inaccurately, that he " had been treated with singular lenity rather than harshness," and that " a merciful disposition had been indulged in towards him," which, had a court-martial been demanded, could not have been shown, and that " his conduct was a violation of all military discipline."

To those who were this most gallant, unfortunate, and injured gentleman's counsel, such information appears truly extraordinary. There never was a dissentient voice in the court, I may say, or at the bar on either side, when his cause was tried at Guildhall before the late Chief Justice, and afterwards on the motion for a new trial, upon the question of his intentions, nor upon the question whether or not he was, even if in a strict legal view wrong, he had not been worthy of the deepest commiseration. No man affected to doubt that he acted from the purest motives. He firmly believed that Colonel Arthur was assuming the command without any right whatever, and up to this hour it is my belief that no authority has been produced.

There were some nice points of military rule and etiquette gone into, and something like a case was attempted to be made for Colonel Arthur having some authority. I still much more than doubt it. The court, to the best of my recollection, was not satisfied with it, and he obtained a verdict upon one part of his case. Whether he has ever received the amount, or even his costs of the action, I know not. For a long time he had not, because Colonel A. had been appointed to a foreign station, and the rule of Government is to defend its officers in court, but not to pay either costs or damages when the verdict passes against them, a rule which, though hard on the unsuccessful party, is

founded on reason; only that it ought to be coupled
with another, viz., not to employ and send abroad officers
against whom verdicts pass, and if they should be abroad
when the decision is pronounced, either to recall them
or to make them pay the costs of their former mis-
conduct.

Now, if Colonel Arthur acted without authority, Lieut.-
Colonel Bradley, so far from violating all discipline, was
bound by every rule of discipline to act as he did. Of this
there can be no doubt. Colonel Arthur's not choosing to
produce his authority, if he had one, gives rise to another
question, namely, whether or not Lieut.-Colonel Bradley had
a right to disregard his assertion and consider him uncom-
missioned? And there is another question still, namely,
whether he might not take the risk on himself of acting
as if Colonel Arthur had no authority, none being produced? How these points were decided at the trial or
afterwards in court I cannot tell, for I find no report of
the very full argument which occupied the court for two
days, or nearly so. But of this I am quite certain, that
every one considered Lieut.-Colonel Bradley, if wrong at
all, to be merely so upon a most rigorous, not to say
harsh, construction of a very nice and unsettled point, and
that nothing like substantial blame could attach to his
conduct.

That he has been most unfortunate; that his case was
one peculiarly fitted for lenity, even if the point of law was
against him; that no lenity has been shown towards him, I
believe no one at all acquainted with the case can for a
moment doubt.

I suppose from the expression he may have been allowed
the price of his commission. If it be so I also am sure
than an officer of his distinguished services may well be
excused for not considering that a very adequate compensation for the utter ruin of all his prospects in his profession,
especially when we have seen so many instances of others
who had been guilty of worse, at least of much more
unquestionable breaches of discipline, restored to the service

even after a court has pronounced their conduct not to have been strictly according to the rules of the service.

Believe me, very sincerely yours, H. BROUGHAM.*

I must repeat that when his case was tried the expressions of all men, of all parties, at the bar were loud and unanimous that Lieut.-Colonel Bradley's was a case of singular hardship, even if the point of law was against him, upon which there was a very great difference of opinion.

It appears from this able and impartial "summing up" by one of the soundest lawyers and most philosophical thinkers of his age, that the Lieut.-Colonel had been sharply dealt with. He had been led into, by somewhat questionable means, the commission of a breach of discipline, and been punished with dismissal from the service. He appears to have been recommended to Mr. Duncombe by a rather celebrated political character, familiarly known as "Place, the tailor," a man of considerable ability, much esteemed by Sir Francis Burdett and the early Reformers. He wrote many political pamphlets, and was a contributor to the *Westminster Review*.

July 5th, 1835.

DEAR SIR,—Colonel Bradley having told me that he has had an interview with you and is to have another, I have taken the liberty to say that I have known Colonel Bradley from the commencement of his troubles, am acquainted with all his proceedings of every kind relating to his case, and am satisfied he has been very unjustly treated.

I, with every one who has taken an interest in the concerns of this gentleman, will be greatly obliged by your interference in his behalf.

Yours, &c. FRANCIS PLACE.

Thomas S. Duncombe, Esq.

* Lord Brougham and Vaux.

It is evident, from allegations in the petition that have never been contradicted, that Lieut.-Colonel Bradley, for refusing to attend a court of inferior officers, was kept in confinement for 312 days; and then the Duke of York allowed him to sell his commission for 2600*l.* There seems reason to believe that the officer of whom he complained had no authority at the time to place him under arrest, but was subsequently supplied with a commission by favour. The other having no interest, though a deserving officer, was broken and dismissed.

Mr. Duncombe could be of little service in such a case. Although he possessed some interest in the Horse Guards, as the breach of discipline had been committed, and the offender had received a fair price for his forfeited rank, the authorities there considered he had been treated leniently.

The next case is equally arbitrary.

The career of a soldier of fortune is sometimes a chequered one, even in cases of particular military talent, and Lothian Sheffield Dickson, when he entered the army in 1825, ought to have been prepared for the usual vicissitudes of aspirants for promotion without influence. Notwithstanding this drawback, he did not fare so badly, for when he proceeded to the East Indies he became aide-de-camp to General Sir Lionel Smith. Though he saw active service in the Deccan and before Kalipore in the 2nd or Queen's Royals, he left India, in consequence of ill-health, two years later, with the highest recommendations of his general and lieutenant-colonel. In 1829 we find him serving as lieutenant in the 51st Regiment, and later as

adjutant at the depôt of the same regiment. In
1835 he joined Sir De Lacy Evans's auxiliary force
in Spain, having raised the 7th Regiment of the
Legion, of which he received the command, and in
1837 was gazetted to the 77th. After this he
retired on half-pay. In the year 1842 he obtained the appointment of civil commissioner and
resident magistrate in the Cape of Good Hope.
Having served three years, he procured leave of
absence and returned to England. He memorialized
the Government for employment at home in consequence of the ill-health of his wife preventing
her residing in Africa, and received encouraging
assurances from Lord Stanley and Mr. Gladstone;
but unfortunately for him a change of Government
took place, and the civil commissioner on making
his appeal to the new Colonial Secretary, Earl
Grey, was refused. He memorialized the Queen;
but as the memorial had to go through the hands of
the Liberal Colonial Secretary, no notice was taken of
it: moreover, his Cape appointment was filled up, his
leave of absence having expired. Thereupon he
printed a pamphlet, with his correspondence and tes-
timonials, as an attack upon Lord Grey, and endeavoured to get into Parliament, associated with the
Marquis of Douro, to join the Opposition, but failed.

The member for Finsbury, as we have already
shown, was a general resource to those who felt themselves aggrieved; but a case was now submitted to
his good offices that his strong sense of justice obliged
him to support, though in opposition to one of his
warmest friends.

In the year 1846 the displaced civil commissioner

was appointed by the Commander-in-Chief (Duke of Wellington) to the majority of the second regiment of the Tower Hamlets Militia, and in 1855 was promoted by his successor, Lord Combermere, to be its lieutenant-colonel. In the spring of 1858 accusations were brought against him by his colonel, Lord Wilton, of alleged mismanagement of the regimental expenditure, and the commander-in-chief wrote a request to the Secretary at War (General Peel) to have him removed: his colonel having written to Lord Combermere a statement of the causes that had induced his lordship to desire this.

On the 17th of July, 1858, Lieutenant-Colonel Dickson called on Mr. Duncombe and stated his case, and it appeared so flagrant a violation of justice, that two days later he in his place in the House of Commons addressed a question to the Secretary at War on the subject. General Peel replied that Lieutenant-Colonel Dickson, in consequence of certain accusations heard before a regimental court of inquiry, had been invited to resign his commission, but had declined so doing. "It is therefore my intention," he added, "to appoint a military board to inquire further into the charges which had been made against that officer."

Three officers, one being president (Colonel Franklin), assembled at the War Office on the 11th of August for this purpose. Their proceedings appear to have been a make-believe, omitting everything that would have rendered the pretended inquiry a real one. They concluded on the 28th.

The previous court had been formed of three of his junior officers in the regiment: a very improper arrangement, as they would all secure promotion by getting the lieutenant-colonel dismissed. Their report, as we have said, was adverse, and each got a step in rank.

In November, 1858, Lieutenant-Colonel Dickson commenced legal proceedings against his colonel for a libel contained in certain letters. In the same month Mr. Duncombe wrote to General Peel in the character of a peacemaker to have a few minutes' conversation "respecting this very unpleasant and every-day-becoming-more-serious affair; as it really appears to me," he added, "that in bringing down your pigeon you will assuredly kill your crow."

An appointment was made, but owing to a severe attack of illness Mr. Duncombe was prevented from keeping it for several days. He then placed several documents in the hands of the minister; these were shortly afterwards returned, with the intimation that Lieutenant-Colonel Dickson would be superseded by Major Walker, the junior officer who had conducted the first inquiry. In communicating this result, Mr. Duncombe expressed to Lieutenant-Colonel Dickson a very strong opinion on the treatment he had received. He also had the following correspondence with the Right Hon. Mr. Walpole:—

9, Grafton-street, November 10th, 1858.

MY DEAR DUNCOMBE,—I have spoken to General Peel about Colonel Dickson's case, and he hardly consented to postpone yesterday's Gazette until he had made some further inquiries about it.

He now tells me that while a regiment of militia is in a disembodied state, it is impossible by law to have a court-martial; that the usual course under such circumstances is to appoint an officer or officers to make an inquiry into the facts; that this has been done in the present instance, and I rather believe at your suggestion, and that the result of the inquiry is so unfavourable that he cannot do otherwise than recommend the appointment of some one else in his, Colonel Dickson's, place.

The only paper which I have read is Colonel Douglas's report, and I must say it is an uncommonly strong one, and the facts there referred to, if they are true, appear to me to leave to General Peel no other alternative than that which his duty has constrained him to take.

Yours ever, very sincerely,   S. H. WALPOLE.

57, Cambridge-terrace, November 11th, 1858.

MY DEAR MR. WALPOLE,—Very many thanks to you for the trouble you have so kindly taken in this painful affair between " Wilton and Dickson ;" you can do no more, and when Parliament meets I shall move for all the papers connected with it, and then the world will judge who is to blame.

You are quite right in saying that I suggested an inquiry, but then I never dreamt that it could be conducted in so one-sided and unfair a manner as the present, the accuser not only declining to appear, but even his letters (which I have seen), and which would be a justification of the accused, not allowed to be put in.

As to Colonel Douglas's report upon the proceedings, &c., upon which you say General Peel has acted, such report in a question of justice is valueless, because the proceedings upon which such report is based are valueless, and other officers of high rank have seen all the papers, with the rejected correspondence, and have come to a totally different conclusion.

Colonel Dickson will of course now take what course he thinks proper; but I suppose, in the interim, the weakest must go to the wall.

Believe me, yours ever faithfully,   T. S. D.

At the Court of Queen's Bench on the 10th of February, 1859, came on the trial of Dickson *v.* Wilton, which lasted five days. Lord Campbell in summing up made some stringent remarks on the constitution of the regimental court of inquiry, and the "inquiry" at the War Office. The jury gave a verdict in favour of the plaintiff, damages 205*l.**

A second action was preferred against the officer who had succeeded him in the lieutenant-colonelcy of the regiment. Here a verdict was given in favour of the plaintiff, with nominal damages and a withdrawal of all imputations.

Having succeeded thus far, Lieutenant-Colonel Dickson now applied to his colonel for restoration to his rank. This was refused. The leading journals in their comments on the trial were extremely severe upon the system that could sanction the injustice which had then been brought to light. Not half of it, however, had yet been disclosed.

The member for Finsbury was determined to leave no stone unturned to get justice done. He appealed to the Prime Minister; with what effect may be seen in the following correspondence :—

Knowsley, December 31st, 1858.

DEAR SIR,—In a correspondence which has been published in almost all the papers of yesterday by Lieutenant-Colonel Dickson (with what propriety at the present moment I do not stop to inquire), I find the following paragraph in a letter from you to him :—" No officer's commission is safe when, to screen the neglect on the part of others, that commission is unscrupulously assailed by the favoured influences of Grosvenor and St. James's-squares." May I

---

* Heavy damages were expected. The solicitor engaged in the case wrote to Mr. Duncombe 9th of February : "If we get a verdict the amount will be *large*."

ask if by this last expression it is intended to convey an impression that I had any part in the transactions to which it refers? I hope that I may receive from you an unequivocal negative. Indeed, my only reason for asking the question is, that considering my near relationship to Lord Wilton, I can put no other construction on your allusion to the "influences of Grosvenor and St. James's-squares." Otherwise I should have been most unwilling to believe that your ideas and mine of what is due from one gentleman to another should be so widely at variance as that you should feel yourself justified in attributing to me gratuitously, and without the slightest shadow of evidence, participation in proceedings which, whether rightly or wrongly, you characterize as "unscrupulous." Of those proceedings the only information that I possess is derived from a ten minutes' conversation with General Peel, a few days before the date of your letter, when he felt it to be his duty to communicate to me, as the head of the Government, the decision he had formed and the course he had pursued in reference to a case with regard to which I was in such entire ignorance, that I either had never heard or had utterly forgotten that there was any question pending between Lord Wilton and Colonel Dickson. I can readily imagine that you did not intend your letter to Colonel Dickson to be made public; but if it conveys the impression to which I have referred I am quite sure that your sense of gentlemanlike feeling will lead you to make the contradiction as public as has been, by no act of yours, the imputation itself.

I have the honour to be, dear Sir, yours faithfully,

DERBY.

T. S. Duncombe, Esq., M.P.

Cambridge-terrace, January 1st, 1859.

DEAR LORD DERBY,—I have the honour to acknowledge the receipt of your letter of yesterday's date, and, in reply to your question—whether, in the sentence of a letter addressed by me to Colonel Dickson on the 11th of last month, I intended to convey an impression that you had any participation in the proceedings to which it refers—I can unequivocally assure you that I did not, and I think, if you will read the paragraph complained of in connexion with my previous remarks upon the court of inquiry, you will at once acquit me of any such intention or desire to give you pain. When I alluded to " Grosvenor and St. James's-squares," that I had " the Prime Minister" in my mind I do not deny, and, therefore, somewhat in my opinion resembled the court of inquiry, which, from what I hear from those who witnessed its extraordinary proceedings, led them to suppose that its object was more to gain the influence and favour of those distinguished localities than to do justice to one whose commission, I still maintain, has been unscrupulously assailed and unjustly withdrawn. If, however, I have, in my published letter to Colonel Dickson, expressed myself ambiguously and given you pain, I much regret it, and you are at perfect liberty to make public this correspondence. As to the propriety of the unhappy moment when the letters in question have appeared in the papers, I must not be held responsible for their publication, as I can truly assure you that no one more sincerely deplores the loss of your lamented relative than I do, from whom I had through life universally received regard and kindness.

I have the honour to be, dear Lord Derby,

faithfully yours, T. S. DUNCOMBE.

The Right Hon. the Earl of Derby, &c., Knowsley.

Knowsley, January 2nd, 1859.

DEAR SIR,—While I thank you for the friendly tone of your explanatory letter of yesterday, and for your unequivocal assurance that you did not intend to impute to me any participation in proceedings which you so strongly condemn, I am compelled to say that I cannot look upon it as entirely satisfactory, for you admit that in the expressions used you had " the Prime Minister " in your mind, and that you meant to convey that " the object of the court of inquiry was more to gain the influence and favour of those distinguished localities, Grosvenor and St. James's-squares, than to do justice." Surely you cannot fail to perceive that this conveys an impression that I had some personal interest in the decision of a case of which I knew nothing, and that my favour and influence, as a Minister, were to be propitiated by taking a particular course, irrespective of the demands of justice.   I feel confident the court of inquiry (I do not even know how it was composed) never allowed such an idea to enter the minds of its members, and I cannot but think that on reflection you will yourself feel that any allusion to my name and position in reference to this matter was gratuitous and uncalled for.   As, however, I am not fond of referring personal questions to the newspapers, I shall, while thanking you for the permission to make our correspondence public, decline to avail myself of it, and shall leave the matter in your hands, to take any step or none at all, as your own sense of honour may dictate to you.   I am gratified by the terms in which you refer to Lady Wilton, and you are aware that I wholly acquitted you of any share of responsibility for the time selected for the publication of these papers.

I have the honour to be, dear Sir, yours faithfully,

DERBY.

T. S. Duncombe, Esq., M.P.

Cambridge-terrace, January 3rd, 1859.

DEAR LORD DERBY,—As I consider (after the publication of my letter to Colonel Dickson, and the inferences that may possibly be drawn from it) your disclaimer of all knowledge of the composition or proceedings of the court of inquiry, so honourable to yourself, that it would be unjust to you in your position to leave the matter in any sort of doubt, I will, with your leave by return of post, take upon myself the publication of our entire correspondence ; as, in consideration of Colonel Dickson's interests, I could not with propriety make public my own individual explanation of your personal complaint.

I have the honour to be, dear Lord Derby,
yours faithfully,   T. S. DUNCOMBE.

To the Right Hon. the Earl of Derby, &c.

Knowsley, January 4th, 1859.

MY DEAR SIR,—I cannot, of course, object to your publication of our correspondence, if you think that the best mode of removing the erroneous impression which your letter of the 11th appeared to me to convey. It must, however, be distinctly understood that in disclaiming any participation in the course taken either by Lord Wilton or the committee of inquiry I do not adopt your views respecting it, nor impute any impropriety to either one or the other.

I am, dear Sir, yours faithfully,   DERBY.

T. S. Duncombe, Esq., M.P.

Lady Combermere in referring to the trial has permitted her affectionate solicitude for the veteran field-marshal to give an air of exaggeration to her statement.* That Lord Combermere did not consider himself unfairly treated during his examination is evident from his subsequently sending Mr. Edwin James an invitation to Combermere Abbey on learning that he was staying in the neighbourhood. There can be no question that his lordship was remarkably amiable, the record of his long and honourable career establishes this beyond the possibility of doubt; but when commander-in-chief, though he acknowledged that he could make neither head nor tail of Lord Wilton's accusations against Lieutenant-Colonel Dickson, he deprived the latter of his commission, and laid himself open to a charge of undue severity.

The *Times* in a leading article thus summed up the merits of the case :—

As soon as time has been given to ascertain if the decision is to be a final one, it is to be presumed that this

* "Memoirs and Correspondence of Field-Marshal Viscount Combermere, G.C.B.," vol. ii. p. 340.

officer's reinstatement in his military position will follow as a matter of course. If not, General Peel must inform the world what are his grounds for differing from a verdict which a jury have brought in under the direction of the Chief-Justice. If Lord Wilton's declarations and expressions were, as the jury have declared them to be, false and slanderous, *Colonel Dickson has as good a right to be in the army as General Peel.* If not, the truth must be shown."

Mr. Duncombe gave his ill-used client a last chance for securing justice by presenting a petition from him to the House of Commons in the month of June, 1859, stating his complaint and praying for a fair inquiry.

Certain facts having, as he alleged, come to the knowledge of Lieut.-Col. Dickson, he in his turn demanded a court of inquiry on Lord Wilton. He engaged Mr. Edwin James as his counsel, when the application was granted. This investigation excited infinitely more interest than the preceding, for it had become known that charges of a peculiar character were about to be preferred against the earl, and that among the witnesses to be examined were the Marchioness of Westminster, the Dowager Marchioness of Aylesbury, and Major-General Peel. The members of the court being of a higher standing suggested more important revelations. This court assembled on the 4th of June, at the Horse Guards, and consisted of Brigadier-General Russell (president), with Colonel Sir Alfred Horsford and Colonel Parke. Intense was the excitement with which the public waited this third trial; still more intense was their disappointment when at the commencement of the proceedings Lieut.-Col. Dickson handed to the president a written statement signed by him, that in compliance with an arrangement entered into between Mr. Edwin James, on behalf of the Earl of Wilton, and Mr. Duncombe acting for himself (Lieut.-Col. Dickson) he had withdrawn the charges he had preferred against his lordship.

He also forwarded the following communication to Lord Combermere, as well as his Royal Highness the Duke of Cambridge, and the Hon. Sidney Herbert:—

10, Stanhope-terrace, Hyde-park, W., 4th June, 1860.

MY LORD,—I have the honour to inform your lordship that I have this day considered it my duty to withdraw the charges I have preferred against Colonel the Earl of Wilton, in consequence of those charges having been fully and satisfactorily explained to Mr. Duncombe, M.P., on my part, and Mr. Edwin James, M.P., on the part of Lord Wilton; to which gentlemen we agreed to refer the case. I have the honour to be, my lord,

Your obedient humble servant,

LOTHIAN DICKSON,

Deputy Lieut., and late Lieut.-Col.
2nd Tower Hamlets Militia.

F. M. Viscount Combermere, G.C.H., &c.

This extraordinary result took every one as usual by surprise, as did the announcement that Lieut.-Col. Dickson's counsel had left his client and gone over to the other side; but the chapter of surprises was far from exhausted. According to the lieutenant-colonel's statement, in one of his pamphlets, " he was advised to place himself unreservedly in the hands of Mr. Duncombe," which he did; and Mr. Edwin James having been accepted as the representative of Lord

Wilton, the following terms of settlement were agreed to :—

First.—That the lieutenant-colonel acknowledges having placed his case in the hands of Mr. Duncombe; and Mr. Duncombe having recommended him to withdraw his charges against Lord Wilton, he shall go before the court of inquiry and do so.

Second.—The referees, on behalf of Lord Wilton, undertake to use their best efforts with the authorities of the War-office and the Horse Guards to restore to Lieut.-Col. Dickson the position he has lost in his profession, and endeavour to obtain for him some employment consistent with his former rank.

Third.—Lieut.-Colonel Dickson having incurred a large expense arising out of the disputes and charges against him, Mr. Duncombe has represented this to Mr. Edwin James, who has agreed on Lord Wilton's behalf to pay Colonel Dickson 600*l.* upon the arrangement being carried out.

After signing this, the referees put an addendum—

If any publication appears connected with the charges, this arrangement is null and void.

The first part of this treaty was carried out, as we have seen; the third article was performed on the 14th of June, when the lieutenant-colonel gave a receipt for a cheque for 600*l.* handed to him by Mr. Edwin James. The completion of the agreement by the fulfilment of the second article Lieut.-Colonel Dickson waited for in vain. Mr. Duncombe remonstrated against Lord Wilton's delay, and on the 8th of November, 1860, suggested that Lord Wilton should write letters to the Commander-in-Chief and to the Secretary at War, recommending the lieutenant-colonel's restoration to his rank. His lordship did nothing of the kind. Mr. Edwin James at last (December 12th) stated his client's reluctance to adopt the plan suggested, and his own determination to withdraw from further intervention. Mr. Duncombe enclosed the communication the next day, considering it very satisfactory; and declined further interference.

Lieutenant-Colonel Dickson, now left to his own resources, threatened to publish the charges he had withdrawn, which brought another negotiator on the scene in the person of Mr. Wyld, M.P., of Charing-cross, who represented himself as being authorized to offer a material guarantee of 5000*l.* for fulfilling proposals then made. Lord Wilton repudiated the negotiation; and Lieut.-Colonel Dickson then published a shilling pamphlet, bearing the title, " Why he Did It," in which he printed the withdrawn charges which in his letters to the Duke of Cambridge, Lord Combermere, and the Hon. Sidney Herbert, M.P., he had acknowledged to have been " fully and satisfactorily explained."

As Mr. Duncombe prudently declined further interference in a quarrel he found it impossible to adjust, we cannot do better than imitate that proceeding. We refrain, therefore, from following the lieutenant-colonel into the scandals he thought proper to make public. A careful perusal of the unperformed article of the agreement will satisfy every unprejudiced mind that Lord Wilton was not bound to fulfil it, even if he had the power, which is doubtful. It only binds the referees to use their " best efforts" for Lieut.-Colonel Dickson's restoration, and to endeavour " to obtain him fitting employment."

There can be no doubt that both Mr. Duncombe and Mr. Edwin James were aware that the conditions they had agreed to did not enable them to go beyond employing their *best efforts*, and *endeavouring*, &c. This having been done, the affair was at an end as far as they were concerned. The responsibility of the publication rests entirely with the author.

In 1859 Lieut.-Colonel Dickson was a candidate for Marylebone, and requested Mr. Duncombe's recommendation to the electors. He gave it (on the understanding that none of his own friends were going to start), to the extent of answering a letter asking " What sort of a character you give the gallant colonel." The candidate then put forward an address to the electors, followed by a memorandum suggesting liberal support and early attendance at the poll, signed "Thomas S. Duncombe, M.P., chairman," unauthorized by Mr. Duncombe, who several days before had addressed a letter to him recommending his withdrawal, as he had no chance of being returned.* The result confirmed these anticipations, Lord Fermoy securing a majority of nearly four to one over Dickson.

We are afraid from the revelations made at the trial that the 2nd Regiment of Tower Hamlets militia was but indifferently officered, and that while it was embodied but little was done by either subalterns or field officers to render it effective beyond the ordi-

* In a letter dated " Cambridge-terrace, Hyde-park, June 28th," he concluded : "I must earnestly recommend you, therefore, not to prolong a canvass, or persevere in a contest which can only terminate in either a ruinous outlay or great disappointment." The whole of this letter was subsequently published, followed by the result of the poll, which proved the soundness of the writer's advice.

nary playing at soldiers had recourse to on such occasions. The mess seems to have been the chief source of interest, and jollifications at Woolwich or Cremorne the principal service thought of. That the mess accounts, therefore, should get into confusion was to be expected; but this did not justify Colonel Lord Wilton in accusing Lieutenant-Colonel Dickson of mismanagement and defalcation, nor in ordering a court of inquiry of juniors to try their superior officer; nor did it justify Lord Combermere—because, as the commander-in-chief acknowledged, he could make neither head nor tail of the colonel's charges—in causing the lieutenant-colonel to be dismissed the service. No one could blame Lieutenant-Colonel Dickson, under such circumstances, in bringing his action against Lord Wilton.

The only thing really surprising in the affair is the inadequacy of the damages awarded by the jury. So miserable a compensation for professional ruin could not be regarded at the Horse Guards as entitling an officer, thus as it were imperfectly acquitted, to restoration to rank: nor could it oblige the colonel to insist on such an *amende honorable.* A shrewd lawyer like Mr. Edwin James could not have been unaware of this himself, or have neglected to represent it to his co-referee; and this view of the case must have made Mr. Duncombe follow Mr. James's example in washing his hands of the affair.

While it was in progress the Government wisely placed his Royal Highness the Duke of Cambridge at the head of the military administration of the country. Never had a change in this important department been so necessary; and it was not long before the

British army, as well as the kingdom generally, felt the advantage of it. His Royal Highness, with characteristic energy, devoted himself to the arduous and responsible employment he accepted, and laboured with such zeal and earnestness of purpose that the confusion and feebleness which had distinguished that branch of the public service since the commencement of the Crimean war, were superseded by a system more worthy of one of the great European powers.

The Duke's profound interest in the service was established by his unremitting endeavours to elevate it in public estimation. If anything could be more praiseworthy than his exertions in this direction, as pre-eminently for the advantage of the men as for that of their officers, it must be found in his solicitude for their moral and intellectual advancement. Under the auspices of his Royal Highness the position of the well-conducted private has become vastly improved, quite as much so as that of the non-commissioned officers; while members of the middle and upper classes entering the army have found that the Queen's commission has secured them a social status equally honourable with that conferred by admission into the most favoured professions.

His labours in behalf of the soldier's widow or orphan equally deserve recognition—in truth, in every way his Royal Highness has earned the title of "The Soldier's Friend." Moreover, his readiness of access, his urbanity, his attention to the reasonable complaints and desires of even the humblest subaltern, render him as popular among the officers as his kindness of heart has made him popular with the men.

It must not be forgotten that while his Royal

Highness has been thus establishing the efficiency of the regular army, he has afforded a cordial and enlightened encouragement to the Volunteer system. To the readiness with which he gave all his influence to that patriotic movement, may be attributed the development it has received. His example put a stop to all display of professional jealousy, and created that kindly interest in the volunteers which the officers of the army, much to their honour, invariably evince.

The Duke's services in the field will not be forgotten by his country; though its attention has of late years been engrossed by the national importance of those in the Cabinet. As an administrator and director of the military department of this empire his Royal Highness stands nearer to the illustrious Wellington than any commander-in-chief who has succeeded him at the Horse Guards.

We have only to add that, for an unusually long period, the Duke of Cambridge remained one of the warmest friends of Mr. Duncombe; who invariably expressed the highest opinion of his Royal Highness's private as well as of his public character.

CHAPTER XII.

THE EMPEROR AND THE DUKE.

Brief communication from Paris—Hostility among the Republicans created by the Emperor's restoration of the Pope—Attempt at Assassination—Captain Felix Orsini—The French Colonels—Complaints of M. Persigny to the English Government—" Conspiracy to Murder Bill "—Mr. Duncombe defends the Emperor in the House of Commons—An indignant radical—The Duke of Brunswick's unrivalled bracelet—" L. N. Paris Notes "—The Jersey Revolutionists and "l'Homme"—Catalogue of the Brunswick diamonds—The Duke sends for his Will—Mr. Duncombe returns it—The Duke's valet absconds with diamonds—Bursting of the bubble—Imperial disappointments.

THE Queen went to Paris this year to return the Emperor and Empress's visit. Mr. Duncombe had few communications from Paris; there was nothing of importance going on there, therefore there was nothing to write about. The emperor seemed to be absorbed in carrying out a grand design for the improvement of Paris, and in collecting materials for his edition of Julius Cæsar. The duke seemed equally given up to diamonds and revenge. If he ever regarded his heir, apparently it was not with any intention of expediting his bequest if he could help it. He cared only to accumulate, and wanted but a reliable method of securing the riches of this world as a provision for the next. There is only a paragraph or two to add respecting him :—

Hotel de Folkestone, Boulogne-sur-Mer,
September 21st, 1855.

With respect to Beaujon we cannot be better; no one
can, or rather could have been, more kind, and, from his
letters, likely to continue so.   He wants me to spend a
little time with him, which I must endeavour to do.   I
quite agree with you about rather trusting French women
than men, and I think with D. B.'s increasing age he is
becoming more steady, and therefore the less cause exists
for family or domestic disagreements; and although it may
never come to pass, as you say, still it is to me a great
satisfaction to keep all right, and I should think I had lost
a great deal if I had lost that chance.

Your view with respect to Ceylon is quite correct; and I
always knew it was a battle of interest, but dared not say
so, for fear you should decline.

There had been no difficulty in this fulfilment of
the Napoleonic programme.   As it was at the call of
the nation that Prince Louis Napoleon had accepted
the Presidency of the Republic, ostensibly at the same
appeal he had mounted the imperial throne.   The
nation had again been put to the vote, and by the
suffrages of the masses he had been elected Emperor
of the French.   This gave mortal offence to the
French Republicans, who from a safe distance assailed
him with the most virulent abuse.   Yet there was a
power much more powerful to Napoleon III., and it
became imperative on him to propitiate it: this was
the influence of legitimacy at home and abroad.   There
could be no difficulty in proving—

I. That an established revolutionary government in
France would be dangerous to the monarchical institutions of Europe.

II. That the support of the French empire would

be a security against a further development of European republicanism.

These ideas obtained general acceptance; and an understanding was soon come to between the old great powers and the new great power, that the Emperor should be maintained in his position on condition that he repressed democracy wherever it became active, and more particularly assist in putting it down in Rome, where a republic had been established under the direction of the triumvirate, Armellini, Mazzini, and Saffi. The entire priesthood of France necessarily became his ardent supporters when made aware that he was about to restore the fugitive head of their church to his dominions. The same support from the same cause was freely extended to him by zealous Catholics of all countries, clerical and lay.

The Holy Father remained at Gaeta, under the protection of the King of Naples. More than one invitation to return had reached him from his revolted subjects; but his holiness prudently bided his time, awaiting the result of pending negotiations with the new ruler of France. The mysterious assassination of Count Rossi had evidently left a profound impression upon his mind; nor were some of the proceedings of the more reckless republicans likely to reassure him. It is true that in the capital, order was said to prevail, but deplorable excesses were committed elsewhere. So rife was assassination at Ancona, fifteen miles distant, that the triumvirs dispatched an officer of theirs to visit that town, armed with their declarations against such crimes. That officer was *Captain Felix Orsini!* and if anything can be more edifying than the secret instructions of the republican government to their commissioner, it is the report of his official proceedings from the commissioner to his government.*

It seemed to be acknowledged by all Catholic monarchical governments having an interest in Italy, that the continuance of the Roman republic was impossible; therefore a French army, with Austrian, Sardinian, and Neapolitan supports, invaded the Pontifical States. It is but justice to acknowledge that the Romans made a defence of their city worthy of their name, General Oudinot having been twice repulsed in an attempt to carry it by assault. It must also be admitted, from creditable testimony, that the triumvirs contrived in this season of tremendous excitement to keep the people under something like control. Three Jesuits were murdered on the bridge of St. Angelo, and about half a dozen priests shot in the barracks of St. Calisto; but these were manifestations of Lynch law with which the government had nothing to do.

It was at last seen that it would be madness to continue to defend the walls against such an overwhelming force, and M. de Lesseps, as the representative of France, began to negotiate with Mazzini for a capitulation. The former wrote to his government announcing that this distinguished republican was putting himself into the hands of the English Protestants, and that he ought to be induced to look to France only as the protector of Italian liberty.† The clever Genoese must have gulled the French ambassador egregiously if he made that gentleman believe that "he was wishing to favour a religious schism!"

* "Actes Officiels de la République Romaine," p. 83.
† Idem, p. 108.

He cared no more for Protestantism than for Popery,
but was anxious to make the best terms he could in
the desperate position in which he found himself
placed.

Terms were arranged, but General Oudinot refused
to respect them. M. de Lesseps indignantly returned
to Paris, and the besiegers recommenced the attack.
After a sharp struggle the defences were carried, and
the French army once more became masters of Rome.
The Emperor of the French had now an opportunity
of assuring the head of the Catholic Church that he
could return to the Vatican whenever he pleased, and
of course was the recipient of the thanks of the entire
Catholic community. The leading republicans lost no
time in making their escape. How the Papal government proceeded when re-established under the protection of a French army of occupation has already been
told.

The Emperor of France certainly did not improve
his relations with his democratic acquaintances of
either France or Italy, by thus stamping out their
first institution; but they found themselves powerless. They hated him, denounced him, abused him,
but could do him no harm. He had recreated an
empire, it was also his ambition to found a dynasty.
He wisely departed from the example of his imperial
predecessor. Having sought a partner—not from
among Austrian archduchesses—not even out of that
little *libro d'oro* the "Almanach de Gotha," but a
very noble woman for all that—one of those rare
women of whom in praise it is impossible to say too
much. An imperial prince in due course blessed the
auspicious union. Again there was a departure from

the Napoleonic programme. He was not proclaimed "King of Rome," though pretensions to the title might have been put forward on his behalf more substantial than were those of his predecessor.

Mr. Duncombe's secretary went backwards and forwards to Paris three or four times this year. A report forwarded in March, 1856, includes the duke's ideas on the condition of Europe. The Austrian terms are curious, if true; his fraternal intentions are equally so; and the supposed treaty with Prussia more singular than either.

St. James's-street, March 28th, 1856.

I met a friend of mine this morning, a French engineer, and spoke with him on the subject of a château in the south, and after explaining as far as was necessary, he said, I know of no place where climate and retirement would so well suit as Bezières, between Narbonne and Montpelier, and to convince how beautiful the climate is, Corneille, when writing of that part, said, " If ever God takes up his abode on earth Bezières will be the place he will choose, for there, and there only, you have and enjoy all that is good of all climates, without having even a shadow of their clouds, and the earth is more fruitful there than in any other part of the world."

My friend tells me that you are there in the centre of the olive and the grape; that partridges, woodcocks, and snipes abound, besides quails; that in two days' journey you can have bear and wolf shooting, and in one hour on horseback you can ride to the shores of the Mediterranean. There is an hotel, the Hôtel du Commerce, at which you can dine at the *table d'hôte*, with wine of ten years old at discretion, and twenty-eight *plats*, for fifty sous *par tête*, and good wine to be had three halfpence per bottle. He says the plan would be to go to the hotel, and from thence make your excursions château hunting. He has given me the address of his friend, a lawyer there, to whom I shall write. The method you will have to adopt is to hire the château and furnish it from the cabinet-maker's by hiring the furniture. There is also a Jesuit living in the town who speaks good English ; he is the only person near who knows or speaks that language. If you look at the map you will see it is much farther south than Pau, and certainly looks to be well situate. I know nothing of the place ; and never heard of it before.

I have received the enclosed from H. J. D. and have acknowledged the receipt. The duke, when I saw him the other day, was quite well, but very busy making a large bracelet, which he wants me to try to show to the queen. It will be the finest bracelet in the world ; and will be of an immense value when finished, and I have got it in my possession. I will show it to nurse, who will, I am sure, admire it ! The regent was rather in high spirits, for it appears that Austria wishing, *sub rosa*, to have the power of deciding the question of the German, *i.e.* Prussian Bund, and feeling desirous not to show her teeth without being sure of being supported by the minor German Powers, has been proposing terms to our regent something to the following effect, viz., that she, Austria, will be very glad to allow him to reside in Vienna, and receive him as a sovereign ; that she will undertake the settlement of his claim upon the following terms : first, that he shall marry, and, secondly, that he shall at once see his brother William and forgive and forget all animosities. There are then some political terms, and so the negotiation ended on their part for the moment, only that the person who brought the news over asked if the regent would have any objection to see the Austrian minister in London if the said minister should seek an interview, to which the regent replied, that at any time upon the minister writing for an audience he would grant one. The regent's reply to the Austrian Government was to this effect, viz., that he had no objection to marry ; that he most decidedly objected to being in any way bound, and would not be, to any act which would compromise his having the power to punish his brother

William both as an usurper as well as a traitor; that he claimed that right as sovereign *de facto*, although by his brother's usurpation not *de jure*; that the punishment for such offences was death by the axe-man, and that he called upon them not to interfere in any way with the "jurisprudence" of Brunswick, and that he begged, if the matter was to be at all entertained, that no interference should take place with respect to the sentence he should pass on his brother; that if he could not find him he should condemn him and punish him *par contumace*, and should carry the final sentence into execution whenever he could catch him; that he should not quit this country without having under his command 6000 troops, natives of Ireland, all officered, and to be called his body-guard. He has also heard from Prussia, I think from the Queen of Prussia, by which it appears that Persigny never mentioned the regent's name while at the Court of Berlin. It appears that his mission to Berlin was to the following effect, viz., that she, France, was desirous of pushing her frontier so far that she might have a small portion of the Rhine; that if Prussia would accord or aid her in obtaining that so-desired frontier she, France, in return would acquiesce in any act of Prussia, either by insisting that Switzerland should give up any refugees Prussia might require, and promised that France should march an army to demand them into Switzerland, and further that she, France, was desirous of entering into a treaty offensive and defensive, to enable them, the two great Powers of Europe, to endeavour to balance the power and at the same time to keep down socialism, *i.e.* liberty. To the honour of Prussia, she refused.

I do not think there is much chance of Austria and the regent coming to terms; but he says if he should be induced to go to Vienna he shall leave his money in my hands: so you see there is, as you may suppose, some little excitement going on.

I dare say we shall soon have to inform the prince of his unhandsome conduct. The regent is waiting for another letter from Prussia.

We have no means of ascertaining whether the un-rivalled bracelet was ever submitted to her Majesty's inspection. The possessor of the koh-i-noor and the crown jewels was not likely to have cared for the or-nament, matchless though it may have been; and after what has been publicly shown in this way in our last Universal Exhibition, and the decorative treasures since completed by Emmanuel and other first-class London and Paris jewellers, and the recent Es-terhazy display, it is difficult to believe in the assump-tion of its supremacy. Nevertheless it is unquestion-able that the duke is the greatest diamond merchant in the world, probably the greatest stock-broker also. This granted, the question naturally arises—If, as he complains, he has been deprived of his private for-tune, whence came this prodigious wealth?

The mystery, we imagine, may thus be explained. The duke did not lose all his private fortune by the revolution at Brunswick. He secured an ample income in England, and being possessed of great financial genius, attempted to rival the Rothschilds—with tolerable success.

The duke's chief occupation at this time was the care of his collection of diamonds, which he watched over with the affection of a parent. Each had a his-tory as well as a value, and he thought of producing a catalogue that should do them justice. He enter-tained no apprehensions for their safety. The pri-soner of Ham was now Emperor of the French, and though he delayed restoring him to his duchy, he might be relied upon for securing the safety of his treasures. But it would be doing him injustice to state that his attention was entirely engrossed by a study of the number of carats in each of these precious acquisitions. He was a keen politician, and as he still believed himself to be a sovereign prince, professed a princely regard for the royalties of Europe.

By the French people the emperor was regarded with enthusiastic devotion, including the army, the clergy, and the industrious classes. The republicans scowled and conspired, but were well looked after by the police. No one seemed to think that there need be any apprehension about them. Suddenly a tremendous explosion in one of the thoroughfares in Paris, into which the emperor's equipage had passed, suggested the fearful idea of another infernal machine. When the cause was ascertained as well as the results, it was found to be an explosive bomb of a very destructive character that had been thrown under the imperial carriage. The emperor escaped, and the missile dealt death among the crowd that had thronged the *pavé*.

The scoundrel who had invented this means of perpetuating the infamy of his name, was discovered to be an Italian, an Italian republican, the identical *Captain Felix Orsini* who in the confidence of Mazzini had been sent to put down assassination in Ancona ! It was moreover ascertained that he had just arrived from London, where the principal Italian republicans had found refuge.

This catastrophe excited a deep feeling of indignation in England, where, notwithstanding the publications of the exiled republicans, the emperor had many admirers. It was on lord mayor's day, 1855, that the French ambassador, M. de Persigny, after the civic banquet, in an admirable speech announced that the Anglo-French alliance was beyond the reach of intrigue. Yet the Orsini plot, under the impression that it had been matured in England, unquestionably gave it a rude shock. Some French colonels presented an address to the emperor of an unquestionably belli-cose nature. The ambassador complained in a letter to Lord Clarendon that the right of asylum had been abused, and asked if hospitality was due to assassins.

At last so much pressure was put upon the Govern-ment that a "Conspiracy to Murder Bill" was brought into Parliament for the purpose of checking the action of reckless republicans. That it was time to repress their sanguinary spirit there could not be any doubt, as publications recommending murder were by no means infrequent.* But the ultra-Liberals in Eng-land opposed the measure in and out of Parliament with the utmost energy. Mr. Gilpin while speaking against it in the House (February 7th, 1858,) referred in strong terms to the Boulogne expedition, and not only accused the director of it of acting precisely as Orsini had done in plotting the overthrow of a foreign government in a state that was affording him an asylum, but charged him with the crime of assassina-tion—a man having been shot in the *mêlée*. The fol-lowing day Mr. Duncombe addressed the House in a powerful defence of the emperor, in which he com-pletely disproved the accusation against him. His pistol had gone off, but the wounded man had re-covered. This statement was challenged by one or two writers in the newspapers on the authority of the "Annual Register" and the "Almanach de Boulogne"; nevertheless it is perfectly true. The member for Finsbury's fidelity to his friend produced the follow-ing declaration from one of his radical constituents :—

* One, "Tyrannicide: is it justifiable?" is worthy of the Reign of Terror.

Sir,—In your speech upon the Conspiracy Bill on Tuesday last you are reported to have said that in the event of certain tactics being pursued by Louis Napoleon the people of England would have given their sanction to the introduction of that Bill, an assertion which I believe to be very far indeed from correct; and then, Sir, you follow up your advocacy of this despot's cause by walking out of the House without evincing the moral courage of giving effect to your voice by your vote. Verily, the people of Finsbury, if not afraid of the fire-eating colonels in the French service, ought to be ashamed of their democratic representative in the company of Disraeli & Co., aiding to inaugurate a system of espionage utterly repulsive to the feelings of Englishmen. Sir, if this report is correct I can never vote for you again.

Mr. Duncombe was certainly in a position of some embarrassment, popular feeling having been excited by the *fanfaronnade* of the French officers. The Liberals were against granting the Executive additional powers, and the exiled republicans were furious against the measure. He could not reconcile himself to neglecting the interests of an absent friend, and did not care to conceal his detestation of the miserable plotters by whom his valuable life was menaced. He therefore took the middle course that lost him the support of a constituent: having successfully defended the emperor from a gratuitous slander, he left the House, without voting for or against the Government measure. We believe that his conduct was not appreciated by Mazzini and his friends. That it did him no disservice in Finsbury was proved in the election of the following year, when he polled the largest number of votes he had ever obtained.

That the frequent visits of Mr. Duncombe's secretary were not always to Beaujon may naturally be inferred. That confidential communications passed through this medium is equally probable from what has already been stated; but written evidence of this has not been preserved. The only document that illustrates this remarkable intimacy at this period is endorsed :—

" Notes of Conversation between L. N. and G. T. S., January 12th, 1859. Seen and approved by L. N., and entitled—' L. N., Paris Notes, January 12th, 1859.' "

L. N. *Paris Notes.*

January 12th, 1859.

That England proposes a Conference for the double purpose of saving bloodshed and settling the question of Italy by diplomacy instead of force of arms, entirely forgetting the position of Austria in Italy. This proposition at first glance appears very plausible, and is likely to have weight with those who only look at the surface of things, but on a closer inspection it will be found quite Utopian, seeing that Austria holds her Italian provinces as conquerors, and it would be hopeless under such conditions of tenure that she would permit, or aid in the slightest degree, any reform, for any such policy introduced by her would be suicidal, and it is absurd to suppose she would aid in her own destruction.

The most remarkable part of this question is the position taken by England, who for the last twenty years has openly instigated and avowedly recognised and protected every insurrectionary movement in Italy that professed to have for its object the liberation of that country, and now that the moment has arrived for carrying out those views she (England) throws obstacles in the way of its success.

There existed about this time a journal in the French language published in the island of Jersey under the title of *L'Homme,* that was the organ of the French democrats, and under the direction of Victor Hugo. On the Queen's return from visiting the emperor and empress at Paris a letter was addressed to her Majesty, printed in the columns of that journal, and signed with the names—"Felix Pyat, Rougée, Jourdain—Council of the Revolutionary Committee." It was not only a gross attack upon the emperor, but called her Majesty to task, she being " a respectable woman," for visiting "the man Bonaparte." It was unquestionably in the worst possible taste, and an outrage on the hospitality these men had obtained when they fled from France. Jersey was within thirty miles of the French coast, and the English Government could no longer endure the responsibility of permitting these acknowledged revolutionists to defy an ally and neighbour and insult their sovereign.

The people of Jersey first took up the matter, and threatened *L'Homme* and its office with destruction. The *Times* denounced the letter of M. Pyat, and the civil authorities of the island then banished the literary staff of the offending paper. Then Kossuth wrote a long letter, not for publication in England, but in the United States. It appeared in the *New York Daily Times.* He expresses disapproval of the offensive letter; nevertheless wrote an apology for the French democrats. The letter concludes with something very like a sneer at England's French alliance, as indicating, he asserts, the "load of a nightmare on the anxious breast of Britannia created by the name of Bonaparte." This communication was reprinted in England, and did great harm to the writer among a large and influential class.

Towards the close of the year 1860 the Duke of Brunswick again had to try the issue of a court of law; but this time *nolens volens*. A man named Welsener had printed a catalogue of the duke's diamonds, *one thousand two hundred* in number, valued at 15,300,000 francs, on the agreement of paying $3\frac{1}{2}$ cents per page for each copy, which made the cost 9830 francs. The duke denied the agreement, and offered to pay 3500 francs. The tribunal, however, awarded 6000 francs. Extensive as is this collection, it was stated in the pleadings that the duke was then in treaty for the purchase of two more gems, one at the price of 1,100,000 francs, the other at 3,000,000 francs.

Mr. Duncombe entertained misgivings respecting his splendid inheritance. Although his secretary was still frequently sent to Paris, the testator and the heir had not seen each other for many years. The latter was kept acquainted with his friend's proceedings, but did not go to Paris. Occasionally he had interviews with the duke's former equerry, Baron Andlau, at whose school his son was educated; but no written communication came from the duke.

We now add a few notes from Mr. Duncombe's ex-secretary. Their tone is somewhat different from previous reports; but the writer was now, or about to become, a gentleman at large :—

December 19th, 1860.

I hardly think it possible to come after Christmas, as I go to Beaujon on the 28th, and think it just possible that Colonel Favé, *aide-de-camp de l'Empereur,* will require my services, at least so he told me before he left with *l'Impératrice*.

L. N., you are quite right, has made a good hit, and had Parliament been sitting I would have given you the opportunity of stating that there was every probability of such a measure being decreed ere long.

"The Pope's Wrongs, &c." is written by a very clever friend of mine, the defender of Radstadt in 1848 against the Prussian army; passed seven years in the prison Spielberg, and wore a leathern mask the whole time. The Introduction I had something to do with. I shall see him on Saturday, and I am sure he will be pleased with your remarks on his work.

You know there is an old adage, that Rome was not built in a day, and it is clearly demonstrated that the Pope cannot be made to quit Rome in a day. Believe me, L. N. is quite right; you must bear in mind that he rules a Catholic nation containing many bigots, and if the Pope would run away all would turn up as you would wish. But it will not do to let Pius IX. become a martyr, which he is seeking to do; you may rely upon it his account will be reckoned up ere long.

Ten years of communication through the secretary elapsed before any more notice was taken by the testator of his remarkable will. In the spring of 1861 the former was sent for as usual, and proceeded to Beaujon, as he had done a hundred times before. Whether the issue of the diamond cause only a few months before had produced an ill effect on the Duke of Brunswick's benevolent intentions, is not known; but it is certain that he had ceased to regard Mr. Duncombe as his heir. It must here be stated that when the duke placed the will in his hands he exacted a promise in writing to restore it when demanded.

We now leave Mr. Smith to make his report:—

21, Rue Beaujon, Paris, March 19th, 1861.

MY DEAR SIR,—On Saturday the 16th I left London by the tidal train, which ought to deposit me in Paris at 11 P.M. I arrived at his Royal Highness's tired, and went to bed.

On Sunday morning his Royal Highness sent to me about 10 o'clock in the morning to say as soon as I was dressed he wished to see me before I went out. As soon as I was ready I went to his Royal Highness, who said, This is a bad day, 17th, and you have arrived twice lately on a 7. I replied, I think, your Royal Highness, I was in the house before 12 o'clock last night. The valet said it was ten minutes past 12. His Royal Highness then said, My reason for sending for you is, that I thought you would not care to run about Paris with the large sum of money you have, and although I am not ready to settle accounts with you (he being in bed), you can seal up the packet, or how you like, and we will settle by-and-bye. He then told me he had been very ill, and that the countess was very ill also. After saying, I wish you could suggest some plan to do away with the " curatelle," his Royal Highness said, I have been thinking a great deal about my testament lately, and I intend to change it, as to its legality, and you must get my testament back from Mr. Duncombe. I replied, Your Royal Highness, that requires an authority from your Royal Highness. He then said, speaking in the plural, you would have less difficulty with a French will than with an English one here in France. The conversation here ended, and I, having some important appointments, left his Royal Highness. I may safely say this is all that passed.

In passing the garden I saw the countess, who was looking very ill, and she said, I was just going to write to you to say that I am so unwell that I cannot do the honours of the table, and as I am sure you would not care to dine here alone when you have so many friends in Paris, I intended to say that you must excuse me and not expect as heretofore our 6 o'clock dinners; to-day will be an exception, as some ladies are coming who will entertain you at table. The dinner hour came; the countess did not come down. We dined, and during the dinner the duke sent twice for me; the second time, dinner being over, I went to his Royal Highness in his dressing-room. I settled my account with him, and said, As your Royal Highness is not going out I

will remain at home and play chess; to which his Royal
Highness replied, I fear it will worry me too much.   He
then said, Did you meet my cousin, the Prince of Wasa, on
the stairs?   I said I did.   He then said, Here is the paper
for Mr. Duncombe.

His Royal Highness threw across the table a paper, of
which the following is a copy:—

"I authorize Mr. George Smith to withdraw my testament from the hands of Mr. Thomas Duncombe, in order
to frame it according to the laws of France.

"Paris, this 18th of March, 1861.   .

"DUKE OF BRUNSWICK."

Now I think, as I find by your letter to-day, the post-
office are playing tricks, you had better hand the document
in question to me on my return to London, and I will bring
it to Paris my next visit here.   I mention this because it
was suggested that you should send it per post.   I have
not seen his royal highness since, but shall write to him in
a few minutes to know his movements to-day.   I can only
add, that his royal highness seems kindly disposed towards
us.

As this narrative is truthful, and the communication
official, you had better write a reply either to his royal
highness direct, or, as I should suggest, through me to his
royal highness.   This you had better do by return of post,
as I shall not be longer than the end of the week.

The precious document was surrendered on the
messenger producing his authority, and nothing more
heard of it.   There is no evidence among Mr. Duncombe's papers that he had any further communication with the duke.

Once more the Duke of Brunswick's name figured
in the French tribunals.   His valet suffered himself
to be tempted by the enormous wealth that was constantly glittering before his eyes.   He fled with a
small Golconda in his pocket; but the electric tele-

graph having been put into requisition, he was over-
taken, seized, tried, and condemned.

Thus for Mr. Duncombe the brilliant bubble burst:
another will was doubtless prepared to produce an
equally dazzling illusion; but he never gave himself
the trouble to inquire. Probably his imperial prospects were equally delusive, for the Emperor seems
doomed to disappoint the expectations of his admirers
—in France after the acceptance of the presidentship,
in Italy after the victory of Solferino, in Rome after
the expulsion of the Pope, and in Mexico after its
occupation by French troops; but great as was the
dissatisfaction created by the *coup d'état* and the
treaty of Villafranca, the abandonment of Maximilian
after so ostentatiously acting as his patron and supporter, created a far greater amount of animadversion,
especially since the miserable tragedy which terminated
the career of that chivalrous young Prince.

CHAPTER XIII.

AUTHORSHIP.

Select reading—Apposite passage from Churchill—Paul Whitehead
and Defoe—Mr. Duncombe attempts verse—" Life at Lambton "
—The Duke of Portland and his friends—Mr. Duncombe mentioned in verse—Frederick Lumley on Gentlemen Jockeys—
" L'Allegro Nuovo "—Presents the Hertford Literary Institution
with " Encyclopædia Britannica"— His poetical " Letter from
George IV. to the Duke of Cumberland "—Prose fragments—
Administrations—Professions of patriotism—Alarm in England
respecting the intentions of the Emperor of France—Mr. Dun-
combe's imaginary dialogue between Mr. Cobden and the Em-
peror—Writes " The Jews of England, their History and
Wrongs "—Letter of Dr. Adler, Chief Rabbi, and reply—
Experience in literary composition—" Le Bon Pays "—" Ma
Chaumière "—" Le délire du Vin."

MR. DUNCOMBE in the early years of his career, when
he had leisure, read much in select literature—particularly history and poetry—copying off passages for
subsequent reference. His taste may be seen in the
following quotation from Churchill's " Rosciad" :—

> Let not threats affright,
> Nor bribes corrupt, nor flatteries delight,
> Be as *one man*—concord success ensures,
> There's not an English heart but what is yours.
> Go forth, and virtue, ever in your sight,
> Shall be your guide by day, your guard by night.

Go forth the champion of your native land,
And may the battle prosper in your hand:
It may—it must—ye cannot be withstood—
Be your heart honest, as your cause is good.

The appropriateness of these lines to his own career must strike every one. He seems too to have borne in mind the graphic lines of Paul Whitehead:—

Thrice happy patriot, whom no courts debase,
No titles lessen, and no stars disgrace!
Still nod the plumage o'er the brainless head—
Still on the faithless heart the ribbon spread:
Such toys may serve to signalize the fool,
To shield the knave, or garnish out the tool;
While you, with Roman virtue, would disdain
The tinsel trappings of the glittering chain!
Fond of your freedom, spurn the venal fee,
And prove he's only great who dares be free.

Often was he enabled to recognise the truth as well as the force of Defoe's description of a sham liberal in his "True-born Englishman":—

Statesmen are always sick of one disease,
And *a good pension* gives them present ease:
That's the specific makes them all content
With any King and any Government.
Good patriots at Court abuses rail,
And all the Nation's grievances bewail,
But when the sovereign balsam's once applied,
The zealot never fails to change his side.

Mr. Duncombe occasionally tried his hand at versification; but his muse never appears to have soared higher than the construction of a poetical quiz. We print a few stanzas of one in MS. The event they chronicle occurred about half a century ago, and nearly all the actors in it have died: the hero, the eldest son of the high sheriff of Durham, of Larting-

ton Hall, in 1835; Frederick Lumley, grandson of
the fourth Earl of Scarborough, in 1831; and the
Hon. Edward Petre (son of Lord Petre by a second
marriage), in June, 1848.

LIFE AT LAMBTON;

OR, THE NOCTURNAL RAMBLES OF HENRY WITHAM, ESQ., AT LAMBTON HALL, OCT. 17, 1822.

The waxlights extinguished one Thursday night,
   The guests had sought rest from their sorrows and joys;
When sudden appeared, like a vision of light,
· Harry Witham, that far-famed promoter of noise.

When lectured for drinking, he often would say,
   " That he never again would exceed what was right;"
But each resolution avowed in the day,
   Like the web of Penelope vanished at night.

To give Duncombe a call now this hero insisted,
   So up to his room he proceeded *toute suite ;*
But when he got there was so terribly fisted,
   That in much quicker time did he beat a retreat.

To the next room he wandered, and found a bed made,
   No questions he asked, but, completely undrest,
Roll'd carelessly in, and down carelessly laid,
   Till its claimant arriving soon ended his rest.

From the couch of John Bentinck's* poor Witham arose,
   Swearing vengeance, " By G——, I *will* have satisfaction;"
This would pass for a joke, so regardless of clothes,
   Out he sallied, exclaiming, " I'm ready for action!"

Shouting, "Lambton for ever! I *will* have a bed,
   Come, open this door, or I quickly will break it!"
The noise soon disturbed the slumbers of Fred,†
   Who, till quite awake, doubted how he should take it.

* Afterwards Duke of Portland.
† Lumley.

In this way the versifier, who was one of the nocturnal revellers, describes their tipsy comrade going from door to door disturbing the repose of the inmates, among whom were the Hon. Edward Petre, Lord William Lennox, Fox (Lord Holland), and Mr. Wyvill, of Constable Burton, who treated the intruder roughly; but at last they found an unoccupied chamber for him, where, having put him comfortably to bed, they left him to sleep off the effects of his potation.

They must have been a particularly jovial crew, the circle of sportsmen who assembled under the same hospitable roof. In another metrical notice of the gentlemen jockeys, written by Mr. Lumley in the same year, we find :—

> Tommy Duncombe comes first, well mounted on Byram,
> Who, by shaking his whip, was able to tire 'em.

The poem, however, like the preceding, betrays signs of haste in the composition.

The following humorous attack on the author of innumerable productions of a similar nature was preserved among Mr. Duncombe's *facetiæ* :—

LONDON POLICE EXTRAORDINARY.

Combination Case.—General Turn Out.

John Scott, Arthur Wellesley, Robert Peel, John Fane, Henry Bathurst, Robert S. Dundas, and Nicholas Vansittart, were brought before the sitting Magistrate, charged with combination, and unlawfully conspiring to prevent George Canning from obtaining employment, contrary to the statute, 6th Geo. IV. cap. 129. From the statement of the prosecutor, it appeared that the persons charged had been for some time in the employment of his father and himself, and had for the most part conducted themselves to their satisfaction, for which they had been amply rewarded, some of them even beyond their deserts; that lately the foreman, who had for many years conducted his affairs, became incapacitated by ill health from continuing longer in his service; and the nature of his business, in which a good deal of complicated machinery was necessarily used, requiring a person of skill and diligence, he had appointed a person, of the name of Canning, who was also in his service, to superintend the works; he was further induced, he said, to make this appointment, as all those persons, both at home and abroad, with whom he transacted business, had great confidence in the skill and integrity of Canning. However, on the accused learning this determination, they turned out, and left their respective avocations without giving any notice of their intention, and declared that the whole establishment might go to the d—l for what they cared, as they would never return to their work if the said Canning was to be their foreman. The complainant further stated, that the workmen, not satisfied with this act, as far as regarded themselves, had also induced three of his domestics, Charles S. Germain, and James Graham, sen. and jun., to quit his service.

George Canning being produced, deposed that, on his acquainting the persons in the establishment that he had been appointed foreman, Scott, Wellesley, Peel, Fane, Bathurst, Dundas, and Vansittart, declared they would not work with him.

The accused being asked what they had to say for themselves, Scott, who is a very old man, replied, that he had been upwards of twenty-six years in the employment of the firm; that he had grown grey in the service of it—(complainant: "and rich, too, old gentleman")—and that he expected he would at least have been consulted in the appointment of foreman.

Magistrate.—What, sir, your master is to consult you who he is to employ to conduct his business; I never heard a more monstrous proposition.

The complainant said, he had great reason to complain of Scott, who had given very little satisfaction to his customers, from the tedious manner in which he did his work, and that several jobs which he had in hand for years, and for which they were anxiously waiting, were still in an unfinished state. He had likewise prevented the introduction of many improvements which the proprietor wished to make in the machinery.

In 1832 there appeared in the *Examiner* a clever burlesque upon Milton's exquisite ode, bearing the title "L'Allegro Nuovo," in which the leading Liberals are thus classed :—

> Haste, ye nymphs, and bring with ye
> A House of Commons fair and free ;
> Thompson, Wood, Burdett, and Hume,
> Gibson, Smith, Macaulay, Brougham,
> Such men as are honest all,
> Right and thorough Radical ;
> Foes to tithe and tax—and worse,
> Foes to duties upon corn ;
> Sheil and *Duncombe*, good at jeering,
> And Dan O'Connell, King of Erin.
> Come, and trip it as ye go
> Through the lobby in a row ;
> And by the right hand lead will ye
> That champion of sweet liberty—
> Thomas Attwood, dubbed M.P. !

Mr. Duncombe was in earnest in his desire to extend the advantages of sterling literature to all able to appreciate them. He showed this when in 1831 he presented the Hertford Literary and Scientific Institution with a splendidly-bound copy of the "Encyclopædia Britannica," in twenty-six volumes. In a letter to the secretary (May 25th) he wrote— "It is to the extension of these societies, and to an extension of the vast mental resources they command, that we must attribute the rapid restoration of our country from the degeneracy that has so long enthralled it." That such societies have rarely succeeded has been owing to the indifference to profit by them shown by a very large majority of those for whose advantage they were created; the most useless contributions to the reading-room having been in eager demand, while the inexhaustible store of knowledge in the "Encyclopædia" was left almost unregarded.

His initials are appended to the following attempt to imitate the *emphatic* phraseology of the king :—

A Letter from George IV. to the Duke of Cumberland,
previous to the Opening of Parliament.

Windsor, February 2nd, 1830.

DEAR ERNEST,—

With pleasure you'll hear, and with pleasure I tell,
The counsels we hate are fast going to ——;
Those detestable rats, that Whig of a beau,
And Peel, that supporter of High Church or Low,
Are both in a funk at the aspect of things;
And swear with distresses my treasury rings,
That counties have met brim full of objections—
And the senseless have broached most disloyal reflections,
Not only on me, but that old —— the Church,
Who I plainly foresee will be left in the lurch.
Some rascals have gone e'en so far as to say,
That I must retrench, or no taxes they'll pay !
Retrenchment be ——!   Can I do with less money ?
No; no more than I can without my dear crony.
By G——, we must stand by the Protestant cause,
Of taxes, of parsons, of tithes, and poor laws.
What's malt-tax or beer-tax to you or to me ?
Maraschino's the stuff—so says Lady C.*

* The Marchioness of Conyngham.

But by G—, that beau Arthur has brought me a speech—
Too civil for Lyndhurst, too pretty for Leech;
It sings praises to Miguel, sends Coburg to Greece
(Who, like Jason of old, now walks off with the fleece):
And, in short, my dear Ernest, my fortunate star
Shines there brighter than ever—by G—,

Yours,   G. R.

In one MS. note Mr. Duncombe has written:—

Since 1827 to this day, we have seen and worn out no less than eight complete sets of honest, able, upright Ministers—not to speak of the present, whom God long preserve! First we had Lord Liverpool's administration—next Mr. Canning's—then Goderich's, and now the Wellington or military administration; then Lord Melbourne, Sir Robert Peel—Lord Melbourne again, and Earl Grey. If, therefore, in plurality of ministers and counsellors consists a nation's safety, how happy, how secure must England be! Eight administrations in the space of eight years — that is, from the time of kissing in and kicking out, eight entire changes, not counting the little amusing episodes of resignations, &c., we were occasionally treated to during each of their respective reigns.

In another:—

It may be said, before a minister came' into power, he declaimed against some particular act or tax, but now everybody ought to know that professions of patriotism are like treaties of peace—only binding till the orator is strong enough to break them.

After the French army had returned from their brilliant campaign in Italy, rumours of great activity in the French arsenals were circulated in England, and the general impression was that the emperor had patched up a hasty peace with Austria, and was now about to commence the mysterious " mission" he is said to have proclaimed when he accepted the Presidentship—this mission, as was generally understood, being to avenge the defeat of Waterloo. It was in vain that sensible men strove to dissipate the widely-spread distrust of his intentions ; it was equally in vain that the emperor expressed assurances of his loyalty and goodwill. The manner in which he had treated the obligations he had voluntarily entered into when he became the chief of the Republic was dwelt upon, and John Bull became more suspicious. It was then that some one—we are not quite certain it was Mr. Duncombe—who had a more intimate knowledge of the emperor's intentions, wrote the following, as a means of allaying the public disquietude :—

A Dialogue supposed to have taken place between Napoleon III. and Richard Cobden, M.P., Dec 21, 1859.—T. S. D.:—

FRANCE AND ENGLAND—(*A Dialogue*).

The Paris correspondent of the *Times* communicates the following conversation, which took place a few days since between two persons—one a Frenchman, the other an Englishman—on the important and absorbing topic of the day. Our readers, after having perused the report, will be able to conjecture perhaps who the interlocutors are likely to have been.

After a few unimportant remarks on ordinary subjects, the Englishman, with characteristic frankness, continued thus :—

You know my sentiments with regard to France, and my sincere desire to see the most complete union always subsist between my country and yours. Judge then of my surprise, and allow me to add my sorrow, at finding that the relations between our respective countries have gradually and profoundly altered—at least, if we may judge from

appearances. I have carefully and conscientiously examined
the state of the public mind in England; I have interrogated
and listened to persons of every class, from the highest to
the very lowest. Well, then, I declare to you, to my deep
regret, I have found with the one as with the other, mistrust
pushed to the point of only believing in menaces on the
part of your country, and fear to that of deeming it necessary to put themselves in a state of defence. I address
myself, therefore, to you, to explain certain facts which are
generally represented in England as flagrant proofs of the
bad intentions of France with respect to us.

Frenchman.—What! you, my dear sir? You, whose
mind is so just and upright; you, whose judgment is so
sound, and whose reason so firm and enlightened—you, too,
caught the contagion? In truth, you would make me
laugh if I did not know you to be serious, and I would
class you among the foolish if I did not know you to be the
contrary. Yes, I declare to you, in the eyes of my countrymen, as in my own, the panic spread abroad in England
is actually folly.

Englishman.—Folly, as much as you please. The fact
does not the less exist; and, as it exists, it must be taken
into serious consideration. Do you not foresee a fatal
result, if so many unfounded rumours are credited? People's
minds on both sides will grow embittered; and the merest
cause will suffice to bring about a rupture, and the slightest
spark to light up a flame.

Frenchman.—The difficulty is to lead back to the truth
those who obstinately wander from it, and to cure the blind
who will not see. Nevertheless, I wish to submit to your
diseased imagination facts that cannot be refuted—to those
phantoms that flit about on the other side of the Channel—
realities which can be easily verified and proved beyond
dispute. Facts shall speak first, and figures after. Now,
the emperor has given to no foreign power more than to
England guarantees of his desire to live in good harmony.
Hardly had he ascended to power, when he dispatched, in
spite of the Assembly, the French fleet to make common

cause with yours in the East. Subsequently he united himself with you in the Crimean war; and when the insurrection which broke out in India employed all your army in Asia, did he profit by the absence of your force to pick a quarrel with you? On the contrary, he offered to give the English troops a passage through France. He sub-scribed—as well as the Imperial Guard—for your wounded, while (be it said *en passant*, and without meaning reproach) our wounded in Italy seemed to find you indifferent. Finally, how many measures for the last ten years have been proposed by divers Governments which might have shocked England? He has rejected them all, and made no merit whatever in your eyes of the rejection. How can so many proofs of a cordiality so constant be all at once for-gotten? And how does it come to pass that mistrust and error are substituted for the legitimate effect which it should have produced? Why should a line of conduct so honest be answered with passionate and mistaken alarm? I look about in vain, and I cannot understand the cause of this sudden terror in England. And, good heavens! what a time has been selected to propagate it! Why, the very moment when the emperor has given a rare example of moderation. From the very day when he proposed and concluded peace people were pleased to attribute to him ambitious designs; he was represented as marching to new conquests when, arresting the impetuosity of his troops, he so resolutely traced the limit beyond which he would not push his victory. There is, then, something insensate in converting into one eager for war the man than whom none can wish to be more pacific; and into a cause of fear what ought to be a pledge of security.

Englishman.—The conduct of the emperor would, I admit, be the most appropriate argument to convince us, and his sympathy for England has never ceased to inspire us with confidence. But the people—but the army! Come now, frankly speaking, do they not both detest us? And will not public opinion force your Sovereign some day to declare war against us?

Frenchman.—To such questions as these I reply—error, error the most grave, my dear sir. It cannot be denied that there is at bottom, in both countries, a remnant of rancour and rivalry which still subsists, but subsists much more in a latent than in an aggressive state. Material interests on one side, liberal ideas on the other, tend incessantly to draw the two countries closer to each other. Moreover, France is more practical than you imagine. What advantage, material or moral, could a war with you bring us? None — absolutely none. Consequently no one desires it. But have you expressed *all* your thoughts? Do you not keep silent as to the cause of this mistrust which is so universal in England against the emperor and his government? Be candid, and I shall be the same.

Englishman.—Well, then, I will be candid. Here is our decisive reason, our principal grievance; the development given to the French navy is out of all proportion to the requirements and the greatness of your country.

Frenchman.—This is another prejudice; is it possible that a man like you should share it? Truly, if instead of being some hours distant from our frontier, England was at the antipodes, one would not find it a greater stranger than you appear to be as to what is passing in France. You speak of our extraordinary armaments, but are you quite sure of the fact? Some journals have printed it; you have read it. Some persons have told you of it; you have repeated it, and you believe it—that's all. Such is the only source of your conviction. Learn, then, what is doing in France, and hold it for certain. Not a centime can be spent without the vote of the Legislative corps, and without the previous examination of the Council of State. Consult the estimates of the navy and army, and you shall find in them no excessive expenditure on the part of the Government.

Englishman.—Your estimates are nothing to me, my dear sir; I am ignorant as to how they are arranged. Figures are easy of handling, and are susceptible of every combination. Facts, on the contrary, are inflexible; and, since you

have appealed to them, I will appeal to them in turn.   At
Toulon and Brest you are building plated ships.   Against
whom can they be intended, if not against us?   At Nantes
you have on the stocks hundreds of flat-bottomed boats.
For what purpose, if it be not to throw 20,000 soldiers on
our coast?   And then your immense supplies of fuel, and
the prodigious activity of your arsenals.   Everywhere you
are building ships; everywhere you are casting rifled cannon
and projectiles of all kinds.   These are so many evident
facts, and of public notoriety.   What answer will you give
me to them?

Frenchman.—The most categorical in the world.   Give
me your attention, for I will now quote laws and regulations, authentic reports, and go back to a period that will
not be suspected by you :—According to a royal ordinance
of the 22nd November, 1846, the total strength of the naval
forces on the peace footing was to be 328 ships, of which 40
·were to be liners, and 50 frigates—sailing vessels.   When
the war in the Crimea came on France had very few steamships; it was easy to see that sailing ships had passed their
time, and that it was necessary to boldly admit the principle
that henceforth every man-of-war must be a steamer.   The
emperor consequently named in 1855, under the presidency
of Admiral Hamelin, a commission to fix the basis of the
new fleet necessary for France.   The commission reported
in favour of transforming the sailing ships, and of appro-
priating to them our ports, giving them especially the yards
and docks which they required.   The report terminated by
demanding that the annual grant for the maintenance of
the *matériel* of the fleet should be augmented by an annual
sum of 25,000,000 francs for thirteen years, the period
judged indispensable to complete their transformation.   Of
that sum 5,000,000 francs were applied to the ports.   The
Council of State, when called upon to give its opinion,
reduced to 17,000,000 francs, for thirteen years, the amount
of extraordinary credits demanded for the navy.   Do not
tire, my dear sir, with these details.   Here is one quite
recent, and not less precise :—In 1859 our fleet consisted of

27 ships of the line (*vaisseaux*) and 15 frigates, screws, completed; and of three plated frigates. We have, then, in order to arrive at the force on a peace footing decided under Louis Philippe, 13 ships of the line to transform, and 35 frigates to build, which, I repeat, will still require ten years at least. As for the plated frigates—the invention of the emperor—nothing is more natural than to construct them as an experiment, since if they succeed they can be advantageously substituted for ships of the line. But this is not all; the necessity of having only a steam fleet entailed on us expenses from which England may be exempted. When our fleet used sails, and we had an expedition to send— as for instance to Africa, to the Crimea, and to Italy—it was easy to find among the trade sailing transports for men, horses, or stores. But at the present day our merchant navy is not sufficiently developed to enable us to find steam transports when we have need of them. We are therefore forced to build them, in order to have at all times a certain number ready, and this imperious obligation is so present to us, that at the very moment I am speaking to you all our transports are proceeding to China; and that we may not be entirely without resources, and be unprovided, the naval department has been obliged to purchase three large steamships in England. You see then I have at heart to convince you that I penetrate without hesitation to the very bottom of things, and I disclose to you the minutest details of our situation.

Englishman.—These categorical explanations begin to reassure me. But have you any such to give me on the supplies of coals and the boats intended for the landing of troops?

Frenchman.—I will continue with the same frankness. Some months back your Tory Ministry was so much opposed to the war in Italy that everything announced its wish to place itself on the side of Austria. It was even on the point of causing coal to be considered as contraband of war. Now, our navy used only English coal. The Minister had then to occupy himself with that semi-hostile attitude of your Ministry, and to look about for the means of supplying, in case of need, the French fleet with French coal. It was his duty not to leave our supplies at the mercy of your Government. With this object, essays were made in changing our boilers, and coal was brought to Nantes, which was to be directed to Brest by the internal canals. Sixty iron barks, of a very small draught of water, were built to facilitate the transport of coals over the docks; but these boats, very different from those which serve for the landing of troops, did not merit the honour of exciting your apprehensions and disturbing your sleep.

Englishman.—Very good. Yet, for all that, you did not the less order from us a very considerable quantity of coal.

Frenchman.—That is perfectly true. The important part, however, is to know for what purpose we wanted this great quantity of coal which frightens you. Well, then, it is exclusively destined to supply our fleet in China and in other parts of the globe. Thus, since the 1st of July we have chartered in France 51 ships, carrying 26,000 tons of coal, to Martinique, to French Guiana, to Senegal, to Gorce, to the island of Réunion, to Mayotte, to Hong Kong, to Shanghae, to Saigon, to the Mauritius, to Singapore. We have chartered in England 25 ships, carrying 31,000 tons of coal, to Hong Kong, Woosung, Singapore, Chusan, St. Paul de Loanda, and the Cape of Good Hope. Of all these details there is not one of which you may not procure the material proof, and then you must agree with me that the apprehensions of your countrymen are chimerical, and without reasonable foundation.

Englishman.—I am willing to admit that what you tell me has the appearance of truth. I have a last objection, and it concerns your arsenals. If, as you assure me, your Government does not contemplate recommencing the war, why does it continue to show such activity?

Frenchman.—I have in vain insisted on one essential point—viz., that, like other countries, we are in a complete state of transformation, but you seem not to wish to comprehend it. We have to change not only all the *matériel* of the navy, but on land also the whole of our artillery; and although the emperor had in Italy 200 rifled cannon, he will still require three or four years to entirely accomplish the definitive transformation.

Englishman.—I thank you for all this information; and I shall turn it to account.

Frenchman.—Permit me one more observation. You have avowed frankly all the apprehensions which my country causes you; but I have not expressed to you the whole of my opinion on yours. If in England people are convinced that France desires to declare war against you, we here are, in our turn, well convinced that the mistrust excited on the other side of the Channel is a party manœuvre. The Tory party, dissolved as you are aware by Sir Robert Peel, seeks the means of reconstructing itself; and, according to it, the best possible one would be by reviving the hatred of France, and by seeking, as in 1804, to form a European coalition against her. The statesmen who at this day take the lead in public opinion cannot be ignorant of all that I have just told you. Among us it is well understood that the Tories, in place of combating these errors, labour to gain them credit, and pursue their policy with traditional perseverance. People ought to take care, however, lest by dint of wishing to deceive others they end by deceiving themselves. There was a certain Marseillaise, whose history occurs to me quite opportunely, and with which I may close a conversation which is already too long. Our Marseillaise, wishing to have a joke at the expense of his fellow-citizens, went about crying out that a whale had just entered the port of Marseilles. His pleasantry succeeded, and every one ran to the port. Soon, drawn on by the example, he himself began to run in the same direction to see, with the others, if his invention was not a reality.

At this point the conversation ended.

During his labours in support of the Jew Bill, Mr.

Duncombe interested himself still further in the subject by superintending extensive researches into the modern history of that ancient race. At last he determined that a work should be written giving an account of the introduction of the Jews into this country, and when a couple of chapters had been completed got them printed, and caused copies to be sent to every one in a position to afford information, requesting it to be returned within a fortnight with corrections and suggestions. The following was the title, " The Jews of England—their History and Wrongs. By Thomas Slingsby Duncombe, M.P." The author first printed a preface and one chapter, forming thirty-two pages post octavo, but subsequently issued ninety-four pages, with a longer preface and copious notes, in demy octavo. The following will show how the work was received :—

Office of the Chief Rabbi, London, January 14th, 5621.

Dear Sir,—I have been favoured with several sheets of your intended History of the Jews in England, and cannot refrain from taking the first opportunity to express my gratification at your successful essay to fill up a void in the literature of this country, which to my surprise was allowed to remain so long. What adds to my satisfaction at the appearance of such a publication is to find it written in the same spirit of toleration and justice which has hitherto prompted you to render such excellent good services to our cause.

In expressing, then, to you my sincere and heartfelt thanks, I do but re-echo the grateful feelings of my whole nation.

You can well imagine that I should like to see the work as perfect and as faultless as possible ; and it is with a view to this that I have requested my son, Mr. Marcus Adler,

M.A., to communicate with Mr. Acland,* and to point out to him some statements which require revision.

I have the honour to be, dear Sir,

Yours faithfully, N. ADLER, Dr.

To Thomas Slingsby Duncombe, Esq., M.P., &c.

February 4th, 1861.

DEAR SIR,—Pray forgive my apparent neglect in not thanking you earlier for your kind and flattering letter, but the fact is, not having visited the Reform Club for some days I did not receive it until yesterday. I hope I need not add that any suggestions you will do me the favour to offer, or corrections you would have the kindness to make, shall be strictly attended to; and I rejoice to say that from the numerous communications I have received from men of all creeds, the proposed publication of a work of this description appears to create much interest, and meets with universal approval. Yours, &c. T. S. D.

Dr. Adler, the Chief Rabbi.

There is a marked difference between the first and second issue of the published portion of the "Jews of England": in the last the preface was extended, as well as the narrative; in the other the first chapter concludes with the establishment of the Jews in Roman Britain, the second brings down the history to their condition in Anglo-Saxon Britain—both are compiled with great care and a comprehensive examination of authorities, indicating no small amount of labour. His attention to this work must have been afforded at intervals of convalescence, when his health was rapidly giving way under the pressure of his political duties. He ought to have been

* The well-known Parliamentary Agent, who afforded important assistance in the collection of the materials and production of the work.

nursing his remaining strength; but having lived a life of continual industry he could not endure even enforced idleness.

Mr. Duncombe had had considerable experience in composition before he attempted his first substantive literary work. His published letters would fill a volume, his published pamphlets another. His correspondence was extensive, and included letters from all classes, from the first minister of the crown to the humblest working-man who chose to recognise the member for Finsbury as "the tribune of the people": a favourite appellation conferred on him by the Liberal press. Almost every great question that had come before the public for more than a quarter of a century he had explained and illustrated by contemporary *brochures*.

Several clever specimens of French verse have been preserved among Mr. Duncombe's private MSS. To them is appended the name of "Chevalier B.," followed by the initials T. S. D., which are always attached to his own compositions. The first may have been a *nom de plume;* but whether these compositions are his own, or those of a friend, it is doubtful whether they have ever been printed :—

LE BON PAYS.

Ah! le bon pays vraiment!
La belle ville que Londres,
Chacun s'écrie en baillant,
Le peuple Anglais est charmant.
On se moque de son roi,
On politique, on raisonne;
C'est là que l'on vit pour soi,
Car on n'accueille personne!

Ici sous l'abri des lois,
    Tout le monde fait fortune ;
On vous fait payer deux fois,
    Ce que l'on n'a vendre qu'une.
        Ah ! le bon pays.

On se procure à grand frais,
    Un logis humide et sombre ;
Et grace aux brouillards épais,
    Du soleil on est à l'ombre.
        Ah ! le bon pays.

Tout est gravement traité,
    Amour, plaisir, bonne chère ;
L'Anglais sans être invité,
    N'ose diner chez son père.
        Ah ! le bon pays.

On avale goulûment,
    De bœuf une large assiette ;
Et pour manger proprement,
    Il faut porter sa serviette.
        Ah ! le bon pays.

Le soir chez soi, petit jeu,
    Au brouillard on fuit la nique ;
Les cartes coutent si peu,
    Quatre shillings l'as de pique.
        Ah ! le bon pays.

Le dimanche tout est divin,
    Ni travail, ni jeu, ni danse ;
On cuit pas même le pain,
    Il faut s'en procurer d'avance.
        Ah ! le bon pays.

Point d'injures ni de coups,
    Les lois protègent la vie ;
Mais en pariant six sous,
    Librement on s'estropie.
        Ah ! le bon pays.

Un watchman reste muet,
   Si dans la rue on s'assomme ;
Mais vous dit l'heure qu'il est,
   Quand vous dormez d'un bon somme.
     Ah ! le bon pays.

L'honneur, et la probité,
   Le génie, et la sottise,
Le serment, et la liberté :
   Ici tout est marchandise.
     Ah ! le bon pays.

Les dames n'aimeront pas
   Cette chanson vendique ;
Des vertus et des appas
   N'offrent rien à la critique.
     Ah ! le bon pays.

Vous illustres favoris,
   De la muse chansonnière ;
Epargnez moi vos mépris,
   Helas ! je bois de la bière.
     Ah ! le bon pays, &c.

                         T. S. D.

December, 1823.

MA CHAUMIÈRE.

Air—" Avec la pipe de tabac."

Lorsque dans ma simple chaumière,
   Parfois je reçois mes amis ;
Près d'eux, ma bouteille, mon verre,
   J'oublie aisément mes soucis.
Un moment je perds la mémoire,
   Je forme mille plans joyeux ;
Je ris, je chante, et verse à boire,
   Au moins un jour je suis heureux.

Dans ce court accès de folie,
  Si l'on veut lui donner ce nom,
Avec du vin, femme jolie,
  Je me crois un Napoléon.
De chacun j'augmente l'ivresse,
  Par quelques traits pleins de gaîté ;
Sans un sou je parle richesse,
  C'est rêver la félicité.

Je choisis aimable compagne,
  Et je lui tiens de doux propos ;
Et sans le secours du champagne,
  Il m'échappe quelques bon mots.
Si de ses yeux muet langage
  Répond aux désirs de mon cœur ;
Vous voyez que mon hermitage
  Devient le séjour du bonheur.

Amis, croyez m'en sur parole,
  La tristesse abrège nos jours ;
Venez, venez à mon école,
  Du temps je sais remplir le cours.
Entre Bacchus et la folie,
  L'amour, quelque fois la raison,
Je dépense gaîement la vie,
  Comme le sage Anacréon.

Par CHEVALIER B.

LE DÉLIRE DU VIN.

Quoi, toujours ce sujet m'inspire !
  Bacchus, je te résiste en vain !
Je prononce dans mon délire,
  Gloire à jamais au dieu du vin !
Sans ce sujet inépuisable,
  Que maint auteur servit petit ;
Et que de beaux esprits à table,
  On verroit souvent sans esprit.

De nectar quand ma coupe est pleine,
  Et que le plaisir la soutient,
Elle devient ma souveraine,
  L'univers alors m'appartient.
Le bonheur lui-même me berce,
  Dans un rêve doux et trompeur ;
Et chaque coup que ma main verse,
  Par degrés accroit mon erreur.

Bacchus, tes effets sont magiques !
  D'un poltron tu fais un héros ;
Père de nos auteurs comiques,
  Ta source est celle des bon mots.
L'amant y court puiser l'audace,
  Qui sert à combler tous ses vœux ;
Et le vieillard que le temps glâce,
  Y vient chercher de nouveaux feux.

L'artisan assis sous la treille,
  Entre sa femme et ses enfans,
Oublie en vidant sa bouteille
  Les rois, les princes, et les grands.
Il goûte une volupté pure,
  Sa bien-aimée est dans ses bras ;
Il se croit roi de la Nature,
  Si sa coupe ne tarit pas.

Lorsque la camarde inflexible,
  Dont la visite nous fait peur,
Viendra d'un air très-peu risible,
  Me dire, Allons donc, vieux buveur !
Je veux tenter de la séduire,
  Par l'effet de ce jus divin :
Cela se peut, car j'entends dire,
  Qu'on ne résiste pas au vin.

Par CHEVALIER B.

CHAPTER XIV.

THE POPULAR MEMBER.

Expediency of abolishing the Tower of London—Make-believe
legislation—Sir John Trelawny on church rates—Letters of
the Right Hon. W. E. Gladstone, Chancellor of the Exchequer
—Mr. Duncombe and the Jews' Bill—Letters of Sir F. H.
Goldsmid, Bart., and Baron Lionel Rothschild—Rise of the
great capitalist—Objections of the House of Lords—Letters of
Lord Lyndhurst and Lord Derby—Mr. Duncombe's popularity
with the Jews—Medical reform—Speech of the member for
Finsbury—Letters of Dr. Maddock and Mr. John Lawrence
—Proposed letter of Liberal members of the House of Commons to Lord Palmerston—Abolition of toll-gates—Mr. Forster
on the turnpike question—Correspondence of Lord Palmerston
and Mr. Duncombe, respecting the consul at Savannah—Mr.
Duncombe's fatal illness.

A STRIKING instance was given by the popular member
of his indifference to sentimental impressions when he
had a public benefit in view. Among the notices of
motion on the paper for February, 1859, the following must have startled some of the members of the
House :—

Mr. Thomas Duncombe. Tower of London. Address for
a Commission to inquire into the expediency of continuing
the present establishment and jurisdiction of the Tower, and
whether the site, together with the lands and property belonging to it, cannot, by sale or otherwise, be converted to
purposes of greater utility with advantage to the public
service.

When he proposed this from his seat there seemed a general disposition to treat it as a joke; but one of the most influential of the daily papers encouraged him to proceed. In a leading article of great ability the editor stated :—

The Tower of London, in its present state, is an anachronism and an anomaly. It professes to be a fortress, and is governed by a kind of martial law, but for any purposes of offence or defence it is useless, and might be escaladed by an Irish hod-carrier, or stormed by a resolute party of coalwhippers.*

The member for Finsbury characteristically looked at the subject from a utilitarian point of view, and ignored historical and poetical associations. He had ascertained that the establishment covered a space of twelve acres and five poles of valuable land, and cost the country yearly in salaries 4255*l*. 9*s*. 7*d*., besides an enormous expenditure in enlargements and improvements. The cry of vandalism, however, was immediately raised by zealous antiquaries, and genuine Conservatives, military and civilian, and the ancient palace, fortress, prison, mint, and cemetery was preserved intact.

In the experimental legislation, for which recent Parliamentary annals are famous, there is much that is make-believe. Members every session introduced resolutions, or submitted bills to the House, that were never intended to become laws. They did so with a perfect knowledge that a discussion on a division would be fatal to their pretensions; but such experiments were made for the constituency, not for the country. It was a pet scheme of particular politicians who

* *Daily Telegraph*, February 9th, 1859.

exercised a considerable influence over the borough, town, or county that had returned the member who had invented it; and the annual attempt was got up to show that he did not neglect his duty. Such is the case with the proposals for the Ballot, the Anti-Maynooth question, the Repeal of the Union, and similar displays of useless oratory.

There were also instances where, to save appearances, some members were uncommonly busy in bringing forward measures they never intended to carry. They were not of the same opinion as their constituents, but it was essential to their interests to appear so—a bill must therefore be framed and advocated; and the local paper was sure to be filled with highly-coloured descriptions of its merit, as well as with glowing eulogiums of the public spirit of their popular and patriotic representative; when, just as everything looked fair for its favourable passage through the House, some unexpected obstacle occurred, and the bill was withdrawn. This appears to have been considered the case with an attempt to reform church-rates—a subject that was sure to meet Mr. Duncombe's approval, in consequence of the large element of dissent in the Finsbury constituency. Such an experiment was made, and he had suggested improvements that elicited the following note:—

Reform Club, March 24th, 1860.

My DEAR SIR,—I should think the following clause would suit the case:—

"And be it enacted, that from and after the passing of this Act, no expenses now legally payable out of the proceeds of a church rate shall be defrayed out of sums accruing from any other rates whatsoever, any present law or custom notwithstanding."

But perhaps Dr. Forster would give you his opinion on it.   Yours truly,   J. S. TRELAWNY.

Thomas Duncombe, Esq., M.P.

Among the working-classes whose grievances the member for Finsbury was called upon to remedy, were the cork-cutters. He met deputations, and got himself well up in their trade statistics, as well as in their causes of complaint, and then brought their case before the House of Commons, by asking a question of the Chancellor of the Exchequer. He generally commenced his parliamentary proceedings in this form; and as sometimes the minister was not prepared with an answer, a correspondence or interview became necessary. The letters here printed will show what amount of interest Mr. Gladstone took in the subject:—

11, Downing-street, June 19th, 1860.

The Chancellor of the Exchequer presents his compliments to Mr. Duncombe, and has just received his letter with the enclosures, which he will take the earliest opportunity of examining. He is not yet precisely aware what were the statements made by him which are complained of, or which it is desired to controvert. He finds that his informants are ready to substantiate, so at least they apprise him, all the particulars which he laid before the House of Commons.

He takes this opportunity of assuring Mr. Duncombe that nothing could have been further from his intention than to have censured Mr. Duncombe for not laying any information on this subject before him instead of taking it direct to the House of Commons. It was only upon Mr. Duncombe's seeming to appeal to him for an immediate acknowledgment of error that he was at once led to observe *why* he could pronounce no opinion on the case at the time. He does not particularly recollect the thanks of which Mr. Duncombe speaks, but he has no doubt he did thank Mr. Duncombe for his courtesy in giving him notice of what was to take place, and in this spirit it was his desire and intention that, with whatever differences of opinion, the subject should continue to be handled.

11, Downing-street, Whitehall, June 22nd, 1860.

The Chancellor of the Exchequer presents his compliments to Mr. Duncombe, and will be much obliged if Mr. Duncombe will inform him on what authority it is imputed to him in the declaration of the master cork-cutters of Liverpool (returned herewith for reference), to have said in the House of Commons " that through the imperfections of workmanship, or tyrannical and arbitrary demands of society-men employed by us respectively, we have been obliged to employ boys." Upon this language appears to be founded the charge of calumny which those gentlemen have thought themselves entitled to make.

In the session of 1860 Mr. Duncombe continued his exertions to put the standing orders in favour of Jews taking the altered oath, into a statutable shape. The House of Lords displayed a disposition to maintain the existing law, with one or two noble exceptions ; the principal of these were Lord Lyndhurst, who was very earnest in his commendation of the proposed measure ; Lord Brougham, who was ever in favour of religious toleration ; and Earl Russell (Lord John), who was quite as active an advocate for Baron Rothschild and his co-religionists in the Upper House, as he had been in the Lower since his return for the city of London. Among the wealthy Hebrew capitalists the importance of the measure was at once admitted.   We print notes from two of the most distinguished :—

14, Portland-place, W., 29th March, 1860.

My DEAR SIR,—Not having had the pleasure of seeing you in the House the last day or two (in consequence, I lament to hear, of your being indisposed), I trouble you with these few words, and forward to you with them a draft (which I think will answer the purpose in view) of the Bill you have obtained leave to introduce for amending the Jews' Relief Act of 1858.

I showed a sketch of the Bill to the Attorney-General, and have since made a slight alteration in it in accordance with a suggestion of his.

I remain, my dear Sir, truly yours,

FRANCIS H. GOLDSMID.

Kingston House, 2 May, 1860.

My DEAR MR. DUNCOMBE,—Lord Lyndhurst has requested me to write to you to say, that it will give him great pleasure to see you respecting our Bill.   He will be at home to-morrow (Thursday) at two o'clock, and hopes that it will be convenient for you to call upon him at that hour.

Pray accept again my thanks for the trouble you are taking in our question, and believe me,

Yours sincerely,   L. DE ROTHSCHILD.

The great capitalist's account of his first rise, as given at a party at Ham House, February, 1834, is worth quoting :—

" I dealt in English goods [at Frankfort].   One great trader came there who had the market to himself.   He was quite the great man, and did us a favour if he sold us goods.   Somehow I offended him, and he refused to show me his patterns.   This was on a Tuesday.   I said to my father, ' I will go to England.'   I could speak nothing but German.   On the Thursday I started; the nearer I got to

England the cheaper goods were. As soon as I got to Manchester I laid out all my money—things were so cheap —and I made good profit. I soon found that there were three profits—the raw material, the dyeing, and the manufacturing. I said to the manufacturer, ' I will supply you with material and dye, and you supply me with manufactured goods.' So I got three profits instead of one; and I could sell goods cheaper than anybody. In a short time I made my 20,000*l.* into 60,000*l.*"*

There were other circumstances that favoured the rise to a position of equal honour and influence of this able financier. In the first place the family of merchant princes, of which his lordship is now the head, obtained their first elevation among European capitalists by a well-established reputation for honour and probity. The confidence thus created helped the favourable development of that genius for successful enterprise which has made the name a power in the commercial, quite as influential as that of Czar or Emperor in the political world. In truth there are some sovereignties that owe their present existence to the timely succour afforded them from the resources of these autocratic firms.

Lord Rothschild differs from many other great speculators in many particulars, but essentially in the quiet exercise of the power for doing good which in the present age is so noble an element of wealth. Many acts of practical benevolence might be set down to his credit account, which the outside world, Christian or Jew, have not been permitted to know. His millions do not flow through so many important channels without affording sustenance and strength

* Memoirs of Sir Fowell Buxton, p. 288.

to whatever strives, however obscurely, to flourish within its influence. The Baron is a promoter of art, of literature, and indeed of every merit that can be put to social profit. As a legislator he has always distinguished himself by the liberality of his principles and readiness to forward any measure intended to promote the public good. He was the cordial friend of Mr. Duncombe to the close of his career.

The objections of the House of Lords to the Jew Bill were still stumbling-blocks in the way of parliamentary success. Mr. Duncombe tried every means of overcoming this difficulty in this session; and having determined on his amendment, communicated with the Premier. We subjoin his reply, and the interesting note that follows:—

St. James's-square, July 4th, 1860.

DEAR SIR,—Before replying to your note of yesterday, I thought it right to communicate with Lord Chelmsford, who entirely concurs with me in thinking the Bill, as you propose to amend it, unobjectionable, as doing nothing more than what was intended by the original compromise. But for the same reason, with all deference to the authority of the Speaker, we cannot see the necessity for it, and cannot understand on what grounds he rests his opinion of the necessity of an annual repetition of the Resolution. But if the House of Commons think the amended Bill necessary, and will be satisfied with it, I shall throw no obstacle in the way of its passing in that shape. I return the Bill, and am,

Yours faithfully,   DERBY.

Folkestone, September 1st.

DEAR MR. DUNCOMBE,—I got tired of the dull drippings at the close of the session, and so left for this place. I return Lord Derby's letter. You have done good service in correcting the blunders of the "Lords' House," and have deserved the thanks not of the Jewish people only, but of all the friends of religious liberty.

Very faithfully, &c.   LYNDHURST.

The popular member now found that his labours in behalf of this great historical race were on the point of being crowned with success. He pressed forward his enlightened views, and with an access of parliamentary support secured a legislative *locus standi* for this nation without a country—an important addition to the various evidences of a generous toleration he had assisted, during his long political career, in placing on the statute-book of the country. Contemporaneously, as we have already stated, he assisted in producing an elaborate attempt to make the wrongs of "the chosen people," during their sojourn in the land in which a remnant of them had sought refuge, familiar to Christian readers. Assuredly he had established an undeniable claim to the popularity he enjoyed among the Jewish community.

Among the beneficial reforms advocated by Mr. Duncombe was one of the laws affecting the medical profession. In the session of 1858 Parliament had before it several attempts at legislation; and during the debate on the second reading of Mr. Headlam's Medical Profession Bill, No. 1, he addressed the House in his happiest vein, exposing their imperfections :—

Mr. T. Duncombe could not understand the argument of the hon. member for Oxford, that they were to consult for the dignity of the profession, as his idea was that they were sent to Parliament to deliberate upon what might be for the welfare of the public at large. Certainly, as concerned their own dignity, it had never been better consulted in medical matters than on that occasion; for, on looking to the paper, he saw first the Medical Profession Bill No. 1. What had become of the Medical Profession Bill No. 2 he knew not, but perhaps it had taken the wrong medicine and was unable to appear. (Laughter.) The next was the Medical Profession Bill No. 3; and after that they had the Vaccination Bill, which was, he believed, intended to repeal the Compulsory Vaccination Act, which had been smuggled through the House in 1853—in fact, to take the parliamentary lancet out of the unwilling arm of the nation. (Laughter.) That was not enough in the way of physicking the House—(renewed laughter)—for they had also the Bill brought in by the hon. member for Cork, called the Medical and Surgical Sciences' Bill. In fact, they only wanted the Sale of Poisons' Bill, which was floundering its way in another place, to complete the list, which was appropriately closed by the order for the second reading of the Burials' Bill. (Great laughter.) They already had a State religion and a State education, and it was now proposed that they should also have State physic. He was determined to vote against both Bills. He would join the friends of No. 3 in their endeavour to defeat No. 1; and, as some requital, he should then help the friends of No. 1 to throw out No. 3, for they were not the reforms the people required. They wanted to see all the members of the medical profession, after they had gone through a qualifying examination, placed upon an equal footing. The Bills before the House he considered as an interference between the public and their medical advisers. As regarded the medical corporations and the universities, they had obtained their exclusive privileges under circumstances which were not adapted to the present times, and as in the reform of the House of Commons they had done away with Old Sarum, so in medical reform they should not respect those obsolete institutions. It was said that they should do away with quackery in medicine; to that he had no objection, provided they did not attempt to do it by legislative quackery.

Now he found that those medical bodies which they were told had done so much to advance the profession, had at all times impeded the march of science. They persecuted the man who invented the tourniquet, and the College of Physicians got Dr. Grenfell, who first applied cantharides to the cure of dropsy, sent to Newgate. After all, as Dr. Carlisle in his lectures said, medicine was an art founded in conjecture and improved in murder. He would, therefore, until some better measure of medical reform was proposed to the House, leave the College of Physicians and the College of Surgeons to operate on and prescribe for each other, and the Society of Apothecaries to drench them both. (Laughter.)

On a division there was a majority of 225 for the bill, and 78 against; it was, consequently, read a second time. The author of a pamphlet, who opposed the bill, Mr. Gamgee, an army surgeon on the staff, thus recognises Mr. Duncombe's services in the cause of medical reform in " Two Letters addressed to Lord Palmerston :"—

You will, I trust, remember that for us pleads the British Athens, for us pleads the University of Young England,—the inspiration, aye under divine permission the creation of Henry Brougham ; for us pleads the Alma Mater of William Harvey, under the chancellorship of our Queen's consort; for us, my Lord Palmerston, pleads the history of your whole life, of the life of William Pitt, John Russell, and Robert Peel—of the lives of the really great ones, of all parties and of all ages ; for us have pleaded in the House of Commons, amongst many others, Mr. Duncombe, Mr. Cowper, Lord Elcho, Viscount Goderich, and the illustrious scion—hope of the future—of the house of Derby ; for us plead all history and all philosophy ; for us pleads the Sense of senses—the Universal—the Common Sense.

Mr. Duncombe was never disheartened by failure

where the interests of the community were at stake, and there seemed a fair prospect for perseverance. He made himself acquainted with the several corporations in the profession, as well as with the profession itself, and returned to the charge again and again. Several eminent practitioners communicated their ideas to him and encouraged him to proceed. We append the letters of two distinguished Fellows of the corporations of physicians and surgeons :—

56, Curzon-street, Mayfair, July 12th, 1858.

Dear Sir,—I cannot sufficiently thank you for your very kind and prompt letter.

In consequence of the suggestion contained in the above, I have renewed my correspondence with Lord Ebury, and am led to hope that he will be induced to introduce in committee an amendment (proposed by him on a former occasion), so as to expunge the retrospective clauses in question. I have also written to my very old friend, Mr. Swanston, Q.C. (formerly my guardian), with a request that he will give me notes of introduction to one or two " law lords" who were personally known to my father, the late chancery barrister. I fear that I have already too far trespassed upon your valuable time ; but well knowing the natural goodness of your heart, and the desire you have ever evinced to protect the "weak from the strong," I am induced to ask whether you would give or obtain me an introduction to a peer who would be likely to grant me an interview, or take into consideration the amendment before referred to.

Again most gratefully thanking you for your great kindness, which I shall endeavour in some measure to repay by serving you more energetically than ever in future elections, I am, with great respect, dear sir, your very faithful and obedient servant,   A. B. Maddock.

P.S.—I duly appreciate the encouragement you give me, but would not the bill as it now stands not only debar me the right of registration, but even the privilege of retaining my title of M.D., with which I have hitherto practised for some twenty years as a physician?

T. S. Duncombe, Esq., M.P.

30, Devonshire-street, Portland-place, April 28th, 1858.

Sir,—I see by to-day's *Times* that you have given notice of motion on medical reform—a motion which appears to me to more deeply touch those questions which it is to the medical corporation's interest to conceal and the public's to bring forward, than any of the medical bills hitherto proposed. And at the risk of appearing intrusive, I am induced to ask you to grant me an interview, which I venture to think would reveal to you some facts which it is as well you should be informed on. The College of Surgeons (*e.g.*) is supposed by the general public to represent the feelings of the surgeons of this country—it really represents the pecuniary interests of a score of men, who are hence endeavouring to thrust on the legislature a series of measures calculated to benefit themselves, and themselves alone. If I were to attempt to foreshadow to you the despotic machinery of the Council of the College of Surgeons I might write *ad nauseam.* Their constant deputations (one yesterday) to Lord Derby indicate that which the whole medical profession knows—their trepidation and anxiety lest any rude legislation rob them of a single examination-fee. This "examination," too—what is it? Simply absurd. It yearly adds shoals of ignorant "surgeons" to the already overstocked profession, as detrimental to this latter as it is to the public. If, sir, you have the boldness (for it is boldness) to unveil this disgraceful state of affairs, you will reveal a countenance which, like the prophet of Khorassan, the corporations have good reason to be ashamed of, and keep from the gaze of the *profanum vulgus.*

And in concluding permit me to assure you I am actuated to address you by no other motive than to see a system exposed which, if endorsed by the legislature, crushes the profession, elevates the corporations, and injures the public good.—And I am, sir, your obedient servant,

JOHN B. LAWRENCE, F.R.C.S., M.B. Univ. Lond.

The treasurer of the "Parliamentary Reform Association," and an influential member of the Liberal party, well known and respected in commercial circles, took a commercial view of our non-interference in the recent war in Italy; but the member for Finsbury, who had listened to the arguments of Mazzini and Kossuth, was eager for the realization of the prospects that had been held out to the patriotic Italians. The treaty of Villafranca was a death-blow to the hopes of the revolutionists; for though Austria was subsequently obliged to surrender her strongholds in Italy, and the French army quitted Rome, those great events were brought about under royal auspices. Victor Emmanuel had the credit of both, and the one great Italian republic of the democrats appeared to be out of the question.

The following communications on the subject were interchanged:—

18, Wood-street, London, January 2nd, 1861.

DEAR SIR,—The accompanying draft of a letter to Lord Palmerston has resulted from a deep conviction of the necessity for a revision of our present national expenditure, and that it is a wise and friendly act earnestly to press this on the attention of the Government, by a private communication, before they prepare the estimates for the ensuing session.

The draft has been cordially approved by several members to whom I have had facilities of showing it. The following are willing to sign, provided forty members unite in doing so:—Messrs. Baines, Baxter, Bristow, Buxton, R. W. Crawford, Crossley, Crum-Ewing, S. Gurney, Rob.

Hanbury, Kershaw, Lawson, Lindsay, Mellor, Moffat, Paget, Pease, Pilkington, J. L. Ricardo, Shelley, Sykes, Turner, Whalley, Wyld.

I am sanguine enough to believe we shall far exceed forty, and I venture to ask you to add your name on the same condition. It is important not to delay the preparation of the document if any use is to be made of it. Your early reply, therefore, will be esteemed a favour. In any case please return the copy to me, lest it should get astray.

I am, dear sir, yours faithfully,   S. MORLEY.

January 4th, 1861.

DEAR SIR,—Constituted as the present Government and House of Commons are, I much fear that communications such as you propose will be but of little avail, and I do not think that I should feel disposed to sign any, unless obtained in the way I have taken the liberty to suggest; for after England's long and loud professions in favour of Italian independence, I cannot admit that our silence has been, or is, "the policy of wisdom," especially as so much more has yet to be accomplished in Rome and Venetia before Italy's freedom can be considered fully established.

I cannot, however, conclude without taking this opportunity of kindly thanking you for these patriotic exertions in favour of liberty and reform, which I have observed with pleasure you so nobly and so constantly are in the habit of making.   Yours faithfully,   T. S. D.

One of the last of the popular member's many useful labours in Parliament was directed to the abolition of toll-gates. As usual he commenced proceedings by asking questions of the minister, Sir G. Cornewall Lewis, and as usual got no satisfactory reply; but the nuisance—in the neighbourhood of the metropolis especially — had become intolerable, and it only wanted a well-directed attack to effect its removal.

On the 22nd of February, 1861, he asked Sir

George Lewis what was intended to be done, and the latter replied that he was in communication with the Metropolitan Roads' Commissioners. As a memorial complaining of the system had been presented to the minister in the March preceding, signed by 407 mercantile firms and professional men, the member for Finsbury thought something ought to be done.

On Monday, June 3rd, he asked the Secretary of State for the Home Department what progress had been made towards the abolition of the toll-gates round London, whether the Metropolitan Roads' Commissioners had held any special meeting to effect this purpose, if they had been summoned how many had attended, and what business had been done. A letter he received the next day afforded him some useful hints on the subject :—

Reform Club, June 4th.

My DEAR SIR,—Having taken a good deal of trouble and interest in the metropolitan turnpike-gate question, I thank you for putting the queries you did to Sir George Lewis last night on the subject, although somewhat surprised at the answer you received from him. Sir George knows very well that the Commissioners have power by the Act to remove the gates without leave from the parties interested in maintaining them. In proof of this I need only mention that in the first year of coming into office they removed twenty-seven gates without asking leave of the parishes in which they stood. Since then, however, the number of gates and bars have been rather increased than diminished. The reason is plain enough : to remove all the gates would put an end to the Commission ! It has a train of officials, solicitors, surveyors, secretaries, and contractors, all banded together to maintain it, and who get up opposition to the removal of the gates in the parishes in which they stand. Perhaps the ratepayers in the Strand or Cheapside would not object to a gate on condition of being relieved from the expense of repairing those streets.

The ready way to perpetuate an abuse is to put it under a Commission which breeds an interest to keep it alive. This Commission is now not only a job but a nuisance.

I am, my dear Sir, yours sincerely, M. FORSTER.

What makes the remissness of the Government as respects this crying evil more remarkable, is the fact that the House of Commons had in 1856 abolished the gates throughout Ireland. An appeal was made to Lord Palmerston to extend the benefit of the Act to London. Lord Granville was referred to, but nothing was done. In the year 1858 the House of Commons passed a resolution for an inquiry, to precede the removal of gates within a circuit of six miles, and the committee took a year in making their report. Although it recommended a change, nothing of the kind was attempted; and all classes of her Majesty's subjects, to whom a horse or a conveyance was necessary, continued to be taxed and annoyed by those stoppages to the traffic. Mr. Duncombe, however, pressed the subject till a gradual extinction of the obsolete custom was conceded.

Another interchange of letters took place between the Prime Minister and the member for Finsbury. Mr. Molyneux, our consul at Savannah, had felt himself aggrieved in consequence of Mr. Duncombe having read in the House of Commons a letter containing statements as to that gentleman's Southern "proclivities," which he totally denied. He addressed a letter to Mr. Duncombe, who, with his customary sense of justice, lost no time in getting for it the

earliest and greatest possible publicity by sending it
for publication in the newspapers, it being too late for
Parliamentary use. He also wrote on the subject to
his correspondent in the United States, as he promised
in his note to the Minister:—

94, Piccadilly, 2nd August, 1861.

My DEAR DUNCOMBE,—The enclosed letter relates to
some statement made by you in the House of Commons,
which appears to have cast an undeserved imputation on
the writer; would you like yourself to give the explanation,
or would you wish me to do so on Tuesday morning?

Yours sincerely,   PALMERSTON.

Eastbourne, August 8th, 1861.

My DEAR LORD PALMERSTON,—Many thanks for your
letter, which has only just reached me. I regret that you
should have been troubled upon the subject, as it appears
to me to belong more properly to the Foreign Department;
but as I have also received a similar communication from
the consul at Savannah, and which appears in the *Times*
of this day, I do not think it will be necessary to take,
at present, any further steps in the matter beyond asking,
as I shall do, for an explanation from my correspondent
at New York, who ought to be, and who I believe is, well
informed upon these matters.

Always yours faithfully,   T. S. D.

The Viscount Palmerston, M.P., &c.

Neither the popular minister nor the popular
member ever corresponded or ever met again. The
career of both was drawing to its close, but the en-
feebled constitution of the latter indicated a speedier
dissolution. He had proceeded to a favourite water-
ing-place at the termination of the session (1861), to
recruit; but having exhausted the skill of the medical

profession, was doomed to find the healing resources of Nature equally inefficacious. In vain all
reputed specifics had been tried one after another : it
became painfully evident that the long overworked
machine was not only out of gear, but worn out.
Over and over again his enforced withdrawal from
political life had been announced by the public journals; but as he had come forward in person to dis-
prove the intelligence, no apprehensions were entertained by his numerous friends.

Unhappily for those who watched over him and
knew him best, he was hastening to his final rest
after half a century of arduous public service.
His life had been devoted, to the requirements of all
who wanted an advocate or a friend, without respect
to creed or nationality—without the slightest reference to social prejudices and partialities. He
ignored the bonds of family alliance, the claims of
long-established friendship, and the sympathies of
political clanship, at the call of duty ; and though this
lost him favour, it never lost him self-respect.

The bold champion of oppressed nationalities was
never bolder than when he refused to countenance
regicides, and disappointed the expectations of the
band of expatriated political schemers who sought to
make him their dupe and their tool. The Mazzinis
and Kossuths since then had withdrawn their confidence from him, for which, there is no doubt, he was
sufficiently thankful. They did more than this—they
forgot their champion and benefactor. This, however,
left the wearied politician a little more leisure to
attend to himself; his condition, however, proved
daily less capable of amelioration from any care.

Mr. Duncombe's illness originated about the year 1845, when he attended a board of inquiry on board the hulks, regarding the treatment of prisoners and the prison system. He caught a severe cold, which was neglected, and symptoms of a worse malady shortly became apparent, the natural consequence of the little attention which he paid to his health when his Parliamentary duties required him to be in his place in the House of Commons. In the space of one year bronchial disease developed into chronic asthma. He was recommended constant change of air and place, but after a few years the locality and the climate were left to his own goodwill. The principal places he visited were Frant, Brighton, Sidmouth, Tunbridge Wells, Pembury, Reigate, Box Hill, Godstone, Preston (Sussex), Cromer, Reigate, and Eastbourne.

Mr. Duncombe tried every system and every medicine which possessed even a doubtful recommendation. He sought the assistance of twenty-eight doctors, all of whom failed in their endeavours to effect a cure. The attacks of asthma were at times of a most severe and painful character.

In the year 1861 he was induced to try Lancing (in Sussex); on the 12th October he went there, and after a short stay seemed to be improving. The rapid change was so marked (at the time he was trying a new medicine), that his medical man came from London to make an examination, and reported favourably. On the 13th November, two days later, his patient suddenly expired, after over fourteen years of suffering. He was in the sixty-sixth year of his age.

The following is the last account of his health, written by himself for the month of October, 1861:—

Breathing a little easier, and got more out in London after leaving Eastbourne; and on the 12th moved to Lancing, between Shoreham and Worthing. Breathing worse, from visit to dentist, I think, and felt rather bilious on arriving at Lancing. Drove out on the 22nd.

26th.—Began "Cannabis Indica Tincture."

30th and 31st.—Walked out a little, ending the month decidedly better than I began it.

Please God it may continue! T. S. D.

Thus closed the career of a public servant of rare integrity and disinterestedness. Many have taken a similar path to popularity with more brilliant qualifications, but few have shown so signally their indifference to social advantages. He was the honorary advocate of the oppressed of every class and creed, and pursued a course of legislation for the sons of toil with no other object than their moral and intellectual advancement. His life was eminently patriotic, and his labours singularly beneficial. To do this he turned his back upon an elevated position and its all-powerful recommendations for State employment—abandoned the allurements of a patrician circle—and devoted himself to an arduous and unprofitable service.

Could he have survived a few years he would have enjoyed the gratification of seeing the principles he had so long and ably advocated embodied in a legislative measure, and carried triumphantly through both Houses of Parliament by his political associates, in conjunction with the great political party to which his family were attached. It would appear, from this important result, that his private conferences with his talented friend at Grosvenor Gate were not without a purpose. Real Parliamentary Reform has at last been secured—pre-eminently by the perseverance, intelligence, and tact of Mr. Disraeli. The Earl of Derby and his Administration will have the credit of obtaining for the people privileges which popular Governments have been content with promising when out of office, and denying when in. We trust that the industrial class, for whose advantage chiefly the new Reform Bill has been framed, will not suffer themselves to be induced, by specious misrepresentations, to prove that they are incapable of exercising these privileges, in the wise and liberal spirit with which they have been conceded.

Mr. Duncombe left a widow to lament her irreparable loss, and an only son to endeavour to imitate the virtues and emulate the self-sacrificing patriotism of so estimable a parent and so good a man. He died poor—rich in the memory of those who esteemed him, as

" HONEST TOM DUNCOMBE."

APPENDIX.

Baron Capelle's Notes upon the State of France since 1830.

LES ministres du Roi Charles X., usant de droit qu'en donnait à la couronne l'art. 14 de la charte constitutionnelle, avaient, pour préserver la royauté d'une conjuration imminente, suspendu pour un court délai quelques-unes des libertés constitutionnelles ; de même qu'on suspend en Angleterre *l'habeas corpus.*

Le Gouvernement élevé par la Révolution de Juillet a supprimé irrevocablement deux fois plus de libertés que n'en avaient suspendu temporairement les ministres de Charles X.

> The Restoration had suspended in France certain liberties ; the Revolution of July has destroyed them since.

Il a interdit le droit d'association, bien que le droit soit fondamental dans tout gouvernement libre ; et l'interdiction a été poussée si loin qu'il n'y a pas jusqu'à aux moindres sociétés littéraires, savantes, ou de bienfaisance, qui ne soient obligées de demander pour exister et se réunir, la permission de l'autorité.

> The right of association has been destroyed even for benevolent and scientific purposes.

Il a par les lois d'intimidation soumis la presse à un esclavage presque absolu sur les matières du Gouvernement.

> The laws against the Press are now worse than slavery.

Il a converti l'institution libérale et protectrice les juries, en une institution arbitraire et tyrannique, en faisant établir par la législation, que les jugements seraient désormais

> Trial by jury, decided by a majority of votes, and by ballot.

rendus à la simple majorité des votes, et que les jurés voteraient entr'eux au scrutin secret.

La conséquence de ces changements fondamentaux dans les lois a été de soumettre la France à un véritable déspotisme, et de la faire rétrograder vers la moyen âge.

Condition of France equal to the dark ages.

La marche du Gouvernement n'a pas été moins tyrannique que les changements faits dans les lois. On a fait plusieurs fois mitrailler les populations de Paris et de Lyon. Les condamnations pour délits de la presse ont été deux cents fois plus multipliées que pendant la Restauration, et toutes beaucoup plus rigoureux.

The measures of the Government have been worthy of those days. Population massacred; parts of Paris and Lyons demolished by the military. The prosecutions against the Press two hundredfold more numerous than in Charles the Tenth's time.

Les visites domiciliaires qui étaient si rares, et qui ne pouvaient être ordonnées que par les tribunaux, et après une procédure préalable, l'ont été, à tout propos, sous le moindre prétexte et en vertu d'un moindre ordre d'un agent du Gouvernement : l'abus en a été si grand, qu'on peut dire que la violation constante et facultative de l'asile des citoyens, a été par le fait substitué au principe de nos lois qui déclarait cet asile inviolable.

Domiciliary visits permitted by an order of the minister, and the abuse of it most terrific.

Enfin, les arrestations préventives ou préalables à tout jugement ont été tellement nombreuses et tellement prolongées, qu'il faudrait remonter au temps les plus réculés pour en trouver des exemples.

En résumé, non seulement la France était à tous égards et sans comparaison cent fois plus libre pendant la Restauration, mais elle était plus libre sous le Gouvernement impérial.

Arrests on presumptive evidence have been innumerable, and many objects of these arrests have been allowed to remain eighteen months and two years in prison waiting for acquittal. In short, the liberty of France was not only much greater before the Revolution of July, but was also so during the reign of Napoleon.

*Letter of the Duc d'Ossuna to Count de Courcy on Mr.
Duncombe's projected Railway.*

Paris, le 16 Mai, 1845.

MON CHER DE COURCY,—Je suis arrivé dans cette ville
depuis trois jours, et au même moment j'ai reçu vos deux
estimables lettres du 21 et 26 Août dernier qu'étaient par-
venues à ma maison de Madrid depuis mon départ ; l'inter-
vale de temps a été long à cause du mauvais état de ma
santé m'a obligé de m'arrêter souvent en route contre
l'habitude que j'ai de voyager avec la rapidité qu'exige mon
caractère actif.

Je me suis empressé d'examiner votre proposition pour
intervenir, moi comme président en homme de la société
directeur du chemin de fer de Madrid à Lisbonne, et en
effet je prevois que ce doit être une bonne affaire pour vous,
si vous pouvez reussir à en obtenir la concession du gouvernement et à réunir assez d'actionnaires pour le mettre en
exécution. Je m'associerais volontiers à cette entreprise
sans autre raison que savoir que vous et le cher d'Orsay en
étiez intéressés ; mais à mon grand regret il se presente un
grave inconvénient qui m'oblige à me dispenser de cette
question avec toute la bon volonté que j'ai de pouvoir y con-
tribuer mon nom. C'est un fait qu'une société formée à
Madrid pour l'exécution du chemin de fer des Asturies à la
mer du nord de l'Espagne m'avait proposé comme directeur
président de la même, et sans l'autorisation de ma part
m'ayant publiquement proclamé tel ; et voilà la raison
pourquoi vous m'avez vu annoncé dans cette qualité, sans
qu'en realité j'en savais rien. En vertu de cette démarche
qu'était faite par quelques personnes de mon amitié intime,
et par quelques-uns de mes collègues députés aux Cortès, je
ne pouvais pas me montrer à eux offensé dans les termes
qu'une pareille action meritait, et je me suis borné à leur
declarer que mon intention n'était pas d'en faire partie et que
je leur priais de vouloir bien effacer mon nom de cette
entreprise, à laquelle d'ailleurs, mes occupations person-
nelles en l'état de ma santé ne me permettraient prêter mes

soins et attentions : en définitive, il a été convenu qu'il en
serait ainsi ; et vous en verrez prochainement les effets dans
les mêmes annonces où vous m'avez vu figurer avant, sans
nulle connaissance de ma part.

Dans cet état de choses, vous concevrez facilement, mon
cher de Courcy, que la démarche de prêter mon nom à un
autre entreprise de pareil objet serait en extrème offen-
sante pour ces messieurs, et je desire ménager l'amitié des
mes collègues et amis, et plus encore l'honneur et la répu-
tation de la conséquence de mes actions et de mon caractère.
Vous même ayant voulu m'annoncer comme président de
votre entreprise sans avoir connaissance de tous les an-
técédens m'aviez placé involontairement dans un embarras
cruel pour mon amitié et ma déférence pour vous : je serais
obligé d'en donner satisfaction aux personnes à qui j'ai
refusé ma co-opération à Madrid, et j'espère que vous voudrez bien publier dans vos annonces qu'une erreur involon-
taire donnait lieu à insérer mon nom comme intéressé à
cette entreprise.

Pour cela il n'empèche pas, mon cher de Courcy, que par-
ticulièrement je fasse tout ce qui dependrait pour favoriser
votre projet; je m'intérresserais en Espagne avec les ministres,
avec mes amis, avec toutes les personnes de ma connaissance
qui puissent être utiles pour la réussite de l'affaire. Je m'intérresserais même pour un nombre d'actions du moment que
vous en aurez obtenu la concession du gouvernement pour
pouvoir les émettre ; enfin, je ferais tout ce qui pourrait
s'opposer à donner une idée d'inconséquence de caractère et
qui pourrait, en outre, vous prouver que je désire ardemment
servir vos intentions et votre amitié.

Veuillez je vous prie en faire part à mon cher d'Orsay, à
qui j'écrirai aussitôt que me le permettra ma santé chance-
lante, qui m'empêche encore aujourd-hui de vous écrire de ma
propre main comme je l'aurais désiré : presentez mes
respects d'amitié et mes hommages de cœur aux aimables
dames de Gore House, et croyez moi toujours votre ami
bien devoué et affectionné,

LE DUC D'OSSUNA ET DEL Y INFANTADO.

P.S.—Je reçois dans ce moment votre autre estimable lettre du 14 courant, à laquelle je ne puis vous dire que répéter tout ce que je viens de vous dire plus haut : je n'ai pas encore vu M. de Guiche, et pour le cas qu'il m'en parlera, je voudrais que vous eussiez m'envoyé les articles ou conditions sous lesquels est fondée votre société.

Letter of Ferhad Pacha.

Septembre 20, 1856.

TRÈS-HONORABLE AMI,—Il est vrai, que je n'ai pas encore votre réponse, mais je ne peux plus l'attendre pour vous écrire nouvellement sur un sujet qui me semble très important.

Dans ma dernière lettre je crois vous avoir signifié que je ne pouvais rester en bonne harmonie avec Omer P. Je souffrais et je tolérais avec une indifférence stoique, mais je voulais servir à mon souverain, et ne pas être le chien d'un général.

Il parait que cela regrettait quelquefois au général, puisque nonobstant son faible savoir, il aime se mêler en tout, même lorsque par hasard il n'a aucune connaissance sur l'affaire. En telle circonstance on a besoin de recourir quelquefois aux lumières des autres, et un certain Bangya Colonel Mehemed Bey, avec l'insigne Lorody, Lieutenant-Colonel Nurry Bey, aide-de-camp et le confidant d'Omer P., se sont donnés la peine d'illuminer brillamment l'esprit d'Omer P. avec mes lumières sur les haras et la police d'état. Pour un petit local il suffit une petite lumière.

Depuis ce temps on me fait la caresse ; Omer avait reconnu, que nous nous pouvions rendre des services réciproques, mais comme tous les hommes misérables, il n'a pas la franchise d'avouer son tort. Pour ma part je ne l'approcherai pas, et en conséquence l'affaire restera dans une correspondance par le médiaire des autres. Ceci comme l'introduction.

Hier donc Bangya m'avait dit : " Lorody était venu plusieurs fois chez lui, et l'avait trouvé tout-à-l'heure. Il

aurait lui raconté : que la santé du Sultan serait telle qu'il
lui sera difficile de survivre l'hiver (I.) que son frère Abdul-
Asis n'étant propre à la succession du trône, puisqu'il est
véhément, obscurant, fanatique et ne se laisse pas guider
(du moins non par ceux qui aimeraient de le faire) ; c'est
pourquoi une coalition s'est formée, afin de changer la succession du trône, et pour l'assurer au Murad, fils ainé du
Sultan. Celui est un enfant faible, épuisé, de 12—13 ans ;
pendant sa minorité y régnerait une coalition, qui saurait
ménager l'affaire de manière pour continuer de régner même
plus tard. A ce fin Omer P. et Reschid P. se sont récon-
ciliés (II.) et Omer se pacifiera-t-il aussi avec Riza P., à quoi,
sans se prononcer clairement, il parait d'avoir besoin de mon
aide, puisque Riza m'est favorable. Omer me faisait dire
' le temps viendra bien vite, qu'il aura besoin de moi, et il
comptera sur moi, comme je peux compter sur lui à l'instant
et pour toujours, et que tout le monde le sait' ; mais en
verité pour le moment ça ne vaut 5 para, si même il n'est
pas d'un avantage négatif. Lorody en outre avait ex-
pliqué : Abdul-Asis compte un parti puissant parmi le
peuple, et il est à craindre qu'il tenterait avec eux et avec
les Ulemas, qui lui sont devoués, un coup contre le gouvernement actuel. Outre cela il haït Omer, Reschid,
Riza, etc. : et commencait par le fait de les accourcir de
7—8 pouces d'en haut. L'on voudrait prévenir la guerre
civile, qui naturellement s'en prendrait fortement aux chrétiens et aux francs, avec une révolution du palais, et l'ambassade Anglaise, par l'égard des chrétiens y donnerait son
consentement. Sur l'observation de Bangya, que Abdul-
Asis enjouisse une santé fleurissante, l'énergie, et un parti
puissant, Lorody répondait : il mourra avant l'Abdul-
Medschid."

Ad (I.) j'ajouterai, qu'il y avait trois jours que j'avais
encore vu sa majesté en parfaite santé, et si forte comme
elle peut être, sans la moindre trace d'une dissolution pro-
chaine.

Ad (II.) j'observerai, que de fait Reschid P. et Omer P.
se sont réunis chez Kiritly Mehemet P. ; comme ils y se

sont conduits, je ne peux savoir, puisque il n'en avait que des muschirs dans la société.

La seule chose qui fait naître en moi des scrupules est l'article connu et déjà vieux du *Times*, dans lequel fut parlé de la caducité du Sultan, comme si on y voulait préparer l'Europe.

Je ne crois pas à cette histoire, puisque Omer. radote souvent, et voit le monde par la bouteille de scherry; Lorody et Bangya ne sont pas des hommes d'une conduite suffisamment nette. Cependant je ne peux pas me passer sans vous participer la nouvelle, toute fraiche comme elle est.

S'il y a quelque chose dans cette nouvelle, il est bon de le savoir, s'il n'y en est rien, ces quelques mots serviront à la charactéristique du tableau.

Dans le reste, il y est une calme—avant la tempête—et les nuages sont dans la question des Principautés.

Apropos d'Omer, il penche fortement et depuis long temps vers la Russie. Qu'il n'ait pas sauvé Kars, ça n'est pas ni sa faute ni son mérite, mais qu'il n'ait pas détruit Moschransky, comme j'avais voulu, ça est sa faute.

Un soir j'avais surpris dans le bois de Tschaitschi les avant-postes Russes, et je massacrais tout le piquet de Cosaques. Le diable aurait en empêché mes hommes lorsqu'ils ont vu que moi-même j'avais donné à un Cosaque du Don une estocade, qui le faisait tomber de son cheval, après avoir 3 fois tiré sur moi et après m'avoir blessé avec un boulet. En rentrant de mon service, Omer P. m'avait dit: "ce n'est pas la manière de faire la guerre, c'est une boucherie; on voit que c'est encore de la Hongrie que vous aviez de rendre quelque chose aux Cosaques. Il faut être chevaleresque envers l'ennemi; qui sait si demain il ne sera pas notre allié?" Ce sont ses propres paroles, que j'avais extraits de mon journal. Dans une autre occasion j'avais seulement blessé un sergent de Cosaques et je l'avais fait prisonnier, les autres soldats ont été massacrés par mes hommes.

Je conclus avec la prière d'une prompte et amicale réponse; si je peux être bon à quelque chose, commandez moi. Votre sincère et humble, FERHAD.

HONORABLE AMI,—Je vous envoie la missive ici-jointe par le ci-devant Lieutenant Keller de l'armée Hongroise, plus tard Capitaine dans l'armée Turque. Il s'etait economisé quelque argent, et a quitté le service pour se dédier à l'agriculture.

Il était très brave soldat et est un très honnête garçon, quoique Israélite par sa naissance. Il n'est pas révolutionnaire, et je vous garantis qu'il ne fait rien, et qu'il n'agite pas contre l'Autriche.

Son idée est de s'établir en Bulgarie, et si vous pourriez lui être utile à quelque chose auprès du Gouverneur, vous feriez un bon œuvre; il désire un terrain inculte, pour y établir une économie rurale.

Je crois qu'il y aura des autres qui viendront en Bulgarie; si quelqu'un sera votre client, les autres le seront aussi, si même ils ne seront que par le problème "que celui-là qui s'établisse, n'est plus dangereux," et Keller ne l'était jamais excepté avec son baïonnette.

Invariable votre, FERHAD.

Je baise les mains à la Baronne.

Letters of General Türr to T. S. Duncombe, Esq., M.P., June 19th, 28th, July 9th, 21st, August 13th, October 2nd, and November 4th, 1857.

16, Leicester-place, Leicester-square,
London, le 19 Juin, 1857.

MON CHER MONSIEUR,—Ayant reçu une lettre de la Circassie, *viá* Constantinople, laquelle me donne la nouvelle suivante :—

Les provinces Mochos, Ademi, Bsheduch, Katugnach, qui ont conclus la paix avec les Russes, parcequ'ils étaient fatigués des atrocités du Naib Emin Pasha, ses sont à present unis avec Sefer Pasha, qui a déjà sous ses ordres les pro-

vinces Netchnats, Adckuma, Csapona, Deniskanarinda To-
nabsa, et Ubuch, et comme Naib Emin Pasha était forcé de
quitter la Circassie ; la province Abazech a aussi juré fidelité
au Prinz Sefer, outre cela les provinces Kabarda et Karatsa
n'attendent que les ordres de Seffer Pasha,—or donc Sefer
Pasha a sous ses ordres 180,000 familles, chaque famille
donnera un soldat, mais en cas de besoin on pourrait obtenir
par familles 3-5 soldats, parcequ'il y a des familles qui sont
en nombre de 50 personnes, et généralement on peut compter
12-15 persons par famille.   Shamyl a sous ses ordres les
Daghistan et les Tseisains, deux tribus les plus guerriers de
tout le Caucase.   Les Russes ont commencé les opérations
contre Shamyl ; le Prince Général Bariatinsky est parti de
Tiflis pour être présent dans la guerre—le Général Philip-
son, Commandant de Trupes Russes à Ekaterindar, a fait
passer la rivière Kuban par 3-4000 soldats Russes, mais
nous nous avons mis imédiatment contre leurs marche 8000
Circassiens, et les Russes ont repassé le fleuve.   J'ai vu
plusieurs lettres chez Seffer Pasha, lesquelles étant écrites par
Lord Ponsomby dans le temps qu'il était Ambassadeur
Anglais à Constantinople ; je vous enverrais avec la première
occasion ces lettres, et vous verrez quelles sortes de promesses
a fait l'Angleterre aux Circassiens.   Prenant tous ça en considération, la question est—Le Gouvernement Anglais et
Turc voient-ils une intérêt à l'aider dans cette guerre d'in-
dépendence ? ou, avec leur insouciance forceront-ils cette
vaillante nation à conclure la paix et l'amitié avec la Russie ?
Dans le dernier cas l'Angleterre, qui devait très bien savoir que
le Caucase est un véritable boulevart contre la Russie (en
conséquence un sauveguarde pour l'Inde) en Asie ; sans cela
la Russie ne lutterait pas si acharnement pour conquérir la
Circassie, et ne perdrait pas chaqu' année 20 ou 30,000
soldats dans cette guerre Caucasienne.   La Turquie aussi
peut avoir la certitude, que si les Circassiens ses soumettront
à l'autorité Moskowil il n'auront pas à lutter contre 40,000
Russes, comme dans la dernière guerre en Asie, mais bien
contre 200,000 soldats, des desquels seront au moins 100,000
soldats Circassiens qui se combatront avec rage contre les

Turcs qui l'ont si injustement abandonnés. C'est la traduction littérale de la lettre reçu de la Circassie ; maintenant je vous joigns ici deux articles, qui sont parus dans les journaux.

Veuillez avoir la complaisance de parler avec le Lord Palmerston, et daignez dire à son Excellence que je suis devoué complètement à l'Angleterre, jusqu'à ce point où la funeste politique ne touche pas à l'Autriche. Je pars demain pour Birmingham et Liverpool, mais je serais de rétour le Lundi soir le 22 Juin. J'écrirais aujourd-hui à S. E. Lord Clarendon pour lui demander un passport.

Acceptez, mon cher Monsieur, les sincères salutations de votre tout devoué et fidèle, ET. TURR.

T. S. Duncombe, Esq., M.P.

Rose Cottage Hotel, Richmond, le 28 Juin, 1857.

MON CHER MONSIEUR,—Vous avez certainement vu dans le journaux un dépêche télégraphique de la Turquie laquelle etait conçu comme suit : " Une lettre conpromettant écrite par Ferhad Pasha à Mr. Roessler, consul d'Autriche à Ruschink, était interceptée."

Je m'empresse de vous envoyer ici-joint la copie de la traduction de la dite lettre interceptée ; la lettre était écrite en Allemagne parceque Ferhad Pasha, Baron Stein, fils du célèbre General Stein [dont la famille est entièrement Allemande], était en 1848 capitaine Autrichien : il avait quitté les Autrichiens et avait pris service dans l'armée Hongroise, mais déjà alors il était soupçonné comme agent secret de l'Autriche, et vous savez que dernièrement dans l'expédition Circassienne il a voulu en toute manière compromettre le Gouvernement Turc, mais heureusement il ne pouvait rien prouver ; et nous autres, quand nous étions demandés par la commission, nous avons tous simplement repondu que nous n'en savions rien;—maintenant il est la question, quand je dois retourner en Turquie. Quelle réponse dois-je donner aux Circassiens ? Si je dis que l'Angleterre ne veut rien faire, alors je suis sûr qu'ils négocieront la paix avec la Russie, et cela sera funeste pour la

Turquie et pour l'Angleterre aussi. Je viendra vous voir dans deux ou trois jours, parcequc ma santé commence à s'améliorer.

Veuillez agréer les sincères homages de votre

Tout devoué, ET. TURR.

Thomas Duncombe, Esq., M.P.

> Hotel de l'Europe, 15 and 16, Leicester-place,
> Leicester-square, London, le 9 Juillet, 1857.

MON CHER MONSIEUR,—Je viens de recevoir la nouvelle suivante :

> Constantinople, le 26 Juin, 1857.

Depuis long temps le Prinz Sefer Pasha avait notifié à ses sujets que tous les navires pouvaient entrer librement dans les ports de la Circassie pour y faire du commerce, les Russes même n'etaient pas exclus de jouir de ce privilège. Une sensible augmentation se fait voir dans le commerce ; plusieurs négociants de Trebisond et même de Constantinople, esperant en vertu des droits internationaux de jouir toute sureté, ont etablis des entrepôts de marchandises dans differents ports de la Circassie.

L'apparition continuelle de navires dans les ports Circassiens éveillait un malaise aux voisins Russes, et jaloux comme ils sont toujours vers chaque pas que les Circassiens essayent de faire dans la voie du progrès, les Russes prirent la décision de couper court avec eux. Par ordre supérieur fut expedié d'Anapa un bateau de guerre à vapeur pour faire la tournée de la côte Circassienne. Ce bateau s'était servi du stratagème de hisser le pavillon Anglais en s'approchant au port de Gelindjek. Arrivé à la portée du canon, le bateau prit position et commencait le feu contre les sandals (barques) qui y se trouvèrent à l'ancorage, et continuait le feu jusqu'à ce que tous les sandals furent coulés au fond. Après avoir accompli cette barbare destruction, le bateau Russe partit pour Soudjuk-Kale, où sachant qu'il n'y a aucune force militaire, les Russes débarquèrent une compagnie, laquelle ravagait tous les magasins et incendiait toutes les marchandises qu'ils ne pouvaient emporter. Avant de quitter le port du Soudjuk-Kale, les Russes avaient brulés tous les sandals, à l'exception de quelques uns qu'ils prirent à la remorque avec eux.

Cette flagrante violation des droits internationaux et l'offense grave commise contre la traité de Paris, qui declarait la neutralité de la Mer Noire, plus encore l'act de la piraterie fait par les Russes, est necessaire de porter à la conaissance de l'Europe pour qu'elle juge la gravité d'un tel fait. Il faut espérer que les congrès qui vont bientôt se réunir a Paris, établiront une loi que à l'avenir sauvgardera les intérêts internationaux et garantira mieux que jusqu'à présent il était le cas, la libre navigation de la Mer Noire.

Je viendra vous voir demain, et daignez agréer les sincères salutations

De votre tout devoué et obligé,   Et. Turr.

Memorandum.

Les Circassiens restèrent independans jusqu'à présent, parce que ils savaient tenir tête à leurs ennemis et maintenir leur droit et leur liberté. L'Europe entière connait le fait. Depuis 30 ans, les Russes faisaient des irruptions violentes dans notre pays, sans aucune raison plausible, et ils furent la cause que d'un côté et de l'autre, que le sang y coulait à torrents, sans que les Russes auraient atteints leur but. Jusqu'à ce qu'il y aura un Circassien, tous les efforts du pays seront mis à l'œuvre, pour la défense de nos droits et de nos libertés. Les puissances de l'Europe qui ne désirent que la paix, comment peuvent elles regarder tranquillement les injustes empiètements que la Russie exerce sur la Circassie ? Que l'Europe jette un coup d'œil sur cette inutile effusion de sang, et pour mettre fin à cet eternel massacre qu'elle prononce haut l'indépendance de la Circassie, comme elle avait par la traité de Paris prononcée la neutralisation de la Mer Noire. En toute confiance sur le traité de Paris, Zan Oghlu Sefer Giraj avait publié une manifesto à ses sujets, par laquelle l'entrée des ports Circassiens furent ouvertes à tous les navires étrangers ; cet ordre fut respecté par les Circassiens, et produisait déjà de bons resultats. Cependant il y a quelques jours les Russes surprirent les ports de Gelendjik et Sodjuk-Kalé, en se servent d'une ruse, c'est à dire, deux bateaux à vapeur Russes arborant le pavillon Anglais entrèrent sans aucune résistance dans les susdits ports, y coulèrent au fond plusieurs sandals et emportèrent des autres, chargés avec du sel. Ce n'est pas tout, leur barbarie allait plus loin, car ils incendièrent à Sodjuk-Kalé plusieurs magasins, dans lesquels, chose regrettable et douloureuse à dire, il y avait plusieurs enfants et des femmes, qui sont restés victimes de l'élements furieux.

Au nom du peuple de la Circassie, le congrès de Paris vient d'être prié de prendre dans cette circonstance une décision qui soit digne du siècle. Pour la tranquillité du pays et de l'Europe, il est nécessaire de déclarer dans le congrès de Paris l'indépendance de la Circassie, et par cet act solènel rétablir une nation qui existent depuis des siècles.

Marseille, le 13 Août.

Mon cher Monsieur,—Je pars aujourd-hui pour Constantinople, je ferai tout mon possible pour retablir ma santé. Les nouvelles des Indes sont toujours désagreables ; si ma santé revienne je demanderai immédiatement le gouvernement Anglais de me permettre d'aller aux Indes avec quelques milles braves soldats. C'est domage que S. E. le Lord Stratford avec une obstination a perdu pour le moment la suprematie Anglaise à Constantinople ; depuis bien temps je vous ai dit que l'amitié Autrichienne deviendra funeste pour l'Angleterre. Voilà le prologue. Le Caimakin Vogoridis n'est pas Moldave mais Grec, et naturalisé Moldave depuis 12 ans. Or, donc on pu voir que toute la nation Moldave était hostile à ce gouverneur excepté le Fanariots (le Grec habitant de Moldavia). Je ne manquera pas de vous envoyer toutes les nouvelles intéressantes de l'Orient. Tachez de faire tout votre possible de barrer le chemin de Russes en Caucase. Si S. E. le Lord Clarendon pourrait me donner une lettre pour un ministre Turc, cela me ferait beaucoup de bien.

Veuillez, mon cher Monsieur, accepter les sincères salutations

De votre tout devoué,   Et. Türr.

Mon adresse est—Col. E. Türr, Poste Restante, Constantinople (viâ Marseille).

Constantinople, le 2 Decembre, 1857.

Mon cher Monsieur,—J'ai reçu votre lettre du 14 Nov., et je vois que vous n'avez pas reçu ma lettre du mois Septembre; je suis bien fâché que cette lettre soit perdue, parce que je vous y ai donné plusieurs renseignements. Je vois avec plaisir que votre santé s'est amelioré, et que vous pourrez prendre la défense de la cause de liberté et justice dans le Parlement. J'ai écrit à Turin pour remercier à M. Valerio, et de le prier pour qu'il vous envoie le nombre des ex. de Neapel et de Rome; cependant son adresse est—Al Signor L. Valerio, deputato, N⁰. 10, Strada Rosa Rossa, à Torino. Quant à l'attaque Russe a Gelindjek, et qu'ils aient hissé le drapeau Anglais, tout ceci est vrai, et vous pourrez citer pour appuyer cette chose que si les Russes n'auront pas hissés le drapeau Anglais, les Circassiens se seraient pas mis en état de défense; mais voyant le bateau Anglais, il se sont mis sur la rive et ont applaudis le bateau, et un moment après les Russes ont tiré, bordé et mitraillé les Circassiens; et autre cela, les Russes ont fait plusieurs attaques sur la côte Circassienne, et non seulment avec le bateau à vapeur, mais aussi avec la barque canonière. Eh bien, comment expliquer cela, et la traité de Paris? Mr. Richards viendra chez vous, en il vous enverra une traduction d'un document lequel était envoyé à chaque Gouvernement, parti du paix de Paris.

Pour l'Inde je peux vous dire que j'ai la nouvelle certaine que le Gouvernement Russe depuis plusieurs années a l'habitude d'envoyer aux Indes des exilés condamnés en Siberie, pour qu'ils fassent de propagandes Russes parmi cette population contre les Anglais, et comme il y a entre les condamnés en Siberie plusieurs des militaires Polonais et Russes or, donc, c'est bien possible que les Indiens soient commandés par des officiers experts. Sur la frontière Perse il y a une

nation qui se nome Turkoman ; là il y a à présent une révolution ; c'est bien possible quelle a été incitée par les Russes,
parceque le Czar a immédiatement offert au Shah de Perse de
lui aider pour étouffer le mouvement des Turkomans, mais
aussi pour récompenser les Russes. Ainsi attrapperons nous
une portion de territoire qui les approchera un pas de plus
vers l'Inde.

La lettre pour Mr. Barklay. Mr. Barklay est ingénieur
en chef du chemin de fer Turc de Kustendgye à Rasova :
entre les directeurs il y a MM. Paget, Wilson, Levy ; un
des ces messieurs est M.P., pour cela je vous ai prié en
cas que vous connaissiez un des ces messieurs de me procurer
une lettre pour Mr. Barklay.

Quant aux finances Turques, ici le lr. str. a la valeur in-
trinsique 115 piastres, et, à présent, un lr. str. est 156 piastres,
or, donc, par lr. str. 31 piastres plus depuis la crise
Européenne.

Le Lord Stratford part dans quelques jours pour
l'Angleterre : l'affaire de Principauté n'est pas encore finie ;
cependant je crois que la rappelle du Lord Stratford amenera
une entente entre la France et l'Angleterre.

Attendant votre bienveillante réponse, veuillez accepter
les salutations sincères de votre tout devoué et fidèle,

ET. TURR.

Constantinople, le 4 Novembre.

MON CHER MONSIEUR,—N'ayant pas reçu une réponse
à ma lettre que je vous ai écrit le mois Septembre, je
craigns que votre santé soit toujours altérée ; pour cela je
vous prie de me donner plus tôt que possible vos nouvelles.
Vous avez vu que la réunion des Empereurs a eu lieu
comme je vous ai écrit dans le mois Mai, 1857. L'affaire de
Principauté n'est pas complètement arrangée. Après les
nouvelles télégraphiques, Delhi est heureusement prise ; il
reste à présent de finir avec la province d'Oude, ou je crois
que les rebelles se sont rassemblés.

Les Russes ont bloqués la côte Circassienne, malgré que la
traité de Paris défende toute hostilité dans la Mer Noire ;
et Lord Palmerston a dit dans la Chambre de Communs

que les Russes pourraient faire des opérations militaires contre les Circassiens; quant à moi, je crois que Lord Palmerston aura pu empêché toutes hostilités Russes dans la Mer Noire contre le Caucase.

Ma santé a commencé à s'ameliorer; mais malheureusement l'hiver commence, et le froid est très nuisible à cette sorte de maladie.

Veuillez accepter, mon cher monsieur, les salutations sincères de   Votre tout devoué et fidèle,   ET. TURR.

P.S.—On a commencé à construire le chemin de fer de Kustendji à Rassova. L'ingénieur en chef est Mr. Barklay; les directeurs sont MM. Wilson, Price, et Paget. Un de ces messieurs est M.P. Si par hasard vous connaissez un de ces messieurs, je vous en supplie de vouloir me faire donner une lettre de récommandation pour l'ingénieur Barklay.

D'avance vous remerciant pour votre bonté,

Votre fidèle,   TURR.*

---

* The writer, we presume, is a much better Hungarian than he is a Frenchman. In several passages we have found it quite impossible to make out his meaning.

THE END.

13, GREAT MARLBOROUGH STREET.

MESSRS. HURST AND BLACKETT'S
LIST OF NEW WORKS.

THE LIFE AND CORRESPONDENCE OF
THOMAS SLINGSBY DUNCOMBE, LATE M.P. FOR FINSBURY.
By his Son, THOMAS H. DUNCOMBE. 2 vols. 8vo, with Portrait. 30s.

Among other Personages whose correspondence will be found in these
volumes are the Emperor Napoleon III.; Princes Schwarzenberg and
Polignac; the Dukes of Beaufort, Brunswick, Buccleugh, Devon-
shire, Newcastle, De Richelieu; the Marquises Clanricarde, Conyng-
ham, Donegall, Normanby, Townshend; Lords Abinger, Alvanley,
Belfast, Brougham, Chelmsford, Clarendon, Derby, Durham, Dun-
cannon, Essex, Enfield, Charles Fitzroy, Glengall, Robert Grosvenor,
Harrowby, Ingestrie, Lyndhurst, Mahon, Melbourne, Palmerston,
Dudley Coutts Stuart, Rothschild, Uxbridge; Barons Capella, De
Falcke, Pœrio, Orsi; Counts D'Orsay, Batthyany, Morny, Walewski,
Montrond, Bismark; Sirs John Easthope, De Lacy Evans, Roland
Ferguson, R. Graham, Benjamin Hall, Rowland Hill, John C. Hob-
house, George C. Lewis, William Molesworth, Robert Peel, John
Romilly; Messrs. Smith O'Brien, Byng, W. Cowper, Feargus O'Con-
nor, Edward Ellice, W. E. Gladstone, G. Grote, Joseph Hume, La-
bouchere, W. Locke, Mazzini, Madden, Spring Rice, Rose, Tom
Raikes, H. G. Ward, Wakley, Kossuth, Haydon, Peake, Arnold,
Morton, Oxberry, Bunn, &c.

SPIRITUAL WIVES. By W. HEPWORTH DIXON,
Author of 'New America,' &c. 8vo. With Portrait of the Author.
(In the Press.)

UNDER THE PALMS IN ALGERIA AND
TUNIS. By the Hon. LEWIS WINGFIELD. 2 vols. post 8vo, with
Illustrations. 21s.

"This book contains a great deal of very useful and interesting information
about countries of which not much is known by Englishmen; and the Author's
stories of personal adventure will be read with pleasure."—*Star.*

"This narrative will be found of great interest. It is filled with reliable information, most of it entirely new to the general reader."—*Observer.*

LORD BYRON. By the MARQUISE DE BOISSY
(COUNTESS GUICCIOLI). 2 vols. 8vo. *(In the Press.)*

CHAUCER'S ENGLAND. By MATTHEW BROWNE.
1 vol. 8vo. With numerous Illustrations. *(In the Press.)*

THROUGH SPAIN TO THE SAHARA. By
MATILDA BETHAM EDWARDS. Author of 'A Winter with the Swallows,' &c. 1 vol. 8vo, with Illustrations. 15s.

MESSRS. HURST AND BLACKETT'S
NEW WORKS—*Continued.*

THE LIFE OF JOSIAH WEDGWOOD; From

his Private Correspondence and Family Papers, in the possession of JOSEPH MAYER, Esq., F.S.A., FRANCIS WEDGWOOD, Esq., C. DARWIN, Esq., M.A., F.R.S., Miss WEDGWOOD, and other Original Sources. With an Introductory Sketch of the Art of Pottery in England. By ELIZA METEYARD. Dedicated to the Right Hon. W. E. GLADSTONE. Complete in 2 vols. 8vo, with Portraits and 300 other Beautiful Illustrations, elegantly bound, price 42s.

"This is the Life of Wedgwood to the expected appearance of which I referred at Burslem."—*Extract from a Letter to the Author by the Right Hon. W. E. Gladstone.*

"An important contribution to the annals of industrial biography. Miss Meteyard has executed a laborious task with much care and fidelity. The book is profusely illustrated, and the illustrations deserve the highest praise. They are executed with extreme beauty.—*Times.*

"We have to congratulate the authoress on the publication of her Life of Wedgwood. We can award her the praise due to the most pains-taking and conscientious application. She has devoted her whole mind and energy to her subject, and has achieved a work not less creditable to herself than it is indispensable to all who wish to know anything about English ceramic art and its great inventor. The two volumes before us are in themselves marvels of decorative and typographical skill. More beautifully printed pages, more creamy paper, and more dainty woodcuts have seldom met our eyes. It is rarely that an author is so well seconded by his coadjutors as Miss Meteyard has been by her publishers, printers, and the staff of draughtsmen and engravers who have contributed the numerous illustrations which adorn this sumptuous book."—*Saturday Review.*

"This very beautiful book contains that Life of Wedgwood which for the last fifteen years Miss Meteyard has had in view, and to which the Wedgwood family, and all who have papers valuable in relation to its subject, have been cordially contributing. In his admirable sketch of Wedgwood, given at Burslem, it was to the publication of this biography that Mr. Gladstone looked forward with pleasure. It is a very accurate and valuable book. To give their fullest value to the engravings of works of art which largely enrich the volumes, the biography has been made by its publishers a choice specimen of their own art as bookmakers. Neither care nor cost have been grudged. The two volumes form as handsome a book as has ever been published."—*Examiner.*

"The appearance of such a work as Miss Meteyard's 'Life of Josiah Wedgwood' is an event of importance in the sister spheres of literature and art. The biographer of our great potter has more than ordinary fitness for the fulfilment of her labour of love. She is an enthusiastic admirer and a practised connoisseur of Ceramic Art, and she brings the pleasant energy of individual taste and feeling to the aid of complete, authentic, and well-arranged information, and the well-balanced style of an experienced *littérateur.* The interest of the book grows with every page. The reader will peruse the numerous interesting particulars of Wedgwood's family life and affairs with unusual satisfaction, and will lay down the work with undoubting confidence that it will rank as a classic among biographies—an exhaustive work of the first rank in its school."—*Morning Post.*

"An admirable, well-written, honourably elaborate, and most interesting book." *Athenæum.*

"No book has come before us for some time so stored with interesting information. Miss Meteyard is a biographer distinguished by a clever and energetic style, by delicate judgment, extensive information, and a deep interest in her subject. The history of the Ceramic Art in England, and the biography of the eminent man who brought it to perfection, have evidently been to her a labour of love; and of the spirit and manner in which she has executed it we can hardly speak too highly. The splendid getting up of the work reflects much credit on the house from which it is issued."—*Dublin University Magazine.*

"In this magnificent volume we welcome one of the very noblest contributions to the history of the Ceramic art ever published. We place it at once and permanently side by side with Bernard Palissy's Memoirs and with Benvenuto Cellini's Autobiography."—*Sun.*

13, GREAT MARLBOROUGH STREET.

MESSRS. HURST AND BLACKETT'S
NEW WORKS—*Continued.*

NEW AMERICA. By WILLIAM HEPWORTH DIXON.
SEVENTH EDITION. 2 vols. demy 8vo, with Illustrations. 30s.

"The author of this very interesting book having penetrated through the plains and mountains of the Far West into the Salt Lake Valley, here gives us an excellent account of the Mormons, and some striking descriptions of the scenes which he saw, and the conversations which he held with many of the Saints during his sojourn there. For a full account of the singular sect called the Shakers, of their patient, loving industry, their admirable schools, and their perpetual intercourse with the invisible world, we must refer the reader to this work. Mr. Dixon has written thoughtfully and well, and we can recall no previous book on American travel which dwells so fully on these much vexed subjects."—*Times.*

"Mr. Dixon's book is the work of a keen observer, and it appears at an opportune season. Those who would pursue all the varied phenomena of which we have attempted an outline will have reason to be grateful to the intelligent and lively guide who has given them such a sample of the inquiry. During his residence at Salt Lake City Mr. Dixon was able to gather much valuable and interesting information respecting Mormon life and society: and the account of that singular body, the Shakers, from his observations during a visit to their chief settlement at Mount Lebanon, is one of the best parts of Mr. Dixon's work."—*Quarterly Review.*

"There are few books of this season likely to excite so much general curiosity as Mr. Dixon's very entertaining and instructive work on New America. None are more nearly interested in the growth and development of new ideas on the other side of the Atlantic than ourselves. The book is really interesting from the first page to the last, and it contains a large amount of valuable and curious information."—*Pall Mall Gazette.*

"In these very entertaining volumes Mr. Dixon touches upon many other features of American society, but it is in his sketches of Mormons, Shakers, Bible-Communists, and other kindred associations, that the reader will probably find most to interest him. We recommend every one who feels any interest in human nature to read Mr. Dixon's volumes for themselves."—*Saturday Review.*

"We have had nothing about Utah and the Mormons so genuine and satisfactory as the account now given us by Mr. Dixon, but he takes also a wider glance at the Far West, and blends with his narrative such notes of life as he thinks useful aids to a study of the newest social conditions—germs of a society of the future. There is not a chapter from which pleasant extract might not he made, not a page that does not by bright studies of humanity in unaccustomed forms keep the attention alive from the beginning to the end of the narrative."—*Examiner.*

"Intensely exciting volumes. The central interest of the book lies in Mr. Dixon's picture of Mormon society, and it is for its singular revelations respecting Brigham Young's people, and the Shakers and Bible Communists, that nine readers out of every ten will send for an early copy of this strange story. Whilst Mr. Dixon speaks frankly all that he knows and thinks, he speaks it in a fashion that will carry his volumes into the hands of every woman in England and America."—*Post.*

"A book which it is a rare pleasure to read—and which will most indubitably be read by all who care to study the newest phenomena of American life."—*Spectator.*

"We are much mistaken if both in America and England Mr. Dixon's volumes do not win for themselves the widest circulation."—*Standard.*

"Mr. Dixon's 'New America' is decidedly the cleverest and most interesting, as it has already proved the most successful, book published this season."—*Star.*

"Mr. Dixon has written a book about America having the unusual merit of being at once amusing and instructive, true as well as new. Of the books published this season there will be none more cordially read."—*Macmillan's Magazine.*

"Mr. Dixon's book is a careful, wise, and graphic picture of the most prominent social phenomena which the newest phases of the New World present. The narrative is full of interest from end to end, as well as of most important subjects for consideration. No student of society, no historian of humanity, should be without it as a reliable and valuable text-book on New America."—*All the Year Round.*

"In these graphic volumes Mr. Dixon sketches American men and women, sharply, vigorously and truthfully, under every aspect. The smart Yankee, the grave politician, the senate and the stage, the pulpit and the prairie, loafers and philanthropists, crowded streets, and the howling wilderness, the saloon and boudoir, with woman everywhere at full length—all pass on before us in some of the most vivid and brilliant pages ever written."—*Dublin University Magazine.*

3

MESSRS. HURST AND BLACKETT'S
NEW WORKS—*Continued.*

A TRIP TO THE TROPICS, AND HOME
THROUGH AMERICA. By the MARQUIS OF LORNE. *Second Edition.* 1 vol. 8vo, with Illustrations. 15s.

"Lord Lorne's 'Trip to the Tropics' is the best book of travels of the season."—*Pall Mall Gazette.*

"The tone of Lord Lorne's book is thoroughly healthy and vigorous, and his remarks upon men and things are well-reasoned and acute. As records of the fresh impressions left on the mind of a young tourist who saw much, and can give a pleasant, intelligent account of what he saw, the book is in every way satisfactory."—*Times.*

"A pleasant record of travel in the Western Islands and the United States. Lord Lorne saw a good deal of society both in the South and in the North. His tone is good, without undue partisan feeling. We can offer him our congratulations on his first essay as a traveller and an author."—*Athenæum.*

"Lord Lorne's book is pleasantly written. It is the unaffected narrative of a traveller of considerable impartiality and desire for information."—*Saturday Review.*

"In no other book will the reader find a more correct and life-like picture of the places and persons visited by the Marquis of Lorne, and no where more frankness and truthfulness in the statement of facts and impressions."—*Examiner.*

WILD LIFE AMONG THE PACIFIC ISLAND-
ERS. By E. H. LAMONT, ESQ. 8vo, with numerous Illustrations. 18s.

"A more curious romance of life and adventure is not to be found in the library of travel. A pleasanter volume of its kind has not been put forth since the year came in. It is a story of wreck and residence in the islands of the Pacific. The author was more than once in peril of being eaten. From some of the natives, however, he received compassion and kindness, and by asserting the superiority of a civilised man, presently arrived at an importance and authority which made him respected, feared, and loved. His accounts of the habits and ceremonies of the islanders are touched with spirit. The details of his essays at escape read almost like lost pages from 'Robinson Crusoe.' His deliverance is related with as much spirit as the best sea chase in Fenimore Cooper's best sea-romance."—*Athenæum.*

THE SPORTSMAN AND NATURALIST IN
CANADA. With Notes on the Natural History of the Game, Game Birds, and Fish of that country. By MAJOR W. ROSS KING, F.R.G.S., F.S.A.S. 1 vol. super royal 8vo, Illustrated with beautiful Coloured Plates and Woodcuts. 20s. Elegantly bound.

"Truthful, simple, and extremely observant, Major King has been able to throw much light upon the habits as well as the zoological relations of the animals with which he came in collision; and his descriptions of the country, as well as of the creatures inhabiting it, are as bright and graphic as they are evidently correct."—*Athenæum.*

"In 'The Sportsman and Naturalist in Canada' we have a full, true, and comprehensive record of all the facts concerning American animals which the author was able in a three years' residence to collect. We have these facts in a goodly volume, splendidly illustrated, and with its contents so well arranged that a reference to any description of bird, beast or fish may be made almost instantly. It is an important contribution to Natural History, and a work the intending traveller will consult once and again, since it gives him the information he most needs, and finds least generally accessible. The book will take its position in the foremost rank of works of its class. The descriptions throughout are written by one who is a master of his subject, and who writes English such as few are able to equal. Of recent British travellers few can vie with its author in close observation of nature, and in those graces of style and scholarship which make the information contained in his volume as pleasant to obtain as it is valuable to preserve. In fact, since the works of Eliot Warburton and Kinglake, no book of travels with which we are acquainted has been written in a style more clear, forcible picturesque."—*Sunday Times.*

4

MESSRS. HURST AND BLACKETT'S
NEW WORKS—*Continued.*

MEMOIRS AND CORRESPONDENCE OF
FIELD-MARSHAL VISCOUNT COMBERMERE, G.C.B., &c.
From his Family Papers. By the Right Hon. MARY VISCOUNTESS
COMBERMERE and Capt. W. W. KNOLLYS. 2 v. 8vo, with Portraits. 30s.

"The gallant Stapleton Cotton, Viscount Combermere, was one of those men
who belong to two epochs. He was a soldier, actively engaged, nearly ten years
before the last century came to its troubled close; and he was among us but as
yesterday, a noble veteran, gloriously laden with years, laurels, and pleasant reminiscences. To the last this noble soldier and most perfect gentleman took
cheerful part in the duties and pleasures of life, leaving to an only son an inheritance of a great name, and to a sorrowing widow the task of recording how the
bearer of the name won for it all his greatness. This has been done, evidently as
a labour of love, by Lady Combermere, and she has been efficiently assisted in the
military details by Captain Knollys. Apart from the biographical and professional
details, the volumes, moreover, are full of sketches of persons of importance or
interest who came into connection with Lord Combermere."—*Athenæum.*

"A welcome and gracefully written memorial of one of the greatest of England's
soldiers, and worthiest of her sons. It is a most interesting work."—*Morning Post.*

"This biography, abounding in letters and other unpublished materials, is all
fresh and trustworthy information, as to the life of a man whose career deserved a
record."—*Examiner.*

A BOOK ABOUT LAWYERS. By J. C. JEAF-
FRESON, Barrister-at-Law, author of 'A Book about Doctors,' &c.
New, Revised, and Cheaper Edition. 2 vols. post 8vo. 24s.

PRINCIPAL CONTENTS:—The Great Seal, Royal Portraits, The Practice of Sealing,
Lords Commissioners, On Damasking, The Rival Seals, Purses of State, A Lady
Keeper, Lawyers in Arms, The Devil's Own, Lawyers on Horseback, Chan-
cellors' Cavalcades, Ladies in Law Colleges, York House, Powis House,
Lincoln's Inn Fields, The Old Law Quarter, Loves of the Lawyers, The Three
Graces, Rejected Addresses, Brothers in Trouble, Fees to Counsel, Retainers
Special and General, Judicial Corruption, Gifts and Sales, Judicial Salaries,
Costume and Toilet, Millinery, Wigs, Bands and Collars, Bags and Gowns, The
Singing Barrister, Actors at the Bar, Political Lawyers, The Peers, Lawyers in
the House, Legal Education, Inns of Court and Inns of Chancery, Lawyers and
Gentlemen, Law French and Law Latin, Readers and Mootmen, Pupils in
Chambers, Wit of Lawyers, Humorous Stories, Wits in Silk and Punsters in
Ermine, Circuiters, Witnesses, Lawyers and Saints, Lawyers in Court and
Society, Attorneys at Law, Westminster Hall, Law and Literature, &c.

"'A Book about Lawyers' deserves to be very popular. Mr. Jeaffreson has
accomplished his work in a very creditable manner. He has taken pains to collect
information from persons as well as from books, and he writes with a sense of
keen enjoyment which greatly enhances the reader's pleasure. He introduces us
to Lawyerdom under a variety of phases—we have lawyers in arms, lawyers on
horseback, lawyers in love, and lawyers in Parliament. We are told of their salaries and fees, their wigs and gowns, their jokes and gaieties. We meet them at
home and abroad, in court, in chambers, and in company. In the chapters headed
'Mirth,' the author has gathered together a choice sheaf of anecdotes from the days
of More down to Erskine and Eldon."—*Times.*

"These volumes will afford pleasure and instruction to all who read them, and
they will increase the reputation which Mr. Jeaffreson has already earned by his
large industry and great ability. We are indebted to him for about seven hundred
pages, all devoted to the history and illustration of legal men and things. It is much
that we can say for a book, that there is not a superfluous page in it."—*Athenæum.*

"The success of his 'Book about Doctors' has induced Mr. Jeaffreson to write
another book—about Lawyers. The subject is attractive. It is a bright string of
anecdotes, skilfully put together, on legal topics of all sorts, but especially in illustration of the lives of famous lawyers. Mr. Jeaffreson has not only collected a large
number of good stories, but he has grouped them pleasantly, and tells them well.
We need say little to recommend a book that can speak for itself so pleasantly.
No livelier reading is to be found among the new books of the season."—
Examiner.

5

MESSRS. HURST AND BLACKETT'S
NEW WORKS—*Continued.*

LIFE IN A FRENCH CHATEAU. By HUBERT
E. H. JERNINGHAM, ESQ. *Second Edition.* 1 vol. post 8vo, with
Illustrations. 10s. 6d. bound.

"Mr. Jerningham's attractive and amusing volume will be perused with much
interest."—*Morning Post.*

"A thoroughly fresh and delightful narrative—valuable, instructive, and entertaining."—*United Service Magazine.*

"A readable, pleasant, and amusing book, in which Mr. Jerningham records his
life among the denizens of the French Château, which extended its courtly hospitality to him, in a very agreeable and entertaining manner."—*Court Journal.*

TRAVELS IN FRANCE AND GERMANY IN
1865 AND 1866: Including a Steam Voyage down the Danube,
and a Ride across the Mountains of European Turkey from Bel-
grade to Montenegro. By Captain SPENCER, author of ' Travels in
Circassia,' &c. 2 vols. 21s.

"This work would at any time be read with pleasure, but at this moment it is
invested with peculiar interest. There is sufficient of adventure for those who
love that which is exciting; sketches of wild and beautiful scenes; glimpses of life,
not only in cities, but in secluded villages, and notes and observations on the social,
moral, and political condition of the countries passed through. The author's
style is lucid and anecdotal, and the range of his book gives scope for much pleas-
ing variety as well as for much useful information."—*Post.*

ENGLISH TRAVELLERS AND ITALIAN
BRIGANDS: a Narrative of Capture and Captivity. By W. J. C.
MOENS. Second Edition. Revised with Additions. 2 vols., with
Portrait and other Illustrations. 21s.

"Mr. Moens had a bad time of it among the Italian Brigands. But his misfor-
tunes are now to himself and to his friends a source of no little entertainment, and
we can say for those who listen to his story that we have followed him in his
adventures with pleasure. He tells his tale in a clear and simple style, and with
that confident manliness which is not afraid to be natural."—*The Times.*

"Mr. Moens has had an experience and an adventure of startling magnitude in
these prosaic times of ours. He has seen what no other Englishman has seen, and
has done what no one else has done, and has written a bright and charming book
as the result."—*All the Year Round.*

"In these volumes, the literary merits of which are numerous, we have the true
story of the capture of Mr. Moens by the brigands. We have no doubt that the
book will be extensively read; we are quite sure that it will do an immense amount
of good. It lets in a flood of light upon the dens of these robbers."—*Daily News.*

A WINTER WITH THE SWALLOWS IN
ALGERIA. By MATILDA BETHAM EDWARDS. 8vo, with Illustrations. 15s.

"A pleasant volume; a genuine, graphic record of a time of thorough enjoyment."—*Athenæum.*

"A fresh and fascinating book, full of matter and beauty. It is one of the most
instructive books of travel of the season, and one of the brightest. It would be difficult to overpraise it."—*Spectator.*

"A bright, blithe, picturesque, artistic book, full of colour and sunshine, and
replete with good sense and sound observation. To the enthusiasm of the book a
great portion of its beauty and its attraction are owing, but solid information and
the reality of things in Algeria are never disguised in favour of the bright land to
which the author followed the Swallows."—*Post.*

TRAVELS AND ADVENTURES OF AN OFFI-
CER'S WIFE IN INDIA, CHINA, AND NEW ZEALAND.
By Mrs. MUTER, Wife of Lieut.-Colonel D. D. MUTER, 13th (Prince
Albert's) Light Infantry. 2 vols. 21s.

MESSRS. HURST AND BLACKETT'S
NEW WORKS—*Continued.*

THE HON. GRANTLEY BERKELEY'S LIFE
AND RECOLLECTIONS. Vols. III. and IV. completing the
Work. 30s., bound.

Among the other distinguished persons mentioned in these volumes are the
Emperors Alexander, Nicholas, and Napoleon III.; Kings George IV., William IV., and Leopold L.; Princes Talleyrand, Esterhazy, Napoleon, Puckler
Muskau; the Dukes of Sussex, York, Cambridge, Wellington, d'Orleans,
d'Aumale, Brunswick, Manchester, Beaufort, Cleveland, Richmond, Bucking-
ham; Lords Byron, Melbourne, Lansdowne, Holland, Brougham, Alvanley,
Yarmouth, Petersham, Craven, Salisbury, Devonshire, Ducie, Glasgow, Malmes-
bury, Castlereagh, Breadalbane, &c. Sirs Robert Peel, T. Lawrence, W.
Knighton, George Dashwood, George Warrender, Lumley Skeffington, Bulwer
Lytton, Count d'Orsay, Count de Morny, the Rev. Sydney Smith, Tom Moore,
Shelley, Thomas Campbell, Beau Brummell, Theodore Hook, Leigh Hunt,
W. S. Landor, James and Horace Smith, Jack Musters, Assheton Smith, &c.
Ladies Holland, Jersey, Londonderry, Blessington, Shelley, Lamb, Breadalbane,
Morgan, Mrs. Fitzherbert, Mrs. Jordan, Miss Landon, the Countess Guiccioli, &c

"A book unrivalled in its position in the range of modern literature."—*Times.*

"A clever, freespoken man of the world, son of an earl with £70,000 a-year, who
has lived from boyhood the life of a club-man, sportsman, and man of fashion, has
thrown his best stories about himself and his friends, into an anecdotic autobiography. Of course it is eminently readable. Mr. Grantley Berkeley writes easily and
well. The book is full of pleasant stories, all told as easily and clearly as if they
were related at a club-window, and all with point of greater or less piquancy."—
Spectator.

LADY ARABELLA STUART'S LIFE AND
LETTERS: including numerous Original and Unpublished Documents. By ELIZABETH COOPER. 2 vols., with Portrait. 21s.

"The 'Life and Letters of Lady Arabella Stuart' is an unusually good specimen
of its class. Miss Cooper has really worked at her subject. She has read a good
deal of MSS, and, what is better still, she has printed a good deal of what she has
read. The book has a real and substantial historical value."—*Saturday Review.*

"One of the most interesting biographical works recently published. The
memoirs have been arranged by Miss Cooper with much care, diligence, and
judgment."—*Post.*

IMPRESSIONS OF LIFE AT HOME AND
ABROAD. By Lord EUSTACE CECIL, M.P. 1 vol. 8vo.

"Lord Eustace Cecil has selected from various journeys the points which most
interested him, and has reported them in an unaffected style. The idea is a good
one, and is carried out with success. We are grateful for a good deal of information given with unpretending good sense."—*Saturday Review.*

HISTORIC PICTURES. By A. BAILLIE COCHRANE,
M.P. 2 vols.

"Mr. Baillie Cochrane has published two entertaining volumes of studies from
history. They are lively reading. 'My aim,' he says, 'has been to depict events
generally known in a light and, if possible, a picturesque manner.' Mr. Cochrane
has been quite successful in carrying out this intention. The work is a study of the
more interesting moments of history—what, indeed, the author himself calls it,
'Historic Pictures.'"—*Times.*

COURT AND SOCIETY FROM ELIZABETH
TO ANNE, Edited from the Papers at Kimbolton, by the DUKE
OF MANCHESTER. *Second Edition.* 2 vols. 8vo, with Fine Portraits.

"These volumes are sure to excite curiosity. A great deal of interesting matter is
here collected, from sources which are not within everybody's reach."—*Times.*

7

MESSRS. HURST AND BLACKETT'S
NEW WORKS—*Continued.*

A JOURNEY FROM LONDON TO PERSE-
POLIS; including WANDERINGS IN DAGHESTAN, GEORGIA, ARMENIA, KURDISTAN, MESOPOTAMIA, AND PERSIA. By J. USSHER, Esq., F.R.G.S. Royal 8vo, with numerous beautiful Coloured Illustrations. Elegantly bound.

"This is a very interesting narrative. Mr. Ussher is one of the pleasantest companions we have met with for a long time. We have rarely read a book of travels in which so much was seen so rapidly and so easily, and in which the scenery, the antiquities, and the people impressed the author's mind with such gentlemanly satisfaction. Mr. Ussher merited his success and this splendid monument of his travels and pleasant explorations."—*Times.*

TRAVELS ON HORSEBACK IN MANTCHU
TARTARY: being a Summer's Ride beyond the Great Wall of China. By GEORGE FLEMING, Military Train. 1 vol. royal 8vo, with Map and 50 Illustrations.

"Mr. Fleming's narrative is a most charming one. He has an untrodden region to tell of, and he photographs it and its people and their ways. Life-like descriptions are interspersed with personal anecdotes, local legends, and stories of adventure, some of them revealing no common artistic power."—*Spectator.*

THE OKAVANGO RIVER: A NARRATIVE
OF TRAVEL, EXPLORATION, AND ADVENTURE. By C. J. ANDERSSON, Author of "Lake Ngami." 1 vol. Illustrations.

TRAVELS IN THE REGIONS OF THE
AMOOR, AND THE RUSSIAN ACQUISITIONS ON THE CONFINES OF INDIA AND CHINA. By T. W. ATKINSON, F.G.S., F.R.G.S., Author of "Oriental and Western Siberia." Dedicated, by permission, to HER MAJESTY. Royal 8vo, with Map and 83 Illustrations.

A PERSONAL NARRATIVE OF THIRTEEN
YEARS' SERVICE AMONGST THE WILD TRIBES OF KHONDISTAN, FOR THE SUPPRESSION OF HUMAN SACRIFICE. By Major-General JOHN CAMPBELL, C.B. 1 vol. 8vo, with Illustrations.

ADVENTURES AMONGST THE DYAKS OF
BORNEO. By FREDERICK BOYLE, Esq., F.R.G.S. 1 vol. 8vo.

YACHTING ROUND THE WEST OF ENG-
LAND. By the Rev. A. G. L'ESTRANGE, B.A., of Exeter College, Oxford, R.T.Y.C. 1 vol. 8vo, Illustrated.

ADVENTURES AND RESEARCHES among the
ANDAMAN ISLANDERS. By Dr. MOUAT, F.R.G.S., &c. 1 vol. demy 8vo, with Illustrations.

SPORT AND SPORTSMEN: A Book of Recol-
lections. By CHARLES STRETTON, Esq. 8vo, with Illustrations.

BRIGAND LIFE IN ITALY. By COUNT MAFFEI.
2 vols. 8vo.

MESSRS. HURST AND BLACKETT'S
NEW WORKS—*Continued.*

A LADY'S GLIMPSE OF THE LATE WAR
IN BOHEMIA. By LIZZIE SELINA EDEN. 1 vol. post 8vo, with Illustrations. 10s. 6d.

"Miss Eden's book will be of great service to those who wish impartially to consider the true aspects of the late war, and will richly repay an attentive perusal. Nor is it to them alone that this work will be valuable. It is not only useful and instructive, but it is interesting and amusing. The work is highly creditable to its authoress."—*Saturday Review.*

MY PILGRIMAGE TO EASTERN SHRINES.
By ELIZA C. BUSH. 8vo, with Illustrations. 15s.

"This work contains a great deal of interesting matter, and it will be read with pleasure by all who are interested in the country to which so many devout Christians have made their pilgrimage."—*Observer.*

THE BEAUTIFUL IN NATURE AND ART.
By MRS. ELLIS. Author of 'The Women of England,' &c. 1 vol. crown 8vo, with fine Portrait. 10s. 6d.

"With pleasure her numerous admirers will welcome a new book by the popular authoress of 'The Women of England.' A very charming volume is this new work by Mrs. Ellis. Its aim is to assist the young students of art in those studies and subjects of thought which shall enable them rightly to appreciate and realise that oft-quoted truth, 'A thing of beauty is a joy for ever.' 'The Truthfulness of Art,' 'The Love of Beauty,' 'The Love of Ornament,' 'Early dawn of Art,' and various chapters of a kindred nature, are followed by others descriptive of 'Learning to Draw,' 'Imitation,' 'Light and Shadow,' 'Form,' 'Colour,' 'Lady's Work,' &c. The work will interest many fair readers."—*Sun.*

GARIBALDI AT HOME: Notes of a Visit to
Caprera. By SIR CHARLES R. MCGRIGOR, Bart. 8vo. 15s.

MEMOIRS OF QUEEN HORTENSE, MOTHER
OF NAPOLEON III. Cheaper Edition, in 1 vol. 6s.

"A biography of the beautiful and unhappy Queen, more satisfactory than any we have yet met with."—*Daily News.*

WILLIAM SHAKESPEARE. By CARDINAL
WISEMAN. 1 vol. 8vo, 5s.

PRISON CHARACTERS DRAWN FROM LIFE.
BY A PRISON MATRON, Author of 'Female Life in Prison.' 2 v. 21s.

"These volumes are interesting and suggestive."—*Athenæum.*
"The author's quick-witted transcripts of living character are studies that nothing can make obsolete or deprive of interest for living men."—*Examiner.*

RECOLLECTIONS OF A LIFE OF ADVEN-
TURE. By WILLIAM STAMER. 2 vols. with Portrait. 21s.

THE GIRAFFE HUNTERS. By CAPTAIN MAYNE
REID. Author of 'The Rifle Rangers,' &c. 3 vols.

MADONNA MARY. By Mrs. OLIPHANT, Author
of 'Agnes,' &c. 3 vols.

"From first to last 'Madonna Mary' is written with evenness and vigour, and overflows with the best qualities of its writer's fancy and humour."—*Athenæum.*

THE NEW AND POPULAR NOVELS,
PUBLISHED BY HURST & BLACKETT.

OLD SIR DOUGLAS. By the Hon. MRS. NORTON,
Author of 'Lost and Saved,' &c. *SECOND EDITION.* 3 vols.

"There is a great deal worth reading in these volumes. The incidents are powerfully and picturesquely told, and we are especially struck by the conception of Margaret Carmichael, who, as a character in which good and evil are blended, is one of the most natural in the book."—*Times.*

"'Old Sir Douglas' is a thoroughly readable and wholesome work of fiction. It is a book that will satisfy the expectations of Mrs. Norton's many admirers, and is worthy of a writer who, having been a personal witness of much that is most brilliant in human society, and a sufferer of much that is most sad in human life, describes with equal candour and vividness the things that she has seen and the sorrows that she has felt."—*Athenæum.*

"A graceful and touching story. Gertrude is a beautiful character, admirably drawn."—*Pall Mall Gazette.*

"The story of 'Old Sir Douglas' is clearly and consistently worked out, with an enchaining interest."—*Post.*

"Mrs. Norton's novel will have a great success. It is sure to be eagerly read and admired.—*Star.*

"A work of surpassing interest; the aim of which is to exalt what is pure and noble."—*John Bull.*

"'Old Sir Douglas' is unquestionably Mrs. Norton's greatest prose work. There can be little doubt that in it she has attained her highest excellence as a writer of fiction. The tale has the advantage over all her other prose works in vigour of interest, in profusion of thought and poetry; and more strikingly still, in variety and singularity of character. It is a work of the highest order of genius."—*Dublin University Magazine.*

GUILD COURT. By GEORGE MACDONALD, M.A.
Author of 'Alec Forbes,' &c. 3 vols.

EDITH'S MARRIAGE. By ARNOLD HEATH. 3 v.

A HERO'S WORK. By MRS. DUFFUS HARDY.
3 vols. *(In Dec.)*

LOVE'S SACRIFICE. By MRS. WILLIAM GREY.
3 vols. *(In Dec.)*

FAIR WOMEN. By MRS. FORRESTER. 3 vols.

"That her fair form may stand and shine—
Make bright our days and light our dreams,
Turning to scorn with lips divine
The falsehood of extremes."—*TENNYSON.*

SIR TRISTRAM'S WILL. By ALICE KING, Author of 'Eveline,' &c. Dedicated to CHARLES DICKENS. 3 vols.

"Miss King's new story is thoroughly interesting. It is well written and shows a great advance in character painting. The wilful girlishness of the heroine is charmingly blended with her nobler qualities."—*Examiner.*

A WOMAN'S TRIALS. By GRACE RAMSAY. 3 v.

"A clever, interesting novel. Mabel Stanhope is as sweet a character as we remember to have met with in the world of romance for a long—for a very long—while."—*Athenæum.*

"The heroine of this book is a most lovable character, and her extraordinary trials and heroic endurance of them constitute a tale which we advise all our readers to procure for themselves. The book is a decided success."—*John Bull.*

IRENE'S REPENTANCE. By CHRISTIAN EYRE. 2 v.

"A very pleasant story. It is well told, and there is a healthy tone throughout. Irene herself is so natural and charming that Mr. Cunningham will be the envy of all unmarried male readers."—*Athenæum.*

THE NEW AND POPULAR NOVELS,
PUBLISHED BY HURST & BLACKETT.

THE HUGUENOT FAMILY. By Sarah Tytler.

Author of 'Citoyenne Jacqueline,' &c. 3 vols.

"The best of Miss Tytler's books. The author of 'The Huguenot Family' is a writer of true, sweet, and original genius; and her book is one of permanent value, the interest of which repeated readings will not exhaust."—*Pall Mall Gazette.*

"We trust our readers will not miss the chance of taking up these volumes to read them, for we have no hesitation in characterizing them as at once the warmest, richest, and sincerest of recent novels. The story is bright with skilfully-contrasted pictures, and full of mellow wisdom. Miss Tytler has in certain passages called to our mind Tennyson and Browning; and has, in one or two instances at least, surpassed the former in truthfulness and breadth of rendering."—*Spectator.*

"A story of great originality and power. From beginning to end the work is genuine, wholesome, and great. Its verisimilitude is perfect. Every character is full of originality, substance, and vitality."—*British Quarterly Review.*

TWO MARRIAGES. By the Author of 'John

Halifax, Gentleman,' 'Christian's Mistake,' &c. 2 vols.

"We have no hesitation in affirming the 'Two Marriages' to be in many respects the very best book that the author has yet produced. Rarely have we read a work written with so exquisite a delicacy, full of so tender an interest, and conveying so salutary a lesson."—*British Quarterly Review.*

"All the stories by the author of 'John Halifax' have an excellent moral; something tangible, real, and satisfactory."—*Pall Mall Gazette.*

"The author of 'John Halifax' cannot help writing gracefully: all her sentiments are pure, refined, and womanly. Her English is always good, and her skill in suggesting the unspoken details of a story, resembles that of the pieces of music called Songs without Words."—*Athenæum.*

RAYMOND'S HEROINE. *Second Edition.* 3 vols.

"'Raymond's Heroine' is a clever and vigorous work. It is a book which deserves to be read, and it will be read. The reader will gallop through it with breathless interest. It is a book which will be guilty of causing careful mammas to say to their daughters—'My dear, do put down that book and go to bed.' It is very smoothly and fluently written throughout. The scenery of the various incidents is vividly painted, the conversations are lively, and the plot is carefully and coherently put together."—*Times.*

"We recommend 'Raymond's Heroine' to those who can appreciate the charms of a novel throughout which there makes itself unmistakeably manifest the impress of generous feeling and of vigorous thought. It is also one through which there runs a vein of humour which at once relieves and heightens its pathos."—*Saturday Review.*

THE CURATE'S DISCIPLINE. By Mrs. Eiloart.

"We recommend this book to the novel-reader. It is better than nine-tenths of this year's works, and the reader will be pleased with it as the production of a lady apparently gifted with a good education, good taste, and, what is still more remarkable, good common sense."—*Athenæum.*

LESLIE TYRRELL. By Georgiana M.Craik. 2 v.

"There are charming traits of character in this book—much of the portraiture is perfect. The contrast between Leslie Tyrrell and Frank Arnold is drawn with wonderful skill."—*Spectator.*

ALEC'S BRIDE. By the Author of 'St. Olave's,'

'Janita's Cross,' &c. 3 vols.

"'Alec's Bride' is a charming book, and possesses the advantage of being written in good English."—*Athenæum.*

THE SISTERS OF SAINTHILL. By Lady

Blake. 3 vols.

"We are rejoiced again to welcome a work of Lady Blake's—one of our most charming novelists. The present volumes fully sustain her reputation. From first to last the tale is natural and lifelike, and the interest well sustained throughout."—*John Bull.*

HURST AND BLACKETT'S STANDARD LIBRARY

OF CHEAP EDITIONS OF

POPULAR MODERN WORKS,

ILLUSTRATED BY MILLAIS, HOLMAN HUNT, LEECH, BIRKET FOSTER,
JOHN GILBERT, TENNIEL, &c.

Each in a single volume, elegantly printed, bound, and illustrated, price 5s.

VOL. I.—SAM SLICK'S NATURE AND HUMAN NATURE.

" The first volume of Messrs Hurst and Blackett's Standard Library of Cheap Editions
forms a very good beginning to what will doubtless be a very successful undertaking.
'Nature and Human Nature' is one of the best of Sam Slick's witty and humorous
productions, and is well entitled to the large circulation which it cannot fail to obtain in
its present convenient and cheap shape. The volume combines with the great recommendations of a clear, bold type, and good paper, the lesser, but attractive merits of
being well illustrated and elegantly bound."—*Post.*

VOL. II.—JOHN HALIFAX, GENTLEMAN.

"This is a very good and a very interesting work. It is designed to trace the career
from boyhood to age of a perfect man—a Christian gentleman, and it abounds in incident
both well and highly wrought. Throughout it is conceived in a high spirit, and written
with great ability. This cheap and handsome new edition is worthy to pass freely from
hand to hand as a gift book in many households."—*Examiner.*

"The new and cheaper edition of this interesting work will doubtless meet with great
success. John Halifax, the hero of this most beautiful story, is no ordinary hero, and
this his history is no ordinary book. It is a full-length portrait of a true gentleman,
one of nature's own nobility. It is also the history of a home, and a thoroughly English
one. The work abounds in incident, and is full of graphic power and true pathos.
It is a book that few will read without becoming wiser and better."—*Scotsman.*

VOL. III.—THE CRESCENT AND THE CROSS.
BY ELIOT WARBURTON.

" Independent of its value as an original narrative, and its useful and interesting
information, this work is remarkable for the colouring power and play of fancy with
which its descriptions are enlivened. Among its greatest and most lasting charms is
its reverent and serious spirit."—*Quarterly Review.*

"A book calculated to prove more practically useful was never penned than 'The
Crescent and the Cross'—a work which surpasses all others in its homage for the sub-
lime and its love for the beautiful in those famous regions consecrated to everlasting
immortality in the annals of the prophets, and which no other writer has ever de-
picted with a pencil at once so reverent and so picturesque."—*Sun.*

VOL. IV.—NATHALIE. BY JULIA KAVANAGH.

"'Nathalie' is Miss Kavanagh's best imaginative effort. Its manner is gracious
and attractive. Its matter is good. A sentiment, a tenderness, are commanded by
her which are as individual   they are elegant."—*Athenæum.*

VOL. V.—A WOMAN'S THOUGHTS ABOUT WOMEN.
BY THE AUTHOR OF "JOHN HALIFAX, GENTLEMAN."

" A book of sound counsel. It is one of the most sensible works of its kind, well-
written, true-hearted, and altogether practical. Whoever wishes to give advice to a
young lady may thank the author for means of doing so."—*Examiner.*

VOL. VI.—ADAM GRAEME. BY MRS OLIPHANT.

" A story awakening genuine emotions of interest and delight by its admirable pictures of Scottish life and scenery. The author sets before us the essential attributes of
Christian virtue, their deep and silent workings in the heart, and their beautiful manifestations in life, with a delicacy, power, and truth which can hardly be surpassed "—*Post.*

HURST AND BLACKETT'S STANDARD LIBRARY
(CONTINUED).

VOL. VII.—SAM SLICK'S WISE SAWS
AND MODERN INSTANCES.

" We have not the slightest intention to criticise this book. Its reputation is made, and will stand as long as that of Scott's or Bulwer's Novels. The remarkable originality of its purpose, and the happy description it affords of American life and manners, still continue the subject of universal admiration.' To say thus much is to say enough, though we must just mention that the new edition forms a part of Messrs Hurst and Blackett's Cheap Standard Library, which has included some of the very best specimens of light literature that ever have been written."—*Messenger*.

VOL. VIII.—CARDINAL WISEMAN'S RECOLLECTIONS
OF THE LAST FOUR POPES.

"A picturesque book on Rome and its ecclesiastical sovereigns, by an eloquent Roman Catholic. Cardinal Wiseman has treated a special subject with so much geniality, that his recollections will excite no ill-feeling in those who are most conscientiously opposed to every idea of human infallibility represented in Papal domination."—*Athenæum*.

VOL. IX.   A LIFE FOR A LIFE.
BY THE AUTHOR OF "JOHN HALIFAX, GENTLEMAN."

" In ' A Life' for a Life ' the author is fortunate in a good subject, and has produced a work of strong effect."—*Athenæum*.

VOL. X.—THE OLD COURT SUBURB.   BY LEIGH HUNT.

"A delightful book, that will be welcome to all readers, and most welcome to those who have a love for the best kinds of reading."—*Examiner*.
"A more agreeable and entertaining book has not been published since Boswell produced his reminiscences of Johnson."—*Observer*.

VOL. XI.—MARGARET AND HER BRIDESMAIDS.

" We recommend all who are in search of a fascinating novel to read this work for themselves. They will find it well worth their while. There are a freshness and originality about it quite charming."—*Athenæum*.

VOL. XII.—THE OLD JUDGE.   BY SAM SLICK.

" The publications included in this Library have all been of good quality ; many give information while they entertain, and of that class the book before us is a specimen. The manner in which the Cheap Editions forming the series is produced deserves especial mention.   The paper and print are unexceptionable ; there is a steel engraving in each volume, and the outsides of them will satisfy the purchaser who likes to see books in handsome uniform."—*Examiner*.

VOL. XIII.—DARIEN.   BY ELIOT WARBURTON.

"This last production of the author of 'The Crescent and the Cross' has the same elements of a very wide popularity.   It will please its thousands."—*Globe*.

VOL. XIV.—FAMILY ROMANCE; OR, DOMESTIC
ANNALS OF THE ARISTOCRACY.
BY SIR BERNARD BURKE, Ulster King of Arms.

" It were impossible to praise too highly this 'most interesting book.   It ought to be found on every drawing-room table.   Here you have nearly fifty captivating romances with the pith of all their interest preserved in undiminished poignancy, and any one may be read in half an hour."—*Standard*.

VOL. XV.—THE LAIRD OF NORLAW
BY MRS OLIPHANT.

" The Laird of Norlaw fully sustains the author's high reputation."—*Sunday Times*.

HURST AND BLACKETT'S STANDARD LIBRARY
(CONTINUED).

VOL. XVI.—THE ENGLISHWOMAN IN ITALY.

"We can praise Mrs Gretton's book as interesting, unexaggerated, and full of opportune instruction."—*The Times.*

VOL. XVII.—NOTHING NEW.
BY THE AUTHOR OF "JOHN HALIFAX, GENTLEMAN."

"'Nothing New' displays all those superior merits which have made 'John Halifax' one of the most popular works of the day."—*Post.*

VOL. XVIII.—FREER'S LIFE OF JEANNE D'ALBRET.

"Nothing can be more interesting than Miss Freer's story of the life of Jeanne D'Albret, and the narrative is as trustworthy as it is attractive."—*Post.*

VOL. XIX.—THE VALLEY OF A HUNDRED FIRES.
BY THE AUTHOR OF "MARGARET AND HER BRIDESMAIDS."

"We know no novel of the last three or four years to equal this latest production of the popular authoress of 'Margaret and her Bridesmaids.' If asked to classify it, we should give it a place between 'John Halifax' and 'The Caxtons.'"—*Herald.*

VOL. XX.—THE ROMANCE OF THE FORUM.
BY PETER BURKE, SERGEANT AT LAW.

A work of singular interest, which can never fail to charm. The present cheap and elegant edition includes the true story of the Colleen Bawn."—*Illustrated News.*

VOL. XXI.—ADELE. BY JULIA KAVANAGH.

"'Adèle' is the best work we have read by Miss Kavanagh; it is a charming story, full of delicate character-painting."—*Athenæum.*

VOL. XXII.—STUDIES FROM LIFE.
BY THE AUTHOR OF "JOHN HALIFAX, GENTLEMAN."

"These 'Studies from Life' are remarkable for graphic power and observation. The book will not diminish the reputation of the accomplished author."—*Saturday Review.*

VOL. XXIII.—GRANDMOTHER'S MONEY.

"We commend 'Grandmother's Money' to readers in search of a good novel. The characters are true to human nature, the story is interesting."—*Athenæum.*

VOL. XXIV.—A BOOK ABOUT DOCTORS.
BY J. C. JEAFFRESON, ESQ.

"A delightful book."—*Athenæum.* "A book to be read and re-read; fit for the study as well as the drawing-room table and the circulating library."—*Lancet.*

VOL. XXV.—NO CHURCH.

"We advise all who have the opportunity to read this book."—*Athenæum.*

VOL. XXVI.—MISTRESS AND MAID.
BY THE AUTHOR OF "JOHN HALIFAX, GENTLEMAN."

"A good wholesome book, gracefully written, and as pleasant to read as it is instructive."—*Athenæum.* "A charming tale charmingly told."—*Herald.*

VOL. XXVII.—LOST AND SAVED. BY HON. MRS NORTON

"'Lost and Saved' will be read with eager interest. It is a vigorous novel."—*Times.* "A novel of rare excellence. It is Mrs Norton's best prose work."—*Examiner.*

HURST AND BLACKETT'S STANDARD LIBRARY

(CONTINUED).

VOL. XXVIII.—LES MISERABLES. BY VICTOR HUGO.

AUTHORISED COPYRIGHT ENGLISH TRANSLATION.

"The merits of 'Les Miserables' do not merely consist in the conception of it as a whole; it abounds, page after page, with details of unequalled beauty. In dealing with all the emotions, doubts, fears, which go to make up our common humanity, M. Victor Hugo has stamped upon every page the hall-mark of genius."—*Quarterly Review.*

VOL. XXIX.—BARBARA'S HISTORY.

BY AMELIA B. EDWARDS.

"It is not often that we light upon a novel of so much merit and interest as 'Barbara's History.' It is a work conspicuous for taste and literary culture. It is a very graceful and charming book, with a well-managed story, clearly-cut characters, and sentiments expressed with an exquisite elocution. It is a book which the world will like. This is high praise of a work of art, and so we intend it."—*Times.*

VOL. XXX.—LIFE OF THE REV. EDWARD IRVING.

BY MRS OLIPHANT.

"A good book on a most interesting theme."—*Times.*
"A truly interesting and most affecting memoir. Irving's Life ought to have a niche in every gallery of religious biography. There are few lives that will be fuller of instruction, interest, and consolation."—*Saturday Review.*
"Mrs Oliphant's Life of Irving supplies a long-felt desideratum. It is copious, earnest, and eloquent. Irving, as a man and as a pastor, is exhibited with many broad, powerful, and life-like touches, which leave a strong impression."—*Edinburgh Review.*

VOL. XXXI.—ST OLAVE'S.

"This charming novel is the work of one who possesses a great talent for writing, as well as experience and knowledge of the world. 'St Olave's' is the work of an artist. The whole book is worth reading."—*Athenæum.*

VOL. XXXII.—SAM SLICK'S TRAITS OF AMERICAN HUMOUR.

"Dip where you will into this lottery of fun, you are sure to draw out a prize. These racy 'Traits' exhibit most successfully the broad national features of American humour."—*Post.*

VOL. XXXIII.—CHRISTIAN'S MISTAKE.

BY THE AUTHOR OF "JOHN HALIFAX, GENTLEMAN."

"A more charming story, to our taste, has rarely been written. In the compass of a single volume the writer has hit off a circle of varied characters all true to nature, and she has entangled them in a story which keeps us in suspense till its knot is happily and gracefully resolved; while, at the same time, a pathetic interest is sustained by an art of which it would be difficult to analyse the secret. It is a choice gift to be able thus to render human nature so truly, to penetrate its depths with such a searching sagacity, and to illuminate them with a radiance so eminently the writer's own. Even if tried by the standard of the Archbishop of York, we should expect that even he would pronounce 'Christian's Mistake' a novel without a fault."—*Times.*

VOL. XXXIV.—ALEC FORBES OF HOWGLEN.

BY GEORGE MAC DONALD, M.A.,

"No account of this story would give any idea of the profound interest that pervades the work from the first page to the last."—*Athenæum.* "This book is full of good thought and good writing. Mr Mac Donald reads life and nature like a true poet."—*Examiner.*

www.ingramcontent.com/pod-product-compliance
Lightning Source LLC
Chambersburg PA
CBHW051526100726
47898CB00005B/1586